M000302477

OXFORD
Redemption

"Oxford Redemption will captivate your undivided attention as you become intrigued with each fascinating high-profile character involved in the possibility of being a murderer! The volatile solution to this murder mystery may catch you completely unaware, yet pleasantly surprised! I am looking forward to reading more novels by this talented writer!"

—Ruth Ann Williams
Retired Educator, Recording Artist, Lay Speaker,
and married to Liles Williams—Parents of four daughters

• • •

"Could not put this book down. I found myself involved hook, line, and sinker. Dan Gibson captures the spiritual and cultural attitude of small town Mississippi like no one else."

—Henry Michel
Commercial Real Estate Broker

• • •

Prepare yourself for a great ride! From the opening scene, you are really drawn into the story. Lorna provides sorrow, trust, faith, and determination in the aftermath of her husband's death. Intrigue, suspense, hope, love...all the qualities of a great novel are included here. (Not to mention, a few plot twists for good measure.)

—Scott Enochs
Sales Consultant

OXFORD
Redemption

To Jan —
looking forward to meeting
you — Come visit us
in Natchez!
Good Bless You — [signature]
6-25-17

A NOVEL BY

Dan M. Gibson

BookPRO Publishing Company

Natchez, Mississippi
www.bookproonline.com

Copyright ©2016 Dan M. Gibson
ISBN 978-0-9979658-0-3

This book is a work of fiction. Names, characters, and events are the product of the author's imagi-nation. Any resemblance to actual persons, living or dead, or events is purely coincidental. No part of this book may be used or reproduced in any manner whatsoever without written permission except in the case of brief quotations embodied in critical articles and reviews.

ALL RIGHTS RESERVED

Library of Congress Control Number
2016914259

Cover Art by Suzi Jochimsen Hood
Printed in the United States of America

BookPRO Publishing Company
705 Washington Street
Natchez, Mississippi 39120
769-355-2422
www.bookproonline.com
www.oxfordredemption.com

For my Father.

Acknowledgments

I WAS BLESSED WITH loving parents, a wonderful family, and supportive friends. For them, I am truly grateful. They were of significant encouragement as I set out to write this book—especially my lifelong friend Liz Enochs, herself a professional writer, who lent her amazing literary talents to me when I was first getting started. Liz helped significantly with character, plot and dialogue development in the early chapters of this book, and without her I may never have made it past the first page! So many others cheered me on…too many to name. I thank God for my son, Clark, who first listened to the plot of this story when he was only eight years old. He is now twenty-two, and he has been the greatest encourager of my life. Most of all, I thank God for His mercy and love. He has richly blessed me. All glory goes to Him.

Contents

Death in Spring

IT WAS A perfect spring evening. Honeysuckle was in bloom. Azaleas formed a pink frame along the railing of the front porch. A mockingbird called from the 160-year-old live oak in the front yard. It was the kind of Friday evening Lorna and Radley had often spent together on the porch swing, where they would sip on lemonades and talk about the week… local developers preying on aging property owners, the rash of break-ins in south Oxford, the latest intrigue at city hall—standard topics of conversation for small-town mayors and their wives.

On this April evening, though, Lorna was at the Ava Hotel, hosting a charity dinner. The empty swing creaked softly in the breeze—its subdued, gentle sound only intermittently audible, mostly drowned out by Roscoe's insistent barking. The old golden retriever, brought home from the animal shelter when Brad was eight years old, paused every few minutes or so to whine and scratch at the door as he tried to get out.

In the driveway, a few yards from the garage behind the mansion, sat Radley's shining Jeep Wrangler. It had been a present from Lorna on the occasion of his fiftieth birthday just a few weeks earlier. She wanted to get him something fancier. A Mercedes or a Jaguar perhaps. But Radley was a simple guy—an oxymoron of sorts, considering he didn't mind living in the city's grandest home. But the Jeep was just his style. And it was still buffed and gleaming, black as the night.

But something wasn't right. The driver's door was ajar, as if Radley had run back into the house to retrieve something he'd forgotten. Only Radley wasn't in the house searching for his cell phone or reading glasses. He wasn't heading to his impromptu meeting at city hall either. He wasn't at all where he was supposed to be.

CHAPTER 1

Burning Walk

Brad could swear the trees were on fire. Everywhere he looked there were flames. Occasionally, the trees would part, revealing a night sky that glowed a rich amber as explosions echoed in his ears. His chest felt like it was caught in a vise grip with someone slowly but mercilessly tightening the handle. He ran for his life through the reddened darkness, gasping for air.

Brad's feet burned every time they touched the ground, his bare soles bleeding from the sharp rocks that marred the forest floor. His heart was racing, his panicked face soaking wet from the sweat and blood pouring from his matted head of hair. His brown locks were now an eerie shade of red: Brad had suffered a nasty fall against a tree. But the accident hadn't slowed him. He had to find water. He had to find safety. He had to find a way out of this tormented scene.

A few yards below him, the forest began to give way to a beautiful spring night. A heavenly glow spread across a small pasture. Stars hung in the brilliant sky. But in Brad's eyes, the world seemed to burn even stronger. In the distance, Brad could make out the lights of civilization. He had no idea where he was, but he knew that these lights were his salvation. He headed straight for them.

Tripping across a tree stump and rolling down the steep incline, Brad's head hit a rock as his exhausted body made a violent splash into a creek below.

After minutes—or was it hours?—The chilly water startled Brad awake. The spring night had turned cold, and he was shivering violently. Lying still along the creek's sandy bank, Brad had enough wits to feel lucky—lucky that the world was beginning to look more familiar. The creek was one he had explored countless times as a child. And across the pasture, he recognized the soft lighting of Pebble Creek, Oxford's newest off-campus development.

But what was it that had brought him to this place? Even in his half-addled state, Brad knew there was something he needed to remember—something just beyond the edge of his consciousness. It was something dark and frightening but, at the same time, important—something that had driven him out to the woods, to a place where he could forget everything.

Brad got to his feet, unsteadily, and rubbed his arms and legs roughly to warm up and get the circulation going again. He took a few deep breaths and inhaled the scent of the forest—a mix of pines and budding hardwoods. He was feeling better—that is, until the nausea started to kick in. It had been a very bad trip, probably his worst.

Bradford Randolph Hamilton had not always been so strung out. His had been a promising start, as the handsome only son of Oxford's first family: a rich, gifted scion, with personality to spare. With his parents as models, Brad had grown up with the sense that it was his destiny to achieve success in whatever endeavor he chose to pursue. His father had been mayor as long as he could remember, and his mother was one of the city's most respected philanthropists.

Not only were they active in their community, the Hamiltons loved their church. Randolph Lee Hamilton II, Radley's great grandfather, had helped organize it back in the 1800s while he was serving as dean of the Ole Miss Law School. Subsequent generations of Hamiltons had all helped to keep it going, and after a 150-year history, Oxford Methodist had become a large and vibrant church. Brad thrived in the Christian environment he was raised in. He went on every youth trip, participated in every summer camp, and had even become a camp counselor during high school.

Speaking of high school, Brad was bright enough to earn As and Bs. But the thing he'd really excelled in was sports. Athletics had come easily to him: He'd scored starting slots on every school basketball, baseball, and football team he'd ever tried out for. He even helped to start a baseball team at church—and with his pitching and leadership abilities, Oxford Methodist won almost every game it played. Lorna had frequently ribbed her husband that their son took after her side of the family.

The Oxford Hamiltons had long been Mississippi "blue bloods," respected for their brains but not for their brawn. Radley could hold his own at golf and tennis, but that was about it. The Ashleys of Boston, on the other hand, were good at just about everything. Whether it was sailing or rugby, they were tough and fiercely competitive. And Brad, despite his name, was very much an Ashley.

He started out, like most Southern boys, playing T-ball. Busy as Radley was being mayor, he took time to coach his son's team, and they went undefeated their first year. Brad eventually progressed to soccer, baseball, and basketball, finally settling on what would become his greatest passion: football.

Brad was a natural quarterback. Though he wasn't as large as other players, he was strong and agile. At 5' 10", he was one of the smaller guys on the field, but with his strong pitcher's arm, he could throw the football with perfect precision. And, if necessary, Brad could run the ball, too, gaining more yards in some games than all of his running backs put together.

In his senior year at Oxford High School, collegiate talent

scouts from every major Southeastern Conference school sat in the stands at every game, eating home-grilled hamburgers and watching Brad work his magic. And the girls found him irresistible. What Brad possessed in physical ability he also possessed in charm and charisma.

But life in the fishbowl wasn't destined to be perfect forever. It was the last play of Brad's high school career: only a few more seconds to go and they would beat Batesville, Oxford's arch rival and one of Mississippi's toughest teams. Brad had his mind on the future: a starting position with the Ole Miss Rebels was already his.

Brad called the play; the snap was made. He had planned to hold the ball and run out the clock. But the unthinkable happened: Batesville's largest linebacker made an illegal sack behind the line, and Brad's rotator cuff would never be right again. And neither would Brad.

Morphine is said to be the only drug that can really dull the pain of a serious shoulder injury. Brad took the doctors at their word. The pain lasted for months, and Brad went from football hero to drug addict.

Those glory-filled days at Oxford High were light years away from this moment late at night on the sandy beach of Pebble Creek. Brad shook his head and lay back down for a minute—just a minute—to let the nausea subside. And then, without warning, he blacked out.

CHAPTER 2

The Ava

"H E'S FINALLY GOT tenure now that he's at Ole Miss!" Lorna was having to listen to her new friend, Myra Sanchez, gush about her husband. Myra and Matt had just moved to Oxford, lured to a lucrative position at Ole Miss. They had already joined the church and quickly installed themselves into Oxford society.

As much as she liked her new friend, it was hard for Lorna to concentrate on exactly what Myra was saying. Her mind was drifting back home with every other sentence. Not that it wasn't a beautiful night to be on the side porch at the Ava Hotel.

For someone wanting to hold an event, the Ava Hotel was the place—especially in the springtime. With its wide verandas and sweeping lawn, the grand old hotel seemed to harken back to a simpler time. One could almost imagine the music of Glenn Miller serenading dancing starlets from the 1940s—not that any big bands or famous celebrities had ever darkened its doors. For all of its beauty, the Ava Hotel was like many Southern hotspots—far nicer now than it ever had been in the old days.

But Lorna longed to be home with her Radley, enjoying their porch and discussing their day.

"Emory kept him in a holding pattern for six years—can you imagine?" Myra continued. "They were always promising next year he'd get a tenure review, and next year always seemed to be next year. Oh well—it's their loss if you ask me. Matt's loving it here. And not only does he have tenure, but he's finally getting to work on marketing some of his research. He's already got five grad students, and the department head told him just the other day how lucky they are to have him here!"

Lorna just nodded and smiled politely, sipping on a mixture of cranberry juice and tonic water—her version of a mixed drink. Her large brown eyes, however, had that faraway look.

"Oh, I'm sorry, Lorna!" apologized Myra, putting her hand to her mouth almost embarrassingly. "You'll have to forgive me. I get to talking and going on so… and I know bragging isn't becoming at all. I guess I'm just too excited. Life is going so well for us here!"

"Oh, Myra—don't you worry about that," Lorna spoke reassuringly, patting Myra's hand. "I totally understand. You and Matt are so blessed. You have every reason to be excited. He's a biologist, right?"

Now granted permission, Myra continued to talk and gush, "Well, he's actually a computational biologist. What that means, I think—I'm never quite sure I've got it exactly right—is that he builds computer models of biological processes. There's something to do with the proteins in cells, but that's about as much as I know about it."

Lorna was trying her best to listen, but she couldn't help but steal a glance at her phone. Radley hadn't texted her back yet. She was still hopeful he might make it to the party, but last-minute city business often seemed to steal him away from the places he would rather be. It was not unusual. But he was always available by text.

Despite her disclaimers about her husband's work, Myra was no ditz. After spending a decade as a buyer and marketing strategist for Anthropologie, a chain of women's clothing stores, she'd started her own business retailing specialty sweaters. She had two

20

factories in China and a list of clients that included Bloomingdale's, Macy's, and, of course, her former employer.

Lorna didn't know the details, but every couple of months or so, she'd hear about Myra jetting off to Guangzhou or Shanghai or some other exotic place to check on her suppliers or seal yet another deal.

Getting to know Myra had almost made Lorna regret her decision to give up her own career to raise Brad. She'd been a successful lawyer up until then and had been thinking about switching from real estate to intellectual property law so that she could eventually work with the scientists at Ole Miss to help them turn their research into new businesses.

Some of Lorna's old friends from her days at Dartmouth were partners at venture capital firms, and they were always telling her about the amazing research professors at Brandeis or MIT or Harvard were doing, and how the entrepreneurs they knew were helping those academics turn their ideas into real businesses.

What a great idea for Mississippi, Lorna had found herself thinking more than once. After they graduated from Ole Miss, or Mississippi State or Millsaps College, the state's best and brightest often flew the coop for better job opportunities elsewhere. If she could work with professors who were doing cutting-edge research to help them get patents and financing and turn their biotech or robotics discoveries into viable businesses, that would create jobs and economic growth for one of the most economically depressed states in the union. She'd not only be making money, learning new things, and having fun all the while—she'd also be doing a service to her adopted state.

But then reality had intruded. She found herself pregnant, and she had to decide: keep working, hire a nanny, and watch her precious baby be raised by someone else? Or give up a promising career, at least for a while, and focus on nurturing and raising this incredible tiny human being?

From the first heartbeat, she had loved Brad. She chose to be a mother instead of an attorney, and, for many years, she had never looked back.

At first, Radley had persisted that a nanny was a great idea, but deep down they both knew that a child needed more than a nanny. And Lorna knew Radley was a traditional Mississippi man who saw taking care of the children as more of a woman's job than a man's. She never resented that. She'd known it when she married him. And it was balanced by the fact that he was the most attentive, considerate, loving man she'd ever met.

So Lorna had decided to step back from her job for a year or two. Two years turned into five, and five into ten. And now here she was, two decades later—and she had never returned to her full-time career. But Lorna Hamilton didn't lack for enterprise. She'd joined half the clubs in town, become a promoter of several charities, and had even put a bit of her own money into a real estate development on the east side of town that had been so successful she'd ended up tripling her investment.

In addition, Lorna found great joy in volunteering at church. As a newlywed, barely even introduced to Oxford, she had at first been reluctant to do anything but sit in the pew on Sunday morning. But a love for music had drawn her into the choir. Next thing you know, she had begun singing solos, and then helping with a children's choir. Eventually, Lorna shared a vision with the pastor of starting a music ministry for Oxford's youth. Harmony Here became the result, drawing kids from challenged and broken homes, and bringing them into fun and fulfilling church activities—all centered around music. A new center was now under construction on the Ole Miss campus, and Lorna couldn't wait for it to be completed.

Every once in a while, in spite of all she was doing, Lorna would find herself regretful. The years had flown by way too fast... that happens when you're busy. And deep down, she couldn't help but agonize that she had inspired a whole community of children while failing in raising her one and only son.

Drug addiction can be a silent killer, and so far, it had killed all hopes that her precious son would ever amount to anything. And family therapy hadn't helped. Brad was not interested in treatment. Grief tore at Lorna's heart. The critical voice in her head nagged at her, *What had she done wrong? Was all this charity and church work really worth it? What had it led to, anyway?*

Lorna sighed.

"Are you all right?" asked Myra. "It seemed as though you were far, far away for a minute there."

"Oh, Myra, I'm so sorry," said Lorna. "I just got a little distracted thinking about all the drug problems at Ole Miss these days. I guess talking about your husband got me off on a tangent. I completely missed the last thing you said."

"Oh, it was nothing," said Myra. "I was just talking about the kids and how they're afraid to play T-ball. I mean, really! As if they could actually get hurt batting a baseball on a stick! But I know what you mean about the drugs. I've been reading about some of the cocaine arrests the police have been making at the university. It's really shocking. Things weren't that bad even in Atlanta. Makes me glad our kids are still young. There's time to clean up the problems before they get old enough to get into trouble."

As soon as the remark slipped, the look on Myra's face showed that she wished she could take it back. In academic and government circles, Brad Hamilton's drug addiction was common knowledge, but Southern courtesy dictated that you never mention it, or even allude to it, to the parents' faces—even if they did bring the topic up themselves.

Myra rescued them from the awkward silence that followed with one of the most tried-and-true methods known to polite society: a discussion of the weather.

"It's a beautiful night, isn't it?" she asked. "Hard to believe a front is moving in later tonight—supposed to rain tomorrow."

"Well, we probably need the rain," replied Lorna. "You know

what they say about April showers…"

"Can you believe how warm it is all of a sudden?" Myra responded. "After the bitterest winter on record, and barely any spring to speak of, all of a sudden here we are—it's April and we're in sundresses at night. I can't believe I finally got to wear my open-toed shoes after what feels like a million months cooped up indoors."

Myra's sandals looked more like flip-flops, Lorna thought to herself, taking a sidelong glance of disapproval at Myra's feet. Then she caught herself, and almost laughed at how staid and Southern she'd become after so many years in Oxford. And it actually made her wish for a moment she was wearing flip-flops— her stylish pumps were beginning to hurt.

"You know, Myra, growing up in Boston, I used to go out sailing on the Charles River up until November or even early December, wearing not much more than a turtleneck and a windbreaker," Lorna said. "Now I've become so accustomed to the Mississippi weather that I turn on the heater in the car when it dips below fifty degrees. You just never know how your life is going to change, and how you're going to adapt to it."

"I suppose that's true," said Myra. "I certainly never imagined I'd end up in Oxford."

"Ha!" laughed Lorna. "Neither did I, Myra. Neither did I. Both of us are in a different world than the ones we grew up in. I'm not sure how it feels for you, but I'm surprisingly glad I ended up here. Mainly because of Radley, and what a wonderful man he is. But over the years I've really come to appreciate Oxford—the beauty of the place, the rich literary history here, the sense that people are really rooted to this town. And our church… it's really been a support to Radley and me."

At just that moment, a voice boomed from behind Lorna: "Why there she is!"

Lorna turned around with a smile on her face. "I should've known you'd be here, Sterling," she said. "This was always the event of the year for y'all."

"I know—I have been thinking about Kathleen all evening. Wouldn't she be having a blast... if she were only here?" Sterling sighed, his upbeat mood suddenly brought low. "Of course, art was always her greatest passion."

Lorna continued, "I know—Kat loved art so much, and she did so much for the artists here in Oxford. Even though she always did say she couldn't draw a lick, I wasn't sure I ever quite believed her. And she always loved events like this—with young artists all around, just beginning to bloom!"

Kathleen had been Lorna's best friend. Early on, they had been like sisters, raising their sons together from diapers through high school. As time passed, Kathleen had grown somewhat distant, but they had remained good friends. They enjoyed singing in the choir together at church, and Kathleen was always there to help Lorna's Harmony Here kids tinker around with the piano. Lorna still couldn't believe she was gone.

"I'll tell you a secret, Lorna," said Sterling. "Kathleen had a little sketchbook she kept hidden away from everyone, even me. Before she died, I had only seen it once or twice, and only after a good ten years or so of marriage! It was full of exquisite little sketches of detailed scenes, like Faulkner's typewriter on his desk at Rowan Oak, the watering can sitting out next to the bower behind our house, where she planted the wisteria—there were even a few of Lance when he was a baby."

"I knew it!" exclaimed Lorna. "I always figured she was hiding her artistic talent, though I don't know why." To herself, Lorna couldn't help but wonder why Sterling had never shown her the sketchbook. They had spent a lot of time together after Kathleen's death, and she would have loved seeing it. Kat's mom had been a well-known portrait painter in Jackson, and Lorna was convinced that she possessed some inherited talent—stored away in her bones somewhere.

"I think she felt overshadowed by her mom, Lorna," Sterling

responded. "Lacey had accomplished so much that I got the sense Kathleen didn't even want to try and compete with her. Not that it had to be a competition, but somehow, with Lacey, it always was."

"I can only imagine," started Lorna, and then broke off as she turned to Myra. "Oh, how rude of me! I seem to have forgotten my manners. Sterling, you remember Myra. She's a clothing designer, and her husband Matt is a professor at Ole Miss. Myra, I believe you've met Sterling Bradford before."

Sterling reached out his hand, and Myra nodded, "Yes, of course I remember you," but Lorna noticed that, even though she was smiling, her eyes were cold.

It was true that Sterling wasn't in top form this evening. The lanky six-foot-two lawyer with the chiseled cheekbones and distinguished salt-and-pepper hair usually charmed the ladies right off the bat. But tonight he seemed subdued and a bit distracted. And Lorna was surprised to see a martini glass in his hand. He rarely drank. And Lorna couldn't remember ever having seen him drink hard liquor. Was he tipsy now? Lorna had never seen him quite like this.

"Sterling, it's a pleasure to see you," said Myra. "But I just remembered there's an urgent matter that I really need to attend to. Would you please excuse me?"

"Of course," said Sterling. "It was nice to see you, too."

As Myra glided away, his shoulders sank, and he ran his left hand through his hair with that funny, scalp-scratching motion Lorna had noticed him use on the few occasions when she'd seen him anxious. Curious that Myra would make him anxious, she thought. Or maybe it was something else.

"Sterling, why don't we step out to the front veranda where we can talk? It's such a lovely night," Lorna suggested.

He gave her a tight-lipped smile. "Yes, that's a good idea. I haven't had enough air tonight—ha! No, I really haven't. Yes, Lorna, that would be nice. It's been a long week—I really need to unwind. And I can never get enough of the smell of fresh-mown

26

grass in the springtime."

As they left the crowded side porch for the Ava's connecting front veranda, Lorna and Sterling settled into a pair of rocking chairs bookended by spider ferns and potted geraniums, the aroma of the freshly mowed lawn, mixed with azaleas and wisteria, was intoxicating. Now alone, Lorna turned to Sterling and said, "I don't mean to intrude, but are you all right? You don't seem quite yourself tonight. Is anything wrong?"

"No, of course not. Of course not. Of course not. Ahhh—that's what I'm supposed to say, right? Nobody ever admits it when anything's wrong in this town, do they? At least not to anybody else's face." Sterling was running his left hand through his hair again. "We all just pretend we're fine and keep on going to polite brunches and charity dinners and Christmas parties and everything is just fine, fine, fine. Well you know what, Lorna; for once I'm going to tell the truth. No, everything is not fine with me. It's hard, is what it is. Life for me is rough right now. It's almost a year since Kathleen died and here I am at one of her favorite parties for one of her favorite charities in the world and all I can think about is how much I wish she was still here with me, how I miss her laugh and that spark she'd get in her eyes when she was working out a new song on the piano, how good her buttermilk biscuits always smelled, and the way she'd tousle Lance's hair and say 'You go get 'em, tiger!' whenever he was heading out to a football game." His grip on the martini glass tightened and the corners of his eyes creased. "No, everything is not fine. Not fine at all."

Lorna sat up straight, and turned toward Sterling. In spite of his fine suit, and famous good looks, Sterling now seemed totally out of place sitting on the Ava's beautiful veranda. She'd seen him get intense when working on a big case, overheard him vent his frustrations with some of the local judges to Radley from time to time, but he'd never actually talked to her directly about anything this personal before. Of course she knew he must have been grieving, but she'd seen little outward sign of it, just tears

27

at Kathleen's funeral and the red rose he left on her grave every week like clockwork.

Bottling everything up inside was bad news, she knew from personal experience. That's how she and Radley had operated the first few years of their marriage, and it had put them on the brink of divorce once. She'd tried to always be happy and perky with him, even when he made her angry or disappointed her, and he'd been hot and cold, sometimes warm, and sometimes distant. Finally, they went to their pastor, who helped them learn to talk to one another about both the bad things and the good, and how to listen instead of being defensive or immediately trying to fix things. Slowly, they'd learned how to communicate better—how to find compromises they could both live with. As a result, they'd eventually grown closer than they'd felt when they first fell in love.

Sterling and Kathleen had seemed happy enough, but Lorna had never seen him display this much emotion about his wife. Or maybe it was just that she wasn't used to seeing him display much in the way of emotions. She didn't know quite how to react to this outpouring.

Being around Sterling made Lorna worry again about Radley. Surely his meeting was over by now. Why hadn't he texted? Why hadn't he called—or shown up by surprise as he often did when city business interfered with spending time with Lorna? Perhaps there was something wrong with her phone, or maybe she was in a dead zone…

She leaned over and put her hand on Sterling's arm. "Sterling," she said, "Kat was a wonderful woman. We all loved her, but I know you're the one who feels her loss more keenly than anyone else. I wish there was something more I could do, but I want you to know that Radley and I are here for you. And our Lord is with you. He has promised to always be with you—to never leave you nor forsake you. And you know you will see Kat again in that beautiful place called Heaven."

Sterling shuddered and pulled his arm away. "Ah, Lorna, if you only knew. If you only knew."

"What I do know is that you're our dear friend and that you can always call on us, day or night, if ever you need help or support in any way." People in the South said things of a similar tenor to one another all the time, never dreaming that the person listening would actually take them up on such an offer. Lorna, however, really meant it. Sterling was her husband's closest friend, and she'd loved Kathleen, too, even though in her last years, they hadn't been as close as Lorna would have liked. But Lorna prided herself on being a loyal, supportive, and steadfast friend, and she knew she didn't plan to stint on that support with Sterling.

Sterling took a deep breath, and another swig from his martini glass. Lorna looked down, saying a quick prayer for Sterling, and the two friends rocked in silence. Lorna felt compassion for Sterling for perhaps the first time. He'd always been a pretty boy who was also smart, athletic, and good at making whomever he was talking to feel like the most important person in the room. Those were a few of the reasons success seemed to come so easily to him, both in his legal practice and in his personal life. Women had always been drawn to him, even though he was always faithful to Kathleen. But in the early years, he'd certainly turned his thousand-watt smile on Lorna when Radley had brought her home from Boston. As a result, she had never entirely trusted that easy charm of his, though. But now, seeing his vulnerable side, made her feel there might be a whole new dimension to his personality that she'd never been aware of before.

After a while, Lorna fancied she saw a few fireflies blinking in the darkness beyond the veranda, though she knew it was too early in the year for them to be active yet.

Finally, Sterling spoke. "Thank you, Lorna. Your support means a great deal to me. You are one kind and gracious lady, and much more generous than you will probably ever realize."

"Now, Sterling!" she admonished. "That's what good friends are for. I can only imagine what you must be going through, but I know that if anything were to ever happen to Radley, it would be like having my heart knocked out of my chest, and I would need all the help and love and support I could get. So I want to make sure you know that we are here for you."

In the dim outdoor light, Lorna could see Sterling reach up with his left hand again, and grasp his forelock so tightly it seemed he would almost rip it out.

Then Sterling's shoulders relaxed and a serene calmness returned to his body as he turned to Lorna and looked straight into her eyes. "I appreciate your kindness," he said. "Right now I'm still feeling a bit overwhelmed with what's going on with me. I think maybe I'd best be calling it a night."

"Of course. You were brave to even come here tonight, knowing what feelings it might stir up. I'd be happy to drive you home if you'd like," said Lorna, eyeing the martini glass.

"No, no, please. You go back to your friends. I'll be fine. I've only had this one. And I am just going to sit here a while before I head home."

"You're sure?" Lorna asked as Sterling nodded. "All right then. I hope tomorrow will be a little bit better for you."

"I'm sure it will. Good night," spoke Sterling softly as Lorna reached over and squeezed his hand. In a matter of moments, feeling the tug of society, Lorna was once again in her place as host of the party.

CHAPTER 3

Trailer Trouble

THE DOOR SLAMMED open just as the pan crashed to the ground. "Larry, what are you doing?"

Kaylee Jones barreled in, hair flying in fifty directions, legs stamping, jaw set. "I thought you had quit messing with that junk. You're gonna get yourself kicked out of yet another rathole trailer, and although there might be an endless supply of rathole trailers around here, there aren't a lot of girlfriends with an endless supply of patience. And my patience is about gone!"

Because he rarely cooked—food that is—Larry's presence in front of the stove triggered an immediate alarm. But Kaylee's protests were mute.

He picked up the last few pieces of what looked like stale popcorn off the kitchen floor, leaving the pan where it had landed, and placed them in a spoon he held over a propane flame. His hands were dirty, and his large fingers seemed ill-suited to be cradling the shiny small spoon.

After an awkward silence, he turned to Kaylee. "Babe, I know, I know. I told you I wouldn't, but I just—well look, Roger scored him a bunch of Sudafed, and he owed me from the last time, so he split the stash with me. And then, well, there it was. And that's about all there is to say, I guess."

"Not again, Larry!" yelled Kaylee, knocking the spoon from Larry's hand before he could reach the syringe by the kitchen sink. "This is exactly why I don't bring Stacie and Josh over here anymore. You were doing so good for a while. And now you're just—first chance for a fix—can't help yourself. I mean, look at that goose egg on your arm—it ain't gettin' any smaller. You want to end up back in the hospital?"

"Babe, I told you, I can take care of it. I'm in control. Anyway, it's just this once, 'cause Roger owed me."

Kaylee ignored him and began digging through the cabinets in the trailer's narrow kitchen. "Where's the rest of it? I know you've got more. Anytime you get a stash, you hide some away, thinking I won't find it. But I always do. Now where is it?"

"Now Kaylee, honey, you cut that out. You ain't gonna find nothing. Might as well quit it. Just come on over here and give me a kiss," he said, offering her his cheek and trying to keep one eye on the stove as he lunged around the kitchen to block Kaylee's access to cabinets and drawers.

"Get out of my way, Larry!" she grunted, pulling out plastic silverware containers from the drawers to check what was behind and underneath them, throwing cabinet doors open, and digging behind pots and pans. It wasn't until she reached above the refrigerator, though, that Larry really sprung into action.

"Darlin', come on over here." He grabbed her hands and tried to drag her into the living room. "Let's talk for a minute."

Kaylee, who at five-eleven had a good three inches on him, shook him off and reached behind the coffee tin for a bag that appeared to be exactly what she was looking for.

Kaylee looked at Larry with disgust. "This what you want? This is how you thank me? Somebody who's trying to help you get ahead in life, maybe even get a decent job, stop jacking cars and lifting speed from the drugstores, and cooking meth? I've reached my limit. I can't take any more. I'm out of here."

Larry started to look queasy. He bit his lip, wrinkled his nose, and dropped his gaze so he wouldn't have to look directly at her any longer.

She turned on her heel and stomped out the door to her faded Trans Am. The screen door swung jaggedly on its one remaining hinge in the wake of the engine's rumble and then roar, as Kaylee floored it out of the gravel path that served as a driveway.

Larry Palmer's arms sagged at his sides and his shoulders slumped as he watched the best thing that had happened to him in years disappear right out of his life. He hoped she didn't really mean it when she said she wouldn't be back, but he'd never known Kaylee to waffle once she made a decision, especially when her pride or that streak of bullheadedness he both hated and loved was involved. Her fierce determination had helped keep him away from meth for the first four months of their relationship—at first because he was so attracted to her and yet she'd refuse to see him if she could detect the faintest whiff of the drug in his demeanor or behavior and then later because he'd grown to really care for her and her two kids and didn't want to disappoint her.

The craving was so strong, though, that one night he'd driven the fifteen miles or so down to Oxford just to hang with some of his old buddies, telling himself all the while that it would just be old home week—he'd have a few drinks, and that would be it. Of course, he'd found it impossible to say no when Roger pulled out that small clear bag of the "good stuff." It wasn't until the next day, when he managed to stagger home, that Kaylee and his roommate found him passed out on the couch.

She'd stayed away for a month then—hadn't said anything. She just got him cleaned up, and sobered up, and then she disappeared.

Larry had known what was going on. And the whole time he knew where she was, and even had the ability to realize why she was so mad at him, but it didn't mean anything to him while he was in the throes. Even worries that she might be in the arms of her ex-boyfriend, Stan Johnson, didn't seem to bother him. She and Stan had been history forever—long before she had met

Larry. But Stan was one of those guys who just couldn't let go, and Kaylee had once admitted to occasionally seeing him when she was still single and lonely.

Under normal circumstances, the thought of Kaylee out with Stan would have driven him into a rage. But during his month-long binge, nothing really phased Larry—as long as he could stay high.

Every night for several weeks he was off to Oxford. And every night things got worse. Then one night he stopped on a turnoff from Highway 6, halfway back to his broken-down trailer near Sardis Lake, and turned off the car.

He climbed out and sat on the hood for a while, then lay back so he was facing up at the stars. He watched them twinkle, listened to the crickets chirp, and thought about what he was doing for the first time since that night he'd gone back to Oxford to get hammered again. He wasn't sure if he was ready to go completely on the wagon, but he kept thinking about Kaylee, and how much he liked it when she brushed the hair away from his face to give him a kiss on the cheek. She was beautiful and tough—all in one awesome package. She cared enough to keep him straight. Life had been good. And he craved being with her again.

Instead of driving home, he'd driven to Kaylee's house. It was 1 a.m., and she was groggy with sleep—but she answered the door and invited him in to talk. He only asked one question—and Kaylee's reply was "no"—she hadn't been out with Stan. At this moment, Larry realized she truly was devoted to him. And it made him love her even more.

Larry appealed to her motherly side. He just wanted help getting sober again, he said. She didn't have to take him back; she could still hate him if she needed to. He only wanted to dry out and stay away from temptation.

It turned out to be the perfect formula, of course. Within a week, they were dating again, and on top of that he did actually stay sober—of his own volition—until this latest incident.

He even had started going to church with Kaylee and her kids. Although she wasn't particularly devout, Kaylee did happen to think that church was the best place to take a family on Sunday.

I'm an idiot, Larry thought to himself as he stood on the barren patch of dirt in front of the trailer watching Kaylee's rear lights recede into the distance toward Sardis Lake. He'd actually meant to just cook up the meth, stash it, and then sell it—not take any himself, but now that Kaylee was gone, what did it matter? He kicked at the dirt and cursed the stars. He wished he could get in a fight and just punch somebody full-on in the nose, and he didn't care who it was. He smashed the side of the trailer with his fist, bloodying his knuckles. But that wasn't satisfying enough.

The growling anger in his chest wouldn't let up, and he began pounding on the trailer like a drum. He banged and smashed away for a good five minutes, wailing against the hollow that was forming in his chest the more he thought about those taillights. All the while, he felt the fury rise and grow within him.

For a moment, he thought he heard a voice—reminding him that it would all be okay. But he chose to ignore it. After a time, he paused to breathe and hide his throbbing hands under his armpits, applying pressure until the pain subsided. The warmth of the night revealed itself in balls of sweat, beading from his forehead, dripping off his cheek. His narrow chest and back were soaking wet. And while the cold of previous weeks might have snapped him back to clarity, the warm weather only added to the irritation and anger Larry felt.

He swiveled on his heel to go back inside where at least he could turn on the air conditioner, rickety as it was, when a gun Larry always kept near the front door caught his attention. It was sitting on a table under the window, just next to an old lamp, in a leather holster. The sight of that dangerous piece of metal clicked Larry's mind back into gear. He felt his anger turn cold, and, as he stared at the gun, he knew what he would need to do next.

CHAPTER 4

Going Home

Lorna looked down at her phone. No message. It had now been three hours, and she still had not heard from him, which just wasn't like him. Even when he was swamped with city business, Radley always found a moment to text or call his wife and let her know that he'd been detained and wouldn't be home until late. This night, his absence was becoming more and more worrisome.

The charity dinner had been a success. But Lorna's heart was elsewhere. After a few last obligatory hellos and goodbyes, she fetched her shawl from the coat room and headed down the Ava's stone steps leading to the parking lot. As she beeped the Audi to unlock it, she pulled her cell phone from her purse and called Radley. It went straight to voicemail. She texted him again—but to no response.

Back at the house, Radley's phone made a vibrating sound. It came from the mayor's new Jeep, humming quietly in the drive-way behind the house. A passerby would have had to step right up to the open door to hear anything else. But just a few feet from the driver's seat, the music drifted out, and Dave Loggins' voice seemed almost dreamlike. "Please come to Boston! She said no, but you come home to me." The spring evening appeared per-fect. Aside from the incessant barking of the old retriever, nothing seemed amiss. Well, almost nothing…

As she climbed into her car, Lorna thought about how much modern technology had changed the way people communicate with one another. At one time, going a few hours without hearing from a loved one was completely normal. But now everyone was so spoiled by being connected and available all the time. She laughed a little at her worrying about Radley and reminded herself that the last time he'd been in a long meeting, he'd simply turned his cell phone off until after the meeting ended.

As she made her way out of the hotel parking lot and onto University Avenue, Lorna lowered her window slightly. It was such a beautiful night—and a Friday at that. The party behind her, the weekend had finally arrived. Hard to imagine it was supposed to rain Saturday. Lorna thought to herself, *Oh well it will be a perfect day to curl up with a good book.*

The smell of azaleas mixed with honeysuckle was almost intoxicating. The cool spring air brought a sudden chill to her as her mind drifted back to memories of a spring evening in Newport. She and Radley were just newlyweds, combing antique shops for the perfect honeymoon souvenir. Her parents offered to send them to Europe, but Lorna and Radley preferred the familiar surroundings of one of their favorite college getaways. There was something magical about Newport—the smell of the ocean, the quaint restaurants, the enchanted mansions with all of their stories.

As she turned onto South Lamar Boulevard, passing the lovely older homes of Oxford, Lorna could almost feel Radley's strong arms embracing her, sheltering her from the damp sea breeze as they swayed to the soulful trumpet of Miles Davis at the Newport Music Festival. What a wonderful evening that had been. Radley was such a romantic. Had it really been twenty-five years?

The Audi seemed to be on autopilot as it proceeded down Old Taylor Road, passing Faulkner's beloved Rowan Oak—a beautiful antebellum home set in a lush forest known as Bailey's Woods.

It is said that Faulkner found inspiration on the forest trails—an urban utopia just south of the Ole Miss campus. A short distance further, barely visible from the road, Somerset, the Hamiltons' glistening white ancestral mansion, was waiting for Lorna. She was almost home.

Lost in thought, she hardly even noticed the beautifully lit lawn in front of the antebellum mansion as she made her way from the open gate, winding her way through the trees and to the garage in back. She was still lost in Newport, enjoying that first weekend with her new husband. Radley's delicate kisses were playing along the lines of her shoulder. She had chills.

The mansion looked ready for a party—the Hamiltons always kept it well-lit at night. The imposing columns seemed ageless as they supported the grand portico of Radley's family home—pure Greek Revival at its best. The house had stood for ages—ever since Radley's great-grandfather, the same one who founded the church, had designed and built it. "It will be here long after I'm gone," Randolph Lee Hamilton II had said. And time had proven him right.

Lorna was glad to be home. There was Radley's Jeep just outside the garage. How silly she felt for worrying. The driver's door was open—he must have just arrived home himself.

As she drove past the SUV on her way to park, she noticed Radley was not visible. Perhaps he was bending down to get something? Or maybe he had taken something inside the house and was on his way back out?

She parked in her usual spot. Anxious to see Radley, she walked out onto the driveway toward Radley's Jeep. The faint strains of Miles Davis' "Funny Valentine" were playing across the yard. How sweet, she thought. Radley must be listening to that CD she had burned for him—all of their special songs.

She called Radley's name. There was no answer. She called over to the house, only to be met by Roscoe's barking. Still no answer.

Nothing could have prepared Lorna for what she saw next.

Lorna stood frozen in the driveway. She blinked, and blinked again. Her hands rose involuntarily to cover her mouth. Finally, it escaped: The scream that had been building in her body since the moment she had approached the driver's door of Radley's SUV and seen the dark pool that indicated something was wrong. Lorna's mouth opened wide, and sounds came out, but they didn't register in her brain. The only thing that registered was the sight, directly in front of her, of her husband's body slumped on the concrete driveway with a hole in his temple.

"Noooooo!" It was all Lorna could say. She repeated it over and over again, staring at Radley's body, still refusing to believe. "Noooooo!" She dropped to the ground, wrapped her arms around her knees, and began to rock back and forth like a child. "No, no, no!" Her dark hair had been pulled back in an elegant bun, but now, without thinking, Lorna loosened her hairband and began to wrench her hands through her chestnut mane, as if the pain of pulling her own tresses away from her scalp would somehow salve the gaping wound that had just opened in her heart.

He couldn't be gone. Not Radley—the man she'd built her life around, moved a thousand miles for, raised a child with, shared countless joys and sorrows with. How could he be gone? How could he leave her?

She looked to heaven and cried… "Lord, how could this happen? How could this happen? Oh, my Lord. Oh, my Lord." And then all she could do was drop her head and sob.

With a sudden anger, Lorna roused herself from her near-catatonic state. The gears in her brain began to turn again, and she realized that Radley had not left her—or at least, that he hadn't been the agent of his own departure. Someone else had been here, and something had gone terribly wrong. She needed to call the police, and call them right away.

Lorna wiped the tears away from her eyes and surveyed her surroundings. It didn't look like whoever had killed her husband was still anywhere nearby, but the thought that such a thing could even be possible frightened her immensely. She didn't want to go anywhere near the house, but her car was already parked in the attached garage, and that's where, not thinking, she had left her cell phone.

She looked at her husband one last time, set her teeth, and steeled herself. Two minutes later, she was on the phone with the 911 dispatcher, who immediately dispatched three units to her address and was advising her to stay in her car with the doors locked until the detectives arrived.

The next ten minutes were the longest Lorna had ever lived. She couldn't get the image of her husband's face out of her mind. It was not the face she wanted to see—the one that had kissed her goodbye when he'd left for work that morning—or the one that lit up any time he saw her walk into a room. No, the image that stayed burned on her retinas was the one that lay before her now—a stone-cold face, pale and lifeless. But somehow, strange as it was, Radley's was a face at peace.

CHAPTER 5

Coming Down

Minutes turned into an hour—and then, two. Brad was completely passed out, oblivious to the world.

As he slept, his mind played pictures of happier times: riding on Radley's shoulders at the State Fair, fishing and jet-skiing at Sardis Lake with his buddy Lance Sterling on Bradford Sterling's boat, and camping with the Boy Scouts at Wall Doxey State Park. Brad's had been an ideal childhood.

His dad really had loved him. The family's favorite joke was that Brad Hamilton's feet never touched the floor until he was about two years old. Radley was always toting him—either in his arms or on his shoulders. The two were extremely close, and a father had never doted on his son so.

Brad always enjoyed the fair. Every October, he, Radley, and Lorna would load up in the family car and drive to Jackson. The rides were fun, the food was delicious, and Brad especially liked seeing all of the colorful lights.

Quite often, Lance would go with them. The two would ride the kiddy rides, each one pretending to steer their own sleek mini-speedboat.

Later, when the boys were old enough to go out on Sardis Lake alone, they would take Sterling's boat and fish all day, returning home sporting fresh smiles and sunburns, always with a few more trophy bass for the freezer. When they weren't fishing, they were skiing, and Sterling and Radley, along with Kathleen and Lorna, would sometimes go along—towing the boys, each of them taking turns skimming across the waves.

When fall would return, they would go to the fair again. But sometimes, the fair had to wait. Brad and Lance were both in Boy Scouts. Radley was their troop leader. Wall Doxey State Park, just thirty minutes north of Oxford, was their favorite place to camp. Something about the old cabins and overgrown forests gave the old place a spooky feel. Legend had it that the Union army had even camped there during the Civil War.

The boys loved to take night hikes, returning to a campfire, marshmallows, and ghost stories. Radley was the best ghost-story teller around, and all of his scouts loved sitting around hearing him spin tales. "Another, Mr. Radley! Another!" Lance especially got into it. He and Radley always had a special bond—Radley was like a second dad to him. Lance never wanted him to stop telling stories, and Radley would continue way past midnight, when it finally came time for everyone to climb into their tents and try to sleep—if they could. Those were fun nights… and Brad was enjoying his dreams…

But the happy scenes slowly began giving way to different reality. A strange delirium had taken hold of him in which he saw himself walking along the edge of the creek—but not on the sand, on the water. Brad was moving very slowly, and he noticed how cool the water felt on the soles of his feet, but when he looked down he was taken aback: The water was blood red, and his feet were stained the same crimson shade.

Brad shook his head, and jerked awake. Suddenly clear-headed, he followed the familiar trail back to the Pebble Creek parking lot where he'd left his truck. But as he reached the old Toyota pickup, he realized his pockets were empty… no keys. *What to do,* he thought to himself. No telling where his keys were—for all he knew they lay in the creek somewhere, never to be found again.

Exhausted and confused, he felt for his cell phone. Relief poured over him. It was still in his pocket. He took it out, sliding his dirty finger across a cracked screen. The battery was low—not unusual. Drug addicts can't seem to ever charge their phones, if they are lucky to have a phone at all. But the battery strength was just enough to get one call out. And without hesitation he called Larry.

Larry and Brad were roommates. They were an unlikely pair, coming from entirely different worlds. And Larry was several years older. But they shared one thing in common—tough knocks coupled with poor decisions had landed them both in a pretty sad place. And they truly cared for one another.

Taking the back roads on the other side of Lafayette County, Larry was driving below the speed limit, keeping his eyes and ears peeled. He had just robbed a convenience store near Batesville, a small Mississippi town about thirty miles west of Oxford.

Strange as it seems, Larry always got a rush from robbery. He never intended to hurt anyone—just scare them. And the money he made off with was not usually very much, just enough to score some weed or a few cases of beer. He didn't do it for the money—just for the rush. And only when he was really stressed. And tonight Larry was stressed. He feared he had lost Kaylee for good this time, and he was truly upset about it.

When his cell phone rang, it startled him at first. Robberies always left Larry feeling on edge afterward—normal, considering.

"Hey, what's up?" Larry answered the phone, not wanting to appear that anything was out of the ordinary. Besides, he was used to calls from his troubled roommate. "No problem man. I'm comin'." Larry did not hesitate. He really didn't relish the idea of going home to an empty trailer—adrenaline was still pumping through his body. A trip into Oxford was actually just what he needed. He was getting low on cigarettes, and with his cash, it just might end up being a decent Friday night after all. "Find some place to sit down and get a grip—I'll be there in a few."

After a fair length of time had passed, Larry pulled into the Pebble Creek parking lot. He saw Brad sitting in the dark, on the far edge of the lot, adjacent to his truck. He looked terrible.

"What the...? You look like you've had a rough night," said Larry, as he came close enough to notice the cut on his friend's forehead and register the fact that he wasn't wearing any shoes. "What in the world, Brad? Get in the car—we'll come back to get your truck later. Surely you've got some extra keys somewhere. I've never seen you like this, man... where're your shoes? What's up with that cut on your head? Looks like you had the snot beat out of you. You okay?"

"Larry, you're not gonna believe..." said Brad, as his room-mate bundled him into the old Oldsmobile. "I'm not even sure..." he said, starting over and failing to gain traction. "What I remember..." he said, clinging to the last word as if it would guide him through the morass in his brain, "What I remember is that I'd just left work—I came over here to get some weed—just like I do every Friday. You know? And everything went blank. And then I was walking through the woods, and it went blank again. Then I was in the woods another time, only this time my whole body hurt, and the woods were on fire. Then I think I was walking on water—or, I dunno, maybe I dreamed that. Then, all of a sudden, I came to and realized I was at Pebble Creek. But I don't really know." he finished, his voice trailing off.

"I know, buddy," said Larry, patting his friend's shoulder. He'd seen enough of Brad's trips—and he was very familiar with the mixture of truth, imagination, and hallucination that was always the result. But, then again, most of Brad's trips took place on the living room couch in the trailer, not out in the woods, shoeless and bloody. Even in his agitated, methamphetamine-craving state, Larry found that combination of circumstances odd. "C'mon, let's get you home."

CHAPTER 6

Help in Time of Need

An eternity seemed to pass as Lorna waited for help to arrive. Finally, two black-and-whites careened into the driveway, followed by the sheriff, who had heard the dispatch call go out over the radio. Serving first as a deputy and later as the first-ever African American sheriff of Lafayette County, Sheriff Jefferson had known Radley ever since Radley had become mayor a dozen years earlier. In spite of a few face-offs over the years, the two men had worked well together. Sheriff Jefferson respected the mayor and had come to see him as more than a colleague, but as a friend. His first thoughts were for the mayor's wife.

"Lorna!" he called as he stepped from his car. The striking brunette, still dressed for a party in her peach blouse and printed skirt, emerged from the garage and moved toward him, looking stricken.

"Oh, Ellis, thank the Lord you're here," she said. "I don't know what to do. I don't know what happened. I'm... helpless."

Sheriff Jefferson knew how much it must have cost Lorna Hamilton to say that. The woman was one of the strongest he'd met, and while she was always pleasant, she was far from a pushover. And when it came to doing the right thing, he'd seen her challenge her husband and half the other men in town, and it was one of the things he most admired about her.

"Lorna," he said, taking her small hand gently into his. He was a large man, neatly dressed in his uniform, smelling of aftershave. His presence was comforting, and Lorna just fell into his arms.

"It'll be all right," he reassured her, in his most reassuring voice. "It'll be all right. Just tell me what happened when you got home."

"Nothing!" she said. "Nothing! Everything had already happened by the time I got here! I parked my car and then came back to look for Radley, and then when I came around the car door, this is what I saw. Oh, Ellis, how could anybody do this to Radley? Whoever it was, please, please find them. We must find them!"

"Lorna, it'll be all right. Please, let's have you sit in the back seat of my cruiser. I'll have someone take you into the house and take your statement once we've had a chance to search it and make sure it's clear. In the meantime, is there anyone we can call to come be with you?"

Just then, headlights of another car appeared in the driveway. It was Lorna's and Radley's pastor, David Burton, and his wife Tricia. In the ten minutes that seemed like hours, Lorna had managed to call them, and here they were.

Upon seeing Tricia, Lorna nearly collapsed. Tricia and David surrounded her, loving arms forming a tight circle. It was a sweet but very sad moment.

"I just can't believe he's gone!" is all Lorna could say, sobbing into Brother David's shoulder. "I just can't believe he's gone."

The Burtons just stood there loving Lorna, neither of them really knowing what to say.

"It's a sad night," is all Sheriff Jefferson could say to the couple.

"Yes, indeed," said Brother David. "We thank you for being here, Sheriff Jefferson. And please know we're here to help in any way we can. It's a tragic situation. But we have our faith, and God will see us through this."

"Lorna," asked Tricia gently, taking her hand and tenderly

looking into her eyes. "Please come and get in the car with David and me. We need to get you off your feet while the sheriff does what he needs to do."

Lorna, whose brain was not functioning at full capacity, nodded and thanked her. She motioned to Sheriff Jefferson with a slight wave of her hand. And turned to walk with the Burtons, walking slowly between them as they helped her to their car.

Sheriff Jefferson immediately turned his attention to the crime scene. Lorna's keen eye had registered most of the relevant details, including the fact that Radley had been shot in his left temple at close range. Sheriff Jefferson was used to the blankness that came with shock: the inattention to detail, the difficulty focusing. But Lorna seemed to have had the opposite reaction, noticing and remembering relevant details and managing to convey that information clearly and concisely when Sheriff Jefferson questioned her about it.

The sheriff joined two local Oxford police officers, who by now were standing over the mayor's body, seemingly lost somewhere between reality and fiction. Even for seasoned law enforcement, seeing their chief executive now dead in his driveway was not something they could ever have been prepared to witness.

Ellis Jefferson remembered when Radley had first been elected mayor, amid a rush of youthful enthusiasm and excitement for change, which his supporters were convinced Radley would bring. Those happy days seemed so very long ago now—and here Radley Hamilton lay. Dead.

Sheriff Jefferson didn't always agree with how the mayor handled everything, but he did appreciate Radley's commitment to fully funding law enforcement—even when others, like the mayor's own chief of police, did not.

"And where in Sam Hill is the chief?" wondered Sheriff Jefferson. "He should have been the first one on the scene." Before he could get more irritated, the sheriff turned his attention to the two detectives who'd responded to the call. They were kneeling near the SUV. "What's the evidence telling us so far, Detective Castelle?" he asked the balding middle-aged officer crouching down closest to the body. "Looks like our killer walked right through the blood after he shot Mayor Hamilton," Jefferson added, indicating reddish brown footprints on the carport, leading away from the car to the side yard.

"So far that's about right," responded the detective. "There's no real sign of a struggle, either, so we're thinking the mayor might have known his assailant, or else he was surprised and overpowered quickly."

"Also, it looks like the mayor was shot twice: once in the temple and again in the abdomen. We'll have to get the medical examiner's word on which was the shot that killed him, though my money's on the head wound. If that was the first shot, it's unclear why the killer would have fired a second, though it could have just been for insurance—to make sure he was dead."

"We'll know more once we get the body in for an autopsy," said the sheriff. As soon as the words left his mouth, he shuddered. Referring to Radley Hamilton, a man he'd known and respected for years, as "the body" felt completely wrong. Usually he was able to maintain an attitude of clinical detachment toward his job, even when investigating murders—not that murders were that common in Oxford, Mississippi. But this time, he couldn't help but be a bit shaken. Not only was Radley his friend, but as the city's top elected official, the mayor had made more than his share of enemies—some of whom didn't cotton much to the sheriff either. If any of those people had targeted Radley, Ellis Jefferson knew full well he could be on their hit list, too.

He roused himself from that line of thought just as another pair of headlights swung into the driveway. *Finally, the police chief's decided to get his lazy self out of the recliner and make an appearance at the murder scene of his own mayor*, thought Sheriff Jefferson. *About time.*

As the car came into view, however, it was clearly not Chief

Buford. It was a silver Mercedes.

Before it could come closer, Sheriff Jefferson quickly walked down the driveway past the Burtons' car and met it, waving his blinding flashlight.

"Excuse me. This is a crime scene," rung out Sheriff Jefferson's forceful voice. "You need to back up and turn around." He couldn't tell who this gawker was—at least not until he got within a few feet of the driver's side window, and Sterling Bradford rolled his window down.

The stern expression on the sheriff's face relaxed and morphed into one of sympathy. "Sterling, this is terrible, and I'm so sorry, but what are you doing here? You know we don't need to be crowding the crime scene."

The lawyer's face tightened, and his eyes sagged as he responded in a clipped voice, "I'm here for Lorna. When she called me, she could barely get the news out between sobs." His voice softened. "I can't let her go through this alone. She needs somebody, Ellis."

"Yeah, Sterling. I guess you're right. Just hang on there a minute. The officers should be just about done clearing the house. You and the Burtons can take her inside so she doesn't have to look at this horrible sight one minute longer. Why don't you park over there in front of the house? I'll be right back."

Before the sheriff could turn to go, Lorna had made her way from the Burtons' car to Sterling. "Thank goodness you're here!" she exclaimed as Sterling stepped from his car and folded her into his arms. "He's gone. Our Radley is gone."

Brother David and Tricia stood back and looked on in silence. Sheriff Jefferson stared open-mouthed. He had never seen Lorna Hamilton break down, lose control, need somebody. Of course, it was a common enough reaction among crime victims whose loved ones had been killed, but he was still stunned to see Lorna Hamilton revealed as all too human.

From everything he'd seen, she was a woman who had the will and the wits to always carry herself with poise and grace. A breakdown simply didn't fit his mental image of her. Yet he knew how much she had loved her husband, and the pain she'd apparently shoved aside when he had arrived at the crime scene was now almost palpable. *It is a good thing she has somebody like Sterling to trust and rely on,* he thought.

The two moved slowly toward the house, with David and Tricia Burton following behind them. The house had been cleared, and once Lorna and her support team were all inside, Sheriff Jefferson turned his attention back to the crime scene.

CHAPTER 7

Cruisin' Oxford

THE FADED TRANS Am with tinted windows was hers. No doubt about it.

Larry hesitated a moment—glued to the seat of his car. In his agitated state of mind, he really hadn't noticed it until he had pulled into the empty space in front of Circle K. It was his regular stop on the way home. He and Brad had not long been driving through Oxford after leaving Pebble Creek—and he desperately needed some cigarettes.

The heavy breathing next to him was almost as loud as his heartbeat. Brad was out cold. And Larry's heart raced in his ears, dancing as it were to the syncopated sounds coming from his roommate.

"Stupid," Larry muttered to himself. "I should've known better than to stop here."

He started to crank the engine, back out, and drive away. It was just too close. And too soon. Kaylee hadn't had time to cool off—and she would probably think he was stalking her. After all, here he was at midnight, pulled up to the Circle K just around the corner from her mother's house.

Maybe that's what I am…, Larry thought, *…one of them "unsub-conscience stalkers," or something like that.* His mind drifted back to an episode of "Unsolved Mysteries" that he had watched as a child, where a paranoid husband used to mindlessly drive through towns at night, searching for his cheating wife. *That's me, all right. I must be half out of my mind comin' to this dump—of all the dumps between Oxford and Sardis, I had to pick this one.*

For a moment, he sat there imagining what her reaction would be if she saw him, half hoping she would break into that beautiful smile like she used to do when they first started dating. Those were the good days—but they were long gone. He knew that wouldn't happen. That was a fantasy. Now, he was lucky to get even half a smile, and tonight, just the opposite was bound to happen.

I'm an idiot, Larry said to himself. *Kaylee was right to leave. And I better go.*

But it was too late. Coming out of the store with a Diet Coke and a pack of cigarettes in her right hand, pushing the door open with her left, Kaylee Jones stopped dead in her tracks. "What are you doin' here?" she asked, a look of pure disgust written across her beautiful face.

"Force of habit, baby," replied Larry through his open car window. "That's all I reckon there is to say. But don't worry your little self 'bout me. I'm goin'. I know I'm the last person you wanna see right now. And that's fine, sugar—Can't say I blame you…"

"Well, at least you got that right," retorted Kaylee, heading straight to her car without another word and not even a glance.

The minute she opened her door and the lights went on, Larry's blood ran cold. There, sitting in the passenger seat of Kaylee's Trans Am, sat another guy. Stan Johnson. Larry went ballistic.

It's hard to explain what happened next. The rage that had been boiling in Larry earlier in the evening returned in full force. Only this time, his pounding was not wasted on a trailer wall, but instead upon a dazed victim, mercilessly dragged from Kaylee's Trans Am and laid out on the parking lot.

"Get off him, Larry! Stop it! Stop it!" Kaylee was screaming, running over to intervene in the ensuing melee.

But with every protest, came another punch—and another and another. Larry was just getting started.

"Stop it, Larry! Stop it!" Kaylee was panicking. Feeling like she must do something, she grabbed Larry by the shirt, but she only succeeded in ripping it. Larry did not even seem to notice.

Suddenly roused by the noise of Kaylee's screaming, Brad got out of the car. He summoned all of the energy he could summon. And began pulling at Larry to get him off Stan.

"It's not worth it, Larry! It's not worth it! Stop before you go too far!" yelled Brad, pulling at Larry's shoulders while his helpless victim just lay on the ground, cowering—his hands shielding his face.

A good parking lot brawl always seems to get the attention of bored college students cruising town on a Friday night. By now a small crowd had gathered at the Circle K. The store clerk pushed his magic button from behind the counter.

Just as a brawl draws out the spectators, law enforcement makes them vanish. And tonight proved to be no exception to the rule. In just minutes, an Oxford police car arrived at the Circle K, blocking Larry's Olds and Kaylee's Trans Am. The small crowd that had surrounded Larry and Stan quickly dispersed. Other than the store clerk, timidly watching from inside the store, no one else was around.

Thankfully for Stan, Brad had succeeded in getting Larry to the curb and making him sit down. Kaylee was holding Stan, beside herself with worry—feeling a mixture of anger, sadness, and fear. Stan would be okay, but at the moment, he had definitely seen better nights.

"What seems to be the trouble here?" asked Deputy Frank Wilson, coolly getting out of his police car sporting a menacing long, black flashlight—blinding everyone as he shined it across the open space. Intervening in fights in a college town was nothing new to the seasoned officer. He had been working night shifts on the weekends in Oxford longer than anyone could remember—and with his experience came enormous respect.

Nobody said a word. Stan couldn't, Kaylee was too upset, and Brad was focused on keeping Larry quiet.

The thin and lanky deputy stood there in silence, scanning each person with his flashlight, studying each face, each line and emotion, waiting for someone to talk. And then he saw Brad—blood still on his face. It was the most awkward of moments.

Enforcing the law is one thing—but enforcing the law against someone whose dad is your ultimate boss, and who is now deceased, is another.

"Bradford Hamilton—of all people, at all places, I find you here," spoke Deputy Wilson in a solemn voice. "How sad this is. You must have no idea what has happened tonight." He dropped his head in grief. He had known Brad almost all his life. He remembered him being a bright and cute kid, always well-mannered. He had watched him grow up and had even seen him play football a few times. In a nutshell, he had witnessed Brad's entire journey from promise to failure. Everyone had. And he pitied him.

Brad looked at Deputy Wilson with a vacant expression on his face. He clearly had no idea what he was talking about.

Dismissing the blood on Brad's face as an injury he must have sustained in the scuffle with Larry and Stan, Deputy Wilson had more pressing business on his mind. "You need to come get in my car. Now. Something has happened. You need to come with me."

At this, Larry spoke up. "No, take me officer. Leave Brad out of it. It's my fault. It's me who started this. And I'm proud of it," Larry said, fixing his eyes at Kaylee in a cold and angry stare. "If you gonna take somebody—anybody—take me."

"I don't care about the fight or what you have done or why, or anything else right now. It looks like your victim got the better end of the deal anyway," said Wilson, pointing to Stan, whose head was now cradled in Kaylee's lap. "Just be quiet, young man, and consider this your lucky night. Go, get in whichever car is yours. I will move and let you out. Cool yourself down, and go home. This is over. I need to talk to Brad, and I don't have time to deal with you." He then looked directly at Brad, his flashlight now pointing down to the ground, no longer menacing, no longer blinding. "Brad, come on. Get in the car. I must talk to you."

At this, Brad did as he was told. He walked barefoot to Deputy Wilson's cruiser, and got in the back seat. Larry and Kaylee watched in complete silence. Stan was too dazed to even care.

CHAPTER 8

Chasing Rabbits

As he scanned the area immediately adjacent to Radley's body, Sheriff Jefferson's attention was caught by a few clods of dirt on the driveway. Looking closer, he saw that the ground next to the concrete was gouged out in a couple of different directions, and in one or two places the scars in the ground almost looked like drag marks. He had just begun to scan the area for more disturbances when his phone rang. Not letting his eyes leave the ground, Sherriff Jefferson reached into his pocket, pulled out his phone, and held it to his ear. "Jefferson here!" he barked.

"Calm down, Sheriff," came the voice on the other end of the line. "It's me, Cyrus. Could you please tell me what in the world is going on? I've got about a dozen missed calls from you and my detectives, and this is my night off. Haven't even been near my scanner. I sure hope whatever is going on is important enough to pull me in."

Sheriff Jefferson saw red. Literally. He closed his eyes and the surge of anger and adrenaline sent a dark shade of vermilion to the inside of his eyelids. He waited a beat, took a deep breath, paused, took another deep breath, and then spoke. "Well, Cyrus, yes, I would say it's important enough for that. Our mayor, Radley Hamilton, has been shot and killed. I'm at his house right now leading the investigation."

"What?" sputtered the chief. There was silence on the phone. The chief was at a loss for words. "What do you mean? Mayor Hamilton is dead? Radley is dead? Oh, my Lord. You're serious, right?"

"Yes, Chief Buford, unfortunately I am."

"I'll be right there."

"That would be good," said the sheriff resisting the urge to throw his phone and yell a few unmentionables. He caught his breath. And then he let himself exhale slowly, willing himself to focus again on the task at hand. *Lord give me strength*, he prayed under his breath. Ellis Jefferson knew he needed a higher power to control his temper and help him get through the rest of the night.

As he extended his visual scan farther away from the house, the sheriff imagined he could make out a strange shape in the grass about one hundred feet away, toward the woods, far beyond the reach of his heavy-duty flashlight.

A minute later, he saw that it wasn't his imagination after all.

A heavy brown work boot, scuffed and splattered with mud, looked like it had been thrown onto the ground, or wrenched off somebody's foot.

As Sheriff Jefferson reached the spot where the work boot lay, he felt in his breast pocket for a handkerchief, pulled it out, and placed it next to the shoe to make the spot easier to find. "Detective Castelle," he bellowed. "I need you to grab the camera and evidence bags, and get over here."

As he waited for Detective Castelle, Sheriff Jefferson scoured the surrounding area with his Maglite, keeping his eye out for the other boot, or anything else that might be laying in the darkness. By the time the fifteen-year Oxford Police Department veteran arrived, the sheriff had the lay of the land. "Derrick," he said. "Take a look at this." Sheriff Jefferson indicated several patches of grass surrounding the boot. "What do these spots look like to you?"

Detective Castelle took a minute to gather his thoughts. "It looks like footprints. Maybe three or four people were here, and there was a struggle. Then somebody got knocked down and was dragged up, then forced against his will into the woods. There, it's tougher to tell what happened, because of the underbrush."

"Good work," said the sheriff. "That's exactly what I think. But what I don't understand is why so many people were here, and how they could be stupid enough to leave such a major piece of evidence as this boot in plain sight."

"I'd say that's a good question," agreed the detective. "But since we don't know the answer just now, why don't we follow the evidence as far into the woods as we can get? You're the best rabbit hunter in Oxford. I bet you can track these killers for quite a distance."

"I bet you're right," said the sheriff, chuckling to himself about Derrick's reference to rabbit hunting. True—Ellis did love to hunt rabbits. He especially enjoyed the memories a good rabbit stew could conjure. His had been a poor upbringing in rural Mississippi, but thanks to hard-working, loving parents, Ellis never knew he was poor. There were always plenty of rabbits to hunt. But tonight, he had no time for chasing rabbits. He was on a mission. Sheriff Jefferson then set off into the woods, sweeping his flashlight in a steady arc ahead of his methodical steps.

"Whoa, Nelly!" said Sheriff Jefferson. "This is just too easy. Can criminals really be this dumb? Detective Castelle, come take a look at this." He shined his light at some car keys, carelessly left in the pathway. Not twenty feet further along, a red baseball cap, emblazoned with the caption "Ole Miss Rebels," hung at a crooked angle from the broken branch of a sycamore tree.

Sheriff Jefferson swung his flashlight back and forth between the two, disbelieving. "Really, Derrick," he said. "You'd think I'd be used to stupid criminals by now. But honestly, I shouldn't be surprised. I can't tell you how many times I've examined crime scenes where the perpetrators have left just the most obvious of clues, with all signs pointing directly to them, and then been shocked—shocked—when we showed up to arrest them. I don't know why I give criminals any credit for intelligence at all."

Derrick smiled as he listened to the sheriff rant. He'd had the same thoughts about some of the cases he'd investigated, and was happy to be working a case with someone who also seemed capable of connecting the dots, especially considering that some of his colleagues in the police department—the chief among them—somehow managed to overlook the most obvious of clues in not a small number of their cases. He'd kept his suspicions to himself, even with the current inner-office scandal swirling around the chief, but he kept a mental score sheet of the cases that had been mishandled, and by his count, about ninety percent of them were drug-related.

"Check this out, sheriff," said the detective. He shined his flashlight on a tree near the baseball cap, illuminating a spot where the trunk had been scratched, a low-lying branch was half-broken off, and a dark smear stretched halfway across the trunk at about head-height.

"Looks like there was a scuffle here," said the sheriff as he stepped over to take a closer look. He pulled a penknife from his back pocket, scraped off some of the dark substance, and held it up to the light. "Definitely looks like blood." He reached into the inside pocket of his jacket for an evidence bag and deposited the scraping inside.

Detective Castelle's radio crackled. "Detective Castelle, come in," croaked a voice at the other end of the channel.

"Castelle here—come on…," responded the detective.

"Well, get it back to the house, now! Sheriff Jefferson isn't in charge of this investigation; I am, and we've still got evidence to process back here," came the response.

"Ten-four, chief," said Castelle, looking at the sheriff with a shrug of his shoulders. "On my way. Over and out."

"That's fine, detective," said the sheriff. "I've got things under control here. You get on back and do whatever the chief needs you to do. About time he showed up."

"I'll let him know what we found here," said Castelle with a nod, and headed back in the direction of the murder scene.

Sheriff Jefferson turned his attention back to the tree trunk, shaking his head and reminding himself to focus on his work—not his opinion of the police chief. *Lord, please give me strength*, Ellis prayed.

CHAPTER 9

Calm During the Storm

Lᴏʀɴᴀ'ꜱ ʟᴇɢꜱ ᴛᴡɪᴛᴄʜᴇᴅ, mimicking the motion of running, even though she was lying down. In her mind she was racing for the football, twisting her head to look back even as her body hurtled forward through the grass. She saw she was short of the ball's arc, pushed her inner "turbo" switch, and doubled her speed to reach the pigskin, finally stretching out her arms in a dive and meeting the ground elbows first, but with her thumbs curled tightly around the well-worn football.

"Ha!" she shouted to her son after she'd rolled over to absorb the force of the dive. "You're going to have to do better than that. Your running backs might be that fast, but you can't count on them meeting your aim when they're so far behind. You've got the throwing arm and the strength, but we've got to work on your precision."

"But dad can catch it when I throw it like that," groused the pre-teen.

"Okay, I get your point," said Lorna. "But you have got to be able to throw the ball to exactly where your receiver is going to be, not where you hope he's going to be. That's the skill that'll get you a scholarship to Ole Miss. Isn't that what you want?"

"Yes," Brad admitted grudgingly. "I guess so. All right, mom, let's try again."

"Good," said Lorna, dusting off her hands and bracing herself for another sprint.

"Bbbbrrrrrriiiiiiinnngggg!"

Lorna lifted off her feet at the incongruous sound, and the bright greens of the spring day seemed to fade slightly, and recede into the background. Sitting beside Lorna's bed, Tricia Burton lovingly patted her friend's hand and encouraged her to drift back to sleep. The sedative they had administered also helped… and pretty soon Lorna was dreaming again.

"Nooo!" came a hissing voice that grew fainter with each moment. "You cannot. She's sleeping."

Standing in Radley's study, across the hall from the master bedroom, Sterling continued his conversation with the reporter from the *Oxford Eagle*. "She's sleeping. Don't you get it?" His voice was shaking. "Her husband has just been brutally murdered, and you have the gall to call in the middle of the night looking for a comment from her? I don't care what your job is, you're still a human being. Don't you have any common decency? This is a woman who desperately needs her rest. Tomorrow is going to be even harder on her than today was."

"What do you mean, can you quote me on that? Of course you can't quote me! Listen to me: I'm speaking to you as one human being to another, not as a source to a reporter. Mrs. Hamilton has just gone through the shock of her life. It's going to take her a long time to recover. At least allow her one night of decent rest. I promise you, she'll take your questions tomorrow—or if she's not up to it, I will, on her behalf. Just leave her alone until the morning; then you can call again."

"Yes, I understand you have a deadline. You can get the facts from Sheriff Jefferson for now, and after 9 a.m., Lorna or I will talk to you. Okay?"

The voice on the other end of the line made a few more remarks, then quieted down, and eventually hung up the phone after getting further reassurance from Sterling that he would pick up the phone promptly at 9 a.m.

"Can you believe that?" asked Sterling, sitting down next to Brother David on Radley's leather sofa. Pictures and mementos covered the walls, and in the bay window looking out onto Somerset's side lawn sat Radley's massive antique desk, a treasure brought back from New England on one of his and Lorna's early anniversary trips. The intricate carvings were exquisite.

"People just don't know how to act in times like this," was David's calm reply. He had been a pastor for twenty-five years, and he had seen it all.

Reverend David Burton was every bit a fine preacher. He called it "being obedient to the Spirit," which meant he never used notes for his sermons, but instead depended on divine inspiration in the very hour of the sermon to deliver exactly what needed to be spoken. Most Sundays, he would already have a sermon text and a topic prepared, but that would be about it. And he was not opposed to changing things up at the last minute. That was just his way.

David handled situations in his ministry in the same manner— just like tonight. He was truly letting the Spirit lead him. Tricia was as well. They made a good team.

David and Tricia Burton had met while David was in seminary at Asbury Seminary in Wilmore, Kentucky. They had married young and had their four children young—and in rapid succession. They now enjoyed a full and rich life in Oxford where David had been appointed pastor eight years ago—quite a run for an itinerant Methodist. Their children were now grown and living productive lives—two of them in ministry as well.

David loved people. That is what drove him and his ministry. He had grown up helping his family operate a small bed and breakfast in Ocean Springs, a beautiful small town on the Mississippi Gulf Coast. He met people from all over, and he grew to love them all. His parents had been active churchgoers, and from an early age, they instilled in him a love also for the Lord. And

God had truly blessed David.

Tricia, on the other hand, had grown up in rural Kentucky just outside of Wilmore. She was actually still in high school, working a summer job in the Asbury campus library when they met. But her upbringing had been similar to David's—and as soon as she began dating him, his love for people was infectious, as was his calling. She knew she was to be a pastor's wife.

"What I have learned, Sterling, is that you have to treat people with love," said Brother David. "Even stubborn reporters who call at the most awkward of times."

"Yes, David, I hear you," replied Sterling. "But unlike you, I am not a man of the cloth, and I can only tolerate so much."

Sterling and David did not know each other very well. Unlike Radley, Sterling had never been much of a churchgoer. It had affected Kathleen's attendance as well, and in recent years she had only half-heartedly participated in choir. Up until finishing high school, however, Lance had been a regular church member, mostly visiting with Brad and his parents. But since graduation, and especially since Brad's decline, he had fallen away from the routine.

"I sometimes worry about your boy, Sterling," said David, changing the subject. "How is Lance doing?"

"You're asking the wrong person, Brother David. It's the saddest thing, but Lance and I have really drifted apart since Kathleen died. I think he blames me somehow… I just don't know. I try and try, but our relationship is strained at best."

"Sorry to hear that," replied David with sympathy in his eyes. "Though I did not know her well, Kathleen was a fine mother and a loving person. She was indeed talented in her music. We loved having her in choir when she came, and she certainly was a help to Lorna with her Harmony Here program. I know it must have been hard on you and Lance having to say goodbye last year."

"Say goodbye? That's one way of putting it," retorted Sterling, seeming to relive the pain of loss all over again in the flash of a brief moment. "It was a tragic accident—all it was. Accidents happen. But we have to move on. I am trying, and I hope Lance will learn that he has to as well."

An awkward silence filled the room. David felt like there was more to say—a prayer to be spoken. And without asking, he reached out and grabbed Sterling's hand. "Father God—I ask you to comfort my brother and His son," he prayed. "Let them feel your love and your peace. And bring them back together in a special way."

Sterling was at first taken aback. He was not used to having someone pray for him. But he was gracious and after saying "amen," he quietly thanked Brother David.

The two men then sat in silence. Sterling began to massage his temples and then ran his left hand nervously through his hair, scratching his scalp. They watched the scene unfold outside the large windows, and David seemed to still be praying. Yet more police had arrived, lights were glaring, and barely distinguishable through the forest along the street, television news trucks had already made their home along the street just outside Somerset's gate.

It had been a rough several hours. Chief Buford had ordered everyone out of his way as he took command of the crime scene. Emotions and tempers were running high. David, Tricia, and Sterling had insisted on getting Lorna to go to bed. It was all simply too much for her to bear.

Sterling hated seeing Lorna this way. It was so out of character for her, and her grief weighed heavy upon him. Leaving Radley's body in the driveway had been horrible. She really didn't want to leave him and come into the house, but with the whole world watching, Sterling knew that she did not need to be in view of cameras and police. He also knew how difficult it was to see your loved one placed into a body bag. He wanted to spare Lorna that pain.

The fact that she was unable to reach Brad made things even

worse. Lorna had nearly rubbed her fingers raw on her cell phone, calling and texting her only son. Of course Brad never answered or replied. This was not unusual. But tonight, it hurt more than normal—in fact it tore at her heart. Sterling and Tricia finally convinced her to give them the phone, take a sedative Sterling happened to have on him for his insomnia, and go to sleep. And she did.

The quiet of Radley's study was strange compared to the commotion taking place outside. A grandfather clock somewhere in the dimness steadily clicked a mesmerizing rhythm. David shifted back in the sofa and closed his eyes. His breathing seemed to match the clock. Sterling studied him for a moment or two, wondering if he was praying or sleeping. He really couldn't tell.

Sterling got up from the couch. There would be no sleep for him tonight. He walked through the study's corniced doorway and down the wide hallway across antique rugs and beneath paintings of various Hamilton icons. He checked the large silver doorknob on the heavy-paneled front door. It was locked.

Sterling then eased open the door to Lorna's bedroom. All he saw was darkness. He could hear Lorna's faint breathing and a syncopated echo. Tricia must be asleep, too. Good thing he thought. Before long, the media hounds would be overwhelming the Hamilton mansion with their incessant, relentless demands for information.

CHAPTER 10

Mountain of Evidence

"WHO IS YOUR boss, Detective? Who is your boss?"

Derrick Castelle was used to public beratings. It happened all the time.

"Sorry, Chief—I was just out there in the woods with Ellis, I mean, Sheriff Jefferson, and we were finding clues. They're all over the place! You really ought to…"

"Shut Up!" stammered Cyrus Buford—his face even redder than usual. Juxtaposed to his completely white hair, even in the dim light, his face was exceptionally red. He had no tolerance for insubordination. Not that Officer Castelle was being insubordinate. Chief Buford's definition for insubordination just happened to be very broad—almost as broad as his ego and his desire to always be in charge. "I don't care one thing about Ellis Jefferson and whatever he calls himself doing up there in the woods. This is not his turf. This is the City of Oxford. This is my jurisdiction. And this is my investigation. Do you understand?"

Detective Castelle just nodded, looking down at the ground.

"What kind of power trip are you on, Cyrus? This is neither the time nor the place." Sheriff Jefferson's sudden intrusion both startled and angered Chief Buford—and Derrick couldn't help smiling.

"Wipe that stupid grin off your face, Castelle!" retorted the chief. "Or I will wipe it off for you!"

"Is this really the way you want to start *your* murder investigation, Cyrus?" continued the sheriff. "Here you finally show up—our mayor is dead—and it's anybody's guess where you've been and what you've been doing. And all you care about is who's in charge. And who's giving you all the credit. It's pathetic."

"Mind your own business," replied Cyrus. "This is my jurisdiction. This is my crime scene—and I don't need you tromping through the woods, disturbing all of the evidence and totally messing up any chance of finding the killer. Why don't you just leave? We have things under control now. Your services are no longer needed. Thank you for your initial appearance. You can go now."

"I've already identified your chief suspect for you, Cyrus…" Sheriff Jefferson smugly replied, "… and you are welcome."

Detective Castelle and Chief Buford both just stared at him—dumbfounded.

"What do you mean, Sheriff?" asked Derrick. "What else did you find?"

Chief Buford just stood there—words escaped him.

"Come with me—and see for yourselves," was all the sheriff had to say. As he spoke, a grim sadness fell over him that caused the other two officers to follow in silence.

Sheriff Jefferson walked much faster than Buford and Castelle. They could hardly keep up. He was determined to bring this night to a conclusion. He was anxious to share with the others the dark secret that at the moment only he knew.

They quickly reached the area where the bloody work boot was still lying, broken and worn grass all around it. "We've already photographed and logged this area. We'll study it further when it's daylight. Keep moving." Sheriff Jefferson's command received no complaint, not even from Cyrus Buford, whose present curiosity outweighed his normal desire to be in charge. He and Derrick

Castelle just followed Ellis Jefferson into the forest.

Now well past midnight, the spring air was cool and fresh, with a slight breeze drifting through the trees. The front was beginning to move in. Fragrant smells from various blooming sources filled the air. Every once in a while, the hoot of an owl joined the chorus of a few crickets, frogs, birds, or whatever else sings at night to a budding spring forest. The fast, loud footsteps of the three law officers seemed out of place in the beautiful woods. But the three men were obviously not on a nature walk—they were on a mission.

They quickly passed the car keys, the baseball cap, and bloody tree. Sheriff Jefferson did not even slow his pace. Chief Buford and Detective Castelle did not slow either. They just kept on walking.

Pretty soon, after a short distance through the woods, the three men climbed a hill leading them onto a wooded ridge separating the Hamilton forest from Pebble Creek. On top of the ridge, the breeze was slightly stronger, and a full moon shown through clearings in the trees. Clouds were beginning to drift in, glowing in the night sky, and occasionally passing across the moon.

Below them, the creek gently rippled, and the ridge trail followed along above it. They continued on, drawing closer to the crossing that would lead them down on the other side of the ridge, across the creek, and into the thin woods bordering its commercial namesake.

And suddenly there it was.

Laying open on the ground in front of them, illuminated by Sheriff Jefferson's black Maglite, was the black leather wallet, a driver's license clearly visible in the plastic sleeve that most wallets are known to have. Crushed leaves lay all around, and a few feet further lay the other work boot, covered in blood. There was no other conclusion for the three men to reach: Bradford Randolph Hamilton had murdered his father.

CHAPTER 11

Arresting Development

D EPUTY FRANK WILSON'S police car smelled like strawberries. It's not that he was a pansy. He was every bit a real man—who believed in air freshener. A couple of hot Mississippi summers in the same Crown Vic, hauling countless sweaty thugs around in his crushed velour-covered backseat had taught him that. Better to smell the strawberries.

Brad Hamilton actually liked the strawberry smell of Deputy Wilson's cruiser. And after the night he had had, the dark comfy velour actually felt good. It hearkened back to the day when he was a boy, catching a ride with one of his friends after school in some grandmother's big old grandkid mobile—air freshener blowing from the open vents. Those were happy times.

For a few moments, the two men just sat there in their respective places—waiting for the other one to talk. Every other second or so, static from the cruiser's radio broke the silence.

"Brad, I've got to take you to your parent's house. Something has happened. And you are needed there." Deputy Wilson's tone was somber. His voice cracked, and he stopped talking. Except for the occasional pop from the radio, a heavy silence permeated the car.

"What is it, Officer Wilson? What is it? What's happened?"

Brad knew from the sound of it that it had to be bad. And he had become used to bad news. His was no longer the sweet and innocent life it once had been.

Without a word, Deputy Wilson put the car in drive and eased out of the Circle K parking lot, headed toward Somerset. A few moments later, he lowered his window a notch and lit a cigarette. "Don't mind if I smoke do you, Brad?" Frank rarely smoked in his car—he hated the smell. But, on this particular occasion, he simply could not help himself.

"Not if you share," replied Brad. He actually was dying for a cigarette himself. It had been an awful night. He still hadn't pieced it all together in his mind. And getting cigarettes was the main reason he and Larry had pulled up to the Circle K in the first place.

Deputy Wilson handed his cigarette to Brad through the metal caging that separated the front seat from the back seat, lowering Brad's windows just a bit, and then lighting another for himself. The simple act of kindness seemed to break the awkward silence, and Frank began talking again.

"I'm glad I happened to find you. You know it's really something—me pulling up and you happening to be there like that." Frank Wilson was making chit chat, and it wasn't working. Brad knew something was not right.

Just then, the cruiser's radio sputtered again. "Coroner Davis here. I'm pulling up to the Hamiltons. How do I..." Deputy Wilson dropped his cigarette as he nearly smashed the radio turning it off. But it was too late. Brad had heard.

"What's happened?" asked Brad. But he got no reply. "Tell me now! What has happened to my parents?" Still no word from Deputy Wilson. He only sped up, continuing down South Lamar Boulevard and then turning right on Old Taylor Road. Just a few miles to go...

Brad went numb. Chills ran down his spine. He could not believe what was happening. For a moment, he could swear he was either dreaming or having an out-of-body experience.

Silence once again flooded the Crown Vic. But this time it was toxic.

After what seemed like an eternity, two words pierced the darkness: "Who died?" Brad had to know—and at this moment, he wasn't all that convinced that he might not be hallucinating.

"Your mom will tell you when we get there. We're almost there." Deputy Wilson had said too much.

Adrenaline rushed through Brad's body. He struggled to maintain calm, but tears were already beginning to flow, and his heart was beginning to race. But he managed to remain calm, and for a few moments, silent.

Nothing could have hit Brad harder. The tears were small at first but increased as the reality of what Officer Wilson had said began to sink in. In complete silence, he just sat there in the darkness, not even able to breathe. And then the silence was broken. His sobs were pouring out, almost choking him with their rapid pace—growing louder and louder. In spite of their recent friction and separation, Brad loved his dad, and he now felt totally lost without him.

Finally, Brad calmed down enough to speak. "What happened? Did he just drop dead? Heart attack? What happened?"

His tears continued, however, only silently as he bit his lip to restrain them.

"Just try to hold yourself together, Brad. We're almost there," answered Deputy Wilson, passing Rowan Oak. Only a couple of minutes to go, and they would be arriving at Somerset.

The Hamilton mansion still looked like it was lit for a party—and the party was a grand one. But of course, this was no party.

Television trucks seemed to be everywhere, reporters illuminated by spotlights standing by the curb, a yellow police line stretched across the gate—a loan Oxford deputy acting as guard.

In the driveway, the coroner's van had just pulled up, and Sheriff Jefferson had graciously stepped aside to allow Chief Buford to orchestrate the removal of Radley Hamilton's body from the driveway of his ancestral home. Tempers had calmed, mostly due to the oppressive grief that now hung over everyone.

"How are we going to break the news to Mrs. Hamilton?" asked Detective Castelle, standing now on the sidelines with Sheriff Jefferson. "I really don't know how anyone is going to do it."

"Derrick—at this point, that's all I've been thinking about," replied Ellis.

All of the evidence (boots, wallet, keys, ball cap) had been photographed and bagged—their previous locations now marked by numbered signs. Some of Ellis's and Cyrus's deputies had even followed the trail to the Pebble Creek parking lot, where Brad's truck, once opened, had yielded a blood-spattered black handgun, carefully placed under the front seat.

Of course there would be wrap-up work to do on Saturday morning, once they had daylight, but in Chief Buford's mind, this was already an open-and-shut case. The only challenge now was to locate and apprehend the perpetrator.

Deep down, Ellis still had some questions. "There are just some facts that don't make sense to me. The ground by the Jeep was all messed up," he had spoken to the chief when they had a moment alone. "And also in other areas, seemed like a scuffle had to have taken place. It had to be more than one person—two or three most likely." But Cyrus dismissed it.

"You're talking nonsense, Ellis," had been his curt reply. In his mind, the case was closed. Cyrus Buford was ready to call it a night.

"Somebody has got to tell Mrs. Hamilton," repeated Derrick. "And I think you should do it."

Ellis was deep in thought thinking about his earlier conversation with the chief.

"You should do it," Derrick repeated himself again, and this time Ellis looked up and nodded that he was listening. "Everyone knows how close you and the mayor were," Derrick continued, "and Mrs. Hamilton was obviously relieved to see you here handling the investigation at first. She has a lot of faith in you, and I think you are the man to tell her."

Derrick almost surprised himself. It was not his nature to be this direct with anyone, especially someone in authority, but he, too, had faith in Sheriff Jefferson, much more faith that he had in his own chief. And deep down, he knew that Ellis would handle the situation much better than Cyrus would.

Before Ellis could respond, everyone around them began turning their attention toward the driveway. Deputy Frank Wilson's cruiser was making its way up to the house. Walkie talkies came to life everywhere as Frank began telling them to make way: he was arriving with Bradford Hamilton in the car.

Of course, there was no way for Frank to know that he was delivering the chief suspect in the murder of Radley Hamilton directly into the arms of waiting law enforcement. His radio had been silent for the last few minutes of the trip over to Somerset. Lost in the awkward silence of his car, he had totally missed the all-points bulletin that had just hit the airwaves.

All at once, Ellis Jefferson knew that his and Derrick's conversation was now irrelevant. There would be no gentle way of breaking the news to Lorna. If Chief Cyrus Buford had his way, Bradford Hamilton was about to be arrested.

CHAPTER 12

Take It Downtown

"WHAT IS IT officer?" Sterling asked as he stood in the kitchen, having answered the persistent knocking at the back door leading to the Hamiltons' garage. He was actually half-asleep, having just drifted off on Radley's couch. His unruly hair and glazed-over eyes gave him the look of a madman.

"I think you better come out here, Mr. Bradford—we need you outside," replied the young deputy dispatched by Sheriff Jefferson.

At that moment, Reverend David Burton appeared behind Sterling. "I will be happy to come as well, Officer."

Lucidness suddenly returned to Sterling. Quickly slipping on their shoes, he and David made their way out to the garage and onto the carport, only to be greeted by the saddest sight anyone could ever witness.

There, in the driveway, a half-circle of officers had formed around the body of Radley Hamilton and his SUV. Just behind them, Sheriff Jefferson and Chief Buford were engaged in an agitated conversation. And through an opening between two of the officers, Sterling saw him—Brad Hamilton was kneeling over the body of his dead father, sobbing. A helpless Frank Wilson stood beside him, his hand on his shoulder.

"Wilson! Get over here! Now!" hollered Chief Buford, angrily pushing away Sheriff Jefferson as he was trying to calm him down.

"We must be respectful of Mrs. Hamilton," came Ellis's protest. "After all, Brad is still her son. Right now, he may be the suspect, but he is still innocent until proven otherwise. We haven't even questioned him yet. There has to be a diplomatic way of handling this."

"Wilson, Wilson! Get over here!" continued the chief, ignoring the sheriff.

Just then, Brad started yelling, "Mom! Mom!" He looked at the officers around him, a panicked look in his eyes. "Where is my mother? Is she all right? I've got to know if she is all right!" His yells were loud and uncontrolled. They bounced off the house and echoed through the yard.

Just as Sterling and David reached the group of men, attempting to reach out to Brad, everyone turned their attention toward the house. There, in the garage, stood Lorna Hamilton. She looked strangely serene, still dressed in the clothes she had worn to the party, though she was now barefoot, and her hair and makeup were a complete mess.

"Sterling, Brother David—come with me," said Sheriff Jefferson. "I must speak to you and Lorna together."

But before the three men could move toward her, Lorna was moving toward them. Only not really toward them, but toward her son. Behind her, Tricia helplessly watched, tears streaming down her face.

Lorna's arms were outstretched. She was choking back tears. For a moment, everyone stood frozen, not really knowing what to do. That is, until Brad began running toward her.

"Mom, Mom!" is all Brad could say as he bolted from the huddle of officers.

Without hesitation, Chief Buford grabbed him from behind, restraining him with the help of Detective Castelle, while Ellis and

Sterling reached for Lorna. Brad began fighting them, screaming for them to let go, but the two men were too strong for him.

"I am sorry, Mrs. Hamilton," spoke Chief Buford, gasping for air. "We have to make sure he is not armed. We can't take the risk of him hurting you."

"Hurting her? What could you possibly mean?" Brad was confused and upset. And Lorna became upset, too. "I would never hurt her!"

"Let him go, Chief Buford!" Lorna answered. "Let him go! He is my son—he would never hurt me!"

Sterling and David just stood by, not knowing what to do.

Sheriff Jefferson quickly, but gently, grabbed her by the arm. "Lorna, it's all right. No one is going to hurt Brad. Sterling and I just need to talk to you a minute."

Sterling and David nodded, assisting Ellis, even though they still had not been told what was going on.

The three men escorted Lorna backward, her eyes still fixed on her son's—and his on hers.

While Cyrus and Derrick did all they could to calm Brad down, simultaneously checking him for weapons, Ellis directed Lorna to a concrete bench, just a few feet away. She reluctantly sat down. And for the first time, she turned her eyes from Brad and looked at Sheriff Jefferson, vulnerability and hurt written all across her wet and reddened face.

"Lorna—we have located evidence that, for the moment, requires us to retain Brad as a possible witness. It is something that we have to do. There is no way around it." Sheriff Jefferson was using every skill of diplomacy that he had ever learned. "We have to take him down to the police station. But I assure you that I will be right there with him the entire time. I will not let him out of my sight, and I can assure you that he will not be harmed."

And then, addressing Sterling and David, Ellis continued, "Mr. Bradford and Reverend Burton, I would like for you to come with us, to give Lorna greater assurance that Brad's best interests will be protected."

David nodded in agreement. Sterling just stared at him.

"You suspect him, don't you?" Lorna's question was brief and direct. Sheriff Jefferson did not know what to say, and he certainly did not intend to answer.

"I will discuss it with you, Lorna, after we've questioned Brad. Sterling and Brother David will be right there with us. I assure you he will be..."

"I'm going with you," Lorna interrupted. "He's my son. Whatever he has to say, I want to be there when he says it." Lorna Hamilton was hurting, yes. But she still had her wits about her. And she wanted to know the truth—regardless of what the truth might be.

"Okay." Sterling made his interjection suddenly and without warning. "Let her go. All of us will go. And I suggest we all ride in the same cruiser with Brad."

CHAPTER 13

Show and Tell

THE RIDE TO the Oxford police station seemed to last forever. Sheriff Jefferson was retracing Deputy Wilson's earlier route for the most part, making his way down Old Taylor Road, onto South Lamar Boulevard, and then turning left onto University Avenue. Oxford's police department was a mile or two from downtown, a few blocks north of the campus. Behind him, Chief Buford and Detective Castelle followed, along with several other patrol cars and reporters taking up the rear.

Ever since leaving Somerset, the back seat of Ellis's car had been silent. Brad's head was leaning on his mother's shoulder, her hand gently cradling his face—both of them silently holding back, and then letting go of their tears. Sterling was sitting very still in his seat beside them, staring out at the barren city, the first drops of a spring rain beginning to hit his window. Brother David was sitting in the front seat of the cruiser, praying. Tricia had opted to return to the parsonage, but she was available if needed. By now it was almost 4 a.m. Everyone was exhausted, but no one was sleepy.

The exit from the Somerset's driveway had been a difficult one. At first, Brad had protested violently against being taken downtown, protesting his innocence even though no one had accused

79

him of anything. Finally, after his mother's assurances that it was simply a routine matter—allowing the police to continue their investigation—he relented.

The coroner had done his work. And even though Sterling had not wanted it seen, it was—both Lorna and Brad were standing by as Radley's charming face disappeared behind the zipper of a black body bag. Brother David stole an opportunity to grab their hands, bringing Brad and Lorna both close to him, and prayed softly for them during this time of great difficulty.

"Father God, we ask for your mighty power and saving grace to cover this family. Give them a peace that passes all understanding. Let them feel your love and your constant care. In the name of Jesus we pray, amen."

The expression on Radley's face was, strangely, one of peace. And this helped Lorna. Seeing him at this moment had not been as upsetting as she thought it would be. Radley was a man of faith. And knowing he loved Christ gave her comfort, as strange as it sounded.

Pulling into the station, Ellis was extremely grateful that the new police department had an underground sally port. When it had first been suggested, he had considered it a waste of taxpayer money, but now he was glad Oxford had it. Being able to unload the Hamiltons away from cameras and nosy journalists was sure to be a blessing.

As they pulled into the tunnel, driving up to the glass doors leading from the loading area into the station, a half-dozen police officers met them, forming a column of sorts between the car and the building. *The City of Oxford will be paying out a lot in overtime tonight*, thought the sheriff. He then chided himself for thinking such a thought. Lafayette County wasn't a huge county—but it was large enough to demand several deputies on patrol each evening. And while it was true that Sheriff Jefferson's overtime budget was already stretched to the limit, now was not the time to be worrying about budgets.

"Watch your step," Sheriff Jefferson said as he reached to help Lorna from the car and onto the curb of the sidewalk. Ellis was determined to take care of his fragile passenger.

But Lorna was not as fragile as she had been earlier in the evening. Somewhere between Somerset and the police department, she had managed to find her strength and poise. She was feeling David's and Tricia' prayers for her. She paused in the car for a moment, checking her face in the small compact mirror she kept in the purse—gently dabbing some fresh powder under her eyes and on her cheeks. She had straightened her hair, and other than a few lines of mascara under her left eye, Lorna actually looked fairly pulled together. That is aside from the blood that was on her shoulder. Brad still looked the same as he had at Pebble Creek, if not worse.

Now in the glaring lights of the sally port, Brad's injury was evident—and shocking. Lorna had already noticed blood on him, but in the dim light and confusion at the house, she had naturally assumed that the blood was her husband's. But now, under bright lights, the gash on Brad's forehead was obvious—and it was red and swollen. Lorna again became distraught, seeing her son this way.

In the car, she had already questioned Brad about his bare feet. His reply had been simple—he had lost his boots. But now, under the lights, his feet seemed unnaturally dirty, with dried blood from his torn soles caked to the edges. And his jeans were also bloody, and his red plaid shirt wrinkled so badly, it looked as if it were made of wadded crepe.

"What has happened to you?" Lorna exclaimed, involuntarily drawing her hand to her mouth, as one would do in seeing a gruesome scene in a horror movie.

"I really don't know, Mom. I honestly don't know." Brad was telling the truth.

Ellis took Lorna's hand and guided her into the station. It was time to get everyone safely inside. Brad, Sterling, and David followed, the officers falling into a line behind them.

Once inside the station, Sheriff Jefferson yielded to Chief Buford. They were now solidly on Cyrus's turf.

The lanky chief escorted everyone down the hall and into a large, brightly lit break room. Once inside, everyone's reflection played in the dark glass windows that completely lined one wall. The scene was surreal—as if an episode from "Law and Order" was playing out on the big screen. A deputy quickly drew the blinds closed.

On the adjacent wall, a granite counter topped with cabinets spanned half of the distance—a stainless refrigerator, water cooler, and coffee area making up the remainder of the wall. And in the wide space between sat several round tables, each one circled by chairs. It was here that Chief Buford motioned for Lorna, Brad, Sterling, and David to take their seats.

"Mrs. Hamilton, Brad, Mr. Bradford, and Reverend Burton," began the chief, feeling every bit as important as the situation demanded. "First, allow me to express my deepest sympathies to you. Mayor Hamilton was a wonderful man—loved by all who knew him. And he will be missed."

Lorna nodded politely, wiping a tear from her cheek, and replying with a soft "thank you."

"Unfortunately for everyone, this has caused us great anguish—and it is for this reason that we are here tonight, or this morning rather. We must get to the bottom of all this, and to do so, we must ask a few questions of Mr. Hamilton. I assure you this is routine—no one is accusing anyone of anything. We just have some questions."

Brad began to squirm in his seat. Lorna patted his hand and rubbed his shoulder. Sterling grabbed his leg and squeezed. Brother David reached over to him, just behind Sterling, and placed his hand on his back.

"We have a room down the hall," Chief Buford continued. "We'd like for Mr. Hamilton to come with us—and, Mrs.

Hamilton, Mr. Bradford, and Reverend Burton, you're invited to watch and listen from right here." Cyrus pointed proudly to a large flat-screen mounted above the windows—the Radley Hamilton Municipal Justice Complex was state-of-the-art.

At this, Brad stood up and started shouting. "You think it was me! You think it was me! This is a setup! I won't go to jail for something I didn't do! I loved my dad... I loved my dad..."

Chief Buford raised his arms to calm everyone. Two deputies moved in to restrain Brad, while Lorna and Sterling tried their best to quiet him.

"No one is arresting anyone, Mr. Hamilton," said Buford. "We just have some questions, and we need for you to cooperate. We're going to take you down the hall, okay? Gonna let you have some coffee. And we will get this over and done with before you can say 'Ole Miss.' Okay?"

Brad made no reply.

The chief quickly motioned to the deputies, and, in a matter of seconds, Brad was escorted from the room.

"Chief Buford," Sterling spoke up, as soon as Brad was out of earshot. "If you intend to question Bradford Hamilton about the death of his father, I insist that a criminal attorney be present. He has his rights."

"Mr. Bradford—you are correct," Chief Buford replied. "And no one is going to violate Brad's civil rights. I can assure you of that. Right now, we just need him out of the room so we can talk. I need to show something to all of you—especially to you, Mrs. Hamilton."

Lorna just sat there.

Chief Buford motioned to Detective Castelle, who quickly came from across the room where he had been leaning up against the granite counter. In his hands, he was holding a large cardboard box.

He set the box down on the table beside Chief Buford.

"Now we don't normally do this," droned on the chief, clearing his throat before proceeding. "But in this situation, I think it best you see it. I must ask you to brace yourselves. This is not going to be easy. Mrs. Hamilton—can I get you some coffee? Or a Coca-Cola perhaps?"

Lorna just shook her head. Better to get this over with.

"How about you, Mr. Bradford? Reverend Burton?" asked the chief.

"Just get on with it." Sterling was growing inpatient—and perturbed.

As the eerie game of show-and-tell began, Sheriff Jefferson eased in behind Lorna, sitting down and reaching to place his hand over hers. Sterling had already moved into the seat beside her and was holding her other hand. Brother David had placed his hand on her shoulder, his eyes closed—praying.

Chief Buford pulled out a clear plastic bag containing Brad's bloody work boot. He made no remark—just pulled out the bag and placed it on the table.

Lorna let out a quiet scream—jerking her hand from Ellis's and placing it over her mouth.

Chief Buford pretended not to notice and continued, pulling out the other boot, and placing it down beside its mate.

He then proceeded to pull out the other clear plastic bags, carefully and methodically revealing their morbid contents one item at a time and slowly placing each one on the table.

When he pulled out the bloody wallet, he finally spoke. "Brad's driver's license is inside. It was found in the woods adjacent to one of the boots."

Lorna was looking down at the floor. She couldn't bear seeing any more. Tears were beginning to form again, and she began fanning her hands—as if needing more air, or needing more space. One of the two. And then she hid her head on Sterling's shoulder and just lay there.

"We've seen enough," replied Sterling. "Please, Chief, enough is enough. We get the picture—can we please have a private office or area for Mrs. Hamilton? I really don't know that she can take any more of this."

Brother David was in complete agreement. "Really, Chief—let's give Mrs. Hamilton some space. This is extremely hard—would be for anyone."

But Chief Buford was on a roll. No one—nothing—would stop him from pulling the last bag out of the box—except Ellis. Just as he began his final move toward the evidence, Sheriff Jefferson reached over and firmly grasped his hand. The two men locked eyes just for a moment. Ellis was angry—and Cyrus relented.

"Mrs. Hamilton, I will spare you the pain of showing it to you," said Chief Buford, removing his hand from Ellis's grasp, and also from the box, "but the last bag contains the murder weapon—a Smith and Wesson handgun. Our officers retrieved it just a few hours ago—from your son's pickup truck."

The words were callous and cruel. And Chief Buford had gotten way too much enjoyment out of sharing them.

But in her heart, Lorna could not dispute the evidence. She just buried her head in her hands, and wished she could disappear.

CHAPTER 14

Used to Bad News

"SHUT UP, DAPHNE!" giggled Brenda. "I did not do whatever it is he says I did. Tom is the biggest liar I ever met, I swear. Please do not tell me—just don't—whatever else it is he's been telling you." She paused.

"Okay, tell me."

As Daphne started in on her recitation of Brenda's ex-boy-friend's many indiscretions, Brenda winked at the waiter, and pointed to her orange juice. She needed a refill. But she wasn't at all interested in putting down her phone to ask for one. Daphne's gossip was just way too interesting. Brenda really didn't care about Tom... and she found it amusing that he was always having bad luck and making stupid choices.

Brenda looked up as the waiter placed a fresh glass, along with her ticket, beside her half-eaten breakfast. She thanked him with a wink and continued her conversation with Daphne. Just then, she noticed a handsome stranger making his way to her table. He was a six-foot-tall blond with quarterback shoulders, cheekbones like a knife edge, and blue eyes that made her think of pools of cool water.

And then she realized he was no stranger.

"Listen, Daphne," she whispered, "I gotta go. Somethin', uh, you know, somethin's come up."

Daphne snorted. She knew Brenda well. And she had a pretty good idea "somethin" involved a "someone."

As she hung up, Brenda flipped her red hair over her left shoulder and turned to face the young man. "Well, hello, Lance Bradford. It has been a while! What has you out on such an early and rainy spring morning?"

Lance eased into the seat across from her. "Just taking care of a few errands, sweetheart. What about you?" he asked. Lance had known Brenda Marshall since childhood, but he hadn't seen her in a while. And he never really considered her the morning type.

As the waiter hurried over to take Lance's breakfast order and pour him some coffee, Brenda continued her queries. "Working those late nights, huh? Looks to me like you've been up awhile. But don't take that the wrong way, handsome. You look better than ever—all grown up. I hardly recognized you!"

"I thank you, Brenda. And so do you—prettier than I remember, I must say!" Lance continued—completely ignoring her comment about his work. He continued, "But you didn't answer my question: What's with the early breakfast? You're the last person I expected to see here."

"I've got a new job at Belk's—at the makeup counter. And we're doing inventory today," replied Brenda, taking a sip of her orange juice and continuing to eat small bites of a blueberry waffle. "Just happened to have a waffle craving on my way to work. Gotta be there by eight. I just hung up with Daphne. She's working there, too." Brenda was delivering facts with rapid fire.

"Daphne—sweet Daphne," Lance soberly stated, stroking his chiseled chin as an aristocrat would do. He really didn't care much for Daphne. She had broken up with him in eleventh grade to date some fraternity boy at Ole Miss—just couldn't make up her mind who she wanted. It was the first and only time he had ever been dumped, and he had taken it hard. "Best thing that ever happened to me—made me into the man I am today," he said sarcastically, sending a beautiful smile across the table to Brenda. In many ways, Lance was indeed his father's son.

"Well, I always thought she was crazy for letting go of you, Lance," said Brenda, finishing off her orange juice. "You've always been the cutest guy in Oxford. Everybody knows that."

Brenda was grabbing her ticket to leave.

"What are you doing?" said Lance, yanking the ticket from Brenda's manicured hand.

"Sorry, handsome—I gotta go!" replied Brenda. "I told you— gotta get to Belk's inventory! The makeup counter is what I'm going to be today. LOL."

"I meant the ticket, sweetheart," flirted Lance, the famous Bradford wink in his eye. "It's against the law in Oxford for a pretty girl to buy her own breakfast. On the house! That is after you write your phone number on the back. It has been a while, Brenda—and I would love to get together with you sometime."

Hardly able to contain her glee at Lance's flattery, Brenda quickly wrote her phone number on the reverse side of the ticket, kissed it with her long-wearing red lipstick, and hurried past him with a smile, her red-tipped fingers playing across his shoulder, her fragrance lingering behind. Before she even reached the door, Brenda had her phone out again—Daphne's number was ringing on the other end.

The waiter brought Lance's breakfast: pancakes and sausage with another cup of coffee—black. It was a wet morning. The spring rain had been stronger than expected, but it had left everything smelling crisp and fresh outside.

Lance hurried through breakfast—he didn't have time to linger. Saturday mornings were busy. There would be lot of pickups to make after last night—the busiest night of the week. After a quick last swallow from his coffee mug, Lance paid his ticket, and went out to unlock his silver BMW. Just as he reached for his key, his phone began ringing. No surprise. It was time for business to resume.

As he climbed into his car's dark leather interior, he touched the screen and answered. Hearing the voice on the other end of the line made his blood run cold.

Nothing ever really scared Lance Bradford. But at this moment, scared couldn't even come close to what he felt. He was terrified.

CHAPTER 15

Madam Mayor

I‌T WAS A beautiful fall day in Oxford. The town was abuzz with excitement. It was game day! Cars lined every street as brightly dressed pedestrians made their way to the Grove—the University of Mississippi's landmark center of campus, just a short distance from Ole Miss's famous Vaught-Hemingway Stadium. There, under the shade of ancient oaks, elms, and magnolias, pre-game picnics had transcended from traditional tailgating into elaborate tented banquets complete with chandeliers and fine china. Celebration was in the air, and the aroma of fine Southern cuisine wafted through the crisp autumn air. The weather was unusually cool for so early in the season. Many Ole Miss/Alabama games had been played in the scorching heat of Mississippi summers refusing to let go... but an unexpected cold front had created the perfect weekend for SEC college football.

The annual match-up between Ole Miss and their Roll Tide rival was something Lorna never missed, and in spite of all that had happened during the long, hot summer, she was there— beautifully dressed in her red and blue, her dark hair perfectly feathered just above her shoulders. Lorna Hamilton looked every bit the UM fan that she was. Only she was really someplace else. Seemed like her fate in life had become to always be present, but not really there… her mind was on all of the events that had led up to this day… and on her Brad.

"Beautiful day, isn't it, Madam Mayor? So glad you could join us!" said Polly Shoemake, who was 'Oxford Enthusiasm' all in one complete package. The director of the town's Chamber of Commerce was a small bundle of dynamite energy whom everyone knew and loved. Polly never met a stranger—her face radiated warmth and fun—and since Lorna's rapid succession to Radley's former position, Polly had become a bulwark of support to her town's new chief executive.

"Mississippi history is full of women leaders who've succeeded their husbands in office," had been her standard response to anyone asking Polly what she thought about the "Draft Lorna Campaign." "She's exactly what Oxford needs, and I am behind her 150 percent!"

It really hadn't been a traditional campaign at all… no one dared challenge the beautiful grieving widow of Oxford's fallen leader. And if anyone had tried, Polly would've been the one to put an immediate stop to it.

"She's already done so much good for our city," she would say. "Consider her program, Harmony Here—and how many young souls have been transformed because of her caring spirit. She's what Oxford needs!"

Myra Sanchez had been an ardent supporter of the "Draft Lorna Campaign" as well. In fact, she was the one who first proposed the idea to Lorna. "This town loves you, and they need you, Lorna," she had protested when Lorna first threw up her hands in total opposition to the idea.

"I know you're grieving right now—but Radley is gone. You can't bring him back. And Brad is unreachable right now. Mississippi has locked him away, and I don't know that there's anything you can do that will ever change that."

Lorna almost resented Myra for saying these things at first. After all, who was this newcomer to Oxford to remind her that her husband was dead—or to tell her what the future held for her and her son? But in the weeks following Radley's death, Myra had proved she was a friend to be counted on. Never did a day pass when Lorna didn't see Myra's Nissan Mirage driving up Somerset's driveway—sometimes at the earliest time of morning and oftentimes at the darkest time of night—when Lorna's loneliness was at its worst.

Myra's cooking was surprisingly good—she seemed to know all of the perfect comfort foods to bring. Muffins, casseroles, fruit salads, homemade chips, and dips—the spreads were always impressive. And Myra always seemed to include a great magazine, inspiring book or movie, and the two acquaintances quickly became extremely close friends. A series of random visits were, for Lorna, transformed into highly anticipated sessions of comfort and fellowship.

The campaign hadn't lasted long. After Radley's funeral, the Board of Aldermen had quickly set a date for a special election to replace him, and by then, without Lorna even lifting a finger, "Draft Lorna" signs went up all over Oxford.

At first, she had protested completely. "I must devote all of my time and energy to helping my son," had been her constant plea. But with the mountain of evidence Chief Buford was parading against Brad, a fast prison sentence, if not the death penalty, seemed highly likely. And Chief Buford's evidence was not the only problem. Lafayette County's District Attorney, Joe Peterson, was a driven young man with a lot of ambition. County elections were right around the corner, and he knew it probably would not be smart politically to drag the case out. No politician wanted to be in the courtroom prosecuting Oxford's fallen first son on the day voters were casting their ballots.

Rumors were already being circulated that Brad had been set up. Parishioners at Oxford Methodist had been in complete shock and denial that a child they had known since birth could be capable of such a vicious act. Friends of Brad had rallied to his support. Even national news outlets had run sensationalized programming with footage of the crime scene at Somerset and pictures of happier days when a handsome Brad Hamilton was the football star of Oxford.

Sheriff Jefferson even had doubts. Even though he had discovered the initial mountain of evidence against Brad, it just didn't feel right. It was too easy. And he couldn't forget the scuff marks in the ground beside the mayor's SUV. He tried to talk to Cyrus about it, but to no avail. He had no real evidence—just a few hunches. And any attempt to go beyond the evidence would not be supported by the bullying Chief of Police. Oxford was not Ellis's venue, and the sheriff's office had no authority to challenge the OPD.

At the end of the day, the cruel truth prevailed: hard evidence convicts. And regardless of what people may think, without solid evidence that contradicts the prosecution, the prosecution always wins. Thanks to a smooth-talking defense attorney brought in by Sterling Bradford, the death penalty had been avoided. But Brad was going to be in prison for the rest of his natural life.

It was Reverend David Burton and his wife Tricia who finally convinced Lorna to run for mayor. David reminded Lorna of one of her favorite Bible stories, "You remember the great old testament hero, Queen Esther?" Of course Lorna remembered. Esther had been one of her favorite Bible characters. She had even led a women's Bible study group once through a devotional based on Queen Esther's life.

David continued, "She was appointed by God for a special time and special task—to root out evil and save her people. We believe that you, just like Esther, have been called and appointed for 'such a time as this.' Lorna, run for mayor. Your people need you."

"But what about Brad?" had been Lorna's immediate response.

"Perhaps it is in this new position that you can best help Brad as well," answered Tricia. "Like you, we all think there's more to all of this. Perhaps as our mayor, Lorna, you can do something to make a difference in Brad's case."

That is what sealed the deal. Lorna was in. Ever since the murder, something Sheriff Jefferson had been saying kept playing in her mind: *There are just some facts that don't make sense to me. The ground by the Jeep was all messed up. And also in other areas, seemed like a scuffle had to have taken place. It had to be more than one person—two or three most likely.*

These words gave her hope that Brad could be freed. And if she could do something to redeem Brad, she was in. Ultimately, this is what drove her to run, and win. Brad—her precious, only son, was never far from her thoughts. And this week had been a hard one—having to say goodbye. He had just been moved from Lafayette County to the State Penitentiary—and she was very worried about him.

"We've got a tremendous spread today, Lorna!" Polly Shoemake's enthusiasm startled Lorna back to the present reality, and to the tent and the elaborate array of food Oxford's Chamber of Commerce had rolled out for game day at the Grove. "Your friend and mine, Ms. Myra Sanchez, is really talented in the kitchen!"

"I know—amazing, isn't it? Who would have known," replied Lorna, sampling a delicious bite-sized crab cake on a homemade cracker. "Back during the summer, she did her best to keep me fit—and I think she even fattened me up a bit," laughed Lorna, patting her left thigh with her free hand.

"Is someone talking about me?" chimed in Myra, playfully. "Don't give me all the credit. Polly can do some amazing cooking all on her own. That's her crab cake you're trying!"

"Oh, my mom always challenged me to think outside the box—Betty Crocker that is!" laughed Polly, and Lorna and Myra laughed as well. Polly really had a way with puns… it was part of her charm.

"Well, they are delicious, Polly—your mom would be proud!" answered Lorna. And then, turning her attention back to Myra, she continued, "But, I just don't know how a world-traveling fashionista and a hard-working adrenaline-pumping chamber director have time to do all this cooking! I'm lucky these days if I find time to cook toast!"

"It's good therapy, Lorna," replied Myra. "I love to fill my downtime with cooking. And Matt seems to get new inspiration for his research every time he eats a plate of my homemade potato chips! I guess they're fuel to his fire, so I just keep cooking!"

"What are you girls chit-chatting about?" A familiar voice came from behind Lorna's back. She turned around just in time to catch a kiss on the cheek from Sterling, dashing in a tweed suit. Walking up behind him was a smiling dark-haired man wearing a preppy red and blue woven sweater. "You remember Chris Jenkins, don't you, Mayor?" Sterling asked, pointing to the tall man.

"Why Sterling—I was wondering when you'd finally show up," replied Lorna, half hugging him and then handing him a crab cake on a cracker. "Here—you've got to try Polly's crab cakes. They're the best ever!" Turning her attention to Sterling's friend, she continued, "And, of course, I remember Chris—the brilliant young contractor. Our fine new police department wouldn't exist if it weren't for you!"

Chris Jenkins gave Lorna a humble nod as he took her small hand in both of his large ones. Indeed, he was the genius behind the Radley Hamilton Municipal Justice Complex. A college dropout turned self-trained architect and successful general contractor, Chris had managed the project of building the new department while Radley was mayor. All of the bells and whistles—the sally port, the fancy granite and closed-circuit television sets—they had all been Chris's ideas.

"Mayor, it's a pleasure," Chris said warmly, looking straight into Lorna's brown eyes. "I'm sorry I haven't seen you since Mayor Hamilton's funeral. Hard to imagine how that could happen in a town the size of Oxford."

"I know," said Lorna. "We just all stay too busy. But it's really nice seeing you, Chris."

"The pleasure is mine, Madam Mayor," Chris replied. "And please allow me to say congratulations on your election and the fine job you're doing. You make us proud."

"You're so kind," replied Lorna, almost blushing. She was getting used to flattery—people seemed to pour it on extra-thick now that she was mayor. But coming from Chris, it almost sounded sincere.

"Wow—you weren't lying!" Sterling's sudden announcement startled Lorna. "This is the best crab cake ever! But I shouldn't be surprised—I've enjoyed Polly's cooking before. She's a real marvel in the kitchen!" replied Sterling. "A year ago when I was having to get used to bachelorhood all over again, she used to bring the tastiest treats and drop them by the office. I miss those, Polly! Especially the asparagus dip. You need to put me back on your delivery list!"

Polly just smiled and blushed. Myra half rolled her eyes, and changed the subject.

"Well, Matt and I were really drawn to Oxford a year ago—on a day very much like this," she said. "I think seeing Ole Miss on game day is what sealed the deal for him to pick up stakes and leave Emory. I mean, who can resist the aroma of the Grove on a day like this?" Myra stopped to take in a deep breath.

"Has it really been just a year ago you and Matt decided to leave Emory?" asked Lorna. "I really thought you had been here longer."

"Yep—a year ago," Myra stated with a long nod of her head. "And really not a year. Matt had to complete his fall semester in Atlanta first. Talk about a crazy Christmas! Selling a house, buying a house, packing up, and moving a few hundred miles. It was something!"

"Speaking of Matt, where is he?" asked Sterling. "I've about finished the work he asked me to do, and he and I really need to get together. You've got a brilliant husband there, Myra, and I'm so glad Lorna introduced me to him. His little idea is going to end up making a mighty fine new client!"

"Well, he has appreciated your advice, Sterling," Myra replied. "He's really into these patents. Thinks he's going to change the world with them, and I think he just might. Oh—and in answer to your question, he's at the lab, of course. I begged him to come out, and he said he would try to meet me at Vaught-Hemingway. Let's hope he does!"

"Well, I'll be looking for him," replied Sterling. "Being a country lawyer isn't all it's cracked up to be, and I need all the clients I can get!"

Lorna and Myra looked at each other, both of them grinning and then looking down as if enjoying some private joke. Everyone in Oxford knew that Sterling Bradford was anything but a struggling country lawyer. He was wealthy—wealthier perhaps than anyone really realized—with clients rumored to exist far and wide, ranging from local entrepreneurs to international corporations.

"That's why I'm palling around with old Chris here," continued Sterling, placing his arm across Chris Jenkins' shoulders and giving him a squeeze. "I'm telling this young man that he needs to take his business to the next level. With talent like his, the sky is the limit!"

"Well, I don't know about that," replied Chris sheepishly. "But I'll take the compliment. I guess it takes a country lawyer to recognize a lucky old country boy when he sees one. I've just been at the right place at the right time. That's all."

Lorna was amused by the game of modesty being played out before her.

"But before Sterling gives me the big head, I better get going," continued Chris. "I'm supposed to meet up with the wife and kids in a minute or two. The church bought some extra tickets for our youth group, and we're all supposed to be sitting together." Just as everyone in Oxford knew Sterling was rich, everyone knew Chris was devoted. He had been married to his high school sweetheart for twenty years, and together they were raising several fine young boys and helping with the youth program in their church.

"Speaking of Vaught-Hemingway, Lorna—are you ready to go?" Sterling asked, looking at his watch. "I know you, and it will take us an hour to get there with all of the people you will have to stop and talk to on the way. We probably should get going."

"You're right," said Lorna with a sigh. "I just hate to leave good company—and good food! But duty calls, and I'm supposed to be there before the kick-off. We've got that special presentation to make—you know, today we announce the opening of our new center on campus—Harmony Here is going to college!"

"That's right, Lorna," said Polly. "I almost forgot! What an exciting day for you!"

"Yes—I only wish Radley and Brad were here to share it with me. But my hope is that God will use it to reach our college students for Christ. They need saving just like the rest of us!"

"Well, you got me," smiled Sterling, placing her arm in his. "And let's get going!"

"And you've got us!" chimed in Polly and Myra almost simultaneously. "And you've got a whole city that loves you!" added Polly.

Lorna paused for a moment to let the moment sink in. In spite of her troubles, she was truly blessed.

CHAPTER 16

Hard Time with Bubba

THE LOUD CLING of trays hitting the floors bounced off concrete and steel. Loud echoes clamored from cell to cell. It was lunch time. All of the ruckus only served to waken Brad from a nap on his cot—and his response was just as it was on previous days. He rolled over, placed his pillow over his head, and went back to sleep.

Sleep was the only thing that Brad wanted to do. Not that prison is the best place for naps. The constant noises, made by hundreds of men locked up in cages, is not conducive to rest. And Brad was exhausted.

"Ain't you goin' to eat?" Bubba Riley asked, happily picking up his tray and beginning to indulge in cornbread and collard greens. "Supper time ain't coming around anytime soon, and lunch is the best food we get up in here. And Lawdy, it's a good lunch today. Better eat up! 'Cause if you don't, it's going either to my stomach or the rats. And we ain't gonna feed no rats."

Brad was ignoring his new roommate. *Who names their black kid Bubba anyway?* he was thinking to himself as he tried to go to sleep. It's not that Brad was prejudiced. Growing up a Hamilton, he had never been given the option to be. Radley and Lorna had taught him to appreciate people for their good qualities and not for the color of their skin. Even in their church, Lorna had challenged tradition by welcoming into membership African American families whose children attended her Harmony Here program. As a result, Oxford Methodist had slowly become integrated. At the time, Brad had been president of OM Youth—and he followed his mother's example by reaching out to older siblings of Harmony kids and inviting them to church.

No—Brad was a lot of things, but he wasn't prejudiced. It's just that growing up in Oxford, all of the Bubbas he had ever known had been white—rednecks from the country or good ole frat boys at Ole Miss. They all had what he liked to call the "Caucasian persuasion." But Bubba Riley was far from Caucasian. He was distinctly and positively African American—and proud of it. And it gave Brad at least one thing to laugh to himself about: In prison he had met his first Black Bubba.

Prison was not going well for Brad. At least he was alive—but he didn't want to be. His trial had been held, and he had been convicted... to life, not death. A sympathetic jury had listened to the pleas of his mother. Deep down, Brad really wished they hadn't. "If only I had died back at the county jail," he thought. Coming off his heroin addiction had been a living hell—and he really thought he was dying. Now, far from home and confined for life, he wished he had.

He knew no one around him—except his new roommate Bubba, of course. Every gray day just faded into the next without any real purpose or reason for living. He was far from home, no friends or family to comfort him and remind him who he was. He was just a number on a shirt, his address now permanently changed to Unit 29, Parchman, Mississippi 38738.

For more than one hundred years, Mississippi's oldest and only maximum-security penitentiary had occupied a former Delta plantation. Originally just under 4,000 acres, the complex had grown to an immense 18,000 acres of barren flat delta land, devoid of any trees or landscape—the state had cut everything down so that nothing could conceal a wayward inmate. Parchman was desolation itself, complete with its own zip code. It was only about seventy-five miles from Oxford, but in Brad's eye, it might as well have been a million. It had only been a week since he had been transferred there from Oxford—but to Brad, it already felt like an eternity.

When he was first processed into the Lafayette County Prison in the spring, Brad really did think he was about to die. He was coming off heroin—and the withdrawal symptoms were hitting him hard.

Fortunately for Brad, Lafayette Corrections was Sheriff Ellis Jefferson's domain—and Ellis did all that he could to help him. As Brad's cold sweats progressed to muscle cramps, seizures, and vomiting, Ellis made sure he was afforded every comfort available for an inmate. Jail nurses made sure he stayed hydrated. Warm blankets and soft pillows were provided to him—not the standard issue for inmates in county prison. Even special soups and bland broths were brought in to make sure he ate at least something.

In time, Brad's convulsions began to lessen, and for the first time in what seemed like years, clarity began to return. But with Brad's new-found clarity came another hell.

Brad became convinced that he really had killed his dad. He couldn't remember any part of it—nothing up to the time he found himself wandering in the woods by Pebble Creek. He did remember that he had gone to Pebble Creek to meet his dealer—a guy named Joe. He had told the police about Joe—didn't know his last name or anything about him, just that he met him like clockwork every Friday. But nothing had come of it. They didn't seem interested in Brad's dealer "Joe"—they were more inter-ested in the fact that his father's blood was on his hands and feet. It was all over his clothes. It was on his hat, boots and keys. And it was on the gun—along with Brad's fingerprints. Knowing this tormented him without end. He loved his dad. He felt lost without him. And he wanted to die.

"Hey man—you gonna eat or not!" Bubba just wasn't going to

let Brad be. "Like I told you, it's either going to my stomach or the rats, and this stuff is too good to waste on a rat."

"You can have it." Brad's response was no more than a silent whisper. He was laying on his stomach, his back to Bubba—his face buried in the fold of his arms.

"Naw man—I ain't gonna do that to you, bro," said Bubba, coming over to Brad's bunk. "You gotta eat. I ain't gonna sit here and watch my homeboy starve himself to death. You gonna eat, and that's all there is to it."

There was only silence from Brad. Bubba just sat there watching him.

"Come on now—you gonna eat," continued Bubba. "That's whatcha gonna do. You gonna eat. Bubba says it. Bubba means it. And that's that."

Bubba Riley was not a man to be ignored. Dark as night, broad in the shoulders, and standing about six feet tall, he was almost intimidating—except for his friendly smile and deer-like eyes. And he was as persistent as he was dark. Bubba took Brad's tray from the floor, eased over to his bunk, reached up and gently swayed it to and fro—as if the smell of collards might perform like the smelling salts of old—and resuscitate the patient back to life.

Again, Brad was motionless. But Bubba was determined.

He held the corner of the tray over Brad and slowly tilted it to one side, allowing green juice to slowly pool in the corner and then drip, one drip at a time, onto his arm.

The cold liquid tickled at first. Brad twitched. Bubba let another drop or two fall. Brad twitched again. This continued until suddenly Brad startled from his bed.

"What are you doing?" hollered Brad as he jumped up, almost hitting his head on the ceiling, his eyes in a daze. It was all Bubba could do to move the tray in time before the whole lunch landed on the floor—and he couldn't help but chuckle a bit.

"I don't even like collard greens," Brad protested. "They're disgusting. All I want is to be left alone. Don't you get it? Leave me alone!"

Depression can bring out the worst in people, and it was bringing out the worst in Brad. Luckily, Bubba understood this. He had grown up in Tunica, Mississippi, in a home with a depressed mother. He knew that when people are depressed, you have to be extra patient. And he was.

Bubba didn't say a word. He just went back to his chair and sat down, gently setting Brad's tray on the floor. He reached for the only book he had, a King James version of the Bible that some visiting Gideons had given him. The book seemed tiny in his large black hands. But it also looked at home there. And Bubba began to read.

Brad just lay there. He felt bad. He knew that his new roommate was only meaning to help. And Lord knew he needed all of the friends he could get.

"Why is your name Bubba?" Brad finally broke the silence with the question he had been dying to ask.

"'Cause it's my name—that's why," responded Bubba, not looking up from his Bible.

"No, that's not your name. I just don't buy it. I've never met any African American named Bubba. What's your real name?"

At that, Bubba saw an opportunity. He grinned his widest grin, and said, "Come on down here and eat all your collard greens—I means all of them! And then maybe ole Bubba will answer your question."

Brad slowly eased down from his bunk. He pulled his chair up beside Bubba, and reached down for the tray. "But you realize I don't like collard greens, right?" he said, pausing to look down at the green juice and cold greens. "But you want me to eat them anyway?"

"A man's gotta start livin' sometime," Bubba replied. "Go ahead—put that fork in your mouth and start livin'."

Brad did as he was told. Something about Bubba just made you do as you were told.

As Brad brought the fork to his mouth, Bubba stared at him—his face looking like it might at any moment crack into laughter.

"You don't have to stare," Brad said. "Just give me some time. I've never tried collard greens before."

"I figured," replied Bubba as he continued to stare—and his grin cracked open into a smile. At that moment, Brad placed the fork into his mouth and began to chew. Bubba just looked at him—a question mark written across his face.

"Well—whatcha think? How is it? Good, isn't it? Goooooodd!!" Bubba was excited!

Brad didn't speak. He just continued to chew and chew, as if doing so would put off the need to swallow. But then he swallowed, and he sat there as if concentrating. Slowly, he took another bite, performing the same ritual as before. Bubba just watched. Bite after bite, chew after chew, swallow after swallow... before long, Brad had eaten the entire plateful, cornbread and all.

Bubba was pleased. "Now that wasn't too bad, was it? I mean really—collard greens are good!"

"You know? They aren't that bad," replied Brad. "Really, not what I expected at all. Good actually..."

Bubba jumped up and clapped his hands and did a dance. "I knew you'd like them—I just knew it! Trouble is, with white folks, they just don't know good eatin'! They think it's all about steaks and pasta and salad and sushi... sushi! What's up with sushi?" Brad couldn't help but crack a smile. Bubba was funny. "And you got all these white little rich girls sayin' 'I don't like me no turnip greens... they're disgusting. But I'll be happy to slurp down some of them raw sardines if you'll roll 'em in rice.' It's crazy, I tell you! Where I come from sushi ain't nothin' but bait!"

By now, Brad was laughing. It was the first time he had laughed in months. Sitting there watching this giant of black man pretending to priss around like an Ole Miss sorority girl, his hands on his hips, gyrating his head like a hen, really did the trick. It was hysterical!

"And give me a little of that bitter-tasting wine to wash it down... I really like wine with my sushi!" Bubba continued his dance. Brad continued to laugh. It was a good moment for them.

"Okay, Bubba—now it's your turn. We have a deal, remember?" Brad was not going to let his new friend off the hook. "What's your real name? I know it's not Bubba."

"You really want to know my real name?" responded Bubba. "C'mon—why don't you try to guess? C'mon—guess!"

"All right—here goes," Brad replied. "How about Steve, or Robert, Gary, Howard, or Frank?"

Bubba started laughing again. "Not any of those—keep trying."

"Milton, Earl, Billy Bob, Joseph, Steven," Brad was starting to struggle.

"You've already said Steve—and, no, it's not Steven either," said Bubba—really enjoying his new little game.

"I don't know," said Brad, "How about Matthew, Mark, Luke, or John—it's gotta be something!"

"Clarence," Bubba suddenly blurted without warning. "My real name is Clarence."

"Clarence? Clarence?" Brad smiled, beginning to laugh. "You mean like Clarence the guardian angel on 'It's a Wonderful Life'?" Bubba just nodded.

Brad, his mom, and his dad had watched the classic Christmas movie every year while he was growing up. It was a family tradition. And Clarence, the good-natured angel sent to set straight George Bailey's life, was the only Clarence he knew. "Not Clarence... really?" he said. "I would have never guessed Clarence—no! Bubba sure does suit you better."

"Yes, it does," replied Bubba. "I don't know why my mama ever called me Clarence. And I hated it in school. Everybody used to make fun of it. That is, until I got big enough to set 'em straight!"

"Well, how did you get the nickname Bubba?" Brad asked, suddenly growing serious. "It's just such a random nickname for a black guy."

"C'mon home—haven't you ever watched 'Forrest Gump'?" laughed Bubba. "Remember Benjamin Buford Blue? Forrest's best friend in Vietnam?"

"No, not really," replied Brad. "I remember the movie, but I don't remember somebody named Benjamin..."

"C'mon! You gotta remember Benjamin... okay, okay—here's a clue," Bubba was getting excited. "I likes me some shrimp, and you can do just about anything with shrimp. You can fry it, boil it, barbecue it..."

Brad exploded with laughter. "Bubba! You're Bubba! I got it now—you look just like him! Why didn't I guess this before? And act like him, too! Ha—makes sense! Bubba—Bubba Gump!"

"Naw—just Bubba. Bubba Gump was the seafood business remember?" replied Brad's new best friend. "You gotta get it right. I'm just Bubba. Bubba Clarence Riley."

CHAPTER 17

Facts Can Be Stubborn Things

THE FALL COLORS were beautiful in the setting sun. The portico of Somerset glowed in the waning light of day—perfectly framed amid the golden maples. To Lorna, home looked like a Southern postcard—and she was glad to see it.

It had been one of those days at the office. Lorna missed having Radley to talk to—their front porch sessions had always been just the prescription for a tough day, or week. And in this case, Lorna felt that it had been the toughest years. And it had been.

As she drove slowly by the place on the carport where Radley had died, she couldn't help but look at the ground beside it. Ellis Jefferson's words played over in her mind like a record. *There are just some facts that don't make sense to me. The ground by the Jeep was all messed up. And also in other areas, seemed like a scuffle had to have taken place. It had to be more than one person—two or three most likely.* A cold chill ran up her spine. But Lorna shook it off. She just couldn't think about that right now.

Roscoe met her at the back garage. She was always so glad to see him at the end of the day, and he always returned her affection with an excited bark and never-ending wags of his golden tail. Roscoe was the closest thing to family she had, now that Radley and Brad were both gone. And she loved that old retriever with every bone in her body, and he knew it.

It's hard to lose the ones you love. And Lorna was far too accustomed to it. Without her faith in Jesus, she certainly would have given up by now. She had been devastated by Radley's death, but, somehow, her faith, along with the new challenge of running Oxford, had kept her going.

She and Radley both were the youngest children in their families. That meant that their parents were older when they were born—and their goodbyes until heaven had come sooner.

For Radley, it happened in his early forties, when his mother succumbed to cancer at the age of eighty and his father, who was ten years older than her, seemed to quickly wear out and pass in his sleep at age ninety. For Lorna, her losses came earlier. Her parents both died in their late seventies of various health complications. She sometimes worried that she, too, would be called home before she was ready, but so far God had blessed her with excellent health.

"Knock on wood," she thought as she put her key in the back door of Somerset and went inside.

The warm kitchen welcomed her with all of the familiar smells an old kitchen becomes known for. Gone were the memories of law enforcement and police tape. Her home was once again her refuge, and she loved it.

She placed her keys and purse on the counter and began to pull out some hamburger meat to defrost. Although Lorna wasn't nearly the cook Myra and Polly were, she was known to dish out a good dinner from time-to-time. With two men to feed over the years, meat and potatoes had become her specialty. And she was about to get some much-needed practice. Sterling and Lance would be coming over in a couple of hours for her delicious hamburger steaks and French fries. And she was looking forward to it.

Roscoe followed her everywhere she went, gentling nuzzling her from time to time just to remind her he was there. She changed from what she jokingly called "mayor's uniform"—a smart black suit, colorful blouse, and pumps—and put on her favorite blue jeans and sandals. Fall might be putting a nip in the air, but she was determined not to pull out her winter shoes just yet.

Before leaving her bedroom for the kitchen, she gave one last look at herself in the mirror. "Better freshen up," she thought. Returning to the bathroom to touch up her face and apply some new lipstick made her feel like a school girl getting ready for her first date. But this was not a date—oh no. Not this soon. While Sterling was handsome and wonderful to spend time with, Lorna was far from ready. She was still in love with Radley, and she just couldn't bring herself to imagine moving on to anyone else. No one would ever be able to take her Radley's place in her heart.

Lorna's mind wandered back to how she and Radley met and actually ended up having their first date the very next day. It was really a funny story still. It was the Monday before freshman classes began at Dartmouth. Lorna had been walking up some steps on her way to an orientation meeting when she dropped a book she had been reading. Radley, the Southern gentleman that he was, hurried up behind her and picked it up. As he handed it to her, their eyes met—and he said he felt like he had seen an angel. He didn't say it to her, of course, but later that day, to his new roommate, Steve Jackson. Steve happened to know Lorna—had grown up with her in Brookline. And he got a real kick out of his new love-struck friend from Mississippi.

The next day, Steve seized upon an opportunity to have a little fun. Standing in line at the Dartmouth cafeteria, he motioned to Radley and pointed to his beautiful brunette friend. Lorna was surrounded by a group of other pretty girls, talking and laughing.

"You see Lorna over there?" he asked in his thick Boston accent. "Can you believe she had the gall to ask me to fix a flat on her Volkswagen this morning? What nerve! What do I look like—an auto mechanic? These pretty girls from Brookline—that's just the way they all are. An entitled bunch if you ask me!"

"Aw man, where is your chivalry? Don't you know how to treat a lady?" Radley had taken the bait. "Watch and you just might learn something."

Mustering up his coolest walk possible, brushing his light brown hair back from his face, Radley walked over to Lorna, and paused a moment until he had her attention, and that of all of the pretty girls standing around her.

"Hi there," Lorna said. "Well if it isn't my Southern gentleman from yesterday. I was just telling these girls about you. How are you doing? Are you enjoying your first day?"

Radley smiled, "You bet I am—I love it up here! But I'm sorry to hear that your day hasn't been going all that well…"

All of the girls, including Lorna, stared at him, wondering what he was talking about. It was awkward.

"What do you mean, Radley?" asked Lorna slowly, a questioning expression on her face. "I'm having a great day."

"Well, a little bird told me your bug has a flat," answered Radley, beginning to feel a little queasy. "And if you're looking for someone to fix it, here I am—I'm your guy!"

Poor Radley. It was truly his most awkward moment. Lorna laughed remembering what she said next: "But I don't have a bug. What are you talking about?"

At the moment, everyone looked at Steve. He about split his side he was laughing so hard. And the group of girls chimed in— they just couldn't help it. Radley turned five shades of red. He wanted to dig a hole and climb in. But Lorna found it sweet and charming.

Taking his arm, she pointed to Steve and said, "Sorry you had to get him for a roommate. I can only imagine what he just did to you. And here is what I want to do in return." Taking out a piece of paper, she wrote a phone number on it and handed it to Radley. "This is the number for the house phone on our hall. I'll be waiting beside it at seven tonight. You're going to call, and I'm going to answer. You're going to ask me to meet you for sodas tomorrow, and I'm going to say yes. How's that? Do we have a deal?"

"Deal!" said Radley, and hurried off before the mental image of him blushing could no longer be erased.

At that moment, Radley was on top of the world—and also on top of Steve in record time. Thus began Lorna and Radley's sweet love story. That first date led to another, and then to another. And before long, the two were inseparable. By the time Radley popped the question, he was sincerely, wholeheartedly in love with her, and he intended to give Lorna the best life he could possibly create for his brilliant Yankee bride.

The ancient grandfather clock chimed in the hallway. It was six o'clock. "Oh, no!" thought Lorna to herself. "They'll be here at seven! I better get busy!"

As she made her way back to the kitchen, Roscoe at her heels, she almost teared up. The memories were too sweet. And the hardest part: they were just memories now. Lorna thought to herself, "Good thing, company is coming. Thank you for Radley, Lord. I look forward to seeing him again one day. Until then, please keep me going."

At promptly seven, the doorbell rang.

"Smells mighty good in here!" announced Sterling as Lorna opened the back door and invited him inside. With a quick hug, he continued, "and don't you smell good, beautiful. Here are some flowers to add to the bouquet."

Lorna smiled and accepted the fall mix of lilies and carnations. Sterling was such a flirt and a flatterer. He just couldn't help himself.

"Where's Lance?" Lorna asked, worriedly looking over Sterling's shoulder before closing the door.

"He said he's got a hot date," replied Sterling, bending down to pet Roscoe. "You know that boy—he just won't do. Ran into an old high school friend of his a while back, and I've hardly seen him since."

"Is that Brenda Marshall?" asked Lorna, cutting the stems of the flowers and placing them in a tall crystal vase. "I saw her at Belk the other day. Such a pretty girl. Love her red hair. Said she and Lance are really having a good time."

"Yep—that's the one. Brenda. And she is pretty, and that's all it takes for Lance. I guess he comes by it honest," winked Sterling as he removed his jacket and hung it on a hook by the door.

"Well, I remember her mainly because of Daphne. Remember how they were always like sisters? And I remember Lance really taking it hard when Daphne dropped him for that older guy. Whatever happened there? I hardly ever run into her anymore."

"Oh, if you've seen Brenda, I'm surprised you haven't seen Daphne," replied Sterling. "They are still joined at the hip—even work together. I guess she was off the day you went by. But you probably wouldn't recognize her. She's a brunette now."

"A brunette? But I remember her as a beautiful blonde. What happened?" responded Lorna, handing Sterling an iced tea.

"Who knows," replied Sterling. "Who knows why any of these kids do the things they do. I really am getting tired of the whole thing. I just wish Lance would grow up and show some responsibility."

Lorna was silent. She didn't know what to say. That's why she had invited Sterling and Lance over together in the first place. She thought a woman's touch and a little time around her kitchen table would be just the thing for Lance and Sterling.

She knew Lance hadn't been the same since his mom's death, and she also knew that he had missed having a mother in his life.

Lance always enjoyed hanging out at Somerset with Brad— and sitting around the Hamiltons' kitchen table had always been a popular pastime for the two boys. "You make the best hamburger steak in America, Ms. Lorna!" she could almost hear him saying as she set the vase of flowers in the center of the large heirloom tiger-oak table that served as the centerpiece for her kitchen. "And your French fries are second to none!" She could almost see young Lance and Brad sitting there with ketchup all over their faces.

"I'm so sorry he couldn't make it. Please tell Lance I miss him," said Lorna. "I cooked his favorites tonight, and I'm going to send some home with you, Sterling, just so he doesn't miss out! I really love that boy. You know I raised him just like I did my own. I remember how Kat and I would even take turns changing their diapers. What a funny memory! And so long ago." Lorna was lost in thought again. Memories—what sweet but sad things they can be…

"I will, Lorna. I will," replied Sterling as he rubbed her shoulder and looked into her eyes with a smile. "Now, enough reminiscing! This old boy is starving for some of that good grub you've been bragging about!"

The hamburger steak really was good. And the fries and sweet iced tea were the perfect accompaniment. Although she had always tried to watch her diet, Lorna was a firm believer in the power of comfort foods. And good ole meat and potatoes sometimes just couldn't be beat.

"Well, I had quite a visit with Ellis today," Lorna said.

"You mean Sheriff Jefferson?" replied Sterling, taking a swig of iced tea to wash down a delicious home-cut fry. "How's he doing? Haven't seen him lately."

"He's doing well," continued Lorna as she cut her hamburger. "He told me something that I just can't believe though."

"What on earth could that be, Lorna?" questioned Sterling. "As the new mayor, I would think you know everything."

"He told me that he thinks he has found evidence that Chief Buford has been interfering with drug cases. Witnesses who were supposed to testify against drug dealers have been told not to appear. And, according to Ellis's sources, Cyrus may have been the one calling them off."

"Wow, that would be quite problem for Cyrus—if it's true," said Sterling. "But I can't imagine him doing that sort of thing. He may be a brute, but he's not stupid."

"I'm not so sure," responded Lorna. "You know, back when Radley died, there had been talk that Cyrus had not been doing his job. I think he and Radley had actually had some heated exchanges behind closed doors. You know how much Radley wanted to get to the bottom of the drug problem. And it frustrated him that so many dealers were always getting off. He really felt something was wrong."

Sterling made no reply. He just kept eating and listening.

The drug problem had always been a hard topic to discuss. It had claimed Brad, and there were even rumors that Lance had become involved in it. This subject was something, however, that Sterling absolutely refused to discuss. Ever.

"I know this isn't particularly your favorite subject, Sterling, but I feel like it's something I need to address," continued Lorna. "Especially if our own police chief isn't taking steps to stop it."

Everyone knew that the working relationship between the new mayor and the crusty, old police chief was icy at best. Try as she did, Lorna just hadn't been able to make peace with Cyrus Buford. She had thought that it might have been her gender. Men like Cyrus probably didn't like having a woman for a boss.

Deep down, Lorna felt that Cyrus was harboring some deep-seated guilt for how cold and stubborn he had been during Brad's prosecution. Very possibly, this made him feel paranoid that she might pose a threat to him, making him hyper-territorial and defensive.

"You know, I've been racking my brain trying to understand why Cyrus is so hard to get along with," Lorna said as she got up to get the tea pitcher. "Maybe this is it. Radley may have been onto something, and now here Ellis is telling me what he's telling me. I've got to get to the bottom of this. And if it's true, Cyrus has got to go."

Hearing this gave Sterling a start. He was not use to hearing such threats from someone as sweet as Lorna. "Now simmer down there, Marsha Dillon! Don't go throwing someone under the jail just yet!"

The corny reference to "Gunsmoke" made Lorna laugh. She had always loved that show. Perhaps it was a Yankee thing, but watching westerns had always been a source of great amusement to her and her dad.

"No one is sentencing anyone—not yet anyway!" Lorna decided she better tone it down a notch. She wasn't at City Hall after all, and there was no reason to sully such a great evening with office politics.

"How about some lemon pie?" Lorna asked Sterling as she removed the dishes.

"Only if you let me do the dishes first, sweetheart," replied Sterling with his trademark wink.

Lorna was not used to this. No one had washed dishes for her in a long time. And before she could even get the pie out of the fridge, there stood Sterling at the sink, masterfully washing every dish and placing them on a drying mat.

"Hey, this house may be old, but we do have a dishwasher," she laughed. "You don't have to wash every single one!"

"Learned this from my dad," replied Sterling. "When a beautiful woman cooks you supper, the least you can do is clean her kitchen. And look—it's nothing but a thing. I am almost done!"

Lorna just smiled and for the first time in a long time, she felt like a cared-for lady. And although she was a little afraid to admit it to herself, it felt good. She sliced two small slices of pie and summoned Sterling to Radley's study. It had become her favorite place to relax.

"I just love this room," Lorna couldn't help but saying as soon as they sat down on Radley's leather couch. "It makes me feel so close to him." Roscoe eased up beside her, placing his head in her lap, looking up at her with sad brown eyes. She patted his head and rubbed his neck. "I think even Roscoe misses him. He hardly leaves my side these days—which is fine with me. I sure do love this dog." She kissed Roscoe on the head. He just sat there still.

Sterling nodded sympathetically, looking around at all of the mementoes on the walls and remembering back to the night he and Brother David Burton had sat on that dreadful spring night, just where he and Lorna were now sitting. A few months had passed, but it already seemed like a lifetime ago.

"I do enjoy working in Radley's old office at City Hall. I left it just as he had it. I'm the one who decorated it after all," Lorna laughed as she began eating her pie. "But this study is far more personal than the office. Look at all of our family history in this one place... it's all around!"

It truly was a fantastic room. In the old days, it might have been referred to as the back parlor, or gentlemen's parlor, where the men would retreat from the women for their cigars, brandy, and stories of hunts and politics.

But Radley had transformed the space into a very private retreat. In addition to the heavily carved desk in the bay window, and the large leather sofa, the room featured wingback chairs, bookcases filled with pictures, soccer balls, old trophies, and souvenirs from Radley's and Brad's scouting days. There were pictures from Radley's childhood, and even a few of him and Sterling.

Rising from his seat, placing his pie on a table, Sterling walked over to examine one. It was an old Polaroid, framed in a simple black frame, depicting two very young men standing on a wooded trail, their arms over each other's shoulders. "I will never forget this as long as I live," reminisced Sterling. "Our first camping trip without our dads—it was awesome! We loaded up Radley's old Mustang with everything but the kitchen sink and drove up to Wall Doxey. I really can't believe our parents let us go. We were only fifteen! We cooked steaks, ate Little Debbie cakes, hiked in the dark, and told funny stories until our sides ached from laughing. I bet nobody in the campground got a wink of sleep that night! Those were good times."

The chiming of the old grandfather clock seemed to interrupt

Sterling. And he just stood there as it chimed eight o'clock. After it was done, a thick silence filled the room, as if Radley had just walked in. Lorna began to tear up, and Sterling quickly found his place beside her, handkerchief in hand.

"I'm all right, Sterling, I really am. I know Radley's in heaven. And I know I will see him again one day," Lorna said, wiping her eyes. "I just wish he were here. I just wish he were here. And what's worse, I miss Brad—and I feel like there's nothing I can do."

Sterling just sat there. He really couldn't find anything to say.

"You know I'm going to see him tomorrow, don't you?" Lorna continued. "It's visitation day at Parchman. David and Tricia are taking me."

"I wish you'd told me," replied Sterling, "I would've been happy to go with you."

"I know you would have," answered Lorna. "But it's not like I haven't seen him. You know I went every opportunity when he was still in Oxford. But this will be the first visit I've been able to make since he was moved to Parchman a couple of weeks ago. And it's been hard. I really need the time with David and Tricia— this has all been so much, and I sometimes worry that I'm losing my faith. And you know what the Bible says, 'where two or more are gathered, He is in their midst.' I know God is with me all the time, even now, but I really think I need the fellowship with David and Tricia tomorrow to help remind me that God is always there. I just need fellowship with other believers."

Lorna suddenly caught herself. She worried that her words had sounded harsh and thoughtless—as if Sterling's company wasn't appreciated. "I'm sorry. I hope you understand. I know it probably doesn't make any sense to you..."

"No, no," said Sterling in his most soothing voice, taking Lorna's hand in his. "Even though I don't go to church, it doesn't mean I don't believe. Don't forget that I've been right where you are—just last year. And even though it didn't drive me back to church, I had my quiet moments with God. And I knew He was there."

Lorna smiled. Perhaps there was more to Sterling than just silver temples and beautiful eyes. She leaned over and placed her head on his shoulder. It was a peaceful moment. Roscoe had drifted off to sleep, his steady breathing intermingled with the clock's ticking, almost made her drift off herself. For a moment, she was back on the couch with Radley, and Brad was upstairs in his room, and all was well in the world. It reminded her of something she wasn't sure she wanted to tell Sterling. But she couldn't keep it in any longer.

"Ellis did tell me something else today that I haven't told you," said Lorna. "Something that very possibly could help bring Brad home I think. It's a long shot, but I've got to believe in something."

Sterling turned his face to hers. His dark eyes opened wide. "What is it, Lorna? What did Ellis say?"

"He has a witness," Lorna replied. "A witness that thinks he saw Brad walking with someone into the woods at Pebble Creek the night Radley died. The witness has been afraid to come forward, but Ellis thinks that he just might be able to get him to."

CHAPTER 18

Mother and Child

SATURDAY MORNING CAME early for Lorna. Saturdays had once been her days to sleep in. She and Radley might not even leave their room until around nine, which for them was definitely sleeping in. After a walk outside with Roscoe, they would gather in their big old Southern kitchen where Lorna would make pancakes and Radley would start one of their old love song CDs on the stereo. He had speakers all over the house, and on Saturdays, the house would be alive with music.

Without Radley, Saturdays were no longer all that special. Lorna rarely found herself able to sleep in anymore, and she usually was up early looking for something to do to get her mind off being alone. This particular Saturday proved to be no exception. Lorna was wide-awake at 3:30 a.m. But unlike other early mornings, it was not her loneliness that had awakened her—but her anticipation. She was going to see Brad today.

She had learned the hard way that lying in bed in the dark with a fully awake brain can be a bad way to start the day. She turned on her bedside lamp immediately and decided to read a morning devotion from a book on her nightstand, which was often her habit. This morning, in particular, she felt that God had a special word of hope and comfort for her.

No sooner had she opened the little book, Lorna found her confirmation. There before her were the words she and Radley had prayed so many times over Brad—Proverbs 22:6: "Train up a child in the way he should go, and when he is old, he will not depart from it."

Lorna felt encouragement flooding her soul, and she closed her eyes and prayed, *Thank you Lord for loving me—and for loving Brad. I know you have never given up on us. You are faithful. Help us to never give up on you.*

She continued to read and pray, and every word of the devotion seemed tailor-written for her, Brad, and for this day. Lorna was excited. She looked at the clock—almost 4 a.m. David and Tricia would be picking her up at six. Might as well start the day.

As she showered and dressed, all she could think about was Brad. She wondered how he would look and if she would be able to touch him or hug him. Visiting hours were very limited—9 a.m. to 2 p.m.—and she knew that the time would fly by in no time.

Lorna made up her bed—it was her habit. She couldn't start her day without completing at least this one simple task. She then headed to the kitchen with Roscoe slowly following behind her. It was still a bit early for the old dog. She smiled as she felt him nuzzle the back of her knee going into the kitchen. As she opened the door to let him out, a chilly breeze blew unexpectedly against her face. It was exhilarating—a beautiful early fall morning. This was going to be a good day!

"I'm going to fix some breakfast," Lorna suddenly decided. "Blackberry Pancakes!" The plan had originally been to stop and eat something on the way to Parchman with David and Tricia, but this sounded like a much better idea.

As she put on her apron and got out the flour, eggs, and oil, Lorna became aware of an oppressive silence. The kitchen seemed barren and lonely all of a sudden, and she could almost hear her own blood circulating through her head. "Music!" she exclaimed, making her way to Radley's old stereo. Instead of choosing an old love song CD, however, she opted for an upbeat worship CD she had recently burned for her kids at Harmony Here. She needed something to usher in the day and provide hope and encouragement.

Pretty soon, she was dancing to the rhythms of inspirational music by a local praise band that had visited her church. "We have hope in our hearts—the good news is here. Shout it out to the world, Jesus will save!" It was exactly what Lorna needed to hear.

She really didn't know why she was in such a good mood. Of course, she was excited about going to see Brad, but she had also been somewhat apprehensive about it. Participating in a visitation day at Parchman wasn't really on any self-respecting mother's wish list. Never in Lorna's wildest dreams would she have ever thought she would have a son in prison. But none of that mattered today. This was her only son—her precious boy. And she couldn't wait to put her arms around him and tell him she loved him.

As she beat the eggs and folded them in with the flour, her thought drifted back to yesterday's meeting with Ellis Jefferson. Was it really possible that he might have a witness willing to come forward and help exonerate Brad? *Who is it?* she wondered. *And what did he see exactly?*

She began to worry that she had told Sterling. Ellis had asked her not to tell anyone. But in her moment of vulnerability, sitting in Radley's study missing Brad so, she just couldn't help it. And Sterling was like family. He had been like a second dad to Brad after all. In fact, Radley had chosen Brad's name because of his love for Sterling—Bradford. She dismissed it. "Just worrying to worry—stop yourself, lady!" she told herself out loud. But she made a promise to herself that she would refrain from speaking of it again, even to David and Tricia. Ellis was putting his neck out—and she needed to respect his wishes.

She began mashing the fresh blackberries. *What a great thing it is to live in a time where you can get fresh blackberries any time you want!* Lorna had always loved blackberries. She used to go with her family to a farm in Vermont every summer where they could pick their own. And her mother had used blackberries in so many things—from muffins to cobblers—and Lorna had become very proud of herself when she discovered that they were delicious in pancakes. *Mom would have loved this,* she thought for a moment.

As she gently stirred the blackberries into the batter, her mind drifted back to Ellis's words: "It had to be more than one person—two or three most likely." A chill ran through her, and she suddenly felt cold—and frightened.

Without her noticing, the kitchen door had swung open, and a cold breeze was filling the room. She felt silly as she went to latch it. Roscoe met her with his dark eyes and wagging tail. "What a great dog!" she said to him, letting him pass as she closed and locked the door behind him. "You are my protector—that's for sure!" He just looked at her, happy and frisky. Roscoe was enjoying the chilly morning, too.

She turned on the warming drawer on her faithful old stainless stove—it was a great place for keeping pancakes warm. As she lit the burners under the large cast-iron griddle, she began thinking about Ellis again. She just couldn't get it off her mind. *Could it have been Larry who the witness saw?* she thought to herself. *No—couldn't have been Larry.* She quickly answered her own question.

Early in the investigation, the police had actually brought Larry Palmer in for questioning. After all, Brad had been a passenger in Larry's car the night of the murder, and blood was found in Larry's car—Radley's blood. Larry was almost charged as an accessory, and it was only an unlikely alibi that kept him from going to prison with Brad. Although Larry was now in prison himself—for armed robbery.

Lorna considered what a strange thing it is that a confession to robbery and a video tape of the crime, with date and time showing,

122

could be such a strong alibi. It definitely protected Larry from a murder conviction. His attorney helped him cop a plea, and he would probably serve, at most, about ten years.

It didn't seem fair. Lorna had always suspected that Larry was a bad seed, but Brad liked him so, and after he moved out, he was on his own. Radley and Lorna no longer had any say in his life.

Just at that moment, she heard another moving song, "Come everyone—come to the cross. Jesus paid it all. Doesn't matter what you've done, He washes you clean. Come everyone—come!"

Lorna suddenly felt ashamed she had been judging Larry. And she said a quick prayer for him.

A knock at the door interrupted her thoughts. She made a quick glance to the clock on the wall—six o'clock. Wow, how the morning had slipped by.

"Good morning, Lorna," beamed a smiling Tricia as Lorna opened the door. Roscoe gave a half bark and then ambled over to say hello. "It's a beautiful and chilly morning! I hope you've got your jacket. David's in the car."

"Good morning, love," grinned Lorna, reaching over to kiss Tricia on the cheek. "Tell David to turn off the car and come inside. See my surprise?" Lorna motioned over to the griddle full of blackberry pancakes. "Uh, oh—I better see to them! Sure don't want burnt pancakes for breakfast!"

In short order, David and Tricia were both seated at Lorna's big kitchen table, and she was serving them hot, blackberry pancakes, along with scrambled eggs, bacon, and organic Vermont maple syrup. "Eat up—and enjoy! I just couldn't resist the urge to cook you both breakfast!"

"They're purple," teased David has he paused to bless the food. "Father God, we thank you for this beautiful day. And we thank you for your mercies that are new each and every morning. Give us grace for today, keep us safe on the road, and let us be Christ to Brad. We thank you for this food you have provided. May it be nourishment to our bodies. In Jesus' precious name, Amen."

"Dig in!" came Lorna's reply, "That was always Brad's response to the prayer. 'Amen and dig in!'"

"Well, if you were feeding him anything like this on a regular basis, I can't say that I blame him," replied Tricia. "These pancakes are delicious! And the syrup is unlike any I've had."

"I order it from Vermont," replied Lorna. "Comes from a little inn that Radley and I used to visit. Vermont is famous for their maple trees, you know—and I do think it's the best syrup in the world."

"Well, it sure beats eating out," replied David. "And Tricia and I thank you, Lorna, for your hospitality."

"It is I who should be thanking you, David," replied Lorna. "Friends like you and Tricia are hard to find—willing to take a beautiful fall Saturday and spend it with me driving to Parchman. That is true friendship."

"There isn't a thing we would rather be doing," Tricia chimed in. "You and Brad are special to us. And God is not through with Brad. He is just getting started. Just you wait and see."

"Yes, I know that," Lorna agreed. "I've been praying that, through all of this, Brad would not only be proven innocent—but that he would return to his faith. Just this morning I read the verse Radley and I have prayed over Brad now for several years: 'Train up a child in the way he should go, and when he is old, he will not depart from it.' I've been holding to that promise—but my prayer is that it happens before he gets too much older—I want to still be around when it happens!"

"You will," David said reassuringly, placing his hand on Lorna's. "You just quoted God's word—and may I remind you of another verse? Comes from Numbers: 'God is not a man that he should lie.'"

David's words brought Lorna great comfort. She was feeling hopeful and encouraged—more so than she had felt in a long time. As she savored a soggy, delicious bite of pancake, David and Tricia continued offering words of encouragement. Lorna caught her mind drifting back to Ellis and his possible witness. Perhaps this was all part of God's plan—and Brad's redemption was on the way.

• • •

The drive to Parchman took about an hour-and-a-half. The first thirty minutes along Highway 278 was very familiar to Lorna. She and Radley had traveled it many times going to Batesville— mostly for games when Brad was in high school. They also went that way whenever they were going to Memphis occasionally, to stay at the Peabody or catch a show at the Orpheum, a historic old playhouse just two blocks off Beale.

Once David passed Batesville, however, the landscape began to look very different. Lorna had not seen the Mississippi Delta in a long time. She and Radley had once traveled to Greenwood for a Mississippi Municipal League meeting. They had enjoyed some delicious barbecue and blues music, but that was about the extent of it.

As large fields began to appear, Lorna found them fascinating. Many were white as snow, stretching for miles it seemed. They were ripe with cotton, and large tractors and mechanical pickers dotted the vista. In the South, cotton was still a major commodity, world-famous for making Mississippi both wealthy and poverty-stricken. Many of the state's pioneers had staked their livelihoods onto the cotton trade. While it brought many of them great wealth in the beginning, the tactics they employed would prove to be their downfall. Slavery had been a blight on the South, and Mississippi still was suffering the consequences.

The time passed quickly as David steered his Explorer onto Highway 49, heading south to Parchman. Only a few more miles to go.

When they first arrived at the main gate, Lorna was surprised by the way it looked. A large metal sign with clean white letters told her she was at the right place. Red brick columns framed the entrance, and a grove of trees shaded the driveway. It gave the impression that one was arriving at a rural retreat, and not a prison.

Once at the gate, however, she knew very well where she was. It was a prison, and guards were already at David's door, asking questions and checking the car for contraband.

"I don't see Tricia Burton on the visitation list," a young female guard reported—almost rudely. "She can't go."

"But she must be on the list if I'm on the list," protested David. "I'm his pastor, and she's my wife."

"I'm sorry, Reverend," the young woman's attitude changed, hearing he was a pastor, but the answer was still the same. "She can go with you into the visitor's center, but once you get on the bus that will take you to the prison, she will have to stay at the center. I'm sorry, but those are MDOC regulations, not mine."

"It's okay, David," Tricia reassured her husband. "It's really you and Lorna he needs to see. I'll just hang out and read a book I brought along. It'll be fine."

Reluctantly, David agreed and proceeded to park the SUV. They then made their way to the Parchman visitor's center—a neat-looking building with a porch across the front. It seemed small, however, compared to "WARNING"—the large red letters on a gigantic sign practically dwarfed the building. Undoubtedly, any visitor caught breaking any of the rules might find their day visit extended by a year or two.

People were everywhere. Apparently, Saturday visitation at Parchman was a well-attended social event. Ladies all done up, older men and women, even children wearing their Sunday best, could be seen making their way through the checkpoints.

Lorna didn't mind the frisking that took place. She knew it was necessary, and she had been careful to look up the rules in advance: no jewelry other than her wedding band and cross pendant. Not much money either and she had to account for it both entering and leaving. Thankfully, she had dressed conservatively in jeans, a sweater, and tennis shoes—nothing set off the wand metal detector as the female guard checked her.

Within an hour, she and David had been processed, said good-bye to Tricia, and ridden a crowded white school bus to Unit 29 where Brad was housed.

As they approached the main prison area, Parchman began to resemble the descriptions Brad had provided in his letters. It was barren—and immense, twenty-eight square miles of nothing but fields and cotton. She had heard that many of the inmates worked long hours in the fields picking cotton. She wondered if this were true. From what she could tell, there was still plenty to be picked.

After walking through gates in intertwining cyclone fences topped with razor-pointed wire, Lorna and David were guided through heavy steel doors and into another checkpoint area. Once cleared, they were escorted to what resembled a large public school cafeteria, and allowed to sit.

In an instant, Lorna was hugging her son—tears streaming down both of their faces. David just stood by, his hand on Brad's shoulder, waiting his turn.

"I can't believe you're here," is all Brad could say, crying on his mother's shoulder. "I can't believe you're here. I can't believe you're here. I've missed you so much, Mom. I've missed you so much."

"There, there," Lorna whispered into his ear. "I'm here. Brother David is here. It's all going to be okay. It's okay, my darling Brad-ford. You're going to be okay."

After a few moments of more hugs, tears, and tender words, Brad finally turned to David and said, "Thank you for bringing her, Brother David. Thank you." He reached out to shake David's hand only to be pulled in close for a hug.

"I'm glad to see you, Brad," said David. "You look good! And I can tell you've been eating!" David playfully patted Brad's gut.

"Yeah," Brad cracked a smile. "You can thank my roommate Bubba for that. He's made me eat all the stuff I used to think was nasty. It's all they give you up here—and I'm learning that it's not half bad."

"Well, you look great, my boy," Lorna said with a smile, squeezing his hand. Brad hadn't let go of it since they sat down.

For what he had been through, Brad actually did look okay. He had put on a little weight even since the last time she had seen him. And gone were the glazed eyes of a drug addict carrying the frail look of death on his face. *Prison might be a hard a place, but it is better than a heroin addiction,* Lorna couldn't help but think to herself, saying a quick prayer of thanks under her breath to God that Brad was alive and not dead.

"Tell me about Oxford, Mom," was Brad's next statement. "How does it feel—your first football season as mayor. I bet you're making all the rounds—just like Dad used to do."

Before Lorna could answer, Brad began to cry. He was missing his dad so much, and guilt was eating a hole in his heart.

"It's nice, Brad," Lorna said, squeezing his hand again and fighting back tears herself. "But I can't say that I'm loving it as much as your dad always seemed to. You know, he was just cut out to be a politician—he had all the right stuff!"

Brad made no reply. He just cried. Lorna continued to squeeze his hand and rub his back while Brother David placed his hand on his shoulder and said, "Brad—mind if I pray with you?"

Brad shook his head at first and then began to nod. "It's okay, Brother David—I mean I don't mind. Please do."

David closed his eyes and was quiet for a moment. All around them people were talking and laughing—some were crying—but Lorna and Brad didn't seem to notice. Neither did Brother David as he spoke his prayer: "God I'm with my brother right now, and I feel his pain. I know he's blaming himself for something he doesn't exactly understand. None of us do. But you do. And we ask you to grant him peace, pardon his sin just as you have pardoned all of us, for, like the Apostle Paul, we have all sinned and fallen short of the Glory of God."

Just then, David turned to Brad and reminded him of a Bible story he had told Brad long ago when Brad was still active in youth. "You remember when Paul and Silas were in prison? They sang songs to the Lord, and God had mercy on them and sent an earthquake to break down the walls and set them free." He then looked Brad square in the eyes and spoke these words, "Brad—Jesus is going to do that for you. Just sing songs and praise Him. That is all you have to do."

Brad did not speak a word. But he nodded and placed his hand in Brother David's, in the form of a handshake, and squeezed it.

With that, David excused himself. "I'm going to find a bathroom and the canteen while y'all have a chance to visit. And Brad—I'm going to bring you back a Coke and a Snickers—how does that sound?"

"Sounds good," Brad said, placing his head once again on Lorna's shoulder and sliding down in his seat.

The busy visiting room suddenly vanished from around them, all of the noise stopped. For a small window in time, for what seemed longer than it actually was, Lorna and Brad were back on their front porch at Somerset, sitting on the swing together in the early morning. He had his head on her shoulder. They were holding each other's hand. And the sun was rising.

CHAPTER 19

Family Business

"I'M REALLY GETTING tired of doing this." Lance was sitting beside his friend and lieutenant, Joe Parker, on the open tailgate of Joe's shiny new Silverado.

"Aw, c'mon, Lance," reassured Joe. "You're the best at this business. You run the routes like nobody else can. You're always straight-up with people, and they respect you. You've got a good thing going. Don't mess it up."

"I know—to all the world it looks like I'm doing fine," replied Lance. "I've got a nice BMW, a beautiful girlfriend, all the clothes and gadgets I want. You're right." Lance paused for a moment, as if he couldn't get out what he really wanted to say. Finally he continued, "But I wake up in fear every single day and night of my life. I'm constantly looking over my shoulder, and it's reaching the point where I can't even go to sleep anymore for fear I won't wake up."

"Man, that's crazy. C-R-A-Z-Y! You know I've got your back!" said Joe sincerely, rubbing his friend's shoulders and patting him on his back. "And you know—I need you to stick around for my own selfish reasons—'cause I know you've got mine."

"Yeah, I know, Joe," agreed Lance. "We have gotten pretty tight. And you know I love you like a brother." Lance placed his hand on Joe's shoulders, returning the gesture of friendship and loyalty.

"But still, I get to thinking deep down there's gotta be a better life," continued Lance. "And Brenda gets to talking about the future, and you know—I almost start believing it when she says it. That we could have a beautiful future together."

"Lance, that's good and all, but may I remind you who your true friends and partners are? Brenda's awesome and beautiful, she is—but how long have y'all been hanging out? Five, six months maybe?"

"Seven to be exact." Lance was smitten.

"Man, you do got it bad. I see what the problem is," Joe started to laugh. "You got a woman on the brain. And once that happens, nothin' else works right. Trust me—I know. Been there. Done that."

"No, it's not just Brenda, Joe," said Lance. "It's me. Even before we started dating, I was having thoughts about getting out of the business. It's just not what it used to be. Too many people involved. Too many levels. And you run yourself crazy watching this hand while the other one is doing whatever it's doing behind your back—or into your back. I feel like you're the only person in this whole organization I can trust. And it's making me paranoid. I really don't like who I'm becoming."

"Okay, my brother. I can tell you're stressed out over this," said Joe. "Just calm down. Take a breather. It's not all that bad—you know it ain't. I've got your back, and so does everybody else. Our ties run deep—we're a family." Joe paused a second or two, not sure if he should say what he was about to say. But he had to. "Lance, bottom line, at the end of the day, you got to remember what CJ says."

"I know—'once you're in, you never can quit,'" replied Lance. "I've heard it a million times."

"Well, it's true, pal. I know it stinks sometimes, but it's true," said Joe. "We ain't runnin' a charity here. It's not all volunteer work where you come and go as you please. You know that. You know the rules. You help enforce the rules—and it is what it is. If you wanted a job you could quit, you should've taken up bagging groceries at Piggly Wiggly."

Lance didn't say a word. He knew his friend was telling him the truth.

"So what do I tell Brenda?" Lance asked.

"Tell Brenda what?" asked Joe. "She your new boss now? Son—don't tell me you're starting to let her call the shots already."

"She's starting to ask questions, Joe." Lance couldn't believe he was saying this, but he was desperate for someone to talk to. "She's always wondering where I am Friday nights and Saturday mornings. I tell her I'm doing stuff for my job and she asks me what job? She doesn't even think I have one—I'm pretty sure. She's always teasing me about my trust fund and stuff. Even though my dad and I aren't even on speaking terms, and she knows that."

There was silence. The woods around them barely even moved, except for the occasional leaf falling from a random breeze. The two friends had chosen an isolated spot for a meeting, but at this moment, Lance was beginning to wonder if meeting with Joe had been a good idea. He caught himself making a quick glance to the forest around him, half expecting someone to jump out with a gun and take him out.

"You got a problem, man," Joe stated coldly, shaking his head. "You got a problem."

"I know," replied Lance. "I should've done like you. No commitments. No one to answer to."

"Remain free," Joe repeated their primary motto. "Remain free so you don't get caught."

Joe paused to let the words sink in. Lance had heard them a thousand times, but they were beginning to take on new meaning now. *But I'm not free. Haven't been for a long time…* Lance decided to keep his thoughts to himself.

Joe continued, "Problem here, man, is you could take us all

down with you. And what would that do? Huh? What would that do? I tell you what—nothin' good would come of it. You got a death wish? You want to spend the rest of your life looking through bars? Or not even looking at all 'cause you're in the ground dead?"

Lance was scared. He glanced sideways at the forest again and then looked at Joe with the most sincere expression he could muster.

"You're right, Joe. Forget I mentioned it," Lance replied. "We're cool, man. I'm gonna break up with her tonight. I swear I am. She's messin' with my head, Brother. I just needed my man to set me straight. Thanks, boss."

The two men shook hands like they always did, with a flourish that was only known to them.

"I love you, man," Joe said, looking Lance straight in the eyes. "And I got your back. You can count on that."

"I know you do, brother." Lance gave him a hug. "And I love you, too. Thanks, man, for listening to me."

After a little more small talk, both men descended from the Silverado and called the meeting a success. Lance said he felt better, Joe said he was glad they talked, and with a final handshake and hug, they parted ways.

Joe's truck kicked up dust as it passed Lance's BMW. But Lance wasn't going anywhere just yet. He wanted to be alone.

As he sat there in the forest, he had a brief urge to drive away and never come back. Before running into Brenda on that fateful Saturday morning in April, he really was considering it. Maybe he should run away—and take her with him.

"No," he thought. "That would never work."

Other than Brenda, there really was nothing holding him back from leaving. With his mother gone, and no contact with his dad, what did he have to lose? No one really cared about him in Oxford anyway.

How had life gotten like this? Lance just didn't have a clue. One minute, he and Brad were having the time of their life. It was the fall of their senior year. They were always doing something fun it seemed—hanging out at Sardis, double-dating to the movies, and playing goofy golf afterward. Corny stuff really—nothing bad and nothing too serious. He and Brad had been good kids, after all, and they just wanted to have an innocent, good time.

And it had all been innocent and good—a totally different time than the time he was having now. For a brief second, his mind went to the last sermon he ever remembered Brother David preach: Choices and Consequences. It had something to do with a verse out of Deuteronomy about blessings and curses. Lance once felt blessed. Now all he felt was cursed.

Thinking about Brother David made him think about Brad again—and all of the fun they used to have. They had been like brothers. The tragedy of Brad's last senior football game quickly played out in his mind. It was like yesterday. At one moment, all was bright and beautiful in the world. At the next, it wasn't. That's where Lance's downward spiral had actually begun—he went down right along with Brad, just in a different way. Instead of becoming the user, he became the supplier. Trying to be a friend at first, he convinced himself he was doing the right thing—just being a good friend. Lance was always a master at convincing himself of what he wanted to believe.

His thought jumped from Brad to Mr. Radley. How he had loved and admired that man. Being parked in the woods brought a quick flashback to the camping trips they had taken in scouts, and all of the great lessons and stories Radley had told him. In many ways, he loved Radley more than he did his own father. Sterling had always been so busy working at his law office that he and Lance never had much of a relationship. Kathleen had taken up all of the slack. And she had done an amazing job. It's probably why he had been so good—he really looked up to her and never wanted to disappoint her. She always called him her "good son"—and he had always tried his best to live up to it.

"Why did she have to die?" Lance suddenly screamed up to heaven, hitting the steering wheel with such force that he bruised his hand. Here lay the primary source of his anguish. His mother had died, and he didn't understand. How could a God who loves have taken his mother away like that? Lance sat and cried for a few minutes, cursing God and hating the life that his had become.

And then he began to think of Mr. Radley again. He felt so guilty. He knew Radley was dead because of him. If only he could take it back. If only he could take it back.

Lance's body became numb. He shut off his brain—this was his best survival skill. He cranked his BMW and headed down the dirt road. Time to breakup with Brenda. *Remain free so you don't get caught.*

CHAPTER 20

Unlikely Friends

THE SOUNDS OF voices filled the new building on the Ole Miss campus. They were voices of all ages—from kindergartners to college students, and they were singing and clapping to the upbeat music of another praise band—"Jesus shine your light, let it light up your world. Let it chase away the darkness and warm with your love. Jesus shine your light, shine your light on your world!"

From her place in front, Lorna Hamilton was totally into the music—clapping her hands, a big smile on her face as she moved to the beat and directed the kids from Harmony Here. It was the first Monday at the new center, and her decision to combine the two programs into one for this inaugural event was proving to be a good one.

"We will arise and shine, shine forth your love. We will arise and shine, shine through the darkness, Jesus shine your light, let us light up your world. Let us light up your world with your love!" The verse was both meaningful and fun to sing, and everyone was into it.

Lorna considered it appropriate that the kids and students be all together for this first session—after all, many of the college students had started out in Harmony Here when Lorna had first begun the program at Oxford Methodist so many years ago. It was amazing to see them now in college and another generation step-ping in to take their place.

"There is no place in this world that can escape your love. There is no place in this world that can remain in the darkness, with you shining your light, shining your light of love."

Lorna couldn't believe she was actually directing children from such a wide span of time and experience at such a beautiful new facility, placed at the very heart of Mississippi's oldest university. The private donations had rolled in, and the state-of-the-art build-ing she had long dreamed of was now a reality.

At first, some had protested the idea of a Christian ministry on a state-owned college campus. But Lorna had been relentless—and with her own legal training and help from the sharp minds of Radley's former law partners, victory had been hers. She had suc-cessfully convinced the state attorney general and college board, along with the courts, that there was no difference in granting Harmony Here the same kind of long-term land lease given to fraternity and sorority houses. Now completed in beautiful stone and brick, the center would surely last for at least one hundred years, and Lorna's prayer was that, by then, someone else would be around to see the lease renewed.

"Let your mighty kingdom reign, let it reign oh God, let it reign in Heaven and Earth." The final song of Monday's afternoon ses-sion was coming to an end. And it had been wonderful.

After the session was over, one by one, children and college students filed past Lorna, hugging her through enthusiastic smiles and laughter. For some, it had been a sweet reunion—Lorna hadn't directed the college kids in many years—not since they had been in her children's choir at OM. She was so glad to see them, choking back tears as she hugged the necks of several who had been Brad's closest friends in childhood. Her only wish now was that Brad and Radley could be here to share this moment. But there really had been no time for sadness and tears—the joy of the day had been too abundant and complete.

"Congratulations, Lorna—what an awesome beginning!" Tricia Burton was not only a great helper—she was a fantastic encourager.

"Thank you, Tricia," Lorna replied, hugging her neck and then looking to the sound booth and waving. "I couldn't have done it without you and Brother David." Reverend David Burton waved back. He had volunteered to run sound, and by the smile on his face it was evident that he had thoroughly enjoyed his task.

"Madam Mayor, I want to thank you for including Stacie today," a young tallish blonde-haired woman, attractive but plainly dressed, was offering her hand out to Lorna. It was Kaylee Jones—Larry Palmer's ex-girlfriend. "What do you say to Ms. Lorna?" She was holding a small boy in one arm. Standing beside her was a small carbon copy of herself, holding her hand and grinning shyly up at the smiling mayor.

"Thank you, Miss Lorna," Stacie said sweetly, pressing against her mother's leg as she said it.

"It was my pleasure!" exclaimed Lorna, looking down at the little girl, gently stroking her soft blonde hair. "I'm so glad you're finally old enough to come to Harmony Here! You're such a big girl!"

Stacie blushed and grinned again at Lorna.

"And your time is coming soon!" Lorna continued, brushing the little boy on his head as he buried his face in his mother's shoulder.

"Josh is a little shy, Mayor," Kaylee said. "But I can tell he likes you." Josh was beginning a game of peek-a-boo with Lorna, and she was loving it. Stacie looked on giggling.

"My name is Kaylee, by the way. I don't think we've ever met. But I really appreciate what you're trying to do for the kids in Oxford," Kaylee continued. "It's really needed—I just wish Harmony Here had been around when I was a kid. I love to sing!"

"Really?" Lorna saw an opportunity. "We really need some help around here, Kaylee. I see you've got your hands full with this little guy…" Lorna was tickling his leg, and Josh was laughing. "…But we have a place for you if you ever have time to volunteer. We'd love to have you!"

"I actually would like that," Kaylee replied. "My mom helps me out with Josh from time to time, and I could easily come along with Stacie on the days she has Harmony. What do you need?"

"Well, now that I've opened this center, I have two programs to keep going—and you know there's also that place called City Hall?" Lorna was smiling, and Kaylee was getting the message.

"You have to be the busiest lady in town!" Kaylee said, shaking her head. "I don't know how you do all that you do."

"I have great help," Lorna said, pulling Tricia close. "Have you met Tricia and David Burton?" By now, David had joined his wife and reached out his hand to Kaylee.

"Hi, Kaylee, I'm Brother David, and this is my wife Tricia," the preacher said, making introductions and shaking hands with Kaylee, Stacie, and Josh.

"I've actually heard you preach a couple of times," Kaylee said through a smile. "I loved it."

"And I think we've met," Tricia said reaching out her hand as well. "You actually sat behind me during one of those sermons, remember? I was late because of Sunday school and sat in the back that day. I still remember how well-behaved your kids were!"

"Well, they better be!" laughed Kaylee. "Or they know they'll catch it! And yes—I remember you, Mrs. Tricia. So good to put a name with a face."

"Well, since you know everybody, I think you're already on your way to fitting in with us at Harmony Here," Lorna said. "I'm going to be looking for you—we actually meet again this Wednesday at the church—just the kids this time—at our normal time. And I'll be looking for you, Stacie!"

Stacie smiled and pressed against her mother. Kaylee smiled, too, and nodded her head, "I'll be there."

"Well, just know you're always welcome at Oxford Methodist,"

David replied, Tricia nodding her head in agreement."

"And you, Stacie and Josh, are always welcome to sit with me," Tricia added, reaching out to pat Kaylee's shoulder. "We would love to have you."

"Thanks," Kaylee replied, her expression then turning serious as she looked at Lorna. "Ms. Lorna, I just want to say… uh, I wanted to let you know… that I'm sorry about what all you've been through—and, um, … I hope Brad is doing okay."

"Oh, you know Brad?" Lorna asked with a suddenly interested look on her face. Brother David could tell Kaylee had something she wanted to discuss privately with the mayor. So he politely excused himself, as did Tricia, saying goodbye to Lorna and leaving the two women and children alone.

"Yes, I know Brad—he's a wonderful guy—and I've really been upset about what he's gone through," Kaylee continued. "You see, I was Larry's girlfriend."

It all came back to Lorna. She now remembered who Kaylee was. Her name had been mentioned as part of Larry Palmer's alibi—and Lorna now remembered that Brad had always spoken highly of her.

"Thank you, Kaylee," Lorna said, reaching for her arm. "And I'm sorry for you, too. I know it had to be hard for you as well—having someone close to you mixed up in all of this."

"Thanks, Ms. Lorna," Kaylee said looking down as if ashamed. "The problem is, I still love Larry, and I just wish there was some way to reach him. I hardly ever hear from him now that he's in prison, and I worry about him every day. Crazy I know. But it has been really hard trying to move on."

Lorna motioned for Kaylee to sit down on the edge of the stage with her—half for Kaylee's sake and half for her own. She had been on her feet all afternoon, and her dress pumps were beginning to hurt. Kaylee sat down beside her and suddenly began to unload.

"My mom thinks I'm crazy. She never liked Larry. And she

doesn't understand why I still care about him," Kaylee was starting to tear up. "But deep down, he has a heart of gold. You must know that he was truly good to Brad—in spite of all of his hang-ups and bad habits."

"I know he was," Lorna replied, trying to put her own feelings about Larry aside. "Brad always considered him to be a good friend. Tell me, where is he?"

"Parchman, actually," Kaylee answered. "I wonder if Brad has seen him? I understand that he's there, too?"

Kaylee's questions stung a little bit. For the brief span of the afternoon, Lorna had almost allowed herself to forget about Parchman and the sad condition of her only son's life. But now, reality hit her, the image of her handsome son in a striped jump-suit playing across her mind.

"Brad hasn't mentioned it," Lorna answered. "But he's only been there a couple of weeks… Have you attempted to reach Larry or go to see him?"

"Yes—actually I've been writing him all along—even back when he was still in Batesville waiting on his transfer. I did go see him a couple of times, and both times he was excited to see me and really sweet. Apologized the whole time. I think he couldn't believe I still cared. He wrote me a few times—the sweetest letters. But I haven't heard from him since he's been at Parchman. And I'm really worried. I tried to go to see him a couple of weeks ago, but my mom put her foot down and refused to keep the kids and dared me to take them with me."

Lorna looked down at Kaylee's sweet children, who were now sitting on the floor quietly watching something on Kaylee's phone.

"Sounds like you and I have a little bit in common here," Lorna said sweetly to her new young friend. "We both have men we love at Parchman, and we're really struggling with it. Every day I miss Brad. He's doing fine—I saw him just Saturday—but in my heart, I really need him to come home."

"And if you, the mayor of Oxford, Mississippi can't get him

home, then I don't know what on earth I can do," responded Kaylee sadly. "It's really just hopeless for me—and I guess I'm just going to have wait for ten years to go by and hope Larry is the same man when he gets out."

"Oh, dear," said Lorna, pulling Kaylee close. "He'll be a better man. He obviously has a lot of things he needs to let go of, and it sounds like he's already repenting. I'm sure he loves you and would be amazed to know that a girl like you is out here waiting for him."

Kaylee smiled and brushed a tear from her cheek. "I'm sorry— I'm actually really tough deep down. Really tough. But this has been getting to me. I feel responsible. If I hadn't walked out on Larry that day, he wouldn't have gone crazy and robbed that stupid store."

"And he wouldn't have had an iron-clad alibi," Lorna continued the thought. "And he'd be sitting in Parchman with my son—for accessory to murder, not for ten years, but for life."

Kaylee was amazed that Lorna Hamilton was the person reminding her of this—with her own son in prison doing life for such a heinous crime. But Lorna was not finished. "And I want to remind you of something I love from the Bible—it's found in Romans: 'And we know that all things work together for good to them that love God, to them who are the called according to His purpose.' This is what's getting me through all of this. It's been horrible— truly horrible. I've lost my husband—and it would seem my son. But I know that some good must come from all of this. And I hope that, ultimately, the good will be the restoration of my son, the redemption of his soul, and the restoration to him of a happy and free life. And that should be your prayer for Larry."

Kaylee didn't say a word at first. She sat there quiet, letting the words of a very wise woman sink deep into her heart. And then she thought of something—not to say but to ask. And she sat there silently, daring herself to ask it—and finally she did. "Ms. Lorna, I have something to ask you, and I hope you won't consider me too forward for asking this. But next time you go to see Brad, would you let me go with you? I don't think my mom would protest if she knew I was going with you."

Lorna smiled, putting her arm around Kaylee. "My dear—consider it done."

CHAPTER 21

Light in This Present Darkness

I<small>T WAS RAINING</small> at Parchman. The inmates didn't mind a bit. For those on work detail outside, rain usually meant a day off. Not that the guards cared if they worked in the rain or not—they just didn't much like the idea of getting wet themselves.

It had been a while since the Delta had seen any rain. All of north Mississippi had been having a dry spell, actually. Old-timers said they needed rain. And they sure were getting what they asked for—bucketfuls.

For Bubba, it had been a good day. Lunch was fine, napping to the sound of rain had been even better, and around mid-afternoon he had beaten his new buddy Brad at a game of dominoes. It had been a loud and rowdy game. Bubba was always loud and rowdy when he played dominoes.

Supper had been simple, served around four thirty, consisting of vegetable soup and cornbread. And now it was time for Bible study. Bubba loved Bible study. It gave him a chance to get out around some of the other inmates he had befriended while at Parchman. And instead of the usual drill of PT time or work time, they actually got to talk. And Bubba loved to talk.

"C'mon home—c'mon to Bible study with Bubba," the overgrown kid-like inmate was trying to rouse Brad into action.

But as was Brad's habit after losing at dominoes and eating supper, he was rolled over on his cot, the pillow over his head.

"C'mon, Brad, my Lad," Bubba persisted. "C'mon now—get up and go with Bubba. You knows you wants to, and it'll make you feel better just to get out of this cage for a while!"

That got Brad's attention. *Anything to get out of this cage,* he thought to himself. Okay—he was in.

The two inmates, now best friends, waited for the guard to come let them out and escort them to the meeting. It was a regular meeting held by a volunteer preacher in the community who had pulled strings with the Department of Corrections Chaplain to come on-site once a week for a voluntary Bible study. Bubba had been attending ever since it began. Tonight would be Brad's first time.

"Good evening, my brothers!" exclaimed a smiling light-complexioned African American Baptist minister by the name of Brother Morris. "Is there life in the house tonight?"

Brad wondered what he had gotten himself into. He looked around the room. His surroundings were familiar. It was the same large room where he had visited his mother and Brother David just a couple of days ago. But the setting was altogether different now. Everyone sat in chairs set in a perfect circle—and some of the guys looked truly scary.

"Do I need to ask it again, brothers?" repeated Brother Morris. "Is there life in the house to-nighttt?"

At that, everyone clapped. Some laughed, some whistled, and a few of the vocal ones, including Bubba, shouted, "Yes! Amen!" And, all at once, the scary guys Brad had been studying didn't look all that scary anymore. They were now smiling back at the grinning Brother Morris. Brad saw a lot of teeth—white, yellow, some gold and flashy—and he saw some smiles that didn't possess any teeth at all. It was a mental image he would not soon be able to erase.

"I have some good news for you, brothers—some good news!"

Brother Morris was the most energetic preacher Brad had ever seen. "Jesus has set you free—yes, you heard me. I say, I saya, Jesus has set you captives FREE! Can I get an 'amen'?"

From all corners of the room came a response of "amens," including some "Preach Its," some "Hallelujahs," and a lot of claps and whistles.

Brad understood why Bubba liked Bible study so much—it was just one big pep rally—right up his ally. Somehow over time, Brother Morris had obviously broken through to these hardened inmates—they seemed to trust him. And everyone seemed to be glad he was there. Bubba was laughing and carrying on just like many of the others. And Brad caught himself actually enjoying it.

"I've got a goooood story for you fellas tonight. A good story!" continued Brother Morris. He was just getting started. "Take your Bibles, and turn with me to Genesis, chapter 25, verse 21. Are you there yet? Are you there yet? C'mon—let me hear you! Who's there?"

Hands raised everywhere, and Brother Morris called on the first one he saw. "Steven—you read that first part."

And from across the room, a small white man with glasses whom Brad had never seen before began to read slowly. "Genesis 25:21: Isaac prayed to the Lord on behalf of his wife, because she was childless. The Lord answered his prayer, and his wife Rebekah became pregnant."

"Pregnant! Talk about a miracle! The man prayed, and his woman was pregnant!" Brother Morris had everybody going. "Bet that's not how it happened for most of you fellahs!" There was laughing from all around the room—especially from Bubba. Brother Morris continued. "Okay, Steven, keep on reading—22 through 23."

Steven continued, "The babies jostled each other within her, and she said, 'Why is this happening to me?' So she went to inquire of the Lord. The Lord said to her, 'Two nations are in your womb, and two peoples from within you will be separated;

one people will be stronger than the other, and the older will serve the younger.'"

By now everyone had gotten quiet and serious. Some knew the story already. It was the story of twin brothers, Esau and Jacob. And the birthright that Esau had, and that Jacob wanted. "Okay," Brother Morris spoke again, "who's going to read next?"

A few hands went up. And Brother Morris chose a large black man sitting just next to Brad. "James, read 29 through 32."

James toyed with his reading glasses to get them just right, and then began to read, "Once when Jacob was cooking some stew, Esau came in from the open country, famished. He said to Jacob, 'Quick, let me have some of that red stew! I'm famished!' Jacob replied, 'First sell me your birthright.' 'Look, I am about to die,' Esau said. 'What good is the birthright to me?' "

"And so Esau sold his birthright to Jacob for a cup of stew," chimed in Brother Morris, barely giving James enough time to finish. "Must've been some mighty fine stew, brothers! I mean something like your grandmamma might've fixed you—with some good old rabbit meat, possum meat, and maybe even a little coon meat! Must've had some carrots, celery, and potatoes stirred in just to give it flavor. Mmmmm, goooood—I can almost taste me some!"

Again, there were smiles and laughs all around the circle. Bubba enjoyed this part the most, his large face broken into a huge grin—Brad was not surprised.

"Okay—we're going to skip over two chapters to chapter 27, verses 22 through 25," Brother Morris continued. "I need a reader! I need a reader!"

This time, Bubba raised his hand high in the air. And Brother Morris called on him. Bubba started to read slowly and very carefully, "Jacob went close to his father Isaac, who touched him and said, 'The voice is the voice of Jacob, but the hands are the hands of Esau.' He did not recognize him, for his hands were hairy like those of his brother Esau; so he proceeded to bless him. 'Are you really my son Esau?' he asked. 'I am,' he replied. Then he said, 'My son, bring me some of your game to eat, so that I may give you my blessing.' "

"This is cruel, y'all! CRUEL!" Brother Morris had his audience right where he wanted them. "Not only is Jacob a thief—he's a liar, too! And his mama is the one who has put him up to it! Rebekah always liked him better than Esau. He was a sissy mama's boy, you know what I mean?"

All around the room guys were nodding their heads—a few of them saying, "Yeah," "Amen," or "Preach it."

"And what his mama did was disguise him so his hands would feel like Esau's—and poor old blind Isaac. He fell for it." Brother Morris hardly paused for a breath. "Read verse 41."

An older man sitting right next to Brother Morris began to read without even being asked to, "Esau held a grudge against Jacob because of the blessing his father had given him. He said to himself, 'The days of mourning for my father are near; then I will kill my brother Jacob.' "

"BOOM!"

The loud clap of thunder brought silence to the room. One could almost have heard a pin drop, had it not been for the violent storm outside. The lights flickered, went dark for a second, and came back on again. The rain was really starting to come down hard outside—so hard that Brother Morris had to raise his voice even louder to be heard.

"Man—God's giving us some sound effects up in here tonight!" he shouted. A few inmates chuckled nervously. And then Brother Morris continued with his lesson, "There's only one thing you can say about Esau. The dude was ticked off!! Esau had finally had it with his boy Jacob! Said he was ready to kill him!" The preacher's eyes were wide and animated—he had his audience right where he wanted them. He definitely had Brad's attention—the loud clap of thunder had actually given him a scare.

"Brothers—after his father died, Jacob skipped town. You

probably would have, too!" Brother Morris continued. "The blessing Isaac had given Jacob was a good one, and he became wealthy and ended up blessed with a large family. How do you think this made Esau feel?"

"Angry!" one inmate shouted out.

"Betrayed!" another one chimed in.

"Ready to kill!" hollered a third one.

"Well, let's find out," replied Brother Morris. "Let's read on to a place where many years have passed. And Jacob has decided to return to his brother. They haven't seen each other in a long time. Young man—read in chapter 33, verse 4."

Brother Morris was looking straight at Brad. It was awkward. He could feel every eye in the room starting at him.

"But I don't have a Bible," replied Brad.

"I bet your neighbor there would let you borrow his," said Brother Morris, motioning to Bubba. He was not going to accept no for an answer.

Bubba smiled, and eased his open Bible over to Brad, pointing to the passage with his large index finger.

Brad began to read. Every man in the room was listening. "Genesis chapter 33, verse 4." At Oxford Methodist, Brad had been taught to always repeat the chapter and verse first. "But Esau ran to meet Jacob and embraced him; he threw his arms around his neck and kissed him. And they wept."

Brother Morris looked like he was going to cry. Nobody said a word. Some just looked down and stared at their Bibles. Others just stared off into space as if contemplating what they had just heard.

"There you go—there it is. Every one of you was sure that Esau was going to go off on this man, that he was going to kill him! But instead, Esau put his arms around the neck of his brother Jacob and kissed him. That's forgiveness brothers. That's forgiveness!"

Brother Morris then laid down his Bible and stood up.

Almost simultaneously, there was another clap of thunder.

BOOM! And this time, the lights flickered, went out, and stayed out. Darkness enveloped the room, save for a lone generator-powered exit light in the hallway beside the canteen. Nobody moved. No one except Brother Morris.

"It's all right, brothers! It's all right!" he reassured everyone. "We have a light in our darkness, a light in this very present darkness! And His name is Jesus! JESUS! He came to set you free! And who the Master sets free is free indeed. FREE INDEED!"

A few "amens" and shouts of praise echoed loudly throughout the dark room—and then, as if perfectly choreographed, the lights came back on. Brad sat there in complete amazement. He had never experienced anything like this in his life.

"Before I go, I have a word for somebody here," continued Brother Morris, continuing to stand and now walking around before the men in the circle, looking each one in the face. "Somebody here needs to hear what I'm going to say."

He continued to walk around the circle. "What we have studied about tonight is forgiveness—a forgiveness that passes all ability for us to understand it. Esau probably could've killed his brother, and nobody would've blamed him. Some of you here have killed folks for a lot less."

You could've cut the silence with a knife. Brad thought to himself, *This man is either crazy or really brave. Or both…*

"But he didn't kill him," Brother Morris continued. "He forgave him and loved him. The two brothers lived the rest of their days in complete peace with each other."

Brother Morris paused for a minute. He stood still and every eye was on him. And then he walked over to Brad.

"But somebody here needs to hear this about forgiveness." Brother Morris was looking straight into Brad's eyes. "What's your name, son? I can tell you're new here. What's your name?"

Brad was taken aback. He didn't expect this. Sheepishly, he answered the preacher. "Brad. My name is Brad."

"Brad—I have something very important to say to you," said

150

Brother Morris—his full attention given to Brad Hamilton. "I want you to listen carefully. This word is just for you."

Brad dared to even look away. The preacher had his attention.

"Forgiving others is good," said Brother Morris, "but sometimes forgiving others is not what it's all about. You have to first forgive yourself."

And with that, Brother Morris turned around, returned to his seat, and grabbed the hands of the two men sitting on either side of him, and began to pray. Everyone joined hands with their neighbor and followed suit.

The prayer the fiery young preacher prayed was one of the longest and most sincere prayers Brad had ever heard. He caught his hands growing numb almost in the hands of his fellow inmates it went on so long. Bubba didn't know how tight his grip was, and Brad actually had to wrench his fingers a little bit to get Bubba to lighten up. Bubba didn't even seem to notice. He just sat there—his eyes shut tight.

"And, Lord Jesus," Brother Morris concluded. "I pray you will help my young brother Brad over there find the strength and courage to forgive himself. Doesn't matter what he's done. You love him anyway. And I love him. And he needs to let it go, and love himself."

And with that, Brother Morris was finished. In a moment he was gone. And the prison guards escorted the inmates back to their cells. It was now bedtime at Parchman.

Back in his cot, Brad lay awake in the darkness—staring up at what he could make of the ceiling above his bunk. Below him, Bubba's snores filled the room. This was not, however, what was keeping him awake. Brad had become accustomed to his new friend's loud snoring—just as one becomes used to the sound of a loud air conditioner running at night. Bubba's night sounds had almost become comforting, a reminder that Brad was not alone.

No, Brad couldn't sleep because his mind was fixed on Brother Morris. The story of Jacob and Essau continued to play in his

151

head—along with everything the young preacher had said and prayed. How could it be that God could still love him? And how could He ever forgive him for what he had done? Brother Morris's words really hit home, "…sometimes forgiving others is not what it's all about. You have to first forgive yourself." The preacher seemed to know exactly what was in Brad's heart as he lay there in the darkness—more than anything else, he needed forgiveness. Brad started to pray—tears began to run down his checks, making his pillow wet. Eventually he felt a calm come over him, and he drifted off to sleep.

CHAPTER 22

Conspiracy?

"Madam Mayor, Sheriff Jefferson is on the line."

Lorna was having to get used to having a secretary. She was more accustomed to doing everything herself—and she much preferred her cell phone to the handset by her desk. But Ellis must have a good reason for calling her office.

"Put him through, Jane," she responded to Jane Sage—Radley's trusted secretary for all sixteen years he had served as mayor. Jane was now doing her best to help Lorna manage her new position.

"Ellis! What a pleasure," said Lorna, picking up her phone. She was excited. *He must be calling about his investigation*, she thought. *And I really can't wait to see what he's found out.*

"Good morning, Madam Mayor—I hope you're doing well! Long time no see!" Ellis sounded extra chipper, but Lorna was confused. She had just seen him privately on Friday, and today was only Thursday—not even a week later. Something must be up. She decided to play along.

"Yes, Sheriff—we're certainly due a visit," replied Lorna. "We need to make that happen soon!"

"Well, Lorna," replied Ellis. "That's why I'm calling. As I understand it, you're supposed to be at the library today reading to a group of second-graders at two o'clock. I'm scheduled for one thirty—how about that? Guess they are hard up for a guy to read to them! Anyhow, I was wondering if we can meet up for a minute before you go in, and you can bring me that handbook I let you borrow a while back? I've just hired a rookie deputy, and we're all out of copies here at the station."

Now Lorna was really confused. Not only was reading at the library not on her schedule for today, but the handbook the sheriff was referring to was a standard-issue handbook for new hires. She had borrowed it a couple of months ago when she was studying up on policies for the police department—checking behind Cyrus Buford to make sure he wasn't abusing his power. While it had been helpful, the book wasn't anything so unusual. *Surely he has more copies,* she thought. *Ellis must be up to something. He must have a good reason. I guess I'll just have to go with it.*

"Sure, Ellis—that's an easy request!" Lorna was proud of her quick thinking. She sounded convincing even to herself. "Sorry I've held on to it so long. I almost forgot I had it. I will be sure to bring it with me to the library. See you at two."

Lorna hung up the phone and looked at her calendar. Thankfully, two was open. She looked at her watch. Eleven fifteen. Less than three hours to go. *Can't wait,* Lorna thought to herself.

After a hectic lunch, meeting and greeting members of the Oxford Chamber of Commerce with Polly, Lorna was on her way to see Ellis. About five minutes ahead of schedule, she walked into the Oxford City Library. He was waiting in the lobby just inside the front door.

"Sheriff, so good to see you," spoke Lorna as if she hadn't seen him in a long time. "Give me a hug, Ellis—you're a sight for sore eyes!"

As they embraced, she felt the sheriff slip a note into her pocket. She pretended not to notice.

"Mayor, you look radiant as ever!" he spoke to her enthusiastically, not skipping a beat. As she handed him the handbook, he continued the game. "And thank you for this little thing. So silly I know. Can you believe I'm out? Got to get on to those clerks who are supposed to be keeping things stocked. Really inexcusable!"

"Well, it happens to the best of us," replied Lorna. "Seems like I can't keep up with anything at my office. Good thing I have Jane to keep me straight! Well, I hate to cut this short, but I better get to those kids. I imagine they are all eager to get on with this so they can go home!"

"Well, I warmed them up for you, Lorna," replied Ellis. "You take care now. Hope to see you soon!"

Lorna walked to the desk and the assistant librarian greeted her enthusiastically. "Madam Mayor, what an awesome surprise! We knew Sherriff Jefferson was coming, but we had no idea you would be here as well. He told us just a few minutes ago. And Miss Kim and the kids are anxious to see you!"

Lorna graciously thanked the young Ole Miss student as she showed her down the hall—such a cute and bubbly girl. And a few moments later, she was greeted by an overjoyed librarian and a room full of rambunctious second-graders. *Ellis Jefferson sure knows how to be a sneak*, she couldn't resist thinking to herself.

Thirty minutes later, Lorna was back in her car, relieved the decoy reading was over. It was not that she didn't enjoy reading to kids. She did it all the time. But with Ellis's note burning a hole in her pocket, she had found it very difficult to concentrate.

Now in the quiet sanctuary of her Audi, Lorna carefully took the note from her pocket, unfolded it and read what it contained. A few hand-printed cryptic words were on the page. And they sent a chill down her spine. "7 p.m. tonight. Wall Doxey. Make sure no one follows you."

Lorna could hardly stand to go back to her office. She was too nervous and excited—all at the same time. But she had to get back. It might look suspicious if she didn't. She had a meeting with Cyrus Buford at 4 p.m. And she knew she had better keep it. He was just the type to read something into a last-minute cancellation. *Lord help me get through these next few hours,* was all she could think to pray. And she pulled her Audi out of the parking lot and headed back to City Hall.

• • •

"But, Madam Mayor, with all due respect, I need you to stop trying to be the police chief and let me do my job!" Cyrus Buford was almost rising out of his chair across from Lorna's desk at City Hall. His face was beat red, and his temples were bulging.

"But, Chief Buford," Lorna protested. "I'm not wanting to do your job. I just want you to. We have way too many kids getting on drugs. Everybody knows it. Everybody's talking about it. And as a mother, I know what can happen when your child gets hooked."

Lorna wished for a moment she could take back that last statement. She had been hearing what Cyrus had been saying about her: *She's got too much baggage to be mayor. Her husband's dead. Her son's a crackhead in prison...* Lorna put the words out of her mind and continued her point.

"All I'm saying, Chief, is that there has to be something you can do. I'm tired of hearing about young people with promise—children I have watched grow up—having their promising young lives cut short because the Oxford Police Department can't get the pushers off the street."

"Lorna, I know you're frustrated," replied Cyrus, his voice now gentle and calm. His temper was again under control. "And we're frustrated, too. We're doing all we can. And the problem really isn't on the street—it's in the home—so many people getting hooked on hydrocodone and oxycontin, and their kids getting into their medicine cabinets and nightstands—and selling it at school and on campus. How do you suggest we stop that?"

Lorna had to admit Cyrus had a point. "You're right, Cyrus," she said, looking him straight in the eye. "It's a problem with our entire society. I sometimes think that Brother David is right when

156

he says, 'Jesus is the only answer.'"

Cyrus stared back at her. "Yes, Brother David probably is right. And, in the meantime, rest assured we are doing all we can do."

Lorna knew the meeting was over. And she was relieved. She never seemed to get anywhere with Cyrus Buford, regardless of how hard she tried.

Thank goodness it's five, thought Lorna looking at her watch. *And not a minute too soon.*

Lorna had decided to run home to feed Roscoe and eat a bite herself before heading north to meet Ellis. Supper didn't take long—just a salad and water. She wasn't very hungry. Roscoe, however, ate well as usual. *Must be nice being a dog,* Lorna thought to herself, watching him eat. *No worries… only trust.* She leaned over and petted him on the ear. He looked at her with a grateful smile, and returned to his dish. She laughed to herself, *And always smiling!*

A short time later, she was in her Audi driving again. The scenery along Highway 7 north of Oxford can be breathtaking in the fall. And at six thirty in the evening, especially when the sun is glowing through trees after a fall rain, the views can be even more stunning.

Lorna caught herself thinking that this may be the last sunset she would be seeing for a while—at least on a weekday. Saturday, it would be October 31—and the end of Daylight Saving Time. Time to get ready for dark drives home after work. She really didn't understand why the time had to change anymore. *Why not just let time run its natural course?* she thought.

Thinking of time, Lorna thought back to how quickly the afternoon had flown by. She actually had anticipated the exact opposite, but somehow the fast pace of City Hall made the minutes just roll on by. And her meeting with Cyrus had not been at all the chore she expected it to be. Even with the occasional outburst, he was actually downright pleasant. *What's up with that?* she thought. *Is he feeling a bit guilty about the way he's been acting? Or is he feeling guilty about something else?*

Her mind then drifted to more pleasant things, such as the previous evening's church service and Harmony Here session. As promised, Kaylee Jones had shown up right on time, her daughter Stacie by her side. She was eager to help, so Lorna tasked her with helping a few older kids with their solos. Kaylee had proven to be quite the singer—she was definitely going to be an asset to Lorna and Harmony Here.

Her mind then drifted to Brad and Larry at Parchman. *I pray that God can reach both of them, even in that dark place.* She caught herself wondering what Brad would end up doing if indeed he did become free. *Could he go back to school? Or maybe find a church job? He's always been great with kids...* She didn't have time to ponder anymore. Twenty-five miles can go pretty fast when you're going seventy. And she was already pulling up to the gate at Wall Doxey.

A sign saying "Park Closes at Dark" greeted her at the guardhouse. The guard had already gone home. *Good thing,* she thought. *The fewer eyes around the better.*

Taking advantage of the smaller sign inviting campers to self-register after dark, Lorna headed on into the park and toward the campground. The old park was deserted. It had been raining for the past couple of days, and Lorna suspected that this had worked into her and Ellis's favor.

Located in the Appalachian foothills of north Mississippi, just a few miles south of the antebellum mansions of Holly Springs, Wall Doxey was indeed a jewel. Home to a woodland trail around a beautiful sixty-acre spring-fed lake, the park had been named for a former United States senator from Holly Springs who had led the efforts to establish it. Built largely by Roosevelt's Civilian Conservation Corps, "CCC", workers during the Great Depression, Wall Doxey was home to beautiful stone structures and quaint cabins and provided a picturesque retreat for hikers, fishermen, and water lovers.

As Lorna drove slowly through the lush forest, she lowered her windows to enjoy the sounds and smells of the freshly washed landscape. The fall rain had done its work, and it was a beautiful, crisp evening.

As she made her way from campsite to campsite, she could almost see Radley and Brad sitting beside a fire—loving life and each other. Lorna let out a heavy sigh. She just couldn't allow herself to go there. Not right now.

Beginning to feel a sudden loneliness coming over her, Lorna was relieved when she saw a smiling Ellis standing beside his white Escalade. All she really could make out *was* his smile. The park was so dark, and with Ellis' dark complexion, Lorna almost couldn't see enough of him to recognize him. In fact, Ellis looked a bit out of place. No cruiser. No uniform. It was kind of strange—but nice to see him as just a normal human being. Normal. Lorna had almost forgotten what normal looked like.

"Evening, Lorna," Ellis said as Lorna got out of her car.

"Sure good to see you, Ellis," replied Lorna shaking his large outstretched hand. "That is if I could see you, ha! It sure is dark out here!"

"Yeah—I know it is. And dark is best right now," responded Ellis. "Sorry to drag you out this far—I hope you understand."

"Oh, yes, Ellis," answered Lorna. "No apology needed. And I can assure you no one followed me. I made sure of that."

"Good." Ellis seemed pleased. "There are just too many eyes and ears around Oxford right now. I think they've even tapped our phones. Not sure—but better safe than sorry."

"Who's they?" asked Lorna abruptly.

"I don't know exactly, but that's why we are here," answered Ellis. "C'mon—I need you to watch something."

Lorna found the interior of the sheriff's SUV very welcoming. It was clean and comfortable. The leather seat was large and plush, and in spite of being an older vehicle, she could tell that it was one that had been well-cared for and appreciated.

A laptop was set on the dashboard, plugged into a charger in the cigarette lighter. Ellis had come prepared.

"Mayor," Sheriff Jefferson had never been so serious. "What you're about to see is an interview I had with a witness this morning. It was just him and me. No one has seen this. No one even knows this recording exists. And it's important—very important that we keep it this way."

"Okay, Sheriff," Lorna replied in a soft voice. "I understand. No one will hear about this from me."

"What you're about to hear is going to change things," continued Ellis. "It offers completely new evidence—evidence that may eventually free your son. And for now, it must remain between you and me. To the world, you must act like you have never heard it."

"You have my word, Sheriff," Lorna replied.

"Okay. Just had to be sure we covered that," replied Ellis. "And before we watch this, let me tell you who this guy is. His name is Leo Robbins. He's a person already known to us as a habitual offender. He's currently sitting in my jail on a possession charge. Marijuana and cocaine. It's not his first time in my jail—in fact, he's been in several times during his lifetime. But this time, it's not just the possession charge. He had a gun on him, and as a convicted felon, all of this violates his parole. He could be headed back to prison, and for a long time."

Lorna sat there frozen, hanging on every word. Ellis continued.

"When we arrested him last week, I suspected that we may have hit pay dirt. He's one of the witnesses who in the past we think Cyrus Buford let slip through the cracks. He knows a lot he's not supposed to know. Up until now, though, he's always been reluctant to talk to me. But with his current situation, along with the fact that his probation officer happens to be my cousin, I think he's finally motivated. I've been dying to get a minute alone with him. This morning, I got my chance. Luckily, he was ready to talk. I recorded this on my phone and then transferred it to my laptop. Like I said, no one knows about this. You're the first person other than me to hear it."

Ellis touched the screen with his finger. It immediately lit up, filling the Escalade with a soft blue light. Looking back at Lorna was the face of a young man, head shaven, with a barbed-wire tattoo on his neck. In the background was nothing but a cinder block wall. His eyes were brown and his nose and chin prominent. Other than the tattoo, he appeared to be clean cut, and even handsome in his own way. The sheriff touched an arrow on the screen, and Leo Robbins began talking.

"My name is Leonard Anthony Robbins. I'm twenty-four years old and I live in Oxford, Mississippi," Leo said in a high-pitched voice and distinctly country accent—more redneck than Southern.

"What is your place of residence exactly?" Ellis's booming voice was unmistakable.

"Yessir. Em, uh, I live at the Pebble Creek Apartments just off University Place, the south side of campus, apartment number 212."

"By that you mean building number two, apartment twelve, is that correct?" asked Ellis.

"Yessir. That is correct, second building on the end, last apartment upstairs," responded Leo.

"Mr. Robbins, would you please describe to me what you were doing at six-thirty on the evening of Friday, April 17 of this year?" asked Ellis.

"Yessir. Um, Uh, I was sitting in my apartment waiting on Joe," answered Leo.

"Who's Joe?" asked Ellis.

"Joe Parker, you know, the dude you and I were talking about," Leo responded.

"Mr. Robbins, how is it that you can remember with complete certainty what you were doing on April 17 at six thirty?"

"'Cause that's what I'm doing every Friday at six thirty. Waiting at the apartment on Joe," answered Leo. "He comes by every

Friday after work. We hang out a little while, you know. Watch sports and stuff."

"Mr. Robbins. You're not telling me everything," persisted Ellis. "What else is it that you and Mr. Parker do? Why is every Friday night at six thirty so important?"

"Aw, Sheriff—you already know. That's why we're talking about this. You know all about Joe," replied Leo.

"Yes, but I need to hear it from you, Leo," said Ellis in a very calm but determined voice. "What is it that you and Mr. Parker do."

"He fixes me up," Leo responded.

Ellis persisted. "By 'fixes me up,' you mean Mr. Parker delivers to you certain items in exchange for money, don't you?"

"Yes," answered Leo.

"What items, Mr. Robbins?" asked Ellis.

There was a long pause. Leo looked down at his hands and then up at the ceiling, letting out a huge sigh. He looked to his left and to his right. And then he looked back toward the screen. "You really going to get your cousin to cop a deal for me, Sheriff? You really going to do that?"

"Mr. Robbins, you already have my word," responded Ellis, "And we're recording this so you have it from me in a taped conversation that I will talk to Mr. John Jefferson, your probation officer, and I will ask him to take into consideration your cooperation with my investigation. You have my word on that."

Leo looked down and didn't say anything. "So please answer my question, Mr. Robbins. What is the relationship between you and Mr. Parker?"

"He's my dealer," responded Leo, his face still looking down.

"And on Friday, April 17, what was it that you were waiting for him to bring you?" asked Ellis.

After another pause, it seemed that answering the previous question had suddenly become lubricant to Leo's testimony. With the initial confession out of the way, he began to talk freely and openly.

"Marijuana and cocaine. That's what I was waiting for," replied Leo. "Joe brought them every Friday 'cause it was pay day. We'd sit around and talk for a few minutes, he'd hand me my stash, I'd hand him a Ben Franklin, and then that would be it. He'd leave, and I wouldn't see him until the next week."

"Is that all he sold you?" asked Ellis.

"Yes," answered Leo. "Joe always offered me other things, like heroin and LSD, but I knew better than to mess around with that stuff."

"Thank you, Mr. Robbins," replied Ellis. "I appreciate your honesty. Now answer for me this question: Why does Friday, April 17 stick out to you? What happened on April 17?"

Lorna was on the edge of her seat. She remembered the name Joe. He was her son's dealer—the one he met every Friday. She could not imagine what she was about to hear. And she wasn't completely sure she wanted to. April 17 had changed her and Brad's life forever. *Am I finally going to hear what happened?* she thought. Nothing could have interrupted her concentration on Leo Robbins. She was hanging on every word.

"Joe didn't show. That's it—he didn't show," Leo responded. "I sat around like I always do, looking at my watch and waiting for Joe. And he never came. I looked out the window, and he wasn't there. And I didn't understand why, but what can you do?"

"What do mean, 'what can you do'?" asked Ellis.

"I mean, what can you do?" answered Leo. "It's not like I've got his phone number or anything. I don't even know where the dude lives. So, I just had to sit there and wait. I mean, what else could I do?"

"Mr. Robbins—what happened next?" asked Ellis. "Please tell me what happened after Joe stood you up?"

"Well, I walked out on the balcony looking for him," said Leo. "Didn't see him. Went back inside and poured me a drink and sat down to watch ESPN. After a little while, I heard some car doors and went to my window and looked out. It was Joe and

Brad Hamilton. They were walking into the woods. I thought it was strange but figured I better mind my business. I expected Joe would come see me once he was done. So I just sat there."

"How did you know it was Brad Hamilton?" asked Ellis. "Do you know Brad?"

"Of course I know Brad," answered Leo with a laugh. "Who in Oxford doesn't know Brad Hamilton? Cool dude. Sorry about what happened to him."

"Were you surprised to see Brad in your parking lot with Joe?" Ellis continued.

"No—not at all. Brad usually met Joe in the parking lot on Fridays around a quarter till. Joe would hook up with him after he saw me."

Lorna made a sudden choking sound. Ellis paused the video. "Are you okay, Lorna? Do we need to stop this?" asked Ellis, genuinely concerned.

Lorna was crying. Ellis handed her his handkerchief and cracked the windows. They had become thick with condensation, and the Escalade was starting to get stuffy. "We don't have to watch anymore if you don't want to," Ellis continued. "I can just explain it all to you."

"No. I'm okay," replied Lorna. "Just hard to hear. I mean, I'm not surprised. I knew Brad said he was buying from a guy named Joe. It's just really tough when you hear it. And you know for a fact what he was doing. But I'm okay. Really, I am. Please start it back."

Ellis touched the play button. And he was asking Leo another question. "So did Joe come see you later on Friday night?"

"No," answered Leo. "He never made it. I walked out on the balcony a few times looking for him, but I never saw him. Brad's truck was still parked at the edge of the lot. It stayed out there all night. But he and Joe weren't there. And I didn't see Joe's Silverado, so I figured he and Brad must've gone somewhere in it."

"So then what did you do?" asked Ellis.

"It's like I said a minute ago, Sheriff," answered Leo. "What can you do? I just finished off a few more drinks and went to bed."

"Did Joe ever make it by with your stash?" Ellis continued.

"Yeah, actually he did," said Leo. "Came by the next day. Apologized. Said he had gotten tied up and couldn't make it Friday night. Gave me my stash, I gave him the cash, and we were square. He's been running like clockwork ever since. Hadn't missed a day. Until this past week, of course. 'Cause I had a schedule conflict." Leo laughed. On the recording, Lorna could hear Ellis laugh, too, and she found the lighter moment extremely welcome. Being locked up in Ellis's jail had most certainly put a strain on the schedules of many over the years.

"Good to know that even thugs can keep their sense of humor," she interjected from her side of the Escalade.

On the video, Ellis continued in his interrogation: "Did you tell Joe you had seen him with Brad?"

"Of course not!" answered Leo. "I may be stupid, but I'm no fool. There are rules, and everyone knows the last thing you do is ask your dealer anything. Not a good idea. Besides, I figured Joe had his reasons, and by then I imagined he didn't care to have it known he even knew Brad. The news about Brad being arrested for shooting his dad was already on every TV station."

"When on Saturday did Joe come by?" asked Ellis.

"Same as on Fridays. six thirty. I figured he didn't come earlier because he didn't want to get mixed up with the cops. Saturday morning, you know, they were all over the place. The parking lot was crawling with them. It wasn't until around two o'clock that they finally towed off Brad's pickup."

Ellis then changed his tone and direction of the interrogation, and asked Leo a very pointed question: "Mr. Robbins—when the police came by your apartment on Saturday, April 18, to ask you if you had seen anything Friday night, why did you lie to them? The record says you told them you had not seen anything suspicious and that you had gone to bed at 9 p.m."

165

"Sheriff, I told you about that," Leo answered. "You never tell the Oxford Police anything. Not like it's going to matter anyway. Unless the chief wants it said, anything you say might as well not be said. Why waste your breath? And besides, I didn't want to say anything about Joe. That wouldn't have gone good for me. He's my drug dealer, after all. I didn't want people knowing I know him. Not that it would matter anyway. Everybody knows they love Joe down at the station. It's like he practically owns the place."

"What do you mean 'owns the place'?" asked Ellis.

"You know—does whatever he wants," replied Leo. "He's Cyrus Buford's boy—nothing's going to happen to him. Everybody knows that."

"Thank you, Mr. Robbins. I appreciate your honesty." Ellis's last words ended the recording.

Lorna sat in her seat stunned. Ellis was motionless, in his seat beside her, not sure what to say. The sounds of the forest slowly began to fill the silence and in the distance, a lonely whip-poor-will could be heard calling for its mate.

Finally Lorna spoke. "Ellis—is this proof that my husband and son were both victims to a conspiracy?"

Ellis paused before answering, thinking of the best words to describe what he wanted to say. "A conspiracy is exactly what I think is at work here. And the scary thing is, all of the players are still in their same places, carrying about their duties just as before."

Silence again filled the air. The whip-poor-will again made its cry.

"So his last name is Parker—Joe Parker?" asked Lorna thoughtfully. "Who is he?"

"He's a young guy under thirty—not even from Oxford. Attended Ole Miss for one semester years ago and then dropped out. He's really not anyone of any prominence at all. Leo exaggerated Joe's importance. I guess he was speaking from his perspective as Joe's junkie. Contrary to what Leo said, Joe doesn't own downtown. But the people he works for do."

Lorna shuddered. She dreaded the answer to the question she was about to ask, but she had to ask it. "And who would that be?"

"I don't know all of the players at this point, but I do know two of them," answered Ellis. "Brace yourself for this, Lorna. Cyrus Buford. And Lance Bradford."

CHAPTER 23

Skiing on Sardis

F<small>RIDAY MORNING CAME</small> early for Lorna. She had hardly slept a wink all night. Her head was full of many voices… *Brad usually met Joe in the parking lot on Fridays…. Unless the chief wants it said, anything you say might as well not be said…. A conspiracy is exactly what I think is at work here…. The scary thing is, all of the players are still in their same places…. It had to be more than one person—two or three most likely.*

Better get up, Lorna said to herself. She had learned that lying in bed awake was not productive. Best to get busy.

Roscoe stirred as her feet touched the floor beside her bed. She sat there a minute, her toes playing upon the sweet old dog's fur coat. Roscoe rolled over, belly up, and Lorna continued rubbing him with her toes. He loved that.

"Sorry, boy," Lorna said to the sad, brown eyes that looked at her longfully when she stopped. "I've got work to do."

Starting her shower, she turned to the music she had saved in her phone. She chose a Christian CD that one of her childhood friends had shared with her back when she was struggling most with her grief. In a few moments, the comforting words of a healing song were echoing through her marble bathroom… "Let the hurting cry out to our God, let them praise the One who is worthy, let them praise the One who is able to give beauty for all of our ashes. Let the hurting cry out to our God, let them praise the One is mighty, let them praise the One who has conquered the grave and set us free."

Lorna raised her hands to heaven while warm water rained down, rejuvenating her tired face. She sang along to every word. *Oh, how I love to sing praises to God in the morning,* she thought. Suddenly, she remembered that for the first time in many months she would be singing the solo at church this Sunday. The thought of leading others to worship brought her great joy. *Let the hurting cry out to our God, let them praise the One who is able.* Praise had now replaced the voices that had plagued her sleep. Lorna's morning already felt better.

A couple of hours later, Lorna was sitting in her office at City Hall. Jane Sage had just come in and placed the morning paper on her desk.

"Mayor, what are you doing here so early?" she asked, looking at her watch. "It's only seven thirty."

"I know, Jane," replied Lorna. "Good morning, by the way. I just thought I'd make an early start of it. I have a lot to get done this morning, and I'm meeting Sterling for lunch. By the way, make sure to keep my calendar free this afternoon. I'm taking the afternoon off."

Lorna had decided to do like Radley used to do—most Fridays at noon, he went off the clock. It was his way of making up for all the nights and weekends he put in as leader of Oxford. Burnout was a common hazard in the business of city government, and Radley often told Lorna that his Friday afternoons are what kept him sharp—not to mention sane.

"I think that's a great idea, Lorna," replied Jane. "You work too hard. You need to take care of yourself!"

"I agree, Jane—I completely agree," nodded Lorna as she studied the papers on her desk.

"Well, I'm right outside if you need anything, Mayor," said Jane.

"Thank you," answered Lorna, her eyes still focused on her reading. "Please close the door behind you if you don't mind."

Lorna turned over a sheet of paper and began reading the next document. "Testimony of Larry Palmer." It was just one of many documents in the folder open in front of her, "Randolph Lee Hamilton V—April 17, 2015—Case File." Asking for this copy had been one of her first acts as mayor. She had scanned it time after time. But up until now, she had found nothing that seemed to make a difference.

Lorna scanned the testimony document. It was neatly typed, the work of a court stenographer undoubtedly. Her eyes quickly focused on a portion of the interview, toward the bottom of the page.

Chief Buford: And so what did Bradford Hamilton tell you when you picked him up?

Mr. Palmer: Nothing really. He seemed very dazed, like he was high or something. I don't know. He just kept saying he really didn't know what happened. That one minute he was there getting weed after work. And next thing he was hurting all over, banged up, and walking through the woods.

Chief Buford: Is that all he said?

Mr. Palmer: No—he said some crazy stuff, too, about walking on water and stuff. I just figured he was really messed up. Bad weed I guess.

Chief Buford: Do you really think "bad weed" is all it was?

Mr. Palmer: Long Pause... I don't know.

Chief Buford: What else did Brad use?

No answer.

Chief Buford: Answer my question. What else did Brad use?

No answer.

Chief Buford: Mr. Palmer, you're in deep trouble, and I'm that close to charging you as an accomplice. Now, listen carefully and answer my question. As his roommate, I want you to verify what I know you know. We already have a toxicology report. That

Bradford Hamilton was a known drug addict, and that he would do anything to get his weekly stash of heroin—and that he would get so high on it that nothing else mattered to him. Mr. Palmer—is this not true?

Mr. Palmer: Long Pause... You want me to tell you what I know? Well this is all I know. That Brad Hamilton is a good guy. That he wouldn't willfully hurt anybody. And if you want to know what he was getting, ask his pusher, some jerk named Joe. I don't know his last name, but I'm sure you probably already do.

Lorna stopped reading. Here before her very eyes might very well be proof that Oxford's police chief, Cyrus Buford, was somehow involved in the murder of her husband. *"Some jerk named Joe." How on earth did I miss that before?* Lorna thought to herself. "Surely Cyrus is not that arrogant," Lorna spoke under her breath. And all at once adrenaline mixed with anger and rage began pumping through her veins. She was breathless.

Lorna began rapidly turning the pages—desperate to find an interview with Joe Parker. *Surely Cyrus followed up on that clue,* she thought as she flew through the rest of the file. Page after page, she turned. Even pictures of the crime scene, which normally would move her to tears, did not slow her determined search. She reached the final page. Nothing. She went back to the beginning of the file and went through every page again. And again—nothing. There was no interview with Joe Parker.

Lorna's first instinct was to pick up the phone and demand that her chief come to her office at once. Or better yet, *I'll just go to him and confront him right there where he sits,* she thought.

And then she remembered Ellis's words spoken just hours earlier. *To the world, you must act like you have never heard it.*

For now, Lorna realized she was helpless to do anything.

She looked at her watch. *Still a few minutes,* she thought to herself, and began looking through the file once again. This time, her attention was drawn to an almost blank sheet of paper with just a few items listed on it under a handwritten heading, "Items

171

on Mayor's Person." Lorna began reading the list. Just ordinary things. "Reading glasses; wallet containing driver's license, three credit cards, $127 in cash, and pictures of Lorna and Brad; eighty cents in coins, small pocket knife, lip balm..." Lorna could recite the list by heart. She both smiled and teared up, and continued down the list. "Handkerchief embroidered with message from wife." A large tear rolled down her cheek. She had almost forgotten about her gift to Radley on their tenth anniversary. He carried it with him always. And then she read the last item: "Cell phone."

It was hard to concentrate on work for the rest of the morning, but Lorna had to persist. There was a meeting with her new Parks and Recreation Director to discuss youth programs and Lorna's desire to get more parents involved. Everyone agreed that just having activities wasn't enough. Entire families had to become engaged and invested in everything Oxford was trying to do for its youth.

Then came a meeting with the Public Works Director to go over the list of projects that had been completed during the week—filling potholes, unclogging street drains, picking up downed limbs blocking roadways... It was also her chance to give him a new list of complaints that she had handled personally on her cell phone, at the grocery store, and anywhere else citizens feel free to grab the attention of their mayor.

Next was a meeting with the alderman-at-large who was getting flooded with complaints about a stray dog problem—and why wasn't Animal Control doing their job? A doglover himself, he hated to see any animal mistreated, so surely a thinking dog catcher could devise a humane solution?

Normally, Lorna would have enjoyed every meeting. She found great fulfillment in being mayor and helping her department heads and aldermen find ways to better serve Oxford's citizens. The busy routine had proved to be amazing therapy—it helped greatly with her feelings of grief over the death of Radley and the imprisonment of Brad. But today, Lorna's mind was not on mayoral tasks, and she was relieved when time came to meet Sterling for lunch.

"You're the prettiest thing I've seen since last Friday," Sterling said, leaning in to kiss Lorna's cheek as they met in the lobby of Ajax Diner, a favorite local restaurant on Oxford's historic downtown square.

"Has it really been a week since I saw you?" asked Lorna, ignoring Sterling's flattery. She was so used to it, she rarely noticed it anymore. "I can't believe we've gone a whole week! That has to be a record!"

"Yes indeed—and a record we shouldn't repeat anytime soon if you ask my opinion," replied Sterling with a wink.

Looking around the popular restaurant, Lorna felt totally at home. Smiling back at her were the faces of many good friends and acquaintances—even people she had forgotten. Ajax had long been a favorite meeting spot for people in search of Mississippi Soul Food. The walls were full of Oxford history, and the booths were always full as well—everyone from Eli Manning to John Grisham ate at Ajax's. The ceiling was littered with toothpicks—blown into the ceiling from straws held by kids, their parents, college students—anyone who felt like leaving their mark on Ajax's ceiling.

"Well what have you been busy doing this week, Madam Mayor?" Sterling asked playfully as they sat down in worn red booth seats at a table adorned with a red-checkered tablecloth. "You've been the elusive stranger lately."

"Oh, Sterling—you know. Just the same old stuff," Lorna replied. She knew she had better keep things light this time. No talking about Leo Robbins, Cyrus Buford, Joe Parker—any of the things she was really dying to talk to him about. She also knew that she couldn't talk about Lance. After last night's revelation, she wondered if Sterling knew... *Is he just lying to himself— trying to pretend Lance isn't a drug dealer?* she thought. Deep down, she felt sorry for Sterling. She of all people knew what it was like to have a son fall from grace.

"I had a great visit with Brad last Saturday!" Lorna felt this was a safe topic of conversation.

"That's great!" replied Sterling, showing enthusiasm, obviously happy that Lorna was happy. "I can only imagine how glad he was to see you, Lorna."

"Glad is not the word," replied Lorna as the waitress poured tea and prepared to take their orders. "I'll have the usual, Laura," Lorna said, giving the pretty young girl her menu.

"And I'll have whatever she's having," chimed in Sterling.

"But you don't know what I'm having," smiled Lorna, as Laura took Sterling's menu and returned to the kitchen.

"All I know is that if you like it, I'm sure to like it," responded Sterling. "You know, Radley and I always shared one main thing in common: We both knew an awesome girl when we saw her."

Lorna was slightly embarrassed and a little taken back by Sterling's statement. Deep down she had always known he harbored a spark for her. And now she worried that there really might be more to it than just flirtation and flattery.

"I mean, if I had met you first, you would never have become Mrs. Hamilton," continued Sterling. "That rascal Radley. I told him he was a fool breaking with family tradition and not going to Ole Miss. Turns out he was the smartest of us all—going all the way to Dartmouth and bringing you home."

"Well, I remember that first Homecoming quite well," Lorna said with half a smile, stirring her tea and then tasting it.

"I know—that was a cheap moment," replied Sterling. "And I later apologized to Radley for it. But you must remember, here you were looking like Jackie Kennedy come to Oxford, and I was really full of myself back then. Besides, Kathleen and I hadn't started dating yet. I mean, we were only nineteen."

For a quick minute, Lorna returned to her first Ole Miss Homecoming, when Radley brought her home to "meet the family." From the first moment she met Sterling, she distrusted him. He

174

was just too charming and easy with the women. And when he kissed her squarely on the mouth after Ole Miss scored a touchdown against Vanderbilt, with his best friend standing right beside her, she had been mortified. Radley actually laughed it off at the time, but she had never forgotten it.

An awkward silence hovered over them for a moment. And then Sterling started laughing.

"What?" asked Lorna. "What's so funny?"

"Life is truly amazing isn't it, Lorna?" answered Sterling. "I mean, that is where we started and here we are now—the best of old friends enjoying lunch at Ajax. Life can really be something, can't it? Here," he said, holding out his red plastic iced tea glass. "Here's to friendship."

Lorna smiled, and returned the toast. "To friendship," she agreed and took a drink of her tea.

"So, what's for lunch," asked Sterling, placing his napkin in his lap. "I'm starving!"

"Southern pot roast, lima beans, and mashed potatoes and gravy," answered Lorna. "I get it every time I come here."

"You are my kind of woman," said Sterling with a smile. "I knew you wouldn't let me down."

As they sat there enjoying the delicious lunch, Lorna changed the subject. "So how are you doing, really?"

"What do you mean, 'really'?" answered Sterling with a puzzled look on his face.

"Well," continued Lorna, "I know that last week at the house, you were worried about Lance and that you weren't seeing much of him. I just want to make sure you're okay." Lorna just couldn't resist the chance to see what Sterling knew about Lance.

"Well, I'm fine. It just is what it is. These kids get headstrong, you know—and they go and do the stupid things they do," replied Sterling, enjoying his pot roast. "I know in time he'll come around."

"Do you think he still blames you for what happened to Kat?" asked Lorna.

"What do you mean, 'blames me'?" Sterling responded. Lorna feared she had struck a nerve.

"Well, that night at the Ava," she replied. "Don't you remember? You were so upset, Sterling. And you said that deep down you thought Lance blamed you for the accident. And it was creating distance between you. A part of me has been worried about you ever since."

"Well, that was a while back, and I'm doing much better now," answered Sterling. "But I am hoping that Lance is coming around. It was a hard time for all of us you know. And maybe I am to blame."

"What are you saying?" asked Lorna. "It was an accident—everyone knows that. Kat should never have been going fast. And you weren't even in the boat."

"I know," replied Sterling. "You're right. It's just that ever since it happened, I have been beating myself up. I should never have let her drive that boat. It was brand-new after all. An Eliminator, one of the fastest on the market. Didn't take but a small touch on the throttle…"

Sterling stopped talking and just stared down at his plate. Lorna felt sorry for bringing up Kathleen. Sterling had been doing so well since his meltdown at the Ava.

Sterling continued, "… but she wanted me to have a turn skiing—you know how I was always the one towing her and Lance. I'll never forget her last words to me: *'Have fun back there, my love—you deserve it.'*"

All of sudden, he grabbed the forelock of his hair, just as he had done at the Ava Hotel the night Radley died. And then quickly, Sterling regained his composure, straightened his hair, and pushed his plate away.

"Well, I think that about does it for me," he stated, all charm and flirtation gone. Before Lorna sat a sad and broken man.

That did it. Lorna felt horrible. She should never have brought up the subject. She had to change the subject and quick.

"Sterling, you know what I found most memorable about you

when I first met you all those years ago?" Lorna asked.

"No, Lorna. What was it?" asked Sterling, his composure quickly restored by his curiosity.

"It was your striking head of hair," Lorna stated—knowing that flatterers enjoy being flattered. "I must say—even George Hamilton doesn't have a mane like you've got!"

Sterling looked down and smiled. He was used to receiving compliments about his hair, and he loved them. He had also gotten the George Hamilton look-alike line a lot—especially when he was younger. Lorna knew just what she was doing.

"Lorna, you really know how to make a guy feel better," answered Sterling. "I thank you for the compliment. And, in answer to your question, I think it comes from my mother's side. She was one-quarter Cherokee Indian. They say her great-great-grandfather had been a chief. She always had course, dark hair. Her father did as well. So I guess I can thank the Cherokees."

Sterling was smiling. Lorna smiled back. And then Sterling changed the subject.

"Well, tell me," he said as they waited for their ticket to come. "How is Ellis's investigation going? Any more word on the witness?"

Lorna felt a lump in her throat. She was completely not expecting Sterling to bring this up. *What a mistake to have mentioned it last Friday,* she thought. But she was quick on her feet.

"Oh, nothing has come of it," answered Lorna. "I think Ellis is just a little overzealous. I really shouldn't have brought it up last week anyway. He just had a hunch is all. Still waiting to see if it leads anywhere. If anything does come of it, I will let you know."

"That's good," replied Sterling as he took the ticket from Laura. "You know I want to get to the bottom of this as much as you do. Time for Brad to come home!"

Lorna appreciated Sterling's concern, but couldn't help thinking, *No one could possibly want this as much as I do.*

After thanking Sterling for lunch followed by a quick hug

and goodbye, Lorna got in her car to head home. She was really looking forward to changing and getting on with her day. She was anxious to see Ellis and show him what she had found in the case file. *But how do I even get in touch with him?* she thought, remembering his warning, *too many eyes and ears around Oxford right now.*

As she left the square, making a right turn on University Boulevard, it occurred to her that she needed some new foundation from Belk. She had just noticed that morning that the bottle was almost empty. *And every Southern lady worth her salt never runs out of foundation.* Lorna Hamilton may have grown up in Boston, but she had become a Southern belle in Oxford.

Just fifteen minutes later, Lorna pulled up at the Oxford Belk—a large department store, part of a large Southern chain, located on the edge of town in a shopping center just next to Home Depot. Driving up to it, Lorna felt proud to see how commercial development was taking off in Oxford. The small college town had really come far in the thirty-one years since her first visit. And, if they could just get past the drug problem, the future would be even brighter.

She parked and walked in, enjoying the fall fragrances that greeted her as she walked between counters in the cosmetic department. *Christmas already?* Lorna thought to herself seeing a display with beautiful snowflakes and a small fir tree laden with lipstick, blush, mascara, and perfume. *They just roll it out earlier and earlier these days.*

"May I help you, Mayor?" asked a pretty voice from behind the counter. It was Brenda Marshall. Lorna would have recognized that pretty red hair anywhere.

"Why Brenda, dear—so good to see you!" Lorna exclaimed. "I almost forgot you worked here. Just in my zone I guess."

"I know," responded Brenda looking down. "I know all about zones."

"Brenda, what's wrong?" replied Lorna, showing concern. She

could tell something was wrong. Brenda was usually so bubbly and fun—she just wasn't acting like herself.

"You know I was dating Lance Bradford, right?" asked Brenda, eager to talk to someone. "We talked about it last time you were in here, remember?"

"Why, yes," answered Lorna. "Of course I remember. You seemed so happy, and I was just talking about it the other day."

"Well he broke up with me a couple of days ago," Brenda said, showing little emotion on her heavily made-up face.

"Oh, Brenda," said Lorna, "I'm so sorry! I can only imagine how hurt you must feel!"

"Oh, I'm going to be okay, Ms. Lorna," replied Brenda. "Daphne told me I'm better off without him, and she's right. He just has too many secrets." Brenda took a tissue from one of the boxes found on every makeup counter and began to touch the corners of her eyes. Fortunately, the store was not very busy, and the only other customer in cosmetics was being helped by Brenda's co-worker.

"But I can tell you are hurt. And that hurts me," said Lorna, placing her hand over Brenda's. "Tell, me. What do you mean Lance has secrets?"

Brenda was happy to answer. Her heart was hurting, but clearly it had not affected her mouth. "Ms. Lorna, you just wouldn't believe it. He was gone every Friday night—on up into the day Saturday morning, I couldn't get a hold of him. And he never gave me one reasonable excuse. Said he was 'doing stuff for his job,' and I know that's not true. He lives off a trust fund, for Pete's sake. He doesn't even have a job. Can you believe it? The whole time we dated we never went out once on a Friday. Never."

Lorna sincerely felt sorry for Brenda.

"But just last Friday, I had Lance's dad over for supper," responded Lorna, "and he said Lance was out with you. Said Lance was crazy about you."

"How would he know?" asked Brenda, rolling her eyes upward,

179

a dot of mascara traveling with them. "He and Lance haven't even spoken since Lance's mom died. They have nothing to do with each other. Absolutely nothing. I've only seen Mr. Bradford once the whole time we've been dating. He came in here a couple of weeks ago asking me questions about Lance, and I refused to talk to him. I figured if you want to know what your son's doing, just ask him yourself?"

"What kind of questions, Brenda?" asked Lorna.

"Questions about stuff he's been doing and about how serious we are and stuff like that," replied Brenda. "I told him I couldn't help him. Lance wouldn't have liked me talking to him."

"I'm sorry, Brenda. I can tell you're really hurting," replied Lorna.

"Yes, I'm hurting. I really loved that handsome fool," responded Brenda, choking back a tear and dabbing her eyes again with the tissue. "And he was just starting to open up to me. The past couple of weeks had been the best ever for us. He was really starting to tell me things, and I could tell he loved me, too."

Brenda stopped talking for a moment. She took a deep breath, dabbed her nose and then her eyes again, blinking them and looking up at the ceiling.

"His dad is a real jerk, you know?" Brenda continued. "More worried about how he looks and what the world thinks about him than his own wife and son. That's why Lance hates him you know—I mean hates him! Lance told me all about it—every detail—just when we were getting the closest. He was really starting to open up."

"What do you mean, Brenda?" asked Lorna. "I know Lance blames his father for the accident. Sterling has even told me so. But Lance shouldn't. She was going too fast. She hit a buoy and lost control. It was an accident. A horrible accident that cost me my best friend. I loved Kat. But it was an accident, and Lance should let it go."

"If it was an accident, then why is Mr. Sterling lying about it?" asked Brenda, her face suddenly red with anger. Lorna was shocked.

"What do you mean he's lying?" asked Lorna.

"Ms. Lorna—he's been lying to everybody about it. Ms. Kat wasn't driving that boat when it crashed. Mr. Sterling was."

CHAPTER 24

Gots to Give It to Jesus

"HURRY UP, SON!" Radley was calling. "This rain's gonna drown us if lightning doesn't kill us first!"

"I'm coming, Dad—I'm coming," answered Brad, gathering a few games and his Gameboy from the tent. Cold rain stung his face as he ran to the safety of the truck, lightning illuminating what just a few hours earlier had been a placid forest on a beautiful fall evening.

"Been a long time since I've seen a storm move in like this," Radley was saying as a soaking Brad climbed up into the old Chevy—an antique that had been in the Hamilton family for ages.

"Reminds me of when I was a kid and we went camping during Hurricane Camille," Radley continued. "All the reports said clear weather for the weekend. Obviously they were wrong. No radars back in those days. We had to take shelter in this old truck then, too—a tree fell on the tent—but luckily we were all okay."

A large boom startled Brad awake. He was no longer in the '57 Chevy. He was in his bunk at Parchman, and a violent storm was raging across the Mississippi Delta outside his window. He pulled the cover over his head, feeling simultaneous emotions of sadness and relief: sadness that Radley had only been a figment of his dreams and relief that rain meant no cotton picking today.

It had been a hard couple of days. The break in the weather earlier in the week had brought with it hard labor—breakfasts at four thirty followed by early-morning bus rides to the cotton fields in the dark. Brad's hands were sore, his back ached, and everything in between seemed to hurt as well.

As he lay there in the silence of night, his mind drifted back to his dream. It had been such a vivid dream—as if he was really back at Wall Doxey with his dad, enjoying a fall campout. He loved camping out with his dad—especially in the fall. Mississippi summers could be brutal, but with every fall came a reset—cool, drier winds chasing away the humidity and ushering in the season of football and all of fall's other great traditions.

It's Halloween, Brad thought to himself—and immediately he felt even sadder. As a child, he loved Halloween. He and his friends, especially Lance, would really get into it. They would dress up in homemade costumes, the scarier the better, and go trick-or-treating all through Oxford. And as they got older, they would pile up together in trucks and trailers filled with hay, and have their own "hayride" of sorts. They would take in the haunted houses, cruise through the Ole Miss campus, and every once in a while go to the old Civil War cemetery, a little-known spot on the edge of campus where dead soldiers from the Battle of Shiloh were buried in 1862.

What made Halloween most special, though, was the campfire Radley would have waiting for the boys in the woods behind Somerset. Regardless of whether it was a weekend or school night, the fire was always going. And Lorna would have fresh pigs-in-a-blanket ready in the kitchen with mustard and ketchup, along with cold drinks, chips, and sweets.

They would all sit around the campfire, plates full of food, listening to some of Radley's famous stories. It was something Brad and his friends always looked forward to—and over the years it had become one of his favorite traditions.

The tradition had stopped after high school. Radley tried to keep it going, but Brad was too busy getting wasted and staying away from home. And now, two years later, there would be no Halloween campfire at all. Because Radley was gone and Brad was in prison. Yes indeed, Bradford Hamilton's heart was broken.

"What you thinkin' about?" Bubba's sudden question interrupted Brad's pity party and stirred him back to reality.

Brad lay there silent for a few moments, and then answered, "Thinking about how this rain is the best thing that's happened to me the whole time I've been in this place. No cotton picking today, no cotton picking today."

"Yep," came Bubba's response. "I'm glad to see the rain, praise the Lord—Bubba's tired."

Brad lay there thinking—he was glad Bubba was his roommate. He counted himself lucky. Many of the guys in Unit 29 weren't the kind of people you really wanted to hang out with on a regular basis. In fact, many of them were scary—but Bubba seemed innocent—almost too innocent really. During the short time they had been roommates, Brad had begun finding it hard to imagine why Bubba was actually in prison. He really didn't seem the type. It's not that Brad hadn't asked him—he had. But all Bubba had said was, "for being stupid… like everybody else here… for being stupid."

Brad still couldn't imagine what it was Bubba had done—and he wanted to know.

"Whatcha doing awake so early, Bubba?" Brad asked, trying to start up a conversation.

"I could ask you the same question," came Bubba's reply.

"Rain's so loud here, who can sleep?" Brad answered. "And besides, it'll soon be time they'll be getting us up for breakfast anyway. Might as well be awake."

"Yep—that's the way I look at it, too," Bubba said. "And besides, I likes the rain—brings back memories of when I was a kid and we'd go stay with my grandmamma. She stayed in this small shotgun house just outside of Louise, Mississippi. You

184

ever heard of it?"

"Louise?" Brad answered. "Used to know a lady at my church named Ms. Louise. She always brought the best strawberry cakes to our potlucks—and I always loved that strawberry cake."

"Well, I don't know if they named Louise after her or not," Bubba continued, "but if they did, it wasn't much of an honor. Not much to speak of in Louise. But my grandmamma's house was home. When my mama was goin' off the deep end—which was a lot—I loved stayin' with grandmamma. She was the best cook in the county, and she kept a nice place. Her house had an old red tin roof on it, and when it rained the sound of raindrops hittin' that old tin woke the whole house up. But nobody would say a word. We'd just lay there listenin' to it. I really miss those days—them was good days."

"Why'd they call it a shotgun house?" Brad asked. "Was your grandmamma packing?"

"Naw, man," Bubba laughed. "She was a little old lady—didn't even have a gun. And she was one of those types, loved Jesus and hated sin. She could give a good whippin' but she couldn't hurt a fly. You know what I mean? Shotgun house was just an expression. Haven't you ever heard of it? They ain't very big—ours only had three rooms, all connected back to back. And you could stand at the front door, and shoot a shotgun, and the bullet could go through all the rooms and out the back door without hittin' nothin'."

"Man, you did that?" Brad asked.

"Naw, Brad," Bubba answered. "Just an old saying—you know—why they'd called it a shotgun house. Never knew anybody who actually did it though, thank the good Lord."

The rain continued to beat upon the roof of Unit 29. But all was quiet. Brad thought to himself, *This must be what Bubba was talking about—everybody awake but nobody saying a word. Wish it was always like this here.*

"Bubba, can I ask you a question?" Brad wanted to know more

185

about his new roommate.

"You just did," Bubba replied. "But go ahead, bro, you can ask Bubba whatever you want."

"Why are you in Parchman?" Brad asked carefully, as if verbally tip-toeing around the subject."

"I told you already," Bubba answered. "For being stupid. Like everybody else here. For being stupid."

"Yeah, I know that's what you said," Brad replied. "But I'd really like to know more about it. I mean, what did you do?"

The rain continued to beat down upon the roof. A clap of thunder sounded in the distance. For a moment, Brad wondered if he had done the right thing prying into Bubba's business. Perhaps it would be better if he didn't know. He lay there for what seemed to be a long time. Bubba was making no response. Minutes ticked by without a word. Brad found it strange that the normally talkative Bubba Clarence Riley wasn't saying a word.

"I was a thief, a liar, a sinner of the worst sort." Bubba's sudden response startled Brad who was beginning to let the sound of the rain lull him back to sleep. "And that's why I'm here—and that's why I deserve to be here."

Brad just lay there listening—daring not to interrupt Bubba's confession.

"At first, I thought it was harmless—even funny," Bubba continued. "I was good at it, too—stalkin' just the right victim, always a woman in a fine car—a BMW, a Lexus—somethin' like that. I'd wait outside the grocery store while she was shoppin', and just as she was loadin' her bags in the car, I'd snatch her keys, jump in her ride, and take off. Of course I picked women because they never put up a fight—and because they usually had the best groceries."

Brad made no response. He just listened to Bubba as the rain continued to pour.

"It was a lot of fun at first—and I made a lot of money sellin' the cars to a chop shop in Memphis—turned 'em fast before anybody could catch me. And the groceries were just icing on the cake—especially when I got 'em at Fresh Market or some place like that. Some mighty good groceries at Fresh Market!"

Brad chuckled quietly to himself. Classic Bubba—as excited about the groceries as he was about the cars.

"But then came that stupid lady—a horrible lady really," Bubba continued. "You will never believe it."

"What?" Brad asked, relieved that Bubba was beginning to engage him in his story.

"Brad—it was awful. I really didn't know anything like this could happen," Bubba continued. "I was at a grocery store in Germantown—the other side of Memphis—it was a cool day in December, a few years ago. I spied this good-lookin' white lady driving a brand-new Mercedes. I couldn't resist it: black and shiny with chrome rims. I had to have it. Just as always, I made myself inconspicuous, pretendin' to pick up trash, straighten buggies, you name it, when this lady walks out with a couple of bags. Just as she put the bags in the back seat, I grabbed her keys from her hand, jumped in the car, and sped off. And she chased me screamin'! I looked back at her—kinda thought it was funny— and then I saw it."

Bubba quit talking. He was waiting for Brad to ask the question.

"What did you see?" Brad obliged.

"A baby. There in the back seat of that fine Mercedes was a car seat, and a baby was sittin' there just starin' back at me—not cryin' or nothin'—just starin'. I will never forget it as long as I live. That lady had left her baby in the car while she went in the grocery store. Can you believe that? And I hadn't taken the time to notice. Never had to worry 'bout no baby before."

Bubba paused. Brad continued to listen.

"Bubba Riley might be a carjacker, but he ain't no kidnapper," Bubba continued. "Wasn't no way I was goin' to take that car with that baby. No way. So I pulled over right there in the parking lot, jumped out, and started runnin'—as fast as Bubba could run!"

"And then what happened?" Brad asked.

"Bubba got caught, that's what happened," Bubba answered. "As luck would have it, a cop was drivin' past the store just as I was runnin' with that lady screamin' and hollerin' and carryin' on. He whipped his car around, and in a flash he was hot on my tail. Even jumped a curb and plowed across a field to keep up with me, and when I heard the gunshot, I stopped. Dropped to my knees and put my hands in the air. I knew I was done."

Silence followed Bubba's story. The rain had begun to lessen. Brad was amazed. He had never heard firsthand a carjacker's confession before. After a few moments, he said what was on his mind. "You did the right thing, Bubba. You did the right thing."

"Yeah, I know I did," Bubba responded, "Best thing that ever happened to me."

Bubba's words took Brad by surprise. He would have expected Bubba to express disappointment, even anger about getting caught—and here he was hearing just the opposite.

Bubba continued. "That day, December 13, 2008, changed ole Bubba's life forever. That day is when Jesus finally got a hold of me…" Bubba paused. There was only the sound of rain pouring down on Parchman. Brad waited for him to continue.

"Brad, it's like this." Bubba was now energized. Brad felt a sermon coming. "I was a terrible person. From the time I could walk, I was always looking out for Bubba—stealin' from neighbors, lying to my mama and grandmamma about it, skippin' school, drinkin' when I was thirteen, smokin' when I was twelve. You name it; I did it. But that wasn't the worst of it. I was a racist. I hated white people. I blamed them for every bad thing that happened in my life—'cause they all had it so good and ole Bubba had it so bad. I used to target white people just 'cause they was white. And I especially hated white women—guess I was jealous of them. They always seemed to have it easy when I saw my mama and my grandmamma havin' it so hard. Never stole no car off a black woman—only white women."

"What changed you?" Brad asked. He really couldn't believe what he was hearing.

Bubba continued. "It's not that I was a bad person deep down—I mean my mama and grandmamma tried, they really did. They raised me in church. I spent every Sunday I can remember at church—and I mean we'd be there all day! We'd start with singing and a sermon—always a long one about Jesus—His love and forgiveness and all that stuff. And then we'd have lunch at the church and start goin' again. Sometimes didn't even get home till dark. I did this every Sunday. But I rejected it—didn't want it. But I did it anyway, up until I got old enough to speak my mind and stop goin'".

"So what changed you?" Brad repeated his question.

"Jesus—He's what changed me," answered Bubba. "While I was doin' all those bad things, I felt awful inside. I knew I wasn't doin' right. But I just couldn't help it. Left me feeling lonely and depressed all the time. I think that's why I got into carjackin'. I got this boost every time I'd do it, but then it'd leave me feelin' lower than before. And then Jesus found me."

"You mean you found Jesus," Brad replied.

"No, man," persisted Bubba, "He found me. Right there in a Memphis jail in December of 2008. I was sittin' there all lonely and depressed—I knew I had really messed up my life. I felt all of this hatred for white people, and I was down on my life, and how I had turned out so bad just because I was black. And all of a sudden I heard his voice speakin' to me."

"What was he saying?" Brad asked.

Bubba answered, "'Give it to me,' that's what He said. 'Give it to me. Give me all your heartaches. Give me all your sins—whatever weights you down. Give me all your jealousy and all your hate.' And that's what ole Bubba did—on Christmas Day in the Shelby County Detention Center in Memphis, Tennessee. I gave it all to Jesus—and I made Him my Lord and Savior.' And he eased my burden—took all that guilt and hate away—and replaced it with His love. I haven't been the same since."

Brad didn't say anything. He just lay there letting Bubba's story sink in. The rain had slowed considerably—and it would soon be time to get up.

"You know that's what you ought to do." Bubba's directness was intentional. "You gots to give it to Jesus. You're carrying a lot of what I used to carry, only the hate you have is for yourself. You blame yourself for every bad thing that's ever happened to you and the people you love. And you hate yourself for it."

Brad had to admit Bubba was right. He did hate himself. He wished that he was the one who had died instead of Radley.

"But you gots to give it to Jesus, Brad. You gots to let it go. Jesus loves you—He wants to bless you and forgive you. He wants to give you a new life and put love in the place of all that hate. Stop trying to do it all alone. Some things you just can't control—you gots to give it to Jesus."

The sound of guards banging their sticks against the bars rattled the silence. It was time to get up. The timing was perfect. Bubba was finished with his confession—and his sermon. It was time to face the day. But his words had had a profound effect on Brad. "Some things you just can't control—you gots to give it to Jesus."

CHAPTER 25

Taped Confessions

THE SUGARY AROMA of Honey Bee Bakery was almost intoxicating. Lorna was finding it hard to resist a fresh, warm petit four as she paid for the homemade bran and blueberry muffins. Locally owned and family-run, Honey Bee had long been her favorite bakery in Oxford. And if she was going somewhere, and food was expected, Honey Bee had always come to her rescue.

"What's the occasion this morning, Madam Mayor?" asked a bright-eyed young girl as she rang up Lorna's order.

"You remember, Heather," replied Lorna, "it's the last Saturday of the month, and I have the OM Circle."

"That's right!" answered Heather. "My mom is always there—you will probably see her in a few minutes. She just left toting a freshly baked coffee cake. We literally just brought it out of the oven!"

"Well, it will be good to see Martha," replied Lorna. "She's always so faithful. I don't think she's ever missed a circle meeting!"

"No—rain or shine, she's going to be there," stated Heather with a grin. "Speaking of rain, it's a shame about Halloween isn't it?"

Overnight, heavy storms had moved into Oxford, and everyone seemed certain trick-or-treating would be a washout. Some indoor activities would be going on as planned, but most outside events had been canceled.

"Really doesn't affect me," answered Lorna. "With all my trees, and being off the road like I am, we never get the first trick-or-treater. I'll probably just curl up with a good book."

"What are you reading?" asked Heather. "I've been looking for a good book to start—just finished 'The Shack.' Really enjoyed it."

"Well, I'm thinking about starting a new Beth Moore Bible study based on the life of Esther," Lorna replied. "You know, the woman who was called for 'such a time as this'? I've been wanting to read it, but just haven't found the time."

Lorna was really just making conversation with Heather. Ever since Radley's death, she had found it hard to sit still long enough to enjoy a good book. And with all of the excitement of the recent days, she doubted that tonight would be any different. However, curling up with a book on a rainy day had always been one of her favorite pastimes, and the study on Esther would surely be inspiring.

"Just in case you're wondering, we just took your muffins out of the oven as well," Heather said, changing the subject and opening the white cardboard box to allow Lorna to inspect her purchase.

"They look delicious!" Lorna exclaimed. "I really can't say which is my favorite—the bran or the blueberry. I guess whichever one I happen to be eating. I know the ladies at church will love these!"

"And I noticed you eyeing the petit fours," continued Heather. She was very good at her job. "We just made them this morning as well, and yours truly decorated them!" Heather was smiling, pointing to little white cakes embellished with small orange pumpkins, black bats, and smiling ghost faces.

"They're so cute," replied Lorna, "but my waistline won't be if I continue indulging. I better pass!"

"Suit yourself," replied Heather with a giggle as she closed the muffins and handed them to Lorna.

In a few minutes, Lorna was pulling up to Oxford Method-ist Church. She parked in a side parking lot, and began walking quickly to the fellowship hall, muffins in hand, balanced on a music book. While she was at the church, she was hoping to prac-tice her solo for Sunday.

"Looks like you came loaded for action," replied a friendly voice coming up behind her.

"Myra Sanchez!" Lorna was happy to see her friend. "I almost forgot you would be here! Shows what a fog I've been in lately. Forgive me for being such a poor excuse for a friend."

"No excuse necessary," laughed Myra. "I've been busy myself. Just got back last night from the Philippines. We've opened a new operation there, and getting it off the ground has been a job and a half! I'm so glad to be back in the states—Southern American accents have never sounded better!"

"Well, I'm surprised you're here," said Lorna. "If it were me, I'd probably be laid up at the house getting over jet lag. My trav-eling shoes aren't what they used to be."

"Oh, I wouldn't miss Circle for the world," replied Myra. "Besides, I had a new quiche recipe I've been dying to try." Myra was pointing to a sealed Pyrex container in her hand. "Fresh mushrooms, peppers, and water chestnuts. I hope everyone likes it."

"Sounds delicious! I know they will," answered Lorna. "It's no mystery why you always get put on the food committee. I hon-estly don't know why they assign something to me every once in a while. Like today, I'm bringing the best muffins money can buy."

"Well that's just it," said Myra smiling. "Because they are the best."

As the two ladies walked into the fellowship hall and placed their items on a waiting table, Myra turned to Lorna, saying, "I have been meaning to call you all week, but service isn't that good in Manila. Matt and I were wondering if you would like to join us for lunch tomorrow after church? Polly is coming over, and we thought it would be fun if you came, too. You don't have to bring a thing—Polly and I have it covered! I'm thinking of inviting Brother David and Tricia as well."

"Myra," replied Lorna, "that's the best invitation I've had all week. I would love to come!"

A few hours later, Circle meeting and singing practice concluded, Lorna was back at her house—the gloom of a rainy Halloween beginning to settle prematurely around the grounds of Somerset. The rain was really starting to come down.

I guess it's not time for the lights, thought Lorna, considering how the lights around the mansion were all on timers. *I do wish they would come on. Everything looks so dark.* She then tagged for herself a mental reminder: *Daylight Saving Time ends tonight. Better turn the clocks back.*

Roscoe, as always, was happy to greet her, wagging his tail and waiting for her to pat his head. He followed her through the house to her bedroom and waited as she exchanged her tasteful fall outfit for some comfy warmups and slippers.

In short order, she and the golden retriever were both back in the kitchen, a Miles Davis CD playing and fragrant candles burning. Lorna was fixing herself a cup of hot chocolate.

Might as well start that book, she thought to herself. It was Halloween, and there was absolutely nothing for her to do. And she dared not allow her mind to stay idle—too many memories of campfires and pigs-in-a-blanket. Oh, how she missed those days with Radley and Brad. They were just memories now.

Curled up on Radley's leather sofa, hot chocolate in hand, Lorna read the description of her new book: "It's Tough Being a Woman. Esther may have been a queen, but her life was no fairy tale. An outsider, a foreigner, and an orphan, she found herself facing an evil plan to destroy her people. And you thought your life was hard!"

No doubt about it: Beth Moore was a brilliant writer. And wow.

The description fit Lorna perfectly. This book must have been written for her. Ever since Radley's death, Lorna had felt every bit an outsider—a foreigner and an orphan. And she knew that great evil was at work to destroy her town, and her family.

Even though Oxford had embraced Lorna, even electing her mayor, she sometimes felt like she was still a new Yankee transplant from Boston. Her siblings, an older brother and sister, still lived in New England and, while they talked occasionally, Lorna had little day-to-day interaction with them. Radley and Brad had become her family—her life. And now alone, without them, she felt very isolated at times, as an orphan might feel.

Yes, everyone in Oxford was lovely and treated her like a queen. But deep down, she missed her family—and at times, she missed the familiarity of her childhood home—sailing on the Charles, attending concerts at Symphony Hall with her parents, darting off to Newport for a weekend.

Roscoe suddenly moved from his place beside the couch and nuzzled Lorna, placing his nose against her book and putting his heavy head on her lap. She smiled, put down "Esther," and began rubbing his ears. *He seems to know when I am hurting most,* she thought. *Dogs have to be angels sent from God.* Angel or no, Roscoe surely enjoyed good ear rubs.

Her mind drifted back to the present threat facing Oxford. She thought, *As if feeling like an orphan isn't hard enough, I'm now looking right into the face of evil—a conspiracy determined to have its way no matter the cost."*

Lorna's mind drifted back to what Brother David had told her just a few months earlier. He had been referring to Queen Esther when he said: "She was appointed by God for a special time and special task—to root out evil and save her people. We believe that you, just like Esther, have been called and appointed for 'such a time as this.' Lorna—run for mayor. Your people need you."

"Oh, Lord, how can I save my people?" Lorna's question was loud and abrupt. Roscoe jumped at the sudden sound of her voice.

Lorna's question was answered by silence. The Miles Davis CD had ended, and aside from the ticking of the old grandfather clock in the hall, all was quiet. But somewhere in that silence, Lorna heard a voice. *Behold, I am with you always. Even unto the end of the world.* The hairs raised up on her neck. She recognized the voice—it was the voice of Jesus speaking through the Holy Spirit, His last words to His disciples as recorded by Matthew. Lorna suddenly felt warm and at peace. She no longer felt alone.

By now, Roscoe had returned to his spot on the floor, and Lorna was no longer content to lay there drinking hot chocolate and reading her book. She began looking around Radley's study, her eyes moving from picture to plaque, memento to keepsake, until her gaze came to rest on a book laying on Radley's desk. She hadn't noticed it lately, and she was puzzled—curious to know what book it was and finding it difficult to remember.

Getting up, Lorna walked over to Radley's large desk and set-tled into Radley's leather office chair, facing the bay window of his study. Beyond the glass, through rain beads rolling down the antique window panes, she could see that the lights of Somerset were now on, dimly lighting the gloomy wet landscape outside. Tonight was certainly a good night for staying home!

Lorna turned her attention to the book. "Of course," she thought, remembering how much Radley loved "David—a Man of Pas-sion & Destiny" by Charles Swindoll. He had owned it for years, sometimes re-reading it for lessons on how "a man after God's own heart" was also prone to being very human and making many mistakes. The story of how David had defeated the giant Goliath with nothing but a slingshot had always been one of Radley's favorite Bible stories. And he also loved reading how God always loved and forgave David—in spite of some of the terrible things that he did.

Lorna thought about Brad. *The same God that loved and for-gave David also loves and forgives you, Brad,* she thought to herself. *I hope you're learning that.*

Sitting at the old desk, Lorna remembered when Radley first spied it on their fifth anniversary trip to New England. Instead of going to Newport, they had settled on a quaint bed and breakfast in Vermont—complete with its own live-in French chef. The vacation had been heavenly—the mild summer days provided a respite from the humidity of Oxford. They had hiked virgin hardwood forests, waded in cold, spring-fed creeks, and strolled villages full of interesting shops, restaurants, and antique stores.

It happened to be in one of these stores that Radley found "the desk." Made of burl walnut, a rare and exquisite treatment showing the unique grain of the American hardwood, the desk had once belonged to a sea captain—or so was the story. Antiques are most enjoyed for the stories they tell—and it was this story that sold Radley the desk.

It was full of drawers and interesting carvings, many of them quite intricate. Legend has it that the old captain used the desk to hide maps to exotic ports of call. There were indeed hidden compartments—Radley had found a few of them and enjoyed showing Lorna—but only Lorna. He always treasured the secrets of his special desk.

I wonder if I remember how to find them, Lorna asked herself, suddenly feeling like a kid again. As a small girl, curiosity sometimes got the best of her, and she would look into the drawers of her father's dresser when he wasn't at home. She loved finding secrets and hidden treasure—old political buttons, souvenirs from his high school days, and old photographs of people she didn't recognize.

Methodically, Lorna began searching the drawers, first removing the visible contents to make her search for hidden compartments easier. One of the drawers contained the items Radley had with him when he died. She had almost forgotten placing them there after the police department had returned them. She let out an audible sigh as she placed Radley's handkerchief and phone on the desk before her. *Too sad.* She quickly put them out of her thought.

Lorna continued her investigation of the drawers. They were in all shapes and sizes, many of them too small to contain much more than a few coins or a deck of playing cards. She remembered that a few had false back panels—revealing extra storage at the rear of the drawer.

"Our first selfie," she laughed opening one of them. There, carefully placed in a small hidden compartment was a small camera roll, containing three small pictures of a very young Lorna and Radley. She was laughing while he was making a goofy face. They had taken it in a photo booth in Gatlinburg. She placed the photo roll on the desk—this was a keeper.

Lorna was enjoying herself. She found several historic keepsakes—such as arrowheads and Civil War mini balls. A few compartments contained old marbles, a pocket knife, and even some antique Boston subway tokens.

Exhausting the drawers, Lorna turned her attention to the carvings. She knew that some moved, triggering hidden compartments that would magically spring forward. *Imagine the ingenuity of the craftsman who made this,* Lorna thought to herself.

Most of the carvings were stationary, but a couple of them did work as she remembered, one of them revealing a small well-folded program from the Newport Jazz Festival. A tear rolled down Lorna's cheek. *Radley—the original, sentimental, romantic,* she thought to herself, looking through the program. Memories flooded her heart, as if it had been yesterday. Miles Davis' "My Funny Valentine" began to play in her head.

And then came the find she was not expecting. Moving a random carved piece of molding to the left caused a small drawer, concealed as a panel, to ease forward. It was a small drawer, perfectly sized to contain its contents: a micro-cassette.

"What in the world?" Lorna asked her reflection looking back at her through the windows. "I haven't seen one of these in years."

Radley had always been one to use his phone to record certain conversations—or memos to himself. It helped him when having to discuss particular issues with aldermen, or recall a detail for a proclamation or speech. But it had been years since Lorna had seen one of his micro-cassettes, his recording tool of choice prior to the convenience of smart phones.

"I've got to see what's on it!" Lorna exclaimed to herself. She was excited, and she knew it must be something important—Radley had carefully hidden it in a place only Lorna would know to look.

Racking her brain, Lorna tried to remember where she had last seen Radley's micro-tape recorder. It occurred to her that she had stumbled upon it a few months earlier in the most random of places—she had even checked to see if it contained a cassette and had been disappointed when she found it empty.

"His dresser!" Lorna remembered. She had seen the small recorder the last time she put up his clothes—clothes that happened to be in the first laundry she washed after Radley's funeral. It had been a very sad day in late April. She folded his clothes and put them away just as she would on any normal day—and she hadn't looked at them since.

In less than two minutes, Lorna had run to Radley's dresser, found the recorder, and returned to his desk. She carefully opened it, inserted the tape, and pushed play. She then put Radley's ear buds to her ear. With great anticipation, Lorna listened—and only silence greeted her. She pushed rewind. And then pushed play again.

Emotion poured over her as she heard Radley's voice. Tears began to flow. It had been months since she had heard that distinct, gentle Southern accent. It was as if he was in the room with her. *But what is he saying?* Lorna repressed her emotions and listened.

"Hello, Lance, come on and get in. We can talk right here," Radley was saying, the sound of a young voice and a slamming car door in the background. Lorna recognized the voice immediately—it was Lance Bradford.

"Hey, Mr. Radley," replied Lance. "I really hate you sticking your neck out like this. But I had nowhere else to turn."

"You haven't been followed, have you?" asked Radley in a calm but very serious tone.

"No sir. I took backroads, and I watched my rearview mirror the whole way. Nobody knows we're out here."

"Well, it's good to see you, Lance. It's been a while," said Radley warmly.

"Same here—I've really missed the good ole days," responded Lance. "Nice ride, by the way. I love Jeeps. If I ever get rid of my Beemer, I might just get me one."

Lorna gasped. *The tape was not that old after all. It had to be recent.*

"Yeah, I love it," replied Radley. "Lorna gave it to me just a few weeks ago. The big five-oh present. She knocked it out of the park if you ask me."

"Well, she's always been the best," Lance said. "And I really miss her cooking. She was always my favorite friends' mom."

Lorna, felt another tear. All of a sudden, she felt great love and sorrow both for Lance—and she felt ashamed that she had not reached out to him much since Kat's death. He just seemed to be in a different world these days, and she had thought it best to leave him be. Maybe she was wrong.

"What's on your mind?" asked Radley, his tone turning serious again.

"Mr. Radley, this is very hard for me. And I hate to involve you in this. But like I said, I have nowhere else to turn," answered Lance.

"It's okay, Lance," replied Radley. "I am glad you contacted me. And I am very interested in what you have to tell me."

"I know you are," said Lance. "You're the only person in Oxford who seems to care about ending this madness, and I want to do whatever I can to help you. I've gotten in over my head, and

I've got to get out."

"Well, I'm here to help you in any way I can," continued Radley, "but understand I cannot make any promises. We can only hope that the authorities will look favorably on your cooperation. And I will be a personal advocate for you to the best of my ability. But first, I want to ask why you haven't reached out to your dad to help you? I've known Sterling my entire life. And I know that, if he knew you were in trouble, he would do whatever he could to help you."

"No he wouldn't," answered Lance bluntly. "With all due respect, Mr. Radley, you may have known him longer than me, but no one knows him better than me. And he is not what you think he is."

"How so?" asked Radley.

"I think he wanted my mother to die," Lance answered. "I'm not saying that he did it or anything, but I know that the last few years of her life were not happy. She withdrew from the world and stayed home all the time because of him. She never told me what it was, but deep down, I think she knew something about him that made him resent her. You know? Like she knew his weaknesses and vulnerabilities or something."

Lance stopped talking for a minute, as if trying to gain courage to continue.

"Go on," Radley encouraged. "Why do you say he wanted your mother to die?"

"They yelled and fought all the time. It started after Brad got hurt, and I kinda went off the deep end, too. It's like she blamed him for it, and I never understood why, but it's like she knew something I didn't. A few times, the arguments got violent, and I saw him hit her. That's when I lost it for him. I attacked him the first night he hit her—I wanted to kill him. But he put me in my place. And it wasn't long after that mama died."

"But your mother's death was an accident," protested Radley. "Your father may not be perfect, but you can't blame him for that.

201

It was just a tragedy. Kat was going too fast in a new boat. And it broke all our hearts… Lorna and I…"

"But that's just it!" Lance interrupted Radley. "Dad never let her drive that boat—said she couldn't handle it. And she didn't even want to go with him that day—he just guilted her into going, saying something about them spending quality time on Sardis and putting their marriage back together…"

Lance stopped talking again. Clearly this was hard for him.

"And when she, she, you know," Lance could hardly get out the words. There was another pause, and then he continued, "… Dad said he wasn't even in the boat, I knew something was up. He wouldn't let her drive like that. He wasn't even into skiing anymore. It just didn't make sense. I think he was driving the boat. And he's just too ashamed to admit it—would rather lie about it. And that's why I don't trust him. Haven't talked to him since the funeral. And don't intend to."

Lorna's mind returned to what Brenda had said just yesterday: "He's been lying to everybody about it. Ms. Kat wasn't driving that boat when it crashed. Mr. Sterling was."

Deep in thought, Lorna almost missed the next sentence or two spoken, but then returned her attention to the tape just as Radley was saying, "So when did you start dealing drugs, Lance?"

There was another pause. Lance was really finding this difficult, and Lorna felt sorry for him again.

"Shortly after Brad got hooked, I started buying stuff on the street for him. I'm sorry you have to hear me say that. I feel horrible about it. But I was just trying to help him out. Never took any of it myself. Just wanted to help Brad. Next thing I know, I'm getting these offers to make some good money—easy money—and I just fell into it. Stupid, I know. And I wish I could take it all back."

"Who are the players?" asked Radley. It was obvious in his tone he was ready to get to the real reason he and Lance were having this conversation. Lorna knew that Radley had been determined to get to the bottom of the Oxford drug problem, but she had no idea he had gotten this involved.

"You know some of them—but I'm going to tell you about all of the ones I know," answered Lance. "But before I do, I want you to know why I'm doing this. And it's like this, Mr. Radley. I'm tired of living the lie. I run myself crazy trying to keep my nose clean and not get caught. I can't sleep at night. I can't even look at myself sometimes. I hate who I've become. I feel paranoid all the time, like someone is about to kill me. And I can't deal with seeing the pain I've caused others—especially Brad and y'all. I want you to know that I'm sorry—from the bottom of my heart— I'm sorry. Please forgive me."

Lance started to cry.

"Of course we forgive you, Lance," Radley said, love and concern evident in his voice. "And what you're doing right now is very courageous. I applaud you for it. And my prayer is that, in doing this, you will find peace. But first, we have to put the bad guys away. So tell me—who are they?"

Lance stopped crying, took some deep breaths, and then got very serious. "None of them can ever know I told you what I'm about to tell you. If they ever find out, I'm dead. They will kill me—no questions asked. Do you understand that?"

"Yes," Radley replied. "And you have my word that I will do nothing that would endanger you."

Lance then began sharing a variety of details—everything you ever wanted to know about the drug trade in Oxford.

"You've heard about Joe Parker already, I know. He's my lieutenant, and he's already worried that you're on to him. You need to be careful. He's dangerous."

"I'm aware of that. Thank you, Lance," responded Radley.

Lorna shuddered. Only two days ago, she had no idea who Joe Parker was, only to hear his name spoken by Leo Robbins during his interview with Ellis Jefferson. And now, here was his name again—very possibly the real murderer of her husband. Lorna repressed a tear, and continued listening.

"The next name I'm going to give you is my boss," continued Lance. "His name is Chris Jenkins. We call him CJ. Used to go to Ole Miss but dropped out a few years ago and went into construction. He's a general contractor now. Do you know him?"

"Yes," is all Radley said. He made no explanation of how he knew him.

But Lorna knew Chris Jenkins—and she was shocked. Chris—the general contractor for the new police department. She had just seen him with Sterling at the Grove a couple of weeks ago. Chris was a pillar of the community, a family man—a churchgoer and respected businessman. *No way,* Lorna thought—she was speechless.

She continued listening.

"I don't know quite how to tell you the next name," replied Lance. "You're going to be shocked."

There was silence on the tape. And then a name: "Chief Buford."

Radley made no response. Neither did Lorna. She actually was not surprised. And by the lack of response from Radley, she suspected that he was not surprised either.

Radley's voice started speaking again. "Are those all the names you can give me?" he asked.

Lance replied yes and then began sharing general details of the drugs that were sold, the shipments that came in, how they were handled and distributed, and so on. Lorna listened in amazement. Here before her was more information on the Oxford drug trade than she ever dreamed possible. She could not wait to get it to Ellis Jefferson.

But the tape wasn't over. Lance was saying goodbye, reminding Radley to be careful, the sound of the Jeep door closing behind him. Then there was silence. Radley was now alone. But the tape was still going. Then came these chilling words from Radley: "Testimony of Lance Bradford, taken at 4:30 p.m., Thursday, April 16, just outside the city of Oxford, Mississippi. Wouldn't have expected this… Chris Jenkins is the missing link."

Lorna gasped. *Thursday, April 16—one day before Radley died,* she thought to herself. *No wonder Lance has been blaming himself. This conversation is why my husband was murdered—and it's a wonder Lance hasn't been killed as well.*

The old clock chimed in the hall. Lorna jumped, the familiar chimes jolting her back to the present. Roscoe stirred from his nap on the floor and eased up beside Lorna, placing his heavy head in her lap. She rubbed the ears of her faithful old dog. Radley's study was still and peaceful. But not so was Lorna's mind—it was racing toward her next move.

CHAPTER 26

GHB?

"**I** PRAY YOU WILL be there to guide us when we can't see our way. To shine a light when the way is dark, to make straight the paths we walk each day." Lorna's soprano voice was soothing to the grateful congregants at Oxford Methodist. It had been a while since they had heard her sing—and she was singing one of their favorites.

"Lord this is my simple prayer, to be my guide and stay. Lord, lead me in your way, the way of peace and love. Hold me, steady me, on the rock of your salvation, and never let me fall. Oh Lord, never let me fall."

As she sang, Lorna was saying the prayer to herself. It was a prayer for guidance—a prayer for safety—and she desperately needed both. Not only for her—but for Brad. He was weighing heavy on Lorna's mind. It had only been one week since she had seen him, but it felt as if it had been a month or two. So much had happened, and there was now so much for her to do. While the revelations that had come with the week seemed positive, positive enough to give Lorna hope that she was about to exonerate Brad, she worried that, in the end, she might not be able to pull it all together. This is where faith had to come in—Lorna had to depend on someone higher than herself to make truth prevail—and to make all things new.

"Yes Lord, this is my simple prayer, to be my guide and stay. So that at my journey's end, I may find myself safely at home, at rest with my Savior, eternally alive in your loving arms." Lorna finished the song and a hush fell over the church. Her ministry in song had its intended effect.

A couple hours later, Lorna was sitting at Myra Sanchez' long dinner table in her stately beige and brown Craftsman bungalow on University Avenue. To her left sat Tricia Burton, Brother David seated adjacent to her at the end of the table. Across from Lorna sat Polly Shoemake and Myra, Myra's husband Matt sitting at table's head. And to Lorna's right, sat the surprise guest: Sterling Bradford.

Sterling had definitely proved to be a surprise visitor at church that morning. "I just had to hear you sing," he had said through his sincerest smile when he hugged Lorna after church, "and I think I heard heaven today." Lorna felt so charmed, and moved by Sterling's sincerity, that she couldn't help asking him to accompany her to Myra's and Matt's. *Perhaps I can reach Sterling today,* she thought, *and help him shed the guilt he must be carrying over Kat.*

"Thank you for that beautiful prayer." Matt Sanchez was a polite host, albeit a bit more reserved than his wife Myra. After acknowledging Brother David's gracious blessing over the food, he lifted a glass to everyone, looked approvingly at his wife, and said, "Now everyone, let's enjoy this amazing smorgasbord. Myra and Polly—you two are something!"

When it came to the food, Matt's statement was no exaggeration. Myra and Polly had prepared a lunch fit for a king: baked turkey and ham, complimented by a deliciously moist Southern cornbread dressing, shoepeg corn, seasoned green beans, and sweet potato casserole.

"It feels like Thanksgiving," remarked Lorna as she placed a dollop of fresh cranberries on her dressing. "This is how we used to eat at every holiday almost."

"Well, it actually is a 'prequel' to Thanksgiving," replied Myra.

207

"Polly gave me the idea. It seems that we always enjoy Thanksgiving just once every November—and toward the end of November at that. With the cooler weather, we just felt it appropriate to give everyone an early taste of what's to come."

"I can't take all the credit," Polly chimed in cheerfully. "Myra had as much to do with it as me. I just suggested turkey because it's always been one of my favorite meats—and my dad always said, 'you are what you eat'—kinda fits don't you think? Gobble, Gobble!"

Everyone laughed at Polly's corny joke. "Besides," she continued, "we do have so much to be thankful for. Why save it for just one day when we will all be scattered here and yonder with our families." Immediately Polly regretted making her last statement. Everyone at the table was aware that both Lorna and Sterling were currently lacking in the family department. She glossed over the comment by continuing to talk, "And besides, I just can't find enough opportunities to pull out my mother's dressing recipe!"

"It's possibly the best I've ever had," replied Lorna, glad to keep the conversation on the food. "It's so moist, Polly. How do you do it?"

"The secret is chicken broth," answered Polly. "Every time we were going to eat dressing, mother would boil a chicken first. She insisted on using fresh chicken broth—in addition to chicken meat—in her dressing. Seems to make it juicier."

"Well, you should put a patent on it," replied Lorna. "It's absolutely fabulous!"

"Speaking of patents, where are we on mine," replied Matt, cutting a piece of ham and looking to his left at Sterling. The question caught Sterling off guard. He had just put a huge piece of turkey in his mouth.

Reaching for his iced tea, taking a quick swallow and awkwardly clearing his throat, Sterling responded, "They should be approved any day now," he replied with a raspy voice. "And when they are, you will be the first person I call."

"That's so exciting," Lorna chimed in, providing some relief to her friend as he took another sip of tea.

"Matt's patents could very well change the world," a proud Myra responded. "It's the whole reason we left Emory to come here. The opportunity to perfect his research and put new science on the market is going to change lives."

"I don't know if I'd go that far," replied Matt modestly, cutting another slice of ham and dipping it into his dressing. Lorna studied him for a moment. He was meticulous in every way. His thinning hair was neatly combed, and his wire-rimmed glasses were perfectly balanced on his nose. A brightly colored bow tie complimented his freshly starched white shirt and tan wool sweater vest. Up until meeting Matt, Lorna had never known a computational biologist. But Matt Sanchez fit her picture of one perfectly.

"It will change the world!" Myra stated emphatically. "Imagine, a new formulary to help drug addicts beat their addictions! It will be revolutionary!" Clearly, Myra was proud of her husband.

Free of the turkey clogging his windpipe, Sterling now felt able to enter the conversation. "It is truly some amazing research," he said, patting Matt on his arm. "What my brilliant client is about to offer the world could very well put families back together—and Oxford, Mississippi, on the map!"

"Tell me more about this," stated Brother David. He was enthralled.

"Anything that would help our children would be a lifesaver," replied Lorna, also looking at Matt encouraging him to talk.

"Well," their studious host began slowly, "...in a nutshell, I have discovered a way to harness neurons in the receptors of the brain and make them respond as we want them to—to medication that is."

Silence followed Matt's statement. That was all he said. Myra stirred him on. "Come on, Matt," she said gently. "Tell them what that means."

"Just as neurons in the brain respond to addictive drugs, I have found a formulary that allows the neurons to respond in a way that is counteractive to the effects of addiction and reverse the addictive processes in the brain."

Silence again followed—silence from a now entranced audience. Matt continued, "And unlike traditional medications used to treat addictions, such as Suboxone and Methodone that substitute one addiction for another, my formulary actually interrupts the brain's cycle of dependency and 're-sets' as it were the brain for normal electrical activity."

"It's a reboot for the brain!" pronounced Myra, unable to contain herself. "Imagine that—just like a computer that no longer works right, you will be able to reset your brain! It will change the world I tell you—change the world!"

"I hope it will," continued Matt, "but the only trials thus far have been with mice in a lab. Until we get approval to go further with our testing, I would be reluctant to oversell the idea. However, I am confident enough in my research and early results to optimistically say it 'could' present a solution—and I'm obviously at a point where I feel the need to file for patents."

"And they are in the works," answered Sterling, clearly relieved to have his voice back. "Both of them. Just remember me when you become rich, Dr. Sanchez!"

Matt smiled and looked down at his plate. He seemed ready to change the subject.

"I can only imagine the impact this could have on families," Lorna replied. "Anything that can help reverse the horror of addiction deserves all of our encouragement and support. Way to go, Matt—I applaud you and wish you well in your work."

"Amen to that," agreed Brother David, and as if on cue, everyone around the table raised their glasses in a mock toast to their intelligent, yet modest host. Matt nodded his head in appreciation, waved their glasses down, and continued cutting his turkey. Everyone seemed to follow suit and silence returned to the table.

Polly seized the opportunity to change the subject back to the food. "Well, what do you think?" she asked, looking across the table at Tricia. "Are those not the best sweet potatoes you ever put in your mouth?"

Tricia straightened her shoulders and looked back at Polly, embarrassingly putting her hand to her mouth. Clearly, her mouth was full of Myra's sweet potato casserole and she was unable to speak. Polly patiently waited for her reply.

"Absolutely the best," came Tricia's answer after a brief moment. "They're the perfect blend of salty and sweet—with just the perfect amount of cinnamon. What's the secret?"

"Myra will have to tell you," replied Polly. "She hasn't even offered to share her recipe with me—but I do hope she will!"

"That's because I don't have a recipe," stated Myra, defending herself and giving Polly a slight pat on the hand. "I just mix it all together and hope for the best."

"Well, you really must write it down for me," said Tricia. "We never cooked it this way growing up in Kentucky—and I would love to serve it to my family this Christmas. Really—what is your secret?"

"The secret is simple—plenty of marshmallows and pecans both," answered Myra proudly. "It's a trick I picked up in Georgia. You know, most people use either one or the other—but I think it's best to use both! And even better if you use the roasted pecans that have been drizzled with cinnamon and sugar. And plenty of butter—that's really all there is to it."

As the food talk continued, Matt excused himself from the table to go to the kitchen for the tea pitcher. Lorna seized upon the opportunity to follow him.

"Mind if I ask you a question," Lorna whispered to him as he was reaching into the freezer for more ice.

"No, Lorna—go right ahead," he replied. "What's on your mind?"

"Just how much experience do you have with drug addiction?" she asked, looking at him with the most serious of expressions. In her conversations with Myra, the fact that Matt's research involved drug addictions had never come up. And Lorna was suddenly intrigued.

"Let's put it this way," Matt answered. "When we lived in Georgia, I volunteered at a local community treatment facility. It was my way of 'giving back' so to speak. I saw things no one should have to see. It broke my heart—and it became my passion. That's why I'm doing what I'm doing—I'm determined to make a difference."

"I know we can't talk long," Lorna continued, "but I need for you to help me. As you know, my son Brad is currently in Parchman—and I don't think he did what they say he did."

"He was drugged," came Matt's sudden reply. Lorna was speechless. Matt seemed to be reading her mind right there in his kitchen. "Myra has given me details, and I have listened to the talk around town and what I've watched on the news and read in the papers. I know this is what you're asking, and you have a right to know."

Matt put down the ice bin and pitcher and gave Lorna his full attention. "Brad did not OD on heroin. If he had, he would not have been lucid just a few hours later. He would have either been unconscious or dead. The only plausible explanation is that he was administered a fast-acting drug that resulted in amnesia and then wore off within just a few hours."

"Like a date-rape drug?" asked Lorna.

"Precisely," answered Matt. "I'm thinking GHB…"

"GHB?" Lorna asked.

"Gamma-Hydroxybutyrate—it traditionally is used to treat narcolepsy. Takes effect in less than fifteen minutes and only lasts four to five hours. Results in amnesia and other symptoms that can be confused for being high or on drugs."

"I've heard of it," replied Lorna. "Some Oxford fraternity boys got in trouble last year trying to spike their dates' drinks with it. Has a salty taste—the girls got suspicious and didn't drink it, thank goodness."

"Yes—that's it. Very common these days, unfortunately," Matt said. "Especially prevalent on college campuses—really sad."

"But it can be injected?" Lorna asked. "That's surprising."

"Any drug can be injected," Matt answered. "And usually with great effect."

"What are you two up to in here?" Myra startled Lorna as she reached around Matt to grab the ice and tea pitcher.

"Just picking your husband's brain," replied Lorna, quickly recovering. "In addition to being a rude guest. Sorry to have stranded Sterling. Is he okay?"

"Seems to be loving those sweet potatoes," replied Myra with a roll of her eyes. "But then again, I think he loves anything he considers sweet." Myra was half winking at Lorna, but Lorna didn't notice. Her mind was elsewhere.

Back in her seat beside Sterling, Lorna found herself suddenly uninterested in the food or company. All she wanted to do was return home so that she could look at Brad's toxicology report in the case file. But doing so was impossible at the moment.

"Bread pudding, Madam Mayor?" Polly was standing over Lorna proudly holding a small silver dish with a dollop of whipped cream visible under a small twig of mint. Before Lorna could answer, Polly had placed the deliciously fragrant dessert on the linen placemat before her.

"Looks delicious," Lorna stated with a smile. Normally, she would have been drooling over a serving of Polly's bread pudding, but today would have to be an act. She really wasn't interested.

"Yep—you might say we're on a roll here with all these good desserts," Polly replied. "Get it, bread pudding? On a roll...?" For once, Polly's joke fell flat.

"I might have to take two, Polly," replied Sterling with a smile—rescuing the corny chef from her terrible pun. "Poor Lance never got to eat the bread puddings you left for him last year back at the house. I'm ashamed to admit it, but I ate every single one—and never regretted it!"

Polly smiled. She loved Sterling's flattery. "Sterling, I will fix you bread pudding anytime you want—all you have to do is say so," she said placing a silver cupful on his placemat. "And we have plenty if you'd like to take some home with you."

Sterling smiled. "Just might have to take you up on that."

Another hour dragged by before Sterling was opening the door of his silver Mercedes for Lorna to step into. Lunch and the customary after-dinner chit-chat were finally over, and Sterling was about to give her a ride back to the church to retrieve her car. At his insistence, she had ridden with him to the Sanchez'—and she now regretted it. She was ready to go home, and a ride back to the church with Sterling was yet another delay. *GHB. Brad drugged. I have to see that report. And I have to get a hold of Ellis... Chris Jenkins... the tape...* Lorna's busy mind was racing.

"I've got a surprise for you, Lorna," Sterling announced, his sudden statement snapping her back to the present. They were cruising down University Avenue, in the opposite direction of the church.

"But Sterling—I really need to get home," Lorna protested flatly. She was not in the mood for any unplanned excursions.

"Aw, c'mon, beautiful," Sterling replied. "What are you going to do at that lonely old mansion of yours? Same thing I do at mine probably? Wander around the halls with all those ghosts? We've got better things to do with our time."

In just a few moments, Sterling was rounding the Oxford Town Square, passing City Hall and proceeding down North Lamar Avenue. Just a couple of blocks further, he turned left into a cobblestone driveway, his stately brick Georgian mansion beckoning in the distance—a jewel of turn-of-the-century craftsmanship. Sterling and Kathleen had purchased the old home as newlyweds, and its restoration had been one of their early joys of marriage. Lorna still remembered the elaborate party they had thrown when it was completed. Everyone in Oxford seemed to be invited, and few social events before or since seemed to compare.

Lorna's curiosity had begun to repress her eagerness to get home. She wondered what Sterling could be up to. In recent years, he and Kathleen had stopped inviting people over—part of the distance that Kat had built between herself and everyone, including Lorna. She actually hadn't been invited to the Bradfords' home since Kathleen's funeral—and that really didn't count as a social invitation.

"Watch your step," Sterling said as he escorted Lorna down a worn and uneven brick walk adjacent to the large home. He opened a small ornately designed iron gate, and they walked hand in hand under an old wire arbor covered in dormant wisteria.

There beyond them was a beautiful back yard, complete with multiple decks, umbrellas, a screened porch, a fire pit, and an elegant outdoor kitchen. "I've been meaning to invite you over for a steak," Sterling said, pointing to the kitchen. "It's the last project Kathleen and I did together—and I've hardly used it since she died."

Lorna's mind drifted back to the one time she and Radley had been invited over to see the new outdoor kitchen. She had been amazed at how the counters were granite—the very granite she and Radley had wanted for their kitchen but had been unable to find time to install. Looking at it now, the granite still looked new.

"We've got an awesome Green Egg—grills the best filet in Oxford," Sterling said. "I can't believe I haven't fixed you one, Lorna. We'll have to put that on the bucket list!"

"What I want to know is what this surprise of yours is," replied Lorna. She really was curious. For the life of her, she couldn't imagine what Sterling was about to do. Her mind drifted back to her conversation with Brenda Marshall at Belk on Friday. *If it was an accident, then why is Mr. Sterling lying about it?* A shiver went down her spine. For a moment she was tempted to be afraid. But she dismissed it.

"You're going to find out in just a minute," Sterling answered her, opening the screen door of the back porch and leading her into a warm, brightly lit room full of art and color. "I just had some new plexiglass panels installed—keeps out the cold," he said, motioning to the large windows.

"You can hardly tell it's plexiglass," Lorna replied, reaching out to touch one of the panels.

"Yep, they've come a long way with plexiglass," Sterling responded. "I think Kathleen would've loved it, don't you? She loved this room so—it was her favorite room in the house. She loved the light—and this is where she did all of her drawings."

"But she never told me," Lorna said with a tone of surprise. "I always suspected that she had an artist in her, but she never let on. Why is that do you think?"

"It's like I told you before," Sterling answered. "With a mother as accomplished as Lacey, I think she just never felt that she could measure up, so she kept it to herself. And don't forget that she had her music—everyone applauded her talent for the piano. The old Chickering I gave her still sits in the parlor. Hadn't been played since she died."

Lorna began looking around the room at pictures—they were snapshots taken of Sterling and Kathleen mostly when they were very young—and happy. In the years that had passed since they were raising their small boys together, Lorna had forgotten just how happy Kat had always been. The person smiling back at her in the pictures did not resemble the woman she had known later in life. Indeed, Kathleen Bradford's happiest years had been her young ones.

"Where's Lance in these pictures?" Lorna asked, noticing that the pictures were all of Sterling and Kathleen.

"Oh, I don't know," answered Sterling. "They're a few in the house, but I think Lance probably took most of them with him to his place. You know he has his own place now."

"Yes—hard to imagine him all grown up and on his own," Lorna said with a sigh. She missed the little boys that now seemed almost like strangers to her. Lost in thought, she almost didn't notice that Sterling was handing her something. "What's this?" she asked, taking an old worn book from his outstretched hand.

"Kathleen's sketchbook," answered Sterling—a tender expression on his face. "I want you to have it."

Lorna immediately sat down on a day bed tucked under the windows and brought the book close to her chest. "What a treasure!" she exclaimed. "I had almost forgotten about it. You told me about it that night at the Ava Hotel. I'm ashamed to say I haven't thought about it since."

"Well, you've had a lot on your plate," answered Sterling. "But I've been meaning to give it to you. I know you of all people would appreciate it."

Lorna carefully opened the book and began turning the pages. There were drawings of a variety of subject: nature scenes, birds, Oxford landmarks. And then there it was: a drawing of Faulkners' typewriter on his desk at Rowan Oak. "I was with her when she took this picture," Lorna said, studying the lines of the detailed sketch. "We toured it on a lark one day. We had just dropped the boys off at kindergarten, and we didn't have anything better to do. She took it with an old Polaroid instamatic. I had no idea she later drew it."

Sterling quietly sat down beside her, not saying a word. Lorna continued to turn the pages. She saw the watering pot that Sterling had described to her, and the drawings of Lance as a child. She even saw one that she was convinced was Brad—he couldn't have been more than six or seven, and he was sitting in a wheel barrow.

Sterling placed his hand on Lorna's. She didn't move or flinch. His warm hand was comforting.

"You know I really miss her," Sterling said, his voice cracking. "She loved this daybed. Used to sleep out here in the summertime. Said it reminded her of her grandmother's porch in Jackson." He grabbed a pillow with his free hand and brought it to his face. "Still smells like her."

Lorna closed the book, leaving it resting in her lap, and placed her arm around Sterling. "We both have loved ones we miss, Sterling. But we will see them again one day."

"I don't know," Sterling replied.

"What do you mean?" said Lorna. "What do you mean you don't know?"

"I mean I don't know," Sterling answered. He was very quiet.

"Sterling, can I ask you a question?" Lorna asked. Sterling nodded. "Were you and Kat okay when she died?"

Sterling was quiet. And then he asked, "What do you mean okay?"

"I mean okay—were you on good terms?" Lorna responded. "I sometimes worry that you have some unresolved guilt when it comes to Kat's death."

Sterling didn't respond. He removed his hand from Lorna's and ran it through his thick silvery hair, grabbing his forelock and then scratching his scalp. Abruptly, he stood up. He walked over to the door as if looking for someone, and then turned around to face Lorna.

"There are things best left alone. And this is one of them," he stated almost coldly. "We can't go back, even if there are things we'd like to change and do over. And yes—there are things I've said, and things I've done that I wish I could take back. But the past is the past. And we have no choice but to leave it there."

Lorna didn't say anything. She really didn't know if she should or not. Sterling was right: there are things best left alone.

"Sterling, I hate to be a party pooper," Lorna changed the subject, "But I really am tired and need to get home. Could we continue this little visit another time? Perhaps over a filet grilled on your little Green Egg? You know, you owe me one!"

Sterling seemed relieved that Lorna was ending the conversation. He reached for her hand and led her back out the screen door and to the car, opening the door for her and making sure she was safely inside before he closed it.

The two old friends were silent as they rode back to Oxford Methodist. But as Sterling wheeled into the parking lot, pulling his Mercedes into the parking place next to Lorna's Audi, he broke the silence. "Lorna, I guess you struck a nerve with that question about Kathleen and me," he said, placing his car in park. "There are some things that do haunt me. And perhaps it would help to talk about them. I know, if there is anyone in this world I can talk to you, it's you. Mind if I drop by one of these days? You just never know—I may wake up tomorrow and decide it's time to unload. Would you be there if I needed to?"

Lorna was touched. "Why of course, Sterling," she answered sweetly, grabbing his hand and squeezing. "I know you carry many hurts. A woman can tell. And I want you to know that I'm here for you—just as you have been here for me. You can feel free to call on me any time."

Sterling looked at her and smiled. He reached over and kissed her cheek. "Thank you," he said.

Lorna smiled—enjoying the moment. She then removed her hand from his, picked up Kathleen's sketch book from her lap and opened the car door. "You are a special friend, Sterling," she replied. "And I can't thank you enough for Kat's book. I will treasure it always. Goodbye."

In a matter of minutes, Lorna was back in her car. She was finally alone and headed home to Somerset.

• • •

The fall day had grown muggy. Mississippi summers always seem to linger like an unwanted houseguest. And even though the date was November 1, this was proving to be one of those days. Lorna was glad to change out of her fall dress clothes and put on some cool pants and a tee-shirt. She gently patted Roscoe on the head as she took a seat on Radley's leather couch, placing Radley's case file in her lap. With a few quick page turns, there it was: Bradford Hamilton's toxicology report. The page was a standard medical form with a list of substances ranging from alcohol to marijuana. Only two items had markings beside them: "Tobacco," which had the word "positive" written beside it, but no percentage, and "Diacetylmorphine (Heroin)," also with the word "positive" along with an amount: ".08 percent".

Lorna didn't understand what .08 percent meant but she knew someone who did. Immediately, she picked up her phone and texted Myra: "Please ask Matt what .08 percent heroin means on tox report."

A few minutes later, she received a reply: "Not possible. Person would be dead—.08 percent is legal limit for alcohol, not heroin."

A couple seconds later she received another text: "Heroin doesn't even stay in the body long. It's usually undetectable just hours later—.08 is impossible."

Lorna put down her phone and stared at the report. A chill ran down her spine. There could only be one explanation: the report was bogus.

A moment later, Lorna was texting again—this time to Ellis Jefferson: "WD at 7". A minute later she received his one-letter response: "K".

CHAPTER 27

A Savior to the Prisoner

"I HEAR THE PRISON walls a crashing, the prison walls a crashing, the prison walls a crashing down into the ground! I hear every chain a breaking, every chain a breaking, every chain a breaking as my Jesus tears it down. Yes He is tearing down my prison, tearing down my prison, He is tearing down my prison, and praise God oh what a sound!! There is POWER IN HIS NAME, POWER IN HIS NAME! POWER IN HIS HOLY NAME!!"

The choir was the loudest Brad had ever heard. To his left, Bubba was really getting into it, eyes closed, his face titled upward and a huge smile across his face. In fact, all around Brad, some of the inmates were moving to the music—a few of them outright dancing as if they were at a concert.

Brother Morris was back in the house. And this time he had brought a full choir with him. And standing there on the platform in the small Parchman chapel was a large woman blessed with some powerful lungs—with at least twenty able pairs behind her. And they were belting it!

While many of the inmates around Brad were, like him, standing there in silence, some were crying out to heaven, "Hallelujah!" "Amen!" "Praise you, Jesus!" And, as the choir was concluding, a fair number of the men were actually singing along—they had heard this song before.

"Thank you, sister! Thank you, choir. And thank you, JESUS!" Brother Morris was as excited as he had been Wednesday—maybe even more.

As the choir took their seats behind him, everyone around Brad began to sit as well. He was relieved to get off his feet. In spite of Saturday's slow pace due to the rain, his body still hurt from picking cotton—and he was glad to enjoy another day of rest. Sundays at Parchman were usually uneventful, unless you were on the visitation list—and Brad was not. He actually had done nothing all morning but lay on his cot, and he really didn't want to come to the impromptu revival meeting. But Bubba wouldn't take no for an answer.

"You knows you wants to, Brad," Bubba had insisted. "You knows you wants to! And Bubba's gone make sure you do!"

"I know we came at you this afternoon as a surprise," Brother Morris was getting wound up again. "But, honestly, I didn't know until this morning that we were going to be able to come. I hope y'all don't mind surprises! I didn't want to lead you on Wednesday night and then be a no- show. How many of you know what I'm talking about? Someone leads you on, tellin' you all this good stuff, and they prove to be a no-show?"

Some of the inmates began nodding their heads—they were ready to get going. "Amen." "Sho'nuff." "We's listening to you, preacher!"

"Well, that's why I'm here talking to you today, my brothers," continued Brother Morris. "And that's why this choir is here singing to you. 'Cause we have a message for you, and it's this: Jesus ain't no NO-SHOW! You hear me? Jesus ain't no NO-SHOW! HE IS IN THE HOUSE!"

Brad heard clapping and whistling. There were a few more "amens" and "preach-its."

"All right, now. All right, fellas…" Brother Morris starting calming them down. A few guys had stood back up and were now again taking their seats. Brother Morris was ready to preach. "I have a message for you this afternoon, and I'm going to start by reading to you from the book of Isaiah. I'm reading from chapter 61. Just a few words from the first verse."

Bubba opened his Bible and turned quickly to Isaiah. He knew his Bible well. He then shared it with Brad and pointed to the scripture.

Brother Morris began to read: "He has sent me to bind up the broken-hearted, to proclaim liberty to the captives, and the opening of the prison to those who are bound."

Brother Morris then closed his Bible and let the quiet overtake the room. Every man in the chapel was still—every eye focused on Brother Morris, waiting to hear what he was about to say.

"Is there anybody here today with a broken heart?" Brother Morris asked his first question. Brad nodded his head without even thinking. Radley's face was emblazoned on his mind. Oh how much he missed his dad. All day Saturday, Brad had been thinking about his father. And the memories of his dad had invaded his sleep that night—dream after dream haunting him with visions of happier times. Brad had awakened Sunday morning with an intense feeling of grief, missing his father more than ever and longing to have him back in his life. *If only I could have had one more day—just one more day,* he thought. And then Bubba's words from Saturday morning ran through his mind again: "Some things you just can't control—you got's to give it to Jesus."

"I want to remind you what the good book says—the words I just read to you," Brother Morris brought Brad's attention back to the sermon. "'He's sent me to bind up the broken-hearted.'" Take that in. Meditate on it. Let the words enter your heart. I'm here because the Spirit of God has sent me and anointed me to bind your broken heart! To make it whole again!"

A few "amens" chorused through the room.

"I don't care what you have done," continued Brother Morris, "or what you haven't done. I don't care what's been done to you, or what hasn't been done to you. There's only one thing that matters. God loves you. He has promised He would never leave you. And He sent His son Jesus to die for you. Why? To heal your broken heart."

A few more "amens" and "hallelujahs" were shouted from around the chapel.

Brother Morris then posed another question, "Is there anyone here today who feels like you are a captive?" Brad thought this was funny. He raised his hand along with a few of the other men in the room, some smiling big smiles as if saying to the preacher, *"No duh!"*

But Brother Morris wasn't laughing. "I don't mean a captive to these prison walls of Parchman, but I mean captive to the prison walls in your heart. Is there anyone here today who is a captive to depression… a captive to addiction… a captive to pornography… a captive to selfishness… a captive to thievery and trickery… a captive to lust and envy… a captive to idolatry and wickedness… a captive to ANYTHING THAT SEPARATES YOU FROM THE LOVE OF THE FATHER?"

Hands went up here and there, and Brad slowly caught himself raising his hand as well. Brother Morris was reading his mail. Ever since he walked away from God and into drug addiction, Brad had fallen victim to every single thing Brother Morris riddled off his list. He had become thoroughly depressed. He had become an addict. He had looked at porn with his buddies and definitely begun living for no one but himself. He was willing to steal to get his fix. He lusted after heroin, and he envied his friends because of where his choices had taken him…. Brother Morris had just described Bradford Hamilton completely!

He sat there feeling ashamed and repulsed at who he had become. *I deserve to be here,* he was thinking. *I'm guilty of all of that.*

"Now some of you are sitting there feeling mighty low right

now. I can see it," Brother Morris spoke slowly and in a serious tone. "And I am not here to beat you down. We have all sinned. You have. I have. I promise even the best person you know has. Let me remind you of what the great apostle Paul said about himself in a letter he wrote a young preacher named Timothy, 'I was shown mercy so that in me, the worst of sinners, Christ Jesus might display his immense patience as an example for those who would believe in Him and receive eternal life.'" Brother Morris paused to let the quotation sink in.

"May I remind you of what I said just a minute ago?" His voice was raised and excited now, and he was talking fast. "I don't care what you have done, what you haven't done, what's been done to you, or hasn't been done to you. The only thing that matters is that God loves you. God loves you. Did you hear what I said? GOD LOVES YOU!"

"Amens" began filling the room from various directions. Some of the choir members rose to their feet and began clapping. And Brad suddenly rose to his feet and began clapping right along with them. He was feeling it! Bubba looked at him, raised to his feet as well, and embraced him.

"But I'm not done yet!" hollered Brother Morris. Everyone laughed and sat back down, waiting to hear what he was going to say next. "I have a third question for you: Is there anyone here today who is bound and wants his prison doors opened?"

Immediately, there were shouts throughout the room. "Yes, Lord!" "Amen!" "Thank you, Jesus!"

Brad was saying "amen" with the others. And slowly, he along with many of the other inmates, rose to their feet clapping. Brother Morris was speaking loudly over their praise, saying, "I don't care what you've done, I don't care what's been done to you. The only thing that matters is God loves you. God loves you. GOD LOVES YOU! He is tearing down your prison! He is setting those who are bound free! He is BREAKING EVERY CHAIN!"

Suddenly, the choir began belting the main chorus of their song again, the big lady singing her part stronger than even before: "I hear the prison walls a crashing, the prison walls a crashing, the prison walls a crashing down into the ground! I hear every chain a breaking, every chain a breaking, every chain a breaking as my Jesus tears it down. Yes He is tearing down my prison, tearing down my prison, He is tearing down my prison, and praise God oh what a sound!! There is POWER IN HIS NAME, POWER IN HIS NAME! POWER IN HIS HOLY NAME!!"

The chorus went on for a while—and jubilation began to overtake some of the inmates in the chapel. But then, all at once, the choir stopped their singing as the piano player continued to play very quietly. A hush fell over the room, and Brother Morris resumed his sermon. "I have one last question for you. One last question and then I'm done. Listen to me very closely. I'm only going to ask this once."

Every man was focused on Brother Morris, including Brad. And Brother Morris was looking straight at him.

"Is there anyone here today..." Brother Morris was speaking very slowly. "...who wants to give his life to Jesus?"

Immediately, Brad began making his way to the front of the chapel. He did not hesitate. He wanted what Brother Morris had. He wanted what Bubba had. He wanted healing for his broken heart, freedom from his sins. He wanted forgiveness. He wanted Jesus to break every chain.

Brother Morris put his arm around Brad and looked him in the eyes. Brad saw at that moment more love than he had ever seen. Not the love of a man, but the love of a savior.

"Brad," Brother Morris remembered his name. "Will you pray with me and with your whole heart pray the words I'm going to pray with you?"

Brad nodded yes, and the two men knelt right there in front of everyone. Brother Morris began to pray, "Heavenly Father, I have sinned against you. I want forgiveness for all my sins. I believe Jesus died on the cross for me and rose again. Father, I give you my life to do with as you wish. I want Jesus Christ to come into my life and into my heart. I ask Him to be my savior. This I ask in Jesus' name. Amen."

Brad repeated every word, he didn't miss one. And as he finished, he opened his eyes. Tears were pouring down his face. And for the first time in his life, on November 1 at Parchman Penitentiary, Bradford Randolph Hamilton felt free.

CHAPTER 28

Mousetrap

W ALL DOXEY WAS dark and vacant. *Perfect,* Lorna thought to herself as she drove past the gatehouse headed for her meeting with Ellis. As before, her mind drifted back to Radley and Brad as she passed the first campsite. She could almost picture the two of them sitting by the empty fire ring roasting marshmallows. *No time for that—must press ahead.* On this night, sentimentality must be put aside—Lorna was on a mission.

As before, Ellis Jefferson was standing beside his white Escalade—parked in the same spot. His smiling face was a welcome sight.

"Evening, Lorna—a little déjà vu, isn't it?" The sheriff's greeting was comforting to Lorna—in her whole circle of friends and acquaintances, he was rapidly becoming her most trusted ally.

"I must say, Ellis—Wall Doxey has become the perfect meeting place. Talk about deserted!" Lorna replied, looking around at the darkness.

"Yep," Ellis responded. "Doesn't get much better than this. As long as no one is following you. You watched behind you all the way here I assume?"

"You better believe it," Lorna said. "These days, I'm beginning to wish I had eyes in the back of my head. On one hand, I'm getting excited that we are getting so close to solving all of this—but on the other hand, it's making me nervous."

"Well, for good reason," Ellis replied, his tone becoming very quiet and serious. "Before we get started, I need to tell you something. Come on—let's get in my car."

The warm leather interior of Ellis's SUV was welcoming to Lorna. As she sat in the plush passenger seat, memories of Leo Robbins' face on Ellis's laptop came flashing back. It had only been a few nights ago that she had sat in the same spot listening to the chilling details of Leo's interview—but it seemed like ages.

"I can't find Joe Parker." Ellis's sudden statement snapped Lorna back to the present. "He seems to have disappeared. It's as if he knew we might be looking for him."

Lorna was shocked. "How on earth could he have known you would be looking for him?" she asked. "You and I are the only ones that knew about Leo's statement."

"I don't know," replied Ellis. "Like everything else about this puzzle, it's a mystery. His address was easy to find—came right up when I ran it on our computer. He lives in an apartment south of town off Highway 7. Nice place. I went to his address and nothing. Nobody there. I checked with the neighbors, and they said they hadn't seen him in a week. I've been back a couple of times and still nothing."

"Maybe he's just laying low," Lorna said.

"But why? There should be nothing to scare him away," Ellis continued. "We have been careful—you and I are the only ones who even knew about Leo and that I was pressing him for information. I made sure no one was around when I taped that interview. And we haven't breathed a word about his connection to Joe. Anyhow, I talked to the apartment manager, and they said Joe is usually around—only works evenings and weekends. She acted surprised that I hadn't been able to find him."

Lorna sat silently in her seat. Ellis was right—she had not mentioned Leo to anyone... except, of course, Sterling and then only in passing. She didn't even know Leo's name at the time, just that Ellis had located a witness.

"I'm sure he'll turn up eventually," Ellis continued, "I just hope he's still alive and in one piece when he does. We really need to get his statement on the record—and these days, nothing surprises me."

"Well, I brought something that just might surprise you," Lorna replied, changing the subject as she pulled Radley's tape recorder out of her jacket pocket.

"What's this?" Ellis asked, taking the recorder from Lorna and studying it closely. "Haven't seen one of these in a while. We used to use them all the time at the office, but computerized versions have now taken their place."

"It's Radley's," Lorna responded. "And just wait until you listen to it. This is why I had to see you tonight. I think we have a smoking gun."

Without hesitation, Ellis pushed the play button and rested the recorder on the armrest between him and Lorna. Radley's voice suddenly filled the darkness of the Escalade. Lorna choked back a tear—it caught her off guard.

"Are you okay?" Ellis asked, concern in his voice.

Lorna nodded yes and pointed to the tape. "I'm okay," she said, "Just listen."

Ellis turned up the volume and turned his full attention to Radley's conversation with Lance. Lorna stared at him, trying her best to study his face in the darkness of the SUV—looking for the reaction she knew was shortly to come.

A short time later, they were listening to Lance's account of his mother's death and Radley's response: "But your mother's death was an accident. Your father may not be perfect, but you can't blame him for that. It was just a tragedy…"

"But that's just it! Dad never let her drive that boat…"

Ellis stopped the tape. "I always thought something was off about that accident," he said. Lorna forgot that as Lafayette

County sheriff, Ellis had been one of the first responders at the scene of Kathleen's boat wreck. "Sterling was plum pitiful—I've never seen him so upset. He kept going on and on about how he shouldn't have let her drive—and that it was all his fault. He described it in perfect detail—said she hit a buoy with the throttle at full speed. I just couldn't believe it—you know? Hard to picture someone as quiet and reserved as Ms. Kathleen going full-throttle in some new boat she'd never driven before. Just didn't make sense."

Lorna made no reply. Ellis pushed the play button and the tape continued.

Lance Bradford's young voice was unloading all he knew about the drug trade—how and when he started dealing, locations, players—details that Ellis Jefferson was eagerly soaking in. "We've got to bring him in," Ellis muttered under his breath. "This boy could break the whole case for us!"

Along came the name "Joe Parker," followed by Lance's eerie warning to Radley about Joe. "We've got to get Parker," Ellis muttered under his breath. "He just might be our trigger man."

And then another name popped off the tape: "Chris Jenkins." Ellis stopped the recording and slapped his steering wheel loudly. "We have him! We have him! I've been waiting for this! Praise God!!" The sudden outburst startled Lorna, and she was confused.

"You mean you already knew about Chris?" she asked. "I had no idea. I was shocked."

"No, we didn't know about Chris," Ellis answered. "But we knew about a guy named 'CJ.' The name has been a blank until now, but it makes perfect sense. Chris Jenkins—that son of gun. I should've known."

Ellis didn't take time to explain. He pushed play, and Lance Bradford began talking again.

"I don't know quite how to tell you the next name. You're going to be shocked... Chief Buford."

Ellis pushed stop again, this time not as excitedly as before. He just sat there in a momentary silence. "Sad, isn't it? Just sad. And the saddest part is that I'm really not surprised."

Lorna made no reply. Ellis pushed play again.

The remaining details were fodder for the sherriff's ears. Lorna could sense that Ellis Jefferson was pleased. Lance Bradford was providing everything necessary to put an end to Oxford's drug problem, and Ellis could not be happier. But then came Radley's sad footnote at the tape's end—the last recorded words of a great man now dead: "Testimony of Lance Bradford, taken at 4:30 p.m., Thursday, April 16, just outside the city of Oxford, Mississippi..."

The tape ended. Silence filled the Escalade as Lorna studied Ellis—waiting to hear what he had to say. Ellis let out a long sigh and reached for Lorna's hand.

"I'm so sorry, Lorna," he said. "But at least now we know why he died. You're right—this is a smoking gun. Your husband has just helped us solve his murder."

"Yes, but we still don't know exactly who or how," Lorna replied. "We clearly have a motive, and we think it's probably Parker, but what about Chris and Cyrus? We've got to make that connection."

"And we will," Ellis answered. "What we have now is a map that points us in the right direction. All we have to do is get these people to talk, and we will have our answers. But we have to be deliberate and very careful with how we go about it."

"The tape is not all," Lorna said, seizing upon the opportunity to bring up her other subject. Taking a folded document from her coat and handing it to Ellis, she stated the obvious: "I have something I want you to look at."

Ellis carefully took the paper from Lorna's hand, opening it as he reached for the reading light in his SUV. It was Brad's drug report.

"What am I supposed to be looking for here?" Ellis asked as he put on his reading glasses to make out the small print in the dim light of the Escalade.

"Have you seen this before?" Lorna asked, again trying to study the sheriff's face for a reaction.

"It's a drug report—Brad's toxicology report—and yes, I believe I remember seeing it in a packet of documents I had Derrick Castelle bring over to me very early on. I never quite trusted Cyrus and called myself looking over his shoulder. Wasn't happy at all with how he handled things, but I have to admit that I never found anything in the file that seemed to help Brad's case."

Lorna was listening intently—she couldn't wait to share with him what Matt had told her earlier, but she was hesitant to interrupt Ellis just yet.

"... And to be honest, I didn't give this report much thought," Ellis continued. "It appeared to me to be what I would call a very condemning piece of evidence—one very hard to refute. And as I remember, it played out just that way in the courtroom... pretty much sealed Brad's fate with the jury."

"I want you to read the number beside Brad's heroin count," Lorna requested. "Do you see it? Right there toward the bottom with the other numbers from his blood test."

".08," Ellis read aloud after he found the number. "Sounds like legal intoxication—only it's heroin and not alcohol."

"Yes, but do you realize this is impossible?" Lorna replied. "I met with Matt Sanchez today. You know, Myra's husband. He's an expert on drugs and drug testing—been working with drug addicts for years and is even working on a way to treat them. He has serious doubts about what made Brad black out the night of Radley's murder—thinks it might be some sort of date-rape drug instead of heroin. I texted him the test results. Here is what he said." Lorna pulled her text conversation with Myra and Matt up on her cell phone and then handed the phone to Ellis.

Ellis again squinted through his reading glasses at Lorna's phone, examining the small print: "Not possible. Person would be dead—.08 percent is legal limit for alcohol, not heroin… Heroin doesn't even stay in the body long. It's usually undetectable just hours later—.08 is impossible."

Ellis was stunned. It was obvious in his voice. "Lorna—this is serious. How did I miss this? What's worse, how did Brad's lawyer miss it? This throws the whole report into question!"

"Yes it does," Lorna agreed. "And it opens the door for getting Brad's conviction overturned. Clearly, this is a setup. Somebody doctored this report, and we now have solid evidence that any jury would have to listen to."

Ellis didn't immediately respond. He was lost in thought, staring at the report but looking straight through it really. His mind was elsewhere. Lorna sat quietly by, waiting to see what he was going to say next. And then it came. In one motion it seemed, he handed the report back to her, turned out the light of the SUV, and cleared his throat.

"Lorna—I want you to listen very carefully to what I'm about to say," Ellis stated in his most serious tone. Lorna nodded in the darkness. He had her full attention. "This is bigger and far worse than either of us ever realized. You and I could very possibly already be in danger. They have killed already, and they are definitely capable of killing again. I don't want to sugarcoat this in any way—this is serious."

Lorna didn't say anything. She just hung on every word, a lump in her throat—her heartbeat beginning to race. She felt a mixture of both fear and excitement. In one respect, she was exhilarated to be getting so close to freeing her son. It was a scary thing, however. She was unaccustomed to being in dangerous situations—and it was beginning to get overwhelming.

"I think they may be on to us. Joe Parker is missing. Someone has either gotten him out of town or something has happened to him. Either way, it does not bode well for us. We have got to bring this thing to a close now—quickly—before time runs out for us and they get wise to the fact that you and I are working together

234

on this and they all disappear. In fact, they may already know. But this tape is golden. Evidence like this can be played one against another—they don't even have to know what's on it. It just might bring about a confession, especially if we can find Parker."

"What are you suggesting we do, Sheriff?" asked Lorna quietly.

"Push them along to making their next move. And push them soon. Make them desperate. Because desperation will lead to a mistake. And just one mistake is all we need." Ellis was beginning to hatch a plan. And Lorna was in without even hearing it. "But I must warn you—desperation not only brings about mistakes. It also brings danger."

"Don't worry about me," Lorna interjected without hesitation. "I'm ready to get to the bottom of this—and I don't care how we do it. Nor do I care about the consequences I may face. Just tell me what we're going to do."

"I've got a plan," Ellis responded. "But it will require that you do something dangerous, and I'm hesitant to ask you to do anything that could compromise your safety. Your wellbeing comes first and foremost. We have to consider that before anything else."

"Go ahead," Lorna responded. "Ask away—I will do anything if it helps bring Brad home and puts my husband's killer away for good."

"How comfortable are you with Derrick?" Ellis seemed to be changing the subject, but Lorna knew he wasn't.

"Derrick Castelle? He's the only police officer right now that I truly trust," Lorna bluntly stated. "I wish I could appoint him chief tomorrow. I will never forget how sensitive and kind he was the night of Radley's murder—and since I have been mayor, he has gone out of his way to show me his support and respect. I think I would trust him with anything. Why?"

"He's going to help keep you safe," Ellis replied. "I've known Derrick for years—a finer man and law enforcement officer you could never find. With your permission, I would like to bring him into our scheme—if I can find a way to get to him without anyone knowing it. But leave that to me—I know I can do it."

Lorna still had not heard Ellis's plan. "Well that's fine with me—but tell me, Ellis. The suspense is killing me. What are we going to do?"

"We're going to draw these monsters into a trap—and we're going to make them desperate enough to walk right into it tomorrow!" Ellis answered. "And you are going to set it first thing in the morning, but only after I give you the signal that we're good to go."

"And what signal is that?" Lorna asked. She was getting inpatient.

"I'm about to tell you. Just hear me out," Ellis answered. "No later than 7 a.m. tomorrow, I'm going to call your house and let the phone ring twice. I will hang up, and that will be your signal that we're good to go and to call me. Make sure you call me from your home phone. And this is what I want you to tell me: that you have just found a tape of Radley talking to Lance about drugs and that you want me to hear it."

"But isn't that just what we DON'T want to do?" Lorna protested. "You said my phone lines are bugged most likely, and do we really want them to know about the tape?"

"Precisely what we DO want," Ellis continued. "Just listen, Lorna—this is it: we're going to make sure they hear about it. It will make them desperate, and we will have them right where we want them. Now when you make the call to me, I'm going to tell you that I can meet you at City Hall around one o'clock—that it's impossible for me to make it any sooner because of pre-scheduled appointments. You're going to say okay, but you're going to ask me to come by the house instead… that you have decided to work from home all day and that you don't want anyone seeing me at City Hall. And then we'll hang up. You will stay at the house. Cancel whatever is on your calendar. I suspect someone will be coming to see you. And rest assured Derrick and I will be in your woods watching—silent, invisible, and ready to arrest anyone who comes looking for you and your tape."

Lorna sat silent in Ellis's plush leather seat—she was taking everything in that the sheriff had just said. Ellis didn't say a word. He just waited for her response… any response. He realized this was a lot to ponder. A few moments passed, and finally Lorna broke the silence. "Ellis, sounds like a good plan to me. Let's do it."

CHAPTER 29

The Good Son

"**I** TELL YOU IT'S impossible, CJ—I can't do my job without him. This weekend has been a total nightmare." Lance Bradford was frustrated. Ever since Monday's meeting with Joe Parker, the week had gone downhill. He had broken up with Brenda and had hardly slept a wink since. To make matters worse, Joe had gone missing—making Lance's life even more complicated.

"If you will just be patient, all of this will blow over," Chris Jenkins was doing his best to calm his young associate.

"Be patient? That's easy for you to say. You aren't out there on the street risking everything every time you leave the house. This wasn't part of the deal. Joe knows the street—not me. I'm not supposed to be out there showing my face and meeting every punk in Oxford looking for their fix." Lance was not happy. "And ever since Joe went AWOL, my phone's been blowing up—you and Cyrus seem to expect me to do it all alone. Well, I can't, I tell you. I can't. There's no way!"

"Calm down, Lance," Chris was not easily rattled. "Joe won't be gone forever. Just a few days while things blow over. I promise you. In the meantime, I'll try to call in someone else to help take up the slack."

"Well, all I want to know is where is he?" Lance asked. "I don't understand why you're not tellin' me. It just doesn't add up. One day he and I are hanging out—same as usual. Next day he's disappeared. And I'm left holding the bag on everything he does along with my stuff, too."

Deep down, Lance Bradford was scared. His paranoia was about to drive him insane, and he really didn't know how much more he could take. He feared that the very thing he dreaded most had happened to Joe. But he couldn't understand why—Joe Parker was solid. If anybody should have had anything to fear, it was Lance. He really didn't understand why he was still alive after what had happened to Mr. Radley—the very day after he had ratted everybody out.

"I promise you this is only temporary," Chris continued. "And that's all I can say. Now my best advice to you is to get yourself home, take a shower, and go to bed. You look like death warmed over, and you obviously aren't thinking straight. The world will look better tomorrow, Lance. And all of this will be behind us—I promise."

Chris started his engine and put his Lexus in drive. The meeting was over.

Lance put his hands over the SUV's open window before Chris could raise it and drive off. He still had something to say. "You gotta understand that everybody knows me in this town. You know who my dad is. I'm not supposed to be on the street. Everything's supposed to be under the radar, remember? That's been our deal. I don't mean it to sound like an ultimatum, CJ, but it is. Next weekend, I'm either back on my old job, or I'm out. That's it—I just had to say it."

Chris made only one comment. "Nobody gives me an ultimatum." And, with that, he sped off, almost taking Lance's hands with him, kicking up dirt, and barely missing his right foot as he left.

Lance dropped his head. His face was red with anger and disgust. He made a fist with his right hand and slowly began punching it into his left palm as he turned to walk back to his car. He wanted to hit somebody. He felt trapped and helpless. And he hated feeling that way.

As Lance started his car, his mind returned to Brenda. He wished he could go see her, unload on her, and tell her everything. He'd then ask her to leave with him. He had to get out of Oxford. And he wanted to take her with him.

He drove down the gravel road, his headlights shining through a thick wall of dust still floating in the aftermath of Chris's speedy departure. He reached the pavement of Highway 7 and started to make a right turn—the direction of Brenda's house. But he hesitated. He rubbed his tired eyes and sat there a minute. His mind was racing. *Brenda's parents will be there. Daphne will be there. They'll all ask questions. Brenda's ticked at me as it is. She won't go anywhere with me. Not a good idea. I better do like CJ said—go home and go to sleep.*

Lance turned left onto the highway and headed into Oxford. In a few minutes, he was parking in the garage of his condo—a beautiful, new upscale development just a few blocks from campus, near downtown Oxford. He locked his car and heard the alarm chirp. The sound always seemed comforting—at least there was some security in his life—something he could control.

Lance walked up a short flight of steps and put his keys in the door. He walked in, turning on a lamp by the door. And then he saw him. Nothing could have prepared him for the scare that came. There sitting in his leather recliner was a red-faced man with completely white hair. It was Cyrus Buford.

"Evening, Mr. Bradford," the pot-bellied chief stated with a flourish, clearly enjoying the look of shock on Lance's face. "Hope you don't mind me enjoying this comfortable recliner you've got here. I like the massage feature—puts my old worn-out La-Z-Boy to shame."

Lance stood there jaw-dropped, taking in the scene before him. He thought for a moment he must be dreaming. And he had never noticed Cyrus's potbelly before. His appearance in a recliner was definitely not a flattering one. But the red face and hair were unmistakable. It was definitely the chief—this was no dream.

"Come on, Lance, have a seat!" Cyrus was motioning to the couch as if it were his own. "Didn't mean to startle you. Just thought it was time you and I had a talk."

Lance did as he was told. He sat down on the couch and managed to compose himself and say a couple of words: "Evening, Chief." Under normal circumstances, Lance would have been angry to find that someone had invaded his home. But these were not normal circumstances. He was firmly in fear's grip. He did not know what to expect.

"I understand it's getting to be too much for you," Cyrus continued, lowering the recliner to its normal position and leaning forward so that he could look Lance directly in the eyes. Lance had never noticed how blue Cyrus's eyes were.

Cyrus continued, "Chris tells me that you're ready to quit. That the pressure is getting to you."

Lance just sat there looking at him. He made no movement and said nothing.

"You know we're all concerned about you," Cyrus said. "There are others in this organization that you don't know about—no one knows about—but they care about you. Chris cares about you. I care about you. And we want to make sure you're okay."

Lance wanted to believe him. What he was saying was comforting to hear. If only it were true.

"I want to assure you that your friend and mine, Mr. Parker, is just fine. Nothing has happened to him." Cyrus Buford had never sounded so sincere. "Some folks here in Oxford are beginning to snoop a little too much. They want to mess up our little game, and we had to send Joe out of town for a little while. But he'll be back—I assure you."

Lance still didn't say anything.

"Lance, we want to give you a little time off," Cyrus continued.

"We're bringing in some new recruits from Memphis to take up the slack for a while. We all know that you're too high-profile in this town to be working the street. It's starting to get crazy out there. So we want you to lay low for a few weeks."

Cyrus reached into his inside coat pocket. Lance flinched. Cyrus pulled out an envelope.

"Calm down, son," laughed the chief. "Nobody's gonna shoot you. You really do need some time off, don't you!"

Cyrus threw the envelope on the coffee table. It landed with a thud. It was narrow but thick—and heavy. Lance reached for it slowly, looking at Cyrus the entire time, and picked it up. Inside was cash—all hundreds.

"Should be enough to get you by till we start working you again," Cyrus smiled. "Take it—enjoy. Relax. Get some rest. Do what Lance wants to do."

Lance didn't know what to say. This was just the opposite of what he expected. He sat there silent for a few moments, playing through the crisp, green bills with his finger while Cyrus looked on—a grin on his face.

"Thank you, Chief," he finally said, not knowing what else to say.

"Don't mention it," Cyrus replied as he got up from the recliner, adjusting the waste of his blue jeans while straightening his shirt. "Like I said, there are people who care about you. Just take care of yourself and wait to hear from us. We'll let you know when it's time."

With that, Cyrus Buford showed himself to the door and walked out into the evening air—gently closing the door behind him. Lance waited on the couch. He heard the chief's footsteps on the stairs and then a car cranking and leaving. Suddenly, he rushed to the door, locking it and placing a large steel bar across it. He was still shaken by the encounter, but reinforcing the door helped bring back a small sense of security.

He returned to the couch and counted the money. It was a

lot—more than he normally cleared in a month. He was tempted to be happy, but he wasn't.

Lance looked around the living room. It was a plush living room for a twenty-year-old. And it was full of pictures from his childhood: pictures of him and Brad, pictures of his mom, and a few of him with both of his parents—even one with Lorna and Radley. He enjoyed looking at reminders of the happier days. He didn't like who he had become.

"If only mama was still here," he said aloud. "Nothing's been right since she died."

He wanted to make his life right again. He wanted to be her "good son" again. Maybe this was an opportunity. Maybe he could get out—these new guys would take up the slack and they would find they didn't need him. But then what would he do? He had to make a living somehow—and, unfortunately, he only knew one way.

Lance decided not to torture himself any longer. He did what CJ had told him to do. He got a shower and went to bed.

CHAPTER 30

Best-Laid Plans

MONDAY MORNING CAME suddenly for Lorna. She was glad she had set her alarm. Her night had been restless. She had been unable to sleep at all up until about 4 a.m. The excitement of her meeting with Ellis, along with some apprehension over what Monday might hold, had kept her wide awake. When she finally caught herself drifting off, she had set her alarm for six—just in case she overslept. Two hours later, she was glad that she did—and the alarm was doing its job.

Lorna hit snooze at first. And then it occurred to her that she didn't have time for snoozing. She had a big day ahead! In spite of only two hours of sleep, Lorna jumped to the floor—adrenaline rushing through her body. It was time to get on with it.

She paused a minute to rub Roscoe who was still laying on the floor by her bed. And then she headed for the bathroom. The hot shower, as always, felt good to her, especially today. But she didn't linger—no time for long showers. In a matter of minutes, she was drying her hair, pulling on some blue jeans and a sweater, and applying a little makeup. No need to go all out—after all, she would be working from home today. *And maybe even solving a crime,* she thought to herself as she dabbed on a little mascara. In spite of her lack of sleep, her dark eyes looked especially large and beautiful today. She was excited.

Very quickly, she made up her bed—nothing could keep her from performing this daily ritual. And then she saw her Bible and devotion book on the night stand. She thought, *Today of all days, I need to call on God's strength and protection.* She lowered to her knees—something she had not done in a while, knelt by her bed and prayed, *Father God, thank you for always loving me and taking care of me. I ask you to please be with me today. Keep me safe from all harm and help us solve this mystery. I pray your safety over Ellis and Derrick as well. And, Lord, please minister in a special way today to my son. Let him feel your love. Keep him from harm and bless him. In Jesus' name, Amen.*

Now dressed and ready to face her day, Lorna looked at the clock. It was five minutes till seven. And suddenly the phone rang. She almost answered it and then remembered not to. It rang a second time and then stopped. This was Ellis's cue.

Without hesitation, Lorna took a deep breath, picked up the phone and dialed call return. The phone rang a time or two and then a man answered, "Hello."

"Ellis?" Lorna spoke into the phone. The voice was familiar, but it didn't sound like Ellis.

"Good morning, Lorna," the voice spoke into her ear. "It's not Ellis—it's Sterling."

Lorna recognized Sterling's rich baritone voice immediately and felt embarrassed. She also was confused—*Why is he calling so early? And why did he only let the phone ring twice?* Before she could ponder her questions any further, Sterling was providing the answers. "Sorry to call you before seven, Lorna. That's why I hung up. I wasn't sure I should be bothering you this early."

"It's okay, Sterling," Lorna assured him. "It's perfectly fine. You should feel free to call me anytime."

"You're sweet," Sterling continued. "I love that about you. Just hearing your voice makes it all better." Sterling Bradford was either pouring it on thick, and early at that, or he was just really in need of a female listener to talk to. Lorna suspected it was a mixture of both. "After our visit yesterday, I haven't been quite myself. I think you aroused some feelings in me that I have been suppressing—feelings of guilt and self-blame over what happened to Kathleen."

"It's okay, Sterling. I promise it is," Lorna spoke softly to her old friend. "I'm sorry I brought on all of this, but if you need to talk, I'm here for you." Just at that moment, she heard call waiting beeping in. She looked at the clock—7 a.m. It must be Ellis. *What should I do? I've got to get off the phone!* she thought to herself.

"Thank you, darling. You're about the only person I know I can talk to," Sterling spoke in a soft tone. He sounded defeated and vulnerable. Lorna felt torn. She wanted to continue talking to him, but she also knew she had to stick to the plan.

"Sterling—it's not a good time right now, though. Roscoe is dying for me to let him out—it's that time of morning you know." Lorna wasn't lying. Roscoe was starting to pace the floor in front of the bedroom door. It was time for him to go outside. "Could we talk a little later today—maybe tonight?"

"Sure thing, Lorna," Sterling spoke quickly, his voice suddenly lightened by the obvious need for Lorna to get off the phone. "I'll call you later. Maybe we can have that steak I owe you."

"That would be nice," Lorna replied, quickly saying good-bye and hanging up the phone. Immediately, she dialed Ellis. He answered on the first ring.

"Ellis Jefferson here. Good morning." The sheriff was fully into the plan. It was game on.

"Good morning, Sheriff," Lorna spoke brightly. "I'm sorry to bother you so early, but it is important that I meet with you today."

"Never too early for our mayor," Ellis responded. "What can I do for you, Lorna?"

"Well, I have found something you must see—and hear," Lorna continued with her script. "It's a tape—a conversation between Radley and Lance about drugs in Oxford. You won't believe what's on it. You must come over... as soon as you can."

"Lorna, that's really something. Of course I will meet with you." Ellis was fully into his role. "I have a full morning, however. But I can come see you right after lunch. How about one o'clock? I'll come to your office."

"No, not my office. I don't want anyone seeing you—or us—together. This is really that serious," Lorna replied. "I'm working from home today. Come meet me here."

"Yes, ma'am—you've got it. I'll see you at one o'clock sharp!" Ellis hung up the phone. The trap was set.

By now, Roscoe was beginning to dance. He really needed to go out. Lorna quickly placed the phone on the receiver and went to let the old dog out at the kitchen door. As Roscoe ran into the yard, Lorna stepped outside and peered all around. It was a beautiful morning, but she was too preoccupied to notice. She was looking for some sign of Ellis and Derrick, but she couldn't see them anywhere. She considered that a good thing. She shouldn't be able to see them. And she felt comfort in knowing that Ellis Jefferson was a man of his word, and he wanted to catch these guys as much as she did. She knew he was out there somewhere—watching and waiting.

After a few minutes, Roscoe came running back, and she ushered the retriever inside and closed the door, locking it behind her. She proceeded to the kitchen. Might as well fix some breakfast. As she got out some eggs and a pan, she dialed City Hall. By now, Jane Sage would be at her desk. She always came in early on Mondays.

"Mayor's Office," the polite and efficient secretary answered the phone the same way every time, usually on the same ring. Lorna had gotten used to it.

"Good morning, Jane," Lorna said. "I'd like for you to clear my calendar for today if you don't mind. I'm going to be working from home."

"Not a problem at all, Mayor," Jane replied in her polished

voice. "You don't have many meetings as it is—won't be a problem at all."

"Thank you, Jane," Lorna said, hurrying off the phone without much conversation. She wasn't in the mood for small talk.

As she ate a plate of scrambled eggs and a couple of pieces of toast, Lorna stared out the kitchen windows. It was indeed a beautiful day. She wondered how long it would take for Cyrus or Chris, or whomever they happened to send, to take the bait. Surely the brief conversation between her and Ellis had created a stir—they were bound to be on the way any minute. This tape could be the very thing to get Lance on the record and send the chief and his crooked contractor to prison. *But will there actually be a link between them and the murder? A link that will free Brad? And where is Joe Parker?* Lorna was deep in thought. She just didn't understand how it would all finally come together—but she had faith that it all would work out somehow, and that her son would finally be home.

The old grandfather clock chimed eight. She could hardly believe an hour had already passed since Ellis's phone call. Her mind then went to Sterling. It was odd that he had called before seven—unlike him to call so early in the morning and to sound so desperate and vulnerable. She must really have touched a nerve asking him about Kathleen. She hoped he would finally open up. *It must be awful carrying such guilt,* she thought to herself.

Dishes cleared and the table clean, Lorna wondered what she should do next. There really wasn't anything she had to do—except wait. But waiting could be the hardest task of all.

She returned to her bathroom to brush her teeth and apply lipstick. As she looked in the mirror, she thought about what Sterling had said about her a few days earlier at lunch. "Jackie Kennedy come to Oxford." The comment, while flattering at first, now struck her as eerie and sad. For the first time, it occurred to her that she now shared more than just appearances with the famous New England beauty she had always been compared to. They had both buried their husbands before their time—both men shot down while trying to do great good for others. She stared at her brunette reflection, sharing a surreal moment with someone who almost appeared to be a stranger. Roscoe's sudden barking broke the spell, and she hurried back to the kitchen.

There at the back door, Roscoe was barking and whining. *Surely that's not them already. They didn't waste any time,* Lorna thought, an excited shiver running down her spine. She braced herself as she looked through the window—but she saw nothing. In the distance, however, she could hear something. It was a car alarm, barely noticeable, sounding through the woods in the distance.

She opened the door and went outside. The day was starting to warm up—a perfect Mississippi fall day. Before she could stop him, Roscoe bolted past her and into the back yard, heading straight for the forest. In the woods she could hear men running, and the dog was close behind them.

"Roscoe, Roscoe—come back!" Lorna screamed. But to no avail. "Roscoe, Roscoe—come now!" Still no response. Roscoe was nowhere to be seen. Lorna had no choice but to go after him. Fortunately, she had thought earlier to put on her tennis shoes instead of house slippers, and she immediately took off for the trail through Faulkner woods.

The trees were beautiful in the morning light—sunlight glanced off leaves of yellow and red. The fall colors were beginning to overtake the forest. As Lorna made it to the ridge, she could hear Roscoe barking and a male voice commanding him to stop. The voice was familiar to her—it was Derrick Castelle.

"Stop, Roscoe—come here. Come here, boy," Detective Castelle was trying to contain the dog before he went barreling through the creek and up the other side to Pebble Creek Apartments.

Lorna continued calling as well. "Roscoe, come here, boy. Come here now." All of a sudden, the old dog stopped running and turned in the direction of her voice and began making his way to her, head dropped as if he were a child who had been scolded. "I've got him, Derrick," she called to the detective. "Go ahead. Do what you need to do."

"I don't know that there's much I can do," replied Derrick. "Ellis told me not to leave the house unwatched—but I knew you loved this dog, and I just couldn't let him get away."

"Thank you so much," Lorna replied. "It's not like him to run off like this. I guess the car alarm going off was just too much for him."

In the distance, the siren was still blaring, much louder now. It was coming from Pebble Creek.

"Speaking of Ellis, where is he?" Lorna asked, reaching down to take hold of Roscoe's collar as she paused to catch her breath. She wasn't accustomed to running through the woods so soon after breakfast.

"He's actually down there at Pebble Creek," answered Derrick, pointing in the direction of the apartments. "I think that's his alarm going off."

"Oh, no!" exclaimed Lorna. "What in the world could be going on?" Just as she spoke, the siren gave one last bleep and shut off. Obviously, Ellis had made it to his vehicle. "Is he in his car?" she asked.

"No," Derrick replied. "He drove us here in his SUV—didn't want his official car drawing attention."

Just at that moment, his walkie-talkie sputtered. "Derrick, do you read? Derrick, do you read?"

"I'm here, Sheriff," Derrick quickly replied into the receiver on his shoulder.

"Listen to me. I want you to check on the mayor. Make sure she's okay. You may even need to get her out of the house. Somebody's ransacked my Escalade, and I'm worried they're trying to draw us away so they can get to her. Go check on her now! Probably best if she's not at the house."

"Actually, Sheriff, the mayor is with me," Derrick replied.

"She chased her dog out into the woods, and we're both standing on the ridge."

"Tell him we're coming to him," Lorna whispered to Derrick under her breath.

"I heard that, Lorna," Ellis replied. "I really don't think you should. Go right now, get in your car, and you and Derrick drive somewhere safe."

"No, we're headed to you." Lorna was determined. A few minutes later, she, Derrick, and Roscoe met the sheriff on the edge of the woods adjacent to the Pebble Creek parking lot. Ellis's white Escalade was parked exactly where Brad's truck had been parked on that fateful April night—its passenger window busted and many of Ellis's belongings strewn about the parking lot.

Lorna looked around the apartment buildings, hoping someone might be standing outside who would prove to be a valuable witness. But being that it was Monday morning in early November, the apartments were practically vacant—most everyone was either at work or at school.

"It appears that this was more than just a distraction," Derrick stated, looking into the SUV to see the glove box almost torn from its hinge and the arm rest standing upright between the leather seats. "They were looking for something—no doubt about it. They were looking for something."

Ellis was shaking his head, his hands on his hips, appearing both frustrated and helpless. Derrick continued his inspection of the sheriff's Escalade.

"Looks like you've been wired," Derrick said with a serious expression on his face. In his hand was a small black cable connected to the corner of the damaged glove compartment. The wire had been cleverly concealed under the dashboard, and it led directly to a tiny mic in a corner of one of the air vents. "Somebody's been listening to everything you've been saying."

Ellis Jefferson did not handle invasion of his privacy well. He rushed over to Derrick, taking the wire into his own large

251

hands. He closed his eyes and a surge of anger and adrenaline shot through his body with a force that could have made a smaller man explode. But he didn't. He waited a minute—took a deep breath—waited another minute or two—and then spoke soberly, "I swore I checked this vehicle over and over for bugs. Orkin couldn't have done a better job."

Lorna smiled at the statement—as serious as the situation was, she found amusement in Ellis's reaction. Any degree of lightness in such a serious moment was a welcome relief. She walked over to the vehicle, Roscoe at her side, and placed her hand on Ellis's shoulder. "Come on now, Ellis—it could've happened to any-body," she said. "We just have to decide on what we do now."

Clearly, today's plan was shot. Someone had been listening to Ellis's and Lorna's entire conversation at Wall Doxey. They had even listened to the tape. And undoubtedly a desperate search for the tape is what had taken place just a few minutes earlier in the sheriff's prized Escalade.

"I still think this may have been a distraction as well," Ellis was back in control. "We need to go to your house, Lorna—and I mean right now! Who knows what may be going on there. If they didn't find what they were after here, they may very well be at your house right this minute, looking for it."

Lorna hadn't considered this—the thought alarmed her. She couldn't bear the thought of Somerset ransacked. Immediately, they climbed into the sheriff's SUV, being careful around the broken glass. Derrick sat up front with Ellis. Lorna and Roscoe climbed into the back. Ellis would return for his belongings later. Right now, he was intent on speeding to Somerset.

On the way over, he was tempted to call for backup. But then he remembered Cyrus Buford—best not to alert the Oxford Police Department to what he was doing just now. In fact, he had taken great care to use a rarely used frequency on the walkie-talkies with Derrick—just in case someone might be listening. *Yes— better to keep this operation quiet for now*, he thought to himself as he sped down Old Taylor Road heading for Lorna's driveway.

In just seconds it seemed, the Escalade was at the gate of Somerset. Ellis threw the SUV in gear and jumped out, blocking the driveway. The gate was closed, but he didn't want to take any chances on someone making a getaway.

"Mayor, I want you to take the dog and go to a neighbor's house and wait for us to call you," Ellis said in his most serious tone. "You don't need to go up here with us."

"But I don't have my phone—you can't call me," Lorna protested. "And besides, I doubt if anybody's home. I wouldn't know where to begin. Roscoe and I will just sit here. We will be fine."

Reluctantly, Ellis gave a small handgun to Lorna, showed her how to turn the safety on and off, and he and Derrick proceeded up the driveway to Lorna's mansion.

The morning sun was now higher in the sky, and Somerset glowed a brilliant white—almost blinding to the two officers as they approached it.

Ellis opted to take cover in the forest to his right—just beyond the long driveway. He advised Derrick to do the same to the left of the front yard. The two men quietly advanced through the forest like trained guerillas on a quest through foreign jungles. They were both expertly trained, and it was in times like this that their skills were best put to use.

As they reached the rear of the house, Ellis noticed that the backdoor was ajar. He proceeded to the woods behind the house, meeting Derrick has he followed a mirrored path from the other side. The two men then paused, studying the garage from a vantage point where the backdoor was clearly visible.

"What should we do now?" Derrick asked the sheriff.

"Just listen," Ellis replied. "Do you hear anything?"

Other than the sound of a breeze drifting through the forest, and an occasional leaf falling to the ground, the two men heard nothing. The house was completely quiet.

"If they were in there ransacking the place, we would hear it,"

Ellis said under his breath. "They are either gone, or they didn't come here at all. Let's go!"

Slowly, the two men made their way to the backdoor in crouched positions, darting from tree to bush, until they were right behind the garage. Still no noises came from the house. It appeared that all was fine.

But it wasn't.

As they made their way into the kitchen, they were shocked to see the mess. Not every dish was broken, but many were. Obviously, the house had been the scene of a desperate search just moments before their arrival.

Ellis ducked down behind the table, his face positioned toward the back door. Derrick took a position just inside the doorway leading to the back hall.

Ellis motioned to Derrick who immediately recognized his signal. "Police! We are armed! Come out now—lay down your weapons, and no one will get hurt!" Derrick's voice echoed throughout the vast halls and rooms of Somerset. But no answer came. The house was silent as a grave.

"I repeat, come out now! Lay down your weapons, and no one will get hurt!" Derrick again recited his announcement. Still no response.

With Ellis's encouragement, Derrick eased around the corner of the doorway and into the back hall. Everything was still. He proceeded down the hall to Radley's study—again hearing nothing. Ellis continued in the same direction, providing cover behind them as Derrick pressed forward. The study was a wreck. They continued across the hall. Lorna's bedroom and closet were ransacked as well. But the mess ended there. Whoever had created this confusion was now gone—and the rest of the house was still in order.

"We must have interrupted them," Ellis declared as Derrick lowered his firearm and began to relax. "They must've heard our car door and retreated out the back and into the woods."

"It was my fault," said Derrick. "I should never have slammed my door. I just wasn't thinking."

"Don't worry about it, Detective," Ellis replied. "We were both so worked up, and I was worrying about Lorna... Lorna! Let's make sure she's okay!"

Without delay, the two men bolted out the front door straight for the gate. To their relief, Lorna and Roscoe were still sitting in the backseat of the Escalade—they were safe.

"What's wrong, Ellis?" Lorna asked getting out of the car. "You look upset."

"It's okay—we're just relieved that you are okay," replied the sheriff. "But your house is not. I'm afraid they ransacked it, too."

Lorna dropped her head and put her face in her hands. This had been her worst fear.

"But it's not a total ransack," Derrick reassured her. "They stopped at the bedroom. The majority of the house is fine."

Lorna immediately started up the hill to her house, Roscoe following closely behind and then running ahead. When she stepped into the front hall and walked into her bedroom, she started to cry. Pictures lay broken on the floor. Her mattresses were upside down, and her bedside tables tossed aside. It was a complete mess.

She rushed to Radley's study. It, too, was a wreck, pictures hanging lopsided on the walls, books pulled from the bookcases and strewn on the floor. She walked over to the desk—its drawers and their contents spilled everywhere. To her relief, however, the molding and secret drawer protecting Radley's tape were still in place. She dared not open it, even in front of Ellis and Derrick—she wanted to keep this secret to herself.

Lorna proceeded to the kitchen, and she couldn't believe her eyes. Dishes that had been in her family for years were carelessly thrown on the counters and on the floor. Many were broken, but to her relief, some were not.

"I'm so sorry, Mayor," Derrick said as he surveyed the damage from the doorway.

Ellis offered his sympathies as well. "It's been a bad day, Lorna—we've been had."

"No, Ellis," Lorna replied. She had stopped crying and was now beginning to regain her composure, along with her strength. "We shouldn't be surprised. It's like you said last night. These monsters are desperate. They know we're onto them. Their days are numbered. They don't have the tape. We do. And more evidence is on the way—I can feel it. They are about to get caught, and my Brad is about to come home."

CHAPTER 31

Friends in Low Places

Monday afternoon was a busy one—Lorna had not exaggerated when she had talked to Jane Sage early that morning. She was definitely working from home today—really working.

Careful not to share details with anyone, especially Oxford's police department and Cyrus Buford in particular, Lorna had decided to handle the cleanup herself with only a few trusted friends. She didn't want her ransacked Somerset becoming the talk of the town.

Ellis and Derrick had stuck around to help. Derrick had even dusted for fingerprints but, to no one's surprise, only found Lorna's. Lorna had called David and Tricia Burton, who dropped what they were doing and immediately came over to help. As always, the two of them could be counted on in a crisis. Lorna had also asked Myra Sanchez over, partly for cleanup help and partly for moral support. Myra had proven to be a great friend during the months after Radley's death, and Lorna truly loved her.

"I just can't imagine anyone doing this to you—you of all people," Myra was saying as she carefully picked up broken dishes off the floor in Lorna's kitchen. "You're the kindest person I know. It's just awful!"

"Well, these people aren't a bit too happy with me right now,"

Lorna replied, dusting off the large wooden table that she had cleared of all debris. "You know I'm beginning to probe—the bogus toxicology report for example. I'm determined to get to the bottom of this, and Brad is coming home!"

"I admire your spirit, Lorna!" Myra grinned as she paused from her work to look at her friend. "You're amazing—and I'm proud to be helping you today."

Lorna blushed, continuing with her dusting. "God is amazing. He has brought me this far, and I know He's going to see me all the way."

"You know, here you talk about God, but most people would be angry at Him," Myra continued. "Here you are, your husband is gone, your son is in jail, and your house is a wreck. And yet your spirit is intact. How do you do it, Lorna? Honestly, how do you do it?"

"I rely on Him," Lorna responded without hesitation. "I live by that verse from Philippians: 'I can do all things through Christ who strengthens me.' He brings me through every trial. He always has."

"But why aren't you bitter about Radley—and Brad?" Myra persisted. "Honestly, if anything ever happened to Matt, I don't know what I would do. I mean, how can you keep your faith even when such terrible things happen? I'm a believer and all. You know I am. Love the Lord. And I love my church. But really. If anything happened to Matt, I… I just don't know…"

"What about what happened to Jesus?" Lorna answered. "Do you think that was easy for people to understand? I mean, his own mother, Mary, watched him die on a cross. He bled out right in front of her. But did she lose faith? Myra—we live in a fallen world. Bad things happen—sometimes to very good people. But we have to remember the big picture. This isn't all there is."

Lorna had stopped her dusting. Her arms were outstretched to the room before her, and Myra was fully enthralled. "I mean this is not all there is! I've lost my husband, yes. I've also lost my parents—both of them. But will I see them again? Yes! Most definitely yes! You see, we live in a fallen world. But thanks to our God and Savior who is perfect, we have a perfect and eternal world waiting on us. Eternal life itself! We just have to believe!"

Myra didn't respond right away. Lorna had said a mouthful—and it was taking a while for it all to sink in.

"How are you two doing in here?" Tricia Burton's smiling face brightened the kitchen. "We're almost finished in the study. It really wasn't all that bad. Just three broken pictures—and you can easily repair that!" Tricia' bright optimism was a welcome comfort in the midst of what could have been a very dark afternoon.

"Mayor Lorna is preaching, Sister Tricia!" Myra smiled back at Tricia. "She really could have another calling. I don't think I've ever been around someone so positive!"

"Not me," responded Lorna, easing over to Myra and placing her arm around her. "…But He who lives in me."

"Amen to that!" Tricia chimed in. "I honestly don't know where any of us would be if it weren't for Him—and He is going to see you through this, Lorna."

"What are you ladies chit-chatting about in here?" asked Brother David teasingly as he joined them in the kitchen. "Don't y'all have work to do?" He was smiling broadly. "By the way—just in case you're interested—we're almost done with the study. The sheriff and Derrick are putting the last of the books back on the shelves right now. Going to be good as new!"

"I can't thank you and Tricia enough," Lorna replied, crossing the kitchen to hug David and Tricia both. "You're always there when I need you."

"We wouldn't be anywhere else," David replied.

"You're family to us, Lorna," Tricia said. "And we're blessed every time—truly, God is good."

"Yes, He is," Lorna agreed.

"But now that you mighty warriors are done with the study, maybe you can help us in here!" Myra said teasingly. "This has been a mess! Obviously taking a little longer than the study. I've never seen so many broken plates."

"But plates are replaceable," Lorna reminded everyone— mostly for her own peace of mind. The sight of her and Radley's dishes broken on the floor could have sunk her spirit for sure. But her faith, along with the hope that she was getting closer to exonerating Brad, helped her press on. "It will be a challenge to replace them, but I know it can be done. And who knows? A change just might do me good anyway."

Everyone looked on sympathetically and began helping Myra. Just then, two more faces showed up at the door.

"Well—they may not be in the order you want them, Lorna," Ellis announced, "… but Radley's books are officially back on the shelves."

"How can I ever thank you, Ellis?" Lorna said as she hugged him and Derrick.

"No thank you necessary," Ellis replied. "We just feel terrible that this happened to you."

"And I feel stupid for slamming that car door," Derrick stated soberly. "We'd have them in jail by now if I hadn't given them the signal."

"Oh, come on now, Detective," Lorna said reassuringly, taking Derrick's arm in hers. "I believe everything happens for a reason. I mean—what if you and Ellis had caught them in the act? These men are desperate. And there is probably no telling what they would do right now if they were cornered."

"Well—it's getting pretty crowded in here," Ellis said, changing the subject. "Lorna—why don't you and Derrick go with me to the bedroom. A lot to do in there, and it looks like you've got plenty of helpers in the kitchen."

"Yeah, y'all go do that, Lorna, we've got this. Probably do you good to have a change of scenery," Myra said, agreeing with Ellis. "Besides, we've even got Roscoe to help us!" Myra bent down to pet the old dog who had suddenly appeared from somewhere in the house. Lorna realized that she hadn't even missed him.

"Roscoe—come to me," Lorna called to him, crouching down. At once the retriever was in her face with licks and wags of his tail. Petting his soft golden mane brought an immediate sense of normalcy to her.

"Well, I see where his loyalties lie," Myra joked as she resumed her cleanup of dishes.

"And I thank y'all so much!" Lorna replied as she and the two men headed toward the bedroom, Roscoe following close behind her, nuzzling her leg gently as they walked.

Once in the bedroom, Ellis closed the door and turned to Lorna. "We need to talk, Lorna." His mood was very serious. "Obviously, right now they are desperate to find that tape. Had it not been for our interruption, they would've torn your entire house apart."

The sheriff paused allowing the sight of Lorna's destroyed bedroom to sink in. And then he continued, "Derrick and I have been talking, and we think that, for your safety, we need to go ahead and get a warrant to arrest Chris and Cyrus. We'll also put an APB out on Joe Parker. Radley's tape is evidence enough—and if we bring in Lance Bradford as a personal witness I think we'll have them. Of course, we will have to arrest Lance as well—but we will cop a deal with him to spill the details on everyone else. We also have Leo Robbins in custody, along with his testimony against Parker. If we work this right, by midnight tonight, we can have the entire operation shut down and every culprit in custody."

Lorna made no immediate response. Her attention was drawn to the sight of her Bible upside down on the floor by her upturned nightstand. She reached down to pick it up and straighten its pages as Derrick quickly uprighted the nightstand, revealing Lorna's devotion book underneath it. Ellis bent down to pick up some items that had fallen out of Lorna's Bible—pictures of Radley and Brad and her parents, some inspirational cards—mementos obviously important to her. The last item he picked up took him off-guard. He felt bad as he handed it to her. Radley's smiling face was on the cover—it was his funeral program.

"Thank you," is all Lorna could say. Tears were forming in her eyes again—this was hard for her. After a few moments, Lorna waded through a pile of dresser drawers and clothes and sat down. "I'm surprised they didn't knock over the chair at least. They seemed determined to destroy everything else."

Ellis and Derrick said nothing. They didn't know what to say. Ellis reached in his back pocket, pulling out a handkerchief.

"It's okay—I've got one," Lorna replied, pulling an embroidered handkerchief from her front pocket and putting it to her eye. "I hate to get mascara on it, but maybe it'll come out. This was Radley's handkerchief. I gave it to him on our tenth anniversary. He had it with him when he died. He always carried it. It was on the floor by his desk when we came in a little while ago. Guess it didn't mean anything to them." She started to cry more at the thought. "Obviously, nothing means anything to monsters like that."

Ellis and Derrick began to straighten the mattresses on Lorna's bed and straighten the other night table. They were trying to give Lorna space.

A few moments later, she was composed and ready to talk. She cleared her throat, dried her eyes again and began, "This is why I'm reluctant to arrest anybody. I'm afraid they'll clam up, and we'll never get a confession on Radley's murder. We can't bluff them into a confession now—they know exactly what's on the tape. Drugs not murder. And without a confession, I don't get what I want. It's not enough to put them in jail. I want Brad to walk free."

Ellis didn't respond immediately. He didn't want Lorna to feel pressured in any way. After a few minutes he replied, "You make a good point, Lorna. And I wouldn't want to do anything that jeopardizes your ultimate goal to bring your son home. What we have, though, is very good evidence. Everything points to them having a motive—the motive of silencing your husband. This was always a problem with Brad's case. I never saw any clear motive. In addition, you have the bogus toxicology report. I still don't understand Brad's attorney by failing to catch that. You have Cyrus's rush to judgment as well. I can testify to that. Even Derrick here can testify to that."

"You better believe I can," Derrick added. "And nothing would satisfy me more than to see Cyrus get what's coming to him. He obviously has been abusing his power—breaking the law! And he's been doing it a while. No tellin' how many folks have suffered in this town because of him."

"But all of that is subjective," Lorna was quick to respond. "You know it is. I don't think any jury would set Brad free on that evidence alone. We need a confession. There's got to be a way."

By now Lorna was back on her feet, replacing her clothes into her dresser drawers and, with help from Derrick, putting them back into their proper place. Ellis in turn was working on the other dresser—clearly Radley's. He felt awkward picking up Radley's clothes. They were all there as if he might return at any minute, and he even recognized some of them. But Lorna didn't seem to mind. It occurred to Ellis that she was probably relieved to have him doing it, and he considered it the least he could do. Missing was Radley's tape recorder. But Lorna didn't mention it—and Ellis had no way of knowing that she had returned it to Radley's top drawer—and it was now gone. She took no time to worry. The tape was in its safe place—that's all that mattered.

"But Lorna, this is the problem we face," Ellis resumed his discussion of the issue at hand. "Because they bugged my Escalade, they clearly know what's on the tape. It's made them desperate, and I believe they are prone to flee. In fact, it wouldn't surprise me if they were already gone. The last thing Cyrus wants is to be locked up with all the thugs he's put in jail. I don't know if he'd even survive. And he's a loner—you know that. He has no family—nothing to keep him from running. And when he's gone, he's gone. We may never get the opportunity to bring him to justice."

"But what about Chris Jenkins?" asked Derrick. "He's married with at least two children. I forget how many. Nice wife—pretty, involved in everything. I just don't see him leaving them."

"Well, who would have ever seen him doing what he's been doing? Running drugs and all?" Ellis responded. "After all I've seen, nothing surprises me. At the end of the day, I guarantee you that all he cares about is himself. And I think he would leave them in a heartbeat if he felt he had to—might even convince himself he's 'doing it for them.' You know? I've seen it before. He might already be on his way to Mexico for all we know."

"Okay," Lorna answered suddenly. "You have a point, Ellis. We can't run that risk. If Chris and Cyrus leave Oxford, all we have is Lance and his tape. And we'll never have a confession. And Brad will stay in prison because all the tape proves is that they're drug dealers—not murderers."

Ellis did not respond immediately. He wanted to make sure that Lorna's decision was truly hers.

"Yes. Do it. I can't wait. Do it now. I will finish cleaning up here, and I have everybody here to help me," Lorna said with a finality in her voice. Her mind was made up.

CHAPTER 32

Sitting in Quick Sand

A SHOWER AND A good night's sleep can work wonders. For Lance Bradford, they brought about a new lease on life and clarity of purpose. Of course, a month off with pay didn't hurt things. And for the first time in a long time, he actually noticed that the sun was shining and the world had color to it. He was feeling good.

As he wheeled his sleek BMW in and out of traffic along University Avenue, Lance's mind was fixed on one thing—or person rather—she was beautiful, red-headed, feisty, and she was all he wanted. But Brenda Marshall was not responding to his calls and texts.

Lance kept looking down at his phone as he drove, hoping to see her pretty face pop up, but to no avail. Slamming on brakes to avoid hitting a car turning left onto Sorority Row got his attention: He better keep his eyes on the road—and on the prize.

Momentarily, he turned right, passing restaurants and strip malls on his way to Belk. He knew where Brenda was likely to be this afternoon, and she was exactly where he expected.

"Lance, what are you doing here?" Brenda whispered, half-mad, and half-glad at the same time, to see him. "You know you shouldn't be botherin' me at work. Belk's don't like it."

Belk was pretty busy for a Monday. With Halloween now past, Christmas was full-on. Even more decorations festooned the counters and ceilings than had been in place the previous week when Lorna had paid her visit. And Brenda's counter was full of paper, ribbon, and small boxes—the complimentary cosmetic gifts all had to be wrapped by someone.

"I know, I know," Lance sputtered out the words. "But it's like this, beautiful—I can't live without you." His inherited charm was fully at work, only with more sincerity. Lance truly meant every word.

Brenda was flattered. Try as she tried, she couldn't stop the blush that was coming across her face—a hazard of being red-headed. And she couldn't hide the smile that was beginning to form on her brilliant red lips either. So she turned her back to him and pretended to be busy.

"Did you hear me, sweetheart?" Lance persisted. "I love you. I've been a fool. Please forgive me. I love you."

Brenda said nothing. To do so would have been a violation of the "Southern Girl's Handbook." In her heart, she knew that she wanted nothing more than to forgive Lance and rush back into his arms. And this she would definitely do in time. But not just yet. She had to make him squirm.

"Quit ignoring me, darlin'! I know I deserve it and all, but I'm puttin' my heart out here. It's yours. You got it?" the squirming was already beginning. "I know what I said and all didn't make any sense. I know I hurt you. But you've got to forgive me. I love you."

Brenda knew that time was now on her side. And she was going to play it for all it was worth.

She started to speak and then stopped—on purpose. She was going to milk this. "That's sweet and all, Lance," she finally said not looking around. "But I'm busy at the moment. Maybe we can talk later." And with that she turned, her composure back in check, and walked past Lance toward the back of the store. Lance followed her at first and then stopped. He had better breeding than would allow him to cause a scene at Belk.

Moments later, he was back in his BMW along with his bruised ego. The world didn't look quite as bright and colorful. Deep down, however, he felt somewhat optimistic. *At least she said we'll talk later... she's just playing me. It'll all work out,* he thought to himself as he cranked his car and sped out of the parking lot back toward University Avenue. Just at that moment, his phone vibrated. *See—it didn't even take her five minutes.*

But it wasn't Brenda's beautiful face showing on his phone. It was a gray silhouette—CJ.

"Meet in 15. Don't be late." The words in CJ's text message stung. Lance's sudden freedom had come to a sudden end. Immediately he gassed the BMW—he was going to have to speed to make it down Highway 7 in fifteen.

"What kept you so long?" Chris Jenkins was not happy. He was not used to waiting for anyone—especially his employees.

"Sorry, CJ," Lance was about out of breath from the stress of driving so fast. "I was clear on the other side of town when you texted me. I did the best I could. I about did eighty..."

"Nevermind," Chris cut him off with a wave of his hand and handed him an envelope through the open window of his Lexus. "Here, this is for you. Take it."

"What's this?" Lance was confused as he opened the large envelope to find another stack of hundreds, about quadruple the size of Cyrus's gift the night before. "But Chief has already given me..."

"Nevermind that," Chris cut him off again. "Just take it and put it with what Chief gave you last night. Don't even bother counting it. Trust me—it's a lot. But there's a catch. You have to leave town right now. Do not attempt to go back to your condominium. Do not even drive back into the city limits of Oxford, or it is likely you will be arrested. You have to leave now. And I mean now—without a trace."

Lance was stunned. The look on his face said it all. He could not believe what Chris was telling him.

"But that wasn't the deal," Lance protested. "Chief didn't say anything about leaving. He said just to take the month off—which I intend to do."

Chris ignored him. "In the envelope there are instructions on where you are to go. Text me when you get there. And don't screw this up. I've got people there expecting you. If you don't show, I will know."

Lance didn't know what to do. He was tempted to throw the envelope back in Chris's face and take off. But he knew he couldn't do that. He didn't want to sell his freedom either—not for any price. Joe Parker's words started to circle in his brain: "Once you're in, you never can quit." Though he hated to admit it, Lance Bradford had already sold his freedom—he had sold it a long time ago.

"Ain't gonna do it, CJ," Lance replied. "You can boss me all you want, but you don't tell me where to live and where to go. That's crossing the line."

"You don't have a say in it. You should know that by now." Chris Jenkins was angry. "Besides, you're the reason we're all in this mess. You don't get a say. You do what you're told."

"I want to talk to Chief," Lance wasn't going to be bullied. "You're goin' against everything he told me…"

"Shut up!" Chris cut him off a third time. "Just shut up!!" Chris paused for a moment to get his anger under control. And then he continued, "Chief isn't going to help you. He isn't even around. He's already gone—left Oxford. The money and instructions are from him anyway. If it were me, you wouldn't be gettin' anything but a bullet in your head."

Lance's blood ran cold. It was the first time he had ever felt openly threatened by Chris. He wanted nothing more than to get away. His right foot began twitching above the gas pedal. But his better judgment forced him to sit still—and quiet.

"Your little stunt with the mayor a few months ago has almost landed us all in jail. I don't know why you're even still alive, but Chief has his reasons. Did you know Radley was taping you?

What kind of fool are you—rattin' on us like that? Do you have a death wish or something?"

Chris's voice was getting stronger and angrier—he was slowly losing control, and Lance was petrified with fear.

"I honestly don't know what you've got on Cyrus—he won't let anybody touch you. If it was me..." Chris stopped talking. He looked down for a minute and then made a sudden motion that startled Lance cold. All at once, without any warning at all, he was staring down the shaft of Chris's handgun, just inches away from his face. He sat there frozen—half-dreaming, thinking for a moment he was either still in bed or having an out-of-body experience.

Chris's eyes were fixed on Lance. He was not kidding. His face was serious. His finger was touching the trigger, and Lance was staring at it, preparing for it to squeeze ever so lightly, and for his life to be over.

"Don't worry, stupid," Chris laughed suddenly, lowering his firearm as quickly as he had raised it. "Just leave now. Check in when you're supposed to check in. And don't screw it up."

As Chris peeled out, kicking up dirt and gravel onto Lance's car, he just sat there—completely dazed. He could still feel his body frozen in the grip of fear. And then his blood began to flow—along with his adrenaline. Lance Bradford was angry— possibly angrier than he had ever been. He slammed his hands against his steering wheel until they stung. He jerked his head backward repeatedly against the headrest until his neck was sore.

There would be no month off. No Brenda. No freedom. No anything. He would never have a life to call his own. He might as well be sitting in quicksand.

"Well, I may seem powerless to them, but I'm not," Lance announced to the world from his BMW. His mind made up, he threw it into drive. Time to end all of this. He was going to see the only person he knew he could trust. He was going to see Ms. Lorna.

CHAPTER 33

"Sunset-Moonrise"

Normally picking cotton is not high on anyone's list. Never has been. But when compared to the activity of sitting inside in a nine-by-twelve concrete cage, getting outdoors on a pretty fall day, even if in a Mississippi cotton field, can actually be seen as a pleasurable experience. At least this is how Brad Hamilton was looking at his new job on this particular Monday afternoon.

Morning had begun before sunrise—as usual on pretty fall days at Parchman. And with the sun now hovering low to the horizon, Brad felt a sense of great accomplishment. He had picked a lot of cotton. He also caught himself relishing a small dose of hopeful optimism—the first he had experienced in a long while. Perhaps it was his newfound perspective on life as what Bubba was now calling him: a "born-again."

The smell of the soil was subtly sweet, warmed earlier by the Southern sun and now beginning to chill in the approaching evening. Fall was indeed a beautiful time of year, and for Brad and Bubba it had been a good day.

"Can't say I ever imagined I'd be doin' this," Bubba stated, a grin emblazoned upon his face as he freed clump after clump of soft white cotton from their brittle brown husks, emptying his sore hands when they were full into the large bag slung across his shoulder.

"Imagined doin' what? Pickin' cotton?" Brad asked as he imitated Bubba's motions. His bag was getting heavy—good thing it was almost quitting time. "I mean, you told me that pickin' cotton was one of your 'specialties'—having grown up a Delta boy and all."

"I don't mean pickin' cotton," Bubba replied. "I've done this a few times—that's for sure. But I can't say that I've ever done it alongside a white prep boy from Oxford, Mississippi—and I sure can't say I ever imagined that I would be liking it!"

"Yeah, I know what you mean," Brad nodded as he paused a minute to look at his new friend. He also was smiling broadly as he wiped his forearm across his face. "Never in a million years would I have ever pictured myself here with you—Clarence Bubba Riley—in a cotton field at Parchman, Mississippi! But the crazy thing is, it's actually been a good day. I definitely have had worse in my life."

"This I can say, Brad Hamilton—and mean it when I say it!" Bubba was talking but not slowing his pace. His breathing was heavy—he had put in a full day. "The good Lord knew what He was doing when He put me here. I was miserable on the outside. Stealing, lying, living a hard life. It took me ending up in a place like this to finally see what life is about. And I consider becoming friends with you to be the icing on the cake!"

Brad smiled. He felt the same way, but, rather than say it, he let his expression reveal his heart.

"But that's what I'm sayin' when I say I never could have imagined me doing this…" Bubba continued. "I mean, ain't nobody gonna believe it when I tell them I picked cotton with a white boy at Parchman and enjoyed it. But truly, brother, it's been a good day!"

"I know what you mean," Brad agreed. "But I have to say—I will be glad to see that cot tonight. My back is starting to feel it!"

"Yeah, mine, too," Bubba replied. "The price we pay for sunshine."

The two fell silent for a few moments, working hard to finish their row before the guards motioned for them to call it a day. The sun was sinking lower. A full moon was beginning to rise in the distance—large and glowing orange in the reflected light of the setting sun.

"Can't say I've ever seen a sight like that," Brad remarked as he took in the beautiful scene.

"What?" Bubba asked, finishing with the last cotton plant and straightening his back as he lowered his full sack to the ground with a grunt.

"The sun setting and the moon rising—all at the same time," Brad answered. "Quite something to see!"

"One of those special things about the Delta," Bubba spoke nonchalantly. "With land this flat, there's nowhere for 'em to hide from each other. It's especially somethin' this time of year. Has somethin' to do with the harvest moon they say."

"Harvest moon? What is that?" Brad asked.

"You know—the harvest moon," Bubba answered. "Happens every fall. The full moon is larger than normal. The old-timers say it's God shinin' the flashlight for us po' folks still workin' in the fields at night. Kinda what it's like. I've always loved it. Used to go gigging for frogs by it when I was a kid. Didn't even need a lantern! And, man—we'd bring home dem frogs and my grandmamma would fry 'em up in a skillet. You talk about good! Funny thing about frogs—their legs would still be hoppin' around in the hot skillet, even after you cut 'em off. Somethin' to do with the nerves in 'em…"

Brad chuckled to himself—just like Bubba to turn the conversation into something about food. Come to think of it, he was starting to get hungry. Bubba was, too. He was sure of that. For a brief moment, he studied the sun and the moon again. It seemed poetic to him—one was setting but another was rising. He was thinking. *Perhaps this was an omen for my life—the end of one chapter? The beginning of another?*

"Round 'em up—head for the bus!" the prison guard's sudden timing couldn't have been more perfect: Brad was emptying his last husk of its cotton. He and Bubba were finished with their last row.

As the two men lugged their heavy bags, dropping them at a designated place before boarding the bus, other inmates began converging on the bus as well. Men in green and whites were coming from everywhere—the work day was ended. Evening had officially begun.

"Brad Hamilton! Is that really you?" A familiar voice sounded in Brad's ear as he took his seat next to Bubba.

"Brad—turn around. It's me, man! It's me!" Brad couldn't believe it. There smiling from the seat immediately behind him and Bubba was a familiar face—albeit thinner and older than the last time he saw it.

"Larry Palmer!" Brad was excited to see his old roommate. "Man, you're the last person I thought I'd see on this bus! What are you doing here?"

"Same as you," Larry chuckled. "Doing time."

The bus jolted into motion and Brad almost lost his footing. "Better sit down, brother," Bubba motioned to him. "Don't want you fallin' out in the isle!"

Brad quickly sat down but continued straining his neck to talk to Larry.

"How are you doing, Larry?" Brad half asked and half exclaimed. He was excited to see his old friend. "Man—you're a sight for sore eyes! I really didn't think I would ever see you again!"

"Yep, funny how things work out, huh?" Larry laughed aloud. "But I knew you were here. Kaylee told me in one of her letters you were, and I been keeping my eyes peeled for you from day one. Today at the fields I thought I spotted you, but you were pretty far away. And man—you look different. I mean, not bad and all, but in a good way. Looks like Parchman has been good for ya!"

"Ha, yeah—imagine that," Brad replied. "By the way, you gotta meet my man, Bubba! Bubba, this is Larry, my one-time roommate back in Oxford. And, Larry, Bubba's my roommate here at Parchman."

The two inmates spoke their hellos all the while not even looking at each other. All Larry could see was the top back of Bubba's head, and Bubba was looking straight ahead, smiling and nodding to everything Brad was saying but keeping his eyes on the guard standing in front of the bus.

"You still talkin' to Kaylee?" Brad asked with a surprised look on his face. "I thought the two of you were history!"

"You would've thought, huh?" Larry replied. "That's one fine woman there. I think she really cares about me. Never had nobody care for me like she does. She writes me all the time. My own mama ain't even written me. Kaylee is one-of-a-kind I tell you. Seems to really miss me. I think she wants to come see me— that's somethin' ain't it?"

"I think it's great," Brad replied. "Man, how long have you been here?"

"Couple of weeks," Larry answered. "They sent me over here from Batesville last month. Can't say I ever saw a place like this. Pretty much a wasteland, ain't it?"

"Yeah, but it could be worse," Brad responded. His hopeful attitude actually surprised himself as he spoke the words. He indeed was feeling different today—and it was a good feeling. "You know, meeting up with ole Bubba here has really been a blessing." He caught himself using the 'b' word. Something was definitely different. "He got his nickname from Bubba Gump," he continued. "You know? Off Forrest Gump? I think it's funny as all get-out!"

"Bubba Gump was the seafood business, remember?" Bubba corrected him. "Bubba's last name was actually 'Blue.'"

"Bubba Blue—doesn't sound right to me. I like Bubba Gump better," Brad laughed. "But, Larry, Bubba's been really great.

Actually got me eating turnip greens. Can you believe it?"

"Man, that's amazin'!" Larry replied with a funny look. "Bubba—you don't know what you done there. I tried and tried to get Brad to eat some good ole turnips a while back, and he wouldn't touch 'em. You would've thought they was rancid or somethin'!"

"Funny what a man will end up doin' when he's wearin' stripes instead of polos!" Bubba said with a smile. "And I'm mighty proud of Brad my Lad—he's already come a long way!"

The bus passed through some bright lights—fencing and barbed wire formed a tunnel of sorts as the driver pulled into Unit 29. The inmates were already home, and it was night.

"Man, you in Unit 29, too?" Brad asked Larry. "I can't believe I haven't seen you until now."

"Yeah—I haven't gotten out much," Larry chuckled. "Been like incarcerated or somethin'."

Brad laughed aloud. He had always found Larry's sense of humor amusing, but it was especially comforting tonight. Larry truly had been one of his best friends on the outside, and it was reassuring to know he was now in the same unit with him. Even though they probably wouldn't see much of each other in their normal routines, it was nice to know at least that he had a friend in Unit 29.

"Larry, I just thought of something!" Brad knew he didn't have much time. They were about to unload the bus and everyone would be sent back to their cells. "Tonight is Monday night, and a really cool preacher is gonna be here. Am I right, Bubba? He comes every Monday right? His name is Brother Morris. You've got to meet him!"

Bubba nodded, still looking ahead but addressing the seat behind him. "You really ought to join us—a good reason to get out of the cage." Bubba wanted to encourage Larry. There was always room for one more in Brother Morris's Bible study.

"I don't know," Larry answered. "Appreciate the invite, but I'm not much into preachers. You know that about me, Brad. Imagine I'll be playin' dominoes with ole Eduardo here."

Brad noticed for the first time that there was a small Hispanic man sitting next to Larry. He was very quiet and didn't really seem to be someone who wanted to be drawn into conversation.

"Don't let him fool you. He acts all shy and all, but get him into a game of dominoes, and he becomes a monster!" Larry began mock-wrestling his roommate's shoulders. Eduardo grinned and looked down, clearly not wanting to be the focus of any attention.

"Hello, Eduardo. I'm Brad," Brad introduced himself. Eduardo half-nodded at him and then looked away. By now the bus was unloading, and everyone was slowly rising to their feet to file out as instructed. Clearly, everyone was tired from the full day of picking cotton.

"I'm gonna be lookin' for ya' though, Brad," Larry said under his breath as they were filing out. "I'm really glad I got to see ya.'"

"Me, too," Brad answered. "Me, too."

CHAPTER 34

Dropped Call

Mᴏɴᴅᴀʏ ᴇᴠᴇɴɪɴɢ ᴄᴀᴍᴇ as a welcome relief to Lorna. It had been a tumultuous day—and she was exhausted. Thanks to the good-natured support of her friends, however, Somerset was now back in order. In fact, it hardly looked like anything had happened to it at all. Of course, to be reminded of the upsetting trespass, all Lorna had to do was open the cabinets in her kitchen, where over half of her prized china was now gone. She put it out of her mind, though. Her home was a retreat—and she desperately needed a retreat after the long Monday she had endured.

The day had been full of bad news. First, of course, was the complete reversal of Ellis's grand scheme to entrap the perpetrators—his plan to drive them to desperate and careless measures. The plan had blown up instead—in Ellis's face with his ransacked Escalade and in Lorna's with her ransacked Somerset. And, to make matters worse, Ellis's fears had proven true. He and Derrick were fruitless in their efforts to arrest Cyrus Buford and Chris Jenkins. Getting warrants had been no problem—they were issued simply on the sheriff's testimony. The actual tape was not even needed. But, by the time he and Derrick had been able to serve them, both Cyrus and Chris were gone—nowhere to be found. In just a few short hours, Lorna's mood had gone from upbeat and hopeful, even in the aftermath of the ransacking of Somerset, to downtrodden and sad.

"I warned you this might happen," Ellis had reported to Lorna just thirty minutes earlier. "We made them desperate all right. But they are both wanted men now—and they are on the run. We can't even find Lance Bradford either. His landlord hasn't seen his car since around noon. Said he's normally home all day on Mondays. He's probably gone, too. They're probably all having dinner with Joe Parker by now—wherever he is."

Lorna was not concerned about Lance. Truth is, arresting him was last on her list. She just couldn't bear the thought of him in jail while the real criminals, in her opinion, were on the run.

Lorna also found it impossible to conceive that Chris Jenkins had left his family. "Men like him don't care about anything but themselves," Ellis had reminded her. "Like I said earlier, he probably thinks he's doing them a favor. And, truth be told, he is. The further away he is from those kids the better."

Lorna found the whole situation disheartening. It had been an awful Monday, and she felt no closer now to exonerating her Brad than she did months before.

"But they'll turn up," Ellis had reassured her. "They always do, people like that. They're like cockroaches. They can hide for the time being, but eventually they will crawl out from the wrong place at the wrong time and 'Wham!' They'll be history!"

Lorna had found Ellis's illustration a bit melodramatic. Truth is, she really wasn't in the mood for talk—she just wanted to be alone. Ellis had gotten the message.

"We're going to keep looking for them, I assure you. I have deputies at Cyrus's house and also at Chris's—just waiting to nab them should they be stupid enough to show up. But I think Derrick and I need to hang out here with you just to make sure you're okay," he had offered. But Lorna was insistent that she would be fine.

"Ellis, you know as well as I do that they are long gone by

now," she had said to him. "And I just don't think I can handle any more today. I'm going to lock the doors, turn out the lights, and go to bed. But thank you for your concern and for all you've done today. Let's regroup tomorrow."

Ellis understood. He had said his goodnight and was now gone.

The grandfather clock began to chime. Once, twice, three times…. It finally stopped at seven. Seven o'clock. Lorna couldn't believe it was only seven. She thought for sure it must be ten—or later.

As she walked from the kitchen into the hall, Roscoe close behind as usual, the phone rang. She started not to answer but then realized that it could be Ellis with news. A small part of her was still hopeful that good news would be coming—even at the darkest moment. She answered the phone, but it was not Ellis. It was Sterling.

"Lorna, are you okay?" Sterling's voice was full of concern.

"Hello, Sterling," Lorna answered. "Yes, I'm okay. I take it you heard?"

"You bet I heard, and I really should be angry with you right now!" Sterling was only half-serious—a playful jest in his tone. But his concern seemed genuine—and sweet. "I would have come over the minute you needed me. You know that, don't you?"

"Yes, Sterling. I know that," Lorna replied. "You're so kind, and I appreciate you. I just didn't want to blow this thing up more than it needed to be. I didn't even call Polly—and when she finds out, I'm sure she's going to be upset with me."

"And rightfully so!" Sterling responded. "There are people in this town who really care about you, Lorna, and I'm tops on that list!"

Lorna just listened. It was nice to be the object of such concern.

"In fact, I know you haven't bothered to feed yourself all day," Sterling continued. "And I understand that your kitchen is a mess."

"Oh, it's all clean now," Lorna interrupted him. "All thanks to a few busy bees who are kinder than words can say."

"Well, since you denied me the pleasure of helping with the cleanup, you will have to indulge me with the opportunity to bring you dinner. I'm picking it up right now—pasta and red wine. Just what the doctor ordered."

Lorna's first impulse was to say no. But pasta sounded good. And though she rarely drank, a little red wine couldn't hurt. And she was surprised to find herself really wanting Sterling to come over—something about his company brought her peace. She felt so alone without Radley and Brad, and the day had truly been a downer.

"I can't wait," Lorna responded. "I can't wait to see you, Sterling. Thank you so much."

Hanging up the phone, Lorna felt suddenly refreshed. She was actually happy that company was on its way—and not just anyone—Sterling Bradford, her husband's best friend and the very person Brad was named for.

She hurriedly freshened up. Lighting a few candles and starting a light jazz CD, Lorna then turned her attention to Radley's desk. Tricia had done a nice job tidying it, but Lorna felt that she might should put some of Radley's things away. His phone and handkerchief were laid neatly out beside his book on King David. His pocketknife, lip balm, and car keys were close by, along with his wallet and change. Lorna felt surprise and relief that the wallet was left behind. It even still contained the money Radley had on him when he died.

For good measure, Lorna quickly checked the secret desk drawer for the tape. Her pulse quickened suddenly as she opened it. *What if it's missing after all?* she thought.

Relief poured over her as she slid the molding to the side and loosed the hidden compartment. The tape was still there.

She then began putting away Radley's personal items. She paused, however, as she picked up his phone. It had been in his possession the night he died, and for the longest time it had been unavailable to her as evidence in the hands of the Oxford Police. After it had been returned, she had closed it up with the other items in his desk drawer. She had not even looked at it—and it suddenly occurred to her that she had never even checked to see what her husband's last calls had been. Her curiosity was aroused. After the crushing day she had had, Lorna was desperate for clues—anything that would break the case and bring her Bradford back home. Her heart rate began to race. She had to look.

Lorna quickly touched the power button. Nothing happened. The battery was clearly dead. Hurriedly returning the other items to the desk drawer, she carried the phone with her to her bedroom and plugged it into the charger on her bedside table. It seemed to take forever to power on. A brief minute felt like ten. But finally the phone came to life.

She felt torn all of a sudden. Part of her knew she should be in the kitchen watching for Sterling. He was surely to be pulling up any minute. But on the other hand, she really wanted to look at Radley's phone. She cast caution aside and opened his text messages.

All at once, that awful April night came back to her—as if she was reliving it right at that moment. There before her, unread, were the countless text messages she had sent to Radley from the Ava Hotel. Lorna began to cry.

She then pulled up his recent calls, and there was a list of familiar names and numbers. Several from Lorna, a few from Jane at City Hall—nothing appeared out of the ordinary. Except for one unknown number. It happened to be the next to last call on his phone—right before the last calls placed by Lorna. It was an incoming call placed to Radley at 5:35 p.m. the night of his murder.

Lorna's intrigue was not to be quenched. Hesitating at first, she threw care and calculation aside and touched "Call Back." In less than a second, the number was ringing. A male voice answered. Lorna recognized the voice and immediately hung up, dropping the phone by accident. She had recognized the voice at once—she

281

had already heard it twice today. It was the voice of the man who was about to be knocking at her door.

A moment later Roscoe began fidgeting—his ears perked. In another second or two, he was headed to the kitchen door barking. Sterling had arrived.

"Hello, beautiful," he said warmly as she opened the door. He looked like a gentleman out of an old romance film. Handsome, smiling, boxes of food in one hand, flowers in the other, and a bottle of wine tucked under his arm. Lorna didn't know what to think.

"Come in, Sterling," she said, trying to sound normal—and calm. "My you have a load! Look at you!" She was doing a good job with appearances, but deep inside she was completely nervous. Something didn't seem right.

"I thought a healthy prescription is just what the doctor ordered," Sterling announced with charm. "And it doesn't get much healthier than pasta, wine, and flowers. Not that I recommend eating the flowers, mind you!"

Lorna laughed at Sterling's joke—partly because it was funny and partly because laughing eased her tension.

As Lorna looked for a vase, Sterling opened the cabinets for plates and wine glasses.

"Lorna, I'm so sorry," he stated, his tone suddenly subdued. "Your plates are practically gone. And your glasses, too. It must have been a mess. I'm so sorry this happened to you."

"Well, what's gone is gone," Lorna replied. "No use crying over it. At least I have a few things left, and I'm sure I can find replacements. Tricia Burton was telling me about a place up in the mountains somewhere where all they sell are replacements for out-of-stock china. I plan to start there."

Lorna was proud of herself. Making conversation was helping to keep her composure, even though inside she was full of questions, and for the first time, suspicion.

"Do you have a lemon?" Sterling asked. "Pasta's always better with a little fresh lemon juice squeezed on it."

"Sure," Lorna replied, acting as normal as possible and retrieving a lemon from the fridge. "They weren't after lemons obviously," she managed to joke. "Still got several."

She handed the lemon to Sterling along with a sharp paring knife. He quickly cut it in fourths and set it on a plate as Lorna placed silverware and napkins on the table.

"Well, I'm going to propose a toast to your strength of character and heroic resolve!" Sterling had found two wine glasses tucked away in an upper cabinet and was opening the bottle, using the paring knife to cut away the foil. He then poured it equally into the glasses. "To you, Lorna Hamilton," he proclaimed sweetly as he offered her a glass and gently touched it with his. "You are truly the strongest woman I know."

In short order, the two were seated at the large kitchen table, pasta placed in front of them, warm candlelight, and soft music giving the kitchen the feel of a romantic bistro in some far- away place. The food was delicious, but Lorna was not particularly hungry.

"You aren't drinking your wine," Sterling said, noticing that Lorna had only taken one sip from her glass. "You should drink up—it's the best—from Argentina. It was the most expensive label I could find."

"I'm not liking it," Lorna replied, taking another small sip from her glass. She touched her tongue to her lips a time or two and then announced, "It's too salty."

Suddenly, Lorna's mind raced back to her conversation with Matt just a day earlier: *"Has a salty taste—the girls got suspicious and didn't drink it."*

An awkward silence flooded the kitchen. Sterling sat there playing with his pasta—and studying Lorna.

Lorna was studying him as well. He had not touched his wine—his glass was still completely full. His dark eyes told nothing—but his fork was fidgeting. Kathleen's face suddenly passed before Lorna's eyes.

"You never opened up to me about Kathleen," Lorna said, breaking the silence. "What is it that has been making you feel so guilty?"

Sterling paused a moment before answering, looking down at his fork and then taking another bite of pasta. He pretended to take a drink from his glass, but Lorna noticed that he didn't swallow any.

"Oh, you know—same as most husbands who lose a spouse, I guess," Sterling began speaking. "I probably should never have let her drive that boat. She didn't know what she was doing. It really was my fault..." His voice trailed off as he looked down at his plate.

Lorna said nothing. Another tide of silence swept into the room. The two just sat there pretending not to notice. And then Lorna broke it: "I just called you. Did you know that was me?"

Sterling looked up. The look of surprise on his face was obvious. "What are you talking about?" he asked. "I called you—remember? About coming over."

"No, I called you," Lorna continued. "But I didn't know it was you. It was an unknown number. On Radley's phone. From the night he died."

Sterling didn't say a word.

Lorna wasn't finished. "It was an incoming call at five thirty-five on Friday, April 17. The night he died." Silence returned to the room. And then she began talking again, "You never told me you talked to Radley that night. I visited with you at the Ava Hotel, remember? You were all upset. But you never mentioned that you had spoken to Radley. Not even later that night, after you found out he was dead. You never said anything about it at all. So what did you talk about? And why was it a number I didn't recognize?"

Sterling looked down at his pasta, fidgeting again with his fork. And then he looked Lorna straight in the eyes. "It really was no big deal—not worth mentioning, Lorna. It's no secret I keep another phone for my clients to call—the ones I don't want to have my regular number. I was just checking in with him. Nothing really. I hardly even remember the conversation."

Lorna felt a sudden pressure enter her chest. Her blood was racing, and her ears were beginning to pound from the pressure. Something was wrong—very wrong. Her instincts were telling her to flee, but she resisted and continued pretending to act as if everything was normal. She glanced at the paring knife laying on the table. Part of her wanted to pull it over close to her. But she didn't.

Just at that moment, someone knocked on the kitchen door. Roscoe barked—rising from his spot on the floor next to Lorna. Lorna felt relief. *Maybe it's Ellis,* she thought to herself, looking up at the door and then rising to answer it. But it was not Ellis. It was a surprise visitor: Lance Bradford.

"I'm sorry to bother you, Ms. Lorna," Lance blurted out, almost breathless as she opened the door and invited him in. "And I sure wouldn't have come over if I knew he was going to be here," he continued, pointing at his father. Sterling said nothing and remained seated.

"Come in, Lance," Lorna said, reaching out to hug the young man. She was relieved to see him—anyone actually. "Come in. You're a sight for sore eyes. Have a seat."

"Uh, I don't know if I should," Lance said, looking at his father. Sterling was looking in the opposite direction—clearly pretending to be someplace else, and not wanting to face his son. "I almost didn't even come over here at all," Lance continued. "Been driving around a while. But I didn't know where else to turn."

Lorna motioned to a chair next to hers as she sat back down. Lance, however, continued to stand.

"I really shouldn't be here," he said. "I know he doesn't want to see me." Lance was looking at his father, but Sterling still was not looking at him.

"And just why is that, Lance?" Lorna asked with a sudden sharpness in her tone. "Could it have something to do with your mother? And the fact that your father has been lying about it?"

Sterling jerked his head toward Lorna with a look of questioned amazement on his face. He then looked away, grabbing the forelock of his silver hair and scratching his scalp. Lorna ignored him.

"I know all about it. He was at the wheel, wasn't he? He was the one driving that boat—not your mother. He's been lying about it all this time, hasn't he?"

"Yes ma'am," Lance said quietly, his eyes still fixed on Sterling.

"Lorna, what's this about?" Sterling asked with a sudden desperation in his voice. Lorna continued to ignore him.

"I just found out he called my husband the night he died and never bothered to tell anyone about it," Lorna continued. "And I swear I think he just tried to drug me. Taste this." Lorna slid her wine glass over to Lance. He put it to his lips as told, taking a small taste and then sliding it back.

"Nasty," is all Lance said, an obvious grimace on his face.

Lorna continued, "He also seemed to know that my house was ransacked today—and at first I just dismissed it as the gossip of a small town. But thinking about it now, I realize that only a few people knew—my inner circle—and I asked them to tell no one. I am certain they didn't violate my confidence. So I ask you: How did he know?"

Roscoe barked again—and all were startled as the kitchen door swung open suddenly.

"Lance Bradford, you're under arrest!" Ellis Jefferson was holding his gun and his badge. Derrick was right behind him.

"Ellis, where did you come from?" Lorna asked with surprise.

"We've been in the woods the whole time. Couldn't leave you unprotected, Lorna," Ellis replied. "And I'm glad we stuck around. Come on, Lance—you're going with us."

"No, Ellis," Lorna said rising to her feet. "You aren't arresting him." Lorna was pointing her finger at Lance. She then moved it slowly to her left until it was directed straight at Sterling. "You're arresting him."

Ellis was dumbfounded. So was Derrick. Sterling started to rise to his feet in immediate protest but was unable to get out much more than a sentence. Lance Bradford had become incensed, and he was erupting. Sterling sat back down and looked away from him.

"So you're it! All this time I've been wondering—and, man, I was stupid! I've been a fool!" Lance was uncontrollable. "You've been it all along! I can't believe I didn't see it! I knew there was somebody else—somebody higher than Chief and CJ. I just knew it! And now it all makes sense. For the first time, it all makes sense! It's been you! The only reason I'm still alive! The reason they gave me all that money to disappear. It came from you! You were the puppet master pulling on everybody's string. Why didn't I see it before? It's been you all along!"

"Shut up, boy," Sterling hollered at Lance, rising from the table with such violence that he knocked his chair over. "You don't know what you're talking about!"

"Oh, yes, I do," Lance shouted, his face red and his eyes bulging. Veins were popping out on his forehead and in his neck. His arms were prostrate, extended from his sides, and tears were beginning to roll down his cheeks. "All those late-night arguments between you and Mom—they were about me! I get it now—it all makes sense! She found out I was selling drugs and that I was doing it for you! I just didn't know it at the time. That's why you killed her; she knew too much! And that's why you had Mr. Radley killed! You're a demon. I've known it was something, something about you I couldn't figure out, but I had no idea you were so evil. Evil itself!"

All at once, Sterling picked up the paring knife from the table and grabbed Lorna, holding it to her throat. "Okay—so you finally know. And yes—I'm the only reason you're alive, boy. The only reason. And you're right—all that money in your pocket—it's from me. All from me. Your mama knew too much. All because of you. And Radley knew too much, too—putting his nose where

287

it didn't belong. And yes, he's dead, too. They're both dead. And it's because of you."

Ellis and Derrick stood frozen. Lance stood frozen as well, his arms tense—ready to attack his father, but hesitant because of Lorna.

"It's not my intention to hurt Lorna, Lance, or anybody," Sterling addressed Ellis, his voice steady and deliberate. "But you have me in a corner, and I'm not accustomed to being cornered." Sterling's gaze was fixed on Ellis and Derrick. He looked crazed and desperate. Forcefully he declared, "Now this is what is going to happen. You're going to put down your weapons." He then turned to Lance. "You're going to sit down and shut up! And I'm going to walk out of here, and none of you will ever see me again!"

All of a sudden, the unexpected happened. Roscoe, a dog known to love everybody, snapped. In one motion, he was on Sterling, his sharp teeth biting with a brutal force. Sterling grabbed his thigh in agony, letting go of Lorna and swiping at the dog with the knife. All at once, seizing upon the opportunity to act, Lance lunged across the table taking his father down with him—the knife falling to the floor as he and Sterling crashed on top of each other. A skirmish ensued.

"This is for Mom!" Lance was screaming as he punched his dad repeatedly in the face. Sterling retaliated by swinging back, but he was no match for his son. "I hate you! I hate you! I hate what you've done to my life! And what you've done to everybody who meant anything to me!"

Ellis and Derrick hurried over to separate the father and son. By now, Sterling was cowering in a fetal position, his back on the floor. He was holding his arms over his face as he attempted to shield himself from Lance's attack.

Lorna stood back in disbelief—reaching down to subdue Roscoe who was barking and wagging his tail from excitement.

Lance continued to pound. His knuckles were bleeding, but it was unclear which blood was his and which was his father's.

"Come on, son! Stop this!" Ellis spoke forcefully as he grabbed Lance by the shoulders. But he could not subdue him. "Come on now; you've got to stop before you kill him!" Ellis persisted but Lance was unfazed.

Derrick began tugging at him as well, but Lance did not seem to notice.

"He deserves to die!" Lance said as he continued his melee. "He deserves to die! Leave me alone! Leave me alone!"

Ellis Jefferson knew it was time to stop things—with whatever force necessary. With his full weight, he placed both arms around Lance and pushed against him as if making a tackle. Derrick pushed as well, trying to keep from hurting the sheriff, and finally the two men wrestled the young man away from his victim. Knowing he was beat, Lance finally gave up and lay on the floor—tears beginning to replace his rage.

Derrick quickly turned his attention to Sterling—but there was no need to worry about any retaliatory action from the silver-haired lawyer. By now, he was nothing but a helpless wretch on the floor, barely even able to move.

The confusion finally over, Derrick placed handcuffs on Sterling's wrists and began reading him his rights. The prisoner made no response.

Ellis began placing handcuffs on Lance as well, but he said nothing. Lance did not resist. By now he was too exhausted.

Lorna began to protest. "What are you doing, Ellis? You can't arrest him—you can't arrest him!"

Ellis calmly responded to Lorna's protest. "For his own protection, Lorna. For his own protection. And only for questioning. I assure you—only for questioning."

With effort, Derrick stood Sterling up and began to escort him to the door. Lorna stopped them and slowly studied Sterling with disgust. Her eyes pierced him from the top of his head to the soles of his feet. He could not face her. He looked different from the man Lorna had always known—she hardly recognized him. He was no longer handsome. Shame was written all over his bloody face.

She moved past Ellis and grabbed hold of Lance, who by now was shaking as if in shock. She pulled the boy toward her with all of her might and placed her arms tightly around him. He fell into her embrace and began sobbing so loudly that Roscoe began barking in response. Lorna began sobbing, too. The two stood there for what seemed like a small eternity. Finally, Lorna's living nightmare was over.

CHAPTER 35

Redemption

THE DRIVE WAS familiar—but the fields were no longer white. Lorna found it amazing how quickly a landscape can change. Just a few weeks earlier, the cotton had been at its peak, but obviously the mechanical pickers had been busy performing their task. Most of the fields lining Highway 49 were now brown, and in a few areas the giant machines could still be seen as they continued to strip the brown plants of their treasured cotton. Along the highway, roll after giant white roll dotted the fields. To Lorna, they seemed to be the size of small houses!

Brother David was driving, and Tricia was seated up front in her usual place beside him. Lorna found it touching that they were holding hands. It reminded her of long rides with Radley.

Lorna was not tempted to be sad, however. She was too excited. And besides, it was a beautiful day, full of hope and promise—and in the back seat beside her in Brother David's Explorer sat a beautiful young new friend: Kaylee Jones.

"I just can't believe you're letting me go with you," Kaylee was saying to Lorna. "I mean, today of all days!"

"Well, I told you the next time I went to see Brad I would be taking you with me," Lorna replied. "And I'm a woman of my word."

"You got that right," David chimed in. "Lorna Hamilton is a woman of her word all right! She told everyone she was going to bring her son home one day, and today she is!"

"Well, I think it's wonderful!" exclaimed Tricia. "And not even a week after solving the crime! Goodness, Lorna, really... how did you pull this off?"

"Well, I give all credit and glory to God," Lorna answered. "'I can of mine own self do nothing,' but 'I can do all things through Christ who strengthens me.'"

"I love those verses," David replied. "Two of the best in the whole Bible if you ask me."

"Well, it's the truth," Lorna responded. "Just Monday we were cleaning up a mess at the house and things looked hopeless. And here we are today, on our way to bring my boy home. God really works in amazing ways, doesn't He?"

"I'm beginning to figure that out," Kaylee said. "I mean, who would've thought that here you and I would be friends—and I'm so grateful that you're taking me to go see Larry. My mom was almost speechless when she heard I was going to Parchman with Mayor Hamilton. I don't think she believed me at first, but when she saw y'all pull up at the house, she had to eat her words. It was great!"

"Well, you go easy on your mother, dear," Lorna replied. "She just loves you and wants the best for you—that's all. I would probably be the same way had it not been for all I've been through!"

"And that's just it, Lorna," Tricia remarked. "You have been through a lot—but it's all served to make you the wonderfully strong woman you are. And God has carried you through all of it—just like He did for Queen Esther."

Lorna smiled at her reflection in the window as she thought about Esther. *For such a time as this... for such a time as this...*

"And so the drugs are off the street?" David asked. "You think catching Cyrus and the rest of them will finally put an end to it?"

"I know it's made quite a dent," Lorna answered. "But I'm

not through yet. Now that we have them all in custody, we're going to have a field day comparing their statements. By the end of this, we should know where every two-bit hustler lives, eats, and sleeps."

"I think it's wonderful how Lance is cooperating," Kaylee replied. "Word has it that he has proven to be quite the hero."

"Lance and my dog Roscoe," Lorna responded with a smile. "If it hadn't been for the two of them, I just might not be here right now. And of course—I couldn't have done anything without the help of Sheriff Jefferson and Detective Castelle. They have been amazing! And this is really the miracle in all of it— Lance had detailed directions to where the others were hiding out in his coat pocket. Chris Jenkins had given it to him just a few hours before he had come over to Somerset. Once he had that, the sheriff was able to track them down in less than two hours. Can you imagine the look on their faces when he, Derrick, and the Memphis police force showed up at their motel door? And they really thought they were going to be tanning on a beach in Mexico this weekend!"

"I understand they fessed up in record time," Tricia stated.

"All of them except Cyrus," Lorna replied. "In fact, he's still not talking, but we know all we need to know—with or without him. Thank goodness for Joe Parker. When he realized he was caught—on a charge of capital murder, no less—he began telling everything. It's really sad. Turns out he was the trigger man. Can you imagine? He and Chris Jenkins drugged Brad, dragged him through the woods all the way to the house and held him up with his hand on the gun—just so his prints would be on it and the residue would be on his skin." Lorna's voice cracked, and she stopped talking. Kaylee reached for her hand, softly patting it.

"It's okay, Mayor," she said, "You don't have to keep talking about it if you don't want to."

Lorna smiled as she pulled a tissue from her purse and began lightly dabbing her left eye. She squeezed Kaylee's hand and continued to look out the window. "But I do want to—in fact it's all I want to talk about. Because I'm so relieved to know the truth. And the truth is setting my Brad free today!"

Silence again filled the car for a few moments, and Lorna began to finish what she had been saying. "What I'm so grateful for is that Brad was drugged and doesn't remember holding that gun. I mean, it's the cruelest thing I can imagine." Her voice began to crack again, but this time, only for a second. She continued talking. "My hope is that Radley recognized in his final breath that it was not his own son squeezing that trigger but Joe Parker."

Silence returned to the SUV. They were getting close to Parchman.

"And I fear for Sterling," Lorna stated suddenly, "…who will one day have to face his maker and answer for what he has done. To imagine that he had Radley on the phone with him at the precise moment he died. He was stalling him just long enough for Parker to get there. Pretended to be driving up to Somerset any minute. It is unthinkable really—completely unfathomable."

Brother David turned right into the brick-columned entrance of Parchman, Mississippi. The large metal sign was still in place— "MISSISSIPPI STATE PENITENTIARY" emblazoned across it in white letters.

A guard met them at the gate—the same young lady that had been on duty a few weeks earlier. This time, Tricia was on the list, as was David, Kaylee, and Lorna. All was well.

"Y'all have a nice day," the female guard stated kindly as she motioned for them to proceed to the visitor's center.

"Must be having a better day," David stated.

Lorna chuckled. "Aren't we all," she said. "Definitely a better day!"

"Well, I had my book ready," Tricia said smiling. "Glad to know I made the list this time. I must be moving up in the world!"

Kaylee made no comment—she was too busy observing the entrance to Parchman. It was not at all what she had expected.

"This really doesn't look all that bad," she said looking at the neat visitor's center with its porch across the front. "They don't want you to miss the sign, though—do they?" She half joked pointing at the huge warning sign that dwarfed the building.

Brother David laughed. "Yep—you really got to be blind to miss that one!" A few minutes later, he had parked the SUV and the four of them were walking into the visitor's center. All around them, as before, there were people—lots of them. And most were dressed in their Sunday best. It was once again visitation day at Parchman.

But this time, things were different. Brad was no longer a prisoner—he was a free man waiting on a ride. In Lorna's hand were his release papers—Joe Patterson, Lafayette County's ambitious district attorney, had moved heaven and earth for Lorna to get the document filed and executed. It was the least he could do after his unbridled quest to indict and convict the young man just a few months earlier. Getting a judge to sign off had not been a problem at all. After hearing word of Joe Parker's confession—not to mention Sterling's own statement to Ellis Jefferson in Lorna's kitchen—they were practically standing in line to do it. "To think Sterling Bradford got a bogus defense lawyer to handle the case," Patterson had said to Lorna. "I should've known it was too easy. Your boy never even had a chance. I'm so sorry."

Lorna had forgiven him without question. He had only been doing his job after all—and now having release papers in hand made up for everything.

"Mom!" Lorna heard a familiar voice—the only one that called her Mom. It was her son—she had no idea Brad would be waiting for her at the visitor's center. But there he was—he had seen her as she walked through the front door. And he looked great!

Brad rushed over to meet her, and she grabbed him—pulling him into her arms just as she had done Lance a few days earlier. Only this time—it was her own son she was embracing—her one and only son. The tears began to pour—there was no stopping them.

"I knew you would do it," Brad began to say through tears of his own.

Lorna interrupted him. "I knew *God* would do it. I never had the slightest doubt."

David, Tricia, and Kaylee stood back—watching while mother and son embraced. They were crying, too.

"Kaylee, you go get on the bus with Brother David and Ms. Tricia—you don't want to miss it," Lorna said to her young friend. "Brad and I will be right here waiting on y'all when you get back."

David, Tricia, and Kaylee gave Brad quick hugs—his face was lit from ear to ear with the widest smile Lorna had ever seen him grin. He looked good—better than she had ever seen him.

"Something is different about you." Lorna couldn't help but state the obvious after she and Brad had settled papers with the attendant and taken seats in the waiting area.

"I found Jesus," Brad replied and then corrected himself. "I mean, he found me. He wasn't the one lost, after all. I was."

Lorna began to cry again—tears of true joy.

"No wonder you look so good," she said. "I knew it was more than just being set free—you've truly been set free now, haven't you?"

"Mom—you have no idea," Brad confirmed. "I thought I was free on the outside, but I found out I was actually in chains—chains from head to toe. But Jesus broke those chains—He broke every single one! He tore down my prison! And now I know what it means to be truly free. And Mom—it is awesome!"

Lorna just sat there quiet, taking it all in. She didn't know what to say—but she knew her joy had never been more complete. The only thing missing was Radley—she thought *if only he could be here to see Brad free.*

"I sure am thankful for Bubba," Brad continued. "God knew just what He was doing when He gave me that crazy roommate. He taught me how good collard greens are—and he also helped lead me to Jesus."

Lorna smiled—she remembered Bubba from Brad's letters—and from their last visit.

"It was hard saying goodbye to him this morning, Mom—I'm really going to miss him." Brad began to tear up again. "But it won't be long and Jesus will be setting him free, too—I mean getting him out of here. You know what I mean…"

Lorna nodded—she understood exactly what Brad meant. She was holding his hand and pulled him in for another hug.

"But I'll be seeing him soon," Brad continued. "I'm signing up for prison ministry. I've decided it's what I want to do!"

"But I was hoping you would help me with Harmony Here," Lorna replied. She couldn't wait to get Brad back to Oxford and put him to work.

"Oh, I'm going to do that, too—don't worry!" Brad was excited. It was the first time Lorna had seen her son excited about anything since his football days at Oxford High. "I will have plenty of time! I plan to go back to school. I want to focus on ministry. And I want to help you with the college program—especially reaching out to drug addicts. And once a week, I want to drive over here and help out with Brother Morris's Bible studies. I've already mentioned it to Bubba, and he said Brother Morris uses volunteers all the time. I want to stay in touch with Bubba—and I really want to reach out to Larry. He needs Jesus, too!"

"Who is Brother Morris?" Lorna asked. She didn't have a clue who Brad was talking about. And he was talking so fast she was having a hard time keeping up.

"He's an angel—that's what he is," Brad replied, his eyes wide open and his face full of light.

Lorna was moved to tears again seeing her only son so free.

"And I'm also going to sign up for AA," Brad continued his outpouring. "Not because I worry I'm going to go back to drugs, but because I want Jesus to use me as a light for others—to help show them the way!"

"I think that's wonderful, my sweet boy," Lorna replied. "I

think that's wonderful—and I will help you all I can."

All of a sudden, Brad became quiet. His brow wrinkled with worry. "How is Lance? I'm really worried about him."

Lorna had been able to give Brad a brief rundown of everything over the phone the night before—and she had shared her concerns for Brad's best friend.

"I'm afraid he's got quite a hill to climb," she replied. "You know, all in one day he found out his dad was a drug lord and a murderer. That has to be a hard pill to swallow. You know that, in addition to arranging for the murder of your dad, Sterling killed Ms. Kat. They suspect that he hit her over the head with a paddle before wrecking the speedboat. She drowned as a result. He tried to make it look like an accident—and he almost got away with it, too. So sad—Kat didn't deserve to die like that."

Brad put his arm around his mother and pulled her close. "It's okay, Mom—I know it has to be hard. I remember how much you loved Ms. Kat. She was a special lady. And I know you and Dad liked Mr. Sterling. I liked him, too. I can't believe he did all that he did—it blows my mind."

"Yes—but we have to forgive him, too," Lorna responded. "Remember how Jesus forgave the thief as they both hung there dying on a cross. We have to forgive even as we have been forgiven. My question is this: Are you going to be able to forgive him, Brad?"

"Mom—I already have," Brad did not hesitate to answer. "In my old state, I would have been ready to kill him. I probably would've ended back in jail—this time for murder—for real! But just last night I was reading in Romans where it says not to avenge ourselves—but to leave vengeance to the Lord. That's what I intend to do."

"And we need to pray that Sterling will find forgiveness in Jesus," Lorna stated soberly. "He is Sterling's Savior, too."

A New and Glorious Morn

O XFORD METHODIST WAS full—it always was on Christmas Eve. The annual candlelight service was a popular tradition, and people of all denominations filled the pews.

For the first time in many Christmases, Lorna was not singing with the choir. Instead, she had chosen to sit with Brad in the congregation. To their right sat Sheriff Ellis Jefferson and newly appointed Oxford chief of police Derrick Castelle, along with their families. Immediately to Lorna's left sat Lance Bradford and Brenda Marshall, along with Kaylee Jones, her mother, and her children Stacie and Josh. In just a few months, Lorna had gone from having an almost non-existent family to having a large one, for she now counted Lance as her own, along with Brenda and Kaylee. Only Roscoe was missing!

Sitting in front of her was Polly Shoemake and Matt Sanchez. Tricia Burton was sitting with them while Myra Sanchez was in the choir.

Brother David Burton was in the pulpit, delivering a Christmas message: "… and so while the traditions of Christmas are indeed wonderful, trees laden with ornaments and tables laden with delicious food, the true beauty of Christmas is more than all this. It is the beauty of love—God's love. 'For God so loved the world that He sent His only begotten Son, so that all who believe in Him should not perish but have everlasting life.'"

Lorna loved this familiar verse—John 3:16. And she thought of her Radley. This would be her first Christmas without him. Yet, after all she had been through, it was hard to be overly sad. Not only because she had solved his murder, and her Brad was now home, but because deep down, she knew that Radley loved Jesus—and he was now enjoying everlasting life with his Father in Heaven. Lorna smiled.

"O Holy Night, the stars are brightly shining," the choir began to sing. "This is the night of the dear Savior's birth. Long lay the world in sin and error pining till He appeared and the soul felt its worth. A thrill of hope, the weary world rejoices for yonder breaks a new and glorious morn."

Lorna grabbed the hands of Brad to her right and Lance to her left and squeezed. The Savior had been born again in her heart. Redemption was not only Brad's—it was hers, too. And the new morning, just now beginning to dawn, would indeed be glorious.

Soli Deo Gloria

About the Author

Dan M. Gibson has been a pastor, a mayor, a lobbyist—even a candidate for governor. He now adds "author" to his resume with this, his first novel—a murder mystery that delivers a surprising message of hope! Now in his tenth year as Executive Director of the Mississippi Association of Self-Insurers (MASI), Dan is a former mayor of Crystal Springs, MS, and a 1987 graduate of Mississippi State University where he served as student body president and received a Bachelor's in Business Administration. He first entered the insurance profession in 1994 as an independent agent, the same year his son Clark was born. As President of Copiah County Insurance Agency, Inc., Dan was named to the *Mississippi Business Journal*'s Top Forty Under Forty at the age of thirty. He was a Republican candidate for Governor of Mississippi in 1999. Dan obtained his Series 7 as an AXA Advisors Financial Consultant in 2001 and started his own insurance consulting company, Dan M. Gibson & Co., Inc., in 2002. As Executive Director for MASI, Dan is a registered lobbyist representing hundreds of employers with millions in annualized self-insured premiums. In addition to his career in public service, Dan enjoys music, architecture and woodworking. He owns homes in rural Rankin County, Mississippi, and in Natchez, Mississippi, where he serves as Associate Pastor of New Direction Outreach Ministry.